*For Hamish, Hector and
Rowan Marsaili Barbour, with love*

Furnace

Muriel Gray is a broadcaster and author. She lives in Glasgow with her husband, son and daughter.

MURIEL GRAY

FURNACE

HarperCollinsPublishers

HarperCollins*Publishers*
77–85 Fulham Palace Road,
Hammersmith, London w6 8jb

This paperback edition 1998

1 3 5 7 9 8 6 4 2

First published in Great Britain by
HarperCollins*Publishers* 1997

ISBN 0 00 649640 7

Printed in Great Britain by
Caledonian International Book Manufacturing, Glasgow

Acknowledgements

Thanks to, Ray Kasicki and his truck *Thumper* for the ride across America, Joan Kasicki, The Owner–Operator Independent Drivers' Association, Dr I. Cullen, Michael Fishwick, Jane Johnson, Bruce Hyman and Hamish.

1

There was no need for her nakedness. Not yet. But as she stood on the rock and looked at the pale hands stretched out before her, she was glad that she had shed her clothes. The dawn light would break over the mountain behind her at any moment, and although the cold was fierce, her shivering was of anticipation rather than physical discomfort. The chill breeze on her skin felt good and the heavy scent of dogwood blossom and wet grass filled her nostrils.

Far below in the dark sweep of the Shenandoah valley, the lights of isolated trucks and cars moved along the highway as though pulled by an invisible link. She opened the fingers of her right hand and moved them across the blackness until they cupped one of those moving lights like a firefly. Perspective. It was incredible to her that it had taken the human beings until the Renaissance to interpret size and the distortion of distance correctly. What did ancient man think when he held up his hand as she was doing now, perhaps to balance a herd of animals on his palm? Did he think that by the visual evidence of their diminished size he became their master? And what made that thought more obtuse than the beliefs of modern man? To his eye, this would be no more than a naked woman standing alone on a hillside, playing an optical conjuring trick that allowed a truck to drive across her opened hand. How long before the next Renaissance-like awakening of intelligence? The awakening that would confirm his mistake in this respect.

As she became aware of the first rays of the new sun back-lighting her hair, she closed her hand slowly and obliterated the lights of the far distant vehicle from her view.

* * *

'Hey, Peterbilt. You got the four-wheeler leg shot ahead of you?'

Josh Spiller smiled before thumbing the CB in response.

'Might do. Might not. How you gonna get that crawling piece of junk past my rig an' find out?'

There was a cowboy whoop from the radio speakers, and as Josh had guessed, the source of the message was the reefer coming up on his left, increasing its speed and pulling level with him. He glanced with measured amusement at the cab of the Freightliner Conventional. It was like he thought. A company truck. Company drivers. A name 'Kentucky Meat and Foul' was painted on the door in fat blue letters, and the leering bearded face of the team driver hovered above them at the window, like he was a painting and the letters below spelled his title. The guy gave Josh a triumphant surfer's thumb and little finger, accompanied by a shit-eating grin as his partner at the wheel came on the radio again.

'Come on there, big truck. Bet you snatched a look at the snatch. Am I right, or am I right?'

Josh rolled his eyes skyward, trying hard to suppress a smile, then looked forward again.

To his right, the great rolling back of the Appalachians was a graceful black cut-out against the lightening sky, and in only a few minutes the first orange arc of a new sun would break across that heavenly silhouette. But to the guys on his left, the sun could come up accompanied by a cloud of naked golden angels sounding trumpets, and all they'd do would be to slap their thighs and guffaw at the fact that they could see some flying bare ass.

He felt a sudden wave of sympathy for the girl in front, still oblivious to the harassment she was about to endure. Channel 19 had been discussing her for the best part of an hour. Sure her legs were long and her skirt short, though if she hadn't left her interior map light on no one would have known. But the bumper sticker on the back of her tiny Honda, that line-drawn fish that declared the driver was a Christian, suggested that light being left on was an innocent error. In Josh's experience Christian ladies didn't flash truckers.

His sympathy was mixed with a strange nostalgic melancholy brought about by the imminent appearance of the sun. He'd been feeling pretty mellow for miles, looking forward to slotting a cassette into the stereo and watching the dawn break over the mountains to the sound of something good. Something carefully chosen to heighten the privileged experience of welcoming the daybreak over gentle but beautiful open country. Now these pencil-dicks had ruined it, and there was nothing he could do. They would get level with her, probably sound their horn and embark on a series of gestures among which a zoologist could find subject matter for a dissertation.

As they inched forward, the reefer struggling to get ahead of Josh's more powerful rig, he sighed and resigned himself to the spectacle, running a hand over the back of his neck to massage away fatigue from the muscles there.

And then the red light winked.

Josh glanced up at the radar detector on his dash and as quickly across at the cab of the reefer.

Company trucks didn't carry radar detectors. Other owner-operators like Josh might just. The damned things were illegal in big trucks but nobody could get you for just riding with one, and Josh knew where to switch it on and where not to. Here, on this stretch of the northbound interstate through Virginia, he was glad it was on. If nothing had changed in the highway patrol's routine since his journey down, then he knew exactly where those bears with the radar were. There was a rest area just ahead on the right before the next exit, and that's exactly where he'd spied a state bear sitting hunting on the way southbound only three days ago. How could the apes in the Freightliner know that? They couldn't. Not without a detector, or that other essential lifeline every trucker relies on. Information from a fellow driver. A driver like Josh. And if Josh chose not to say anything, there weren't a whole lot of trucks packing out this road right now who'd blow those bears' cover instead. The highway was so quiet it could have doubled as a runway. On the dash the red light was going crazy, and Josh pressed simultaneously on his brakes and the talk button of the CB mike, a smile nearly cutting his face in two.

'Yeah, you're on it, guys. I looked for sure. And let me tell you, she's askin' for it. Since she been showin' us so much leg there, why don't you fellas give her a look at some of them Kentucky chicken pieces of your own.'

He looked across as the cab of the Freightliner started to pull away by virtue of his own subtle braking, and watched the bearded

3

guy slap the dash and give a thumbs up in appreciation of the joke.

'Come on, asswipes,' Josh whispered as he saw the rest area up ahead.

The truck drew level with the Honda, and as the window of the Freightliner started to wind down he could just make out the nose of the patrol car, peeking out from behind a clump of scrubwood, still expertly hidden from anyone who wasn't looking for it. Josh's smile couldn't get much wider, but he tried.

The timing was close to perfect. The Honda swerved a little as two fat white buttocks poked out of the Freightliner's window, a finger sticking grotesquely into its own rectum, precisely as the three vehicles glided past the parked patrol vehicle. To the two cops sitting glumly in their car, wishing that dawn would break and bring the end of their shift closer, it looked like a circus act that had taken a lifetime to perfect. They exchanged no more than a brief and weary glance before snapping on the siren and pulling out.

Now it was Josh's turn to slap the wheel in glee as the Freightliner edged back and pulled over, falling prey to the police car like an antelope brought down by hyenas. Josh was alone with his good Christian lady again, and part of him wished she had CB so he could share the joke, and more important so that she could thank him for his betrayal of colleagues in the name of chivalry. But the exit ahead seemed to be the one she wanted, maybe from choice, or maybe just to get off the highway and away from her persecutors. She started to brake and signal. Josh braked in response and was surprised when she slowed to a crawl. There was nothing for it but to pass, so he swung the rig out and changed down accordingly. As the bulk of the Peterbilt moved past the woman's tiny car, now peeling away at a snail's pace towards the exit ramp, Josh Spiller threw a look across at her.

From her open window an elegant arm emerged in farewell, and on the end of that arm, stabbing the air repeatedly like it was trying to puncture an invisible skin, was a deeply un-Christian middle finger.

He'd fumbled in the plastic ledge above the dash for a good thirty seconds, initially finding only an evil knot of Jelly Bellies that had fused together in the heat of the cab, before his fingers closed on the cassette he wanted. The sun was almost visible now, and Josh urgently wanted to get his chosen track lined up before it was too late.

He flipped the tape out of the plastic junk-filled canyon and slotted it quickly into the stereo. It came on half way through some terrible and elderly Doors number. Wrong. So wrong he wished he'd never included the track on this jumbled and hastily assembled compilation. He pressed fast forward, waited and then let it play again.

Aerosmith. He cursed silently. That meant that it was rewinding, not going forward.

The sky to his right was now growing light so fast that a ridiculous mixture of anxiety and frustration tightened his chest. He took out the tape and reinserted it. The machine didn't like the way he did it and slid it back out at him again. The sky had now gone way past pink, turning into the luminous aquamarine that heralds the first glorious golden shards of sunlight, as he slammed the troublesome cassette back in and pressed fast forward again. Two pauses and he was there.

Josh couldn't say why he fancied this track most to greet the dawn, but he did. It was old but it was tranquil. A song off some weird album by a British band called The Blue Nile that Elizabeth's kid brother had loaned him.

It started with a slow drum then this really sad guy came on and sang like he would break your heart. You had to be in the mood or you couldn't take it. Josh was in exactly the right mood. It was just what he wanted for the big event, the arrival of the sun after this nine-hour non-stop homeward haul from Tennessee. And it was going to work this time. It was going to be a peach. The track was lined up, the sun was maybe only seconds from view, and he was northbound in the right lane with nothing obstructing his view across the dew-soaked fields to the dark rolling back of the Appalachians.

That was important to the full enjoyment of the moment, the absence of anything man-made in between him and the sunrise. No buildings. No human junk. Nothing that would spoil his view with another reminder, particularly after his disappointment in the reluctant maiden he'd rescued, that sometimes people didn't deserve another day graced by anything as beautiful and indiscriminately benevolent as the sun. He waited, his hand ready to press play, glancing every three or four seconds out of the passenger window to catch the first sight.

Up ahead, the highway stretched empty before him, an artery of stone that fed America its life-blood. Or was it a vein that circulated the disease of man and his junk around the once untouched and healthy body of this delicate continent?

Josh gazed out front, contemplating it for a second, knowing that whatever the answer, he was a part of it. The rare sight of clear road made him suddenly feel exposed, an alien object moving without permission upon an ancient and secretive landscape.

And in those few moments of inattention as Josh dreamily regarded the road ahead, the sun betrayed him and sneaked up over the rim of the hills. He whipped his head to the east as the first orange beam hit the side of his face, shifted in his seat and stabbed the play button on the stereo.

The tape hissed and then the song began.

How could he have known? Even with the benefit of the height that he enjoyed from the truck Josh couldn't see the entire landscape ahead, couldn't see the mark of man that was waiting for him, nestling smugly between mountains and highway. So at that religious and significant moment when the sun rose, it rose not over unsullied meadows and hills, but from behind a forest of four tall masts, one tipped by golden horns, another by the Cracker Barrel sign, the other two proclaiming Taco Bell and Burger King.

Josh blinked for a second, his mouth slightly open until an excited voice on the CB crackled over the gentle song playing on the tape and brought him back.

'Man, oh man! Any of you northbounds see that?'

Josh glanced across at the source of the enthusiastic message; a lone R-Model Mack pulling a covered wagon on the southbound highway.

Gratefully, Josh picked up the handset. 'Sure as hell did, big truck. Glad there's someone else out there with a soul.' He flicked off the tape, ready to receive the reply, and it came right back at him with its enthusiasm intact.

'Yeah? Man, I can't believe they's only askin' two dollars ninety for a chargrill, family bucket of fries, soup and a free soda. That's a whole dollar less than the joint at exit 19. Sure gonna work for me!'

Josh Spiller stared ahead for a second or two, then gently replaced the handset, let out the remains of his breath and started to chuckle. He shook his head and carried on laughing until a tiny rogue tear rolled down one cheek and he wiped it away with the back of a greasy hand.

'Shit. Know what, America? You are one fucked-up country.'

2

She'd been awake for at least two hours. Now that the dawn was bleeding through the drapes, she shifted under the covers and ran a hand over her warm belly. She had to get up. No choice. But here, in the dark that was gradually being corrupted by light, it was safe and warm to think, and everything outside that cocoon seemed impossibly cold.

Josh's face. She closed her eyes and thought about it. Sometimes, if it had been a long time, she had trouble remembering the exact contours. But even if it was difficult to visualize she could always recall how it felt beneath her lips. She held on to that now, breathed in through her nose as she thought about the smooth soft skin over his cheekbones, the thick curl of eyelashes and the rough texture of bristle around mouth and chin.

With her eyes still shut, she swung her legs out of the bed and sat up.

The bedroom mirror greeted her with her own reflection when she raised her head and looked towards it. Despite her hunched posture, even she would admit that her breasts looked enticing. They were fuller and firmer than she'd realized, and her hands came up in an unconscious gesture to cup them gently.

Elizabeth Murray let her hands move up to her face and then spoke in a whisper to the mirror, the delicate planes of her cheeks and forehead sculpted by the grey dawn light.

'What now?'

Josh waited impatiently outside the phone booth. There were only three private booths at this Flying J truck stop, all occupied by frowning men who looked like they were making talking an Olympic event. He sighed and leaned heavily against the wall, toying with his Driveline calling card.

The big black guy next to him was holding the phone against his ear with his shoulder, passing a rubber ball restlessly from hand to hand as he listened, his eyes glazed like he was hearing bad news.

Josh guessed what he might be hearing. The guy's dispatcher would have put him on hold, and the profound expression of misery was most likely induced by an age of listening to the theme from *Love Story* reproduced electronically by a sadistic phone company. He looked at his boots. All he wanted to do was to call Elizabeth and tell her he was less than an hour from home. No filthy talk like you sometimes heard and wished you hadn't, but he wanted privacy when they spoke, and if he didn't get a free phone soon he'd miss her. He'd already gone past that delicious time when she would pick up the phone beside the bed and answer in a sexy, sleepy way. Right now she'd have a mouth full of Cheerios and be pulling on a jacket ready to go to the store, pleased to hear from him, but with a tone of urgency in her voice that meant he was making her late. Five more minutes and she'd be gone.

The door of the centre booth opened but infuriatingly the guy hadn't stopped yakking.

Josh made a move towards him and the guy held up a hand without looking at him.

'Uh huh? Well it ain't okay with me.'

A listening pause.

'No, it ain't my last word. This is my last word. Okay, two words. Fuck you.'

He slammed the phone down, got up off the small plastic seat and pushed past Josh.

Josh grinned at him, and gesticulated at the phone. 'It's a drag always havin' to call your grandmother, ain't it?'

The man looked for a moment like he might throw a punch, but something in Josh's eyes held his clenched fist by his side, and he satisfied himself with a 'Yeah, funny guy' muttered beneath his breath.

Josh smiled at the man's back and entered the booth, his grin deforming into a grimace at the blush of sweat those substantial buttocks had left on the plastic. But he needed to make that call. He decided to stand, and as he punched in the code for the card he shook his head. Seemed like all truck drivers did was drive and then get mad with someone for no other reason than they didn't like driving.

Choose any truck stop, any row of phones and mostly all you'd hear was a chorus of deeply discontented men. Some of it was just plain moaning, but enough of it was from the heart to make hearing it uncomfortable. Why drive if you hated it so much? Josh liked it fine. Just fine. And he loved Elizabeth. If the seat was clammy with his sweat after he'd talked to her, it wouldn't be from stress.

The vacant computerized woman on the phone thanked him in a monotone for calling Driveline and informed him in a voice that suggested she was painting her nails that he had seven dollars and fifteen cents left to make his call. He punched in their number.

It rang eleven times and just as he was about to hang up Elizabeth came on, out of breath, and sounding angry.

'Yeah?'

'Hey. You should get into telephone sales, honey.'

She tried to change the tone, but there was still something there. Something at the back of her throat.

'Hey yourself! Where are you?'

'On the pike. Near enough home to smell next door's mutt.'

'Well get back here. I missed you.'

It was familiar small talk. But she said the last bit as though she really meant it.

'You okay?'

'Sure.'

'Big day, huh?'

'Yeah. Big.'

A melancholy tone reaffirmed that something was wrong. Now, in this tiny booth with two guys already waiting outside, wasn't the time to find out what it was.

'Want me to come straight by the store?'

'How you going to park Jezebel?'

'Normally I just pull on the brakes and shut her big ass down.'

'And screw the Pittsburgh morning traffic?'

'For you I'd leave her standin' in the middle of the Liberty Tunnel at five-thirty Friday night.'

She laughed, and hearing her was like he'd swallowed something warm and sweet.

Elizabeth sounded more like herself when she spoke next. 'Then come on by and make a traffic cop's day.'

'See how it goes.'

'Love you.'

'Love you too.'

He hung up and left the booth. Had he imagined it or had she really sounded uneasy? Understandable. Today, she and Nesta started their new career. A sackload of tasty redundancy pay blown on their crazy business.

Josh would have spent it buying something a man could use, like a decent flat-bed to switch with the trailer he was pulling so he could haul bigger sections of steel when he needed to. But it was Elizabeth's choice, her money. She didn't spend much of his, and he certainly didn't spend any of hers.

Fifteen years as a machinist hadn't made her rich but facing a new day, every day, sewing nylon umbrella sleeves, cheap bags for storing shoes and suit covers, had given her plenty time to think about her life. She and her buddy were about the only girls not weeping when the scrawny, acne-covered floor supervisor told them they were out. With a little shame, Josh admitted to himself that he didn't really know if the costume ball hire shop was Nesta's idea or Elizabeth's. But he sincerely hoped the name 'All Dressed Up' was Nesta's. It was seriously crap.

Of course Elizabeth would be scared today. The door would be opening in a couple of hours for the first time, and she'd be praying, fruitlessly Josh thought, that there'd be a queue of customers round the block, ready to part with cash to dress up in the ridiculous costumes she and Nesta had been sewing for the last three months.

Costume balls baffled him. To Josh, the idea of standing around at a party with a beer in your hand talking to someone about real estate or kit cars seemed pretty attractive. But not if you were dressed like Pinocchio and the guy you were talking to was trying to make an earnest point in a fun-fur kangaroo suit. But if it made money, then so what?

What bugged him was that Elizabeth's tone had sounded more than just anxious. Sounded like she was sad.

He wandered out of the phone lobby and through the shop

towards the restaurant. Maybe he should buy her something.

Truck stops nearly always boasted carousels full of junk that skulked near the cash desk like muggers, offering a variety of garbage for the guilty driver to take home and pacify his sweetheart. But until now Josh had never really looked at it.

The days when he'd done things he'd have to say sorry for were the days he hadn't had someone steady like Elizabeth waiting at home. Now he had her, he didn't do much on the road except drive, eat, sleep and shit.

Pausing for the first time at the cylindrical stand like it was a confession box, Josh let an embarrassed gaze drift over the assortment of tacky merchandise. He found himself looking quizzically at some round balls of fluff with eyes and feet made of felt, sporting cloth ribbons that said everything from 'I Love You' and 'You're Cute' to statements of coma-inducing inanity like 'I've been to West Virginia'. A gentle push of his forefinger sent the display turning slowly round to reveal badly-made plastic boxes covered in lace hearts that had been hastily glued to the lids, and some dusty-looking dolls dressed as cowgirls.

Josh glanced around, anxious in case anyone had seen him looking at this stuff, only to discover the woman behind the counter already had. She smiled when he caught her eye. Maybe someone had given her one of those fluffy balls once, with a message on the ribbon that she wanted to hear. He lowered his eyes, and wandered casually over to the display of Rand McNally road atlases, flicked through a couple like he'd never seen a map of America before.

Men like Josh Spiller didn't look right poking at dolls and lacy boxes. Six feet and one hundred and sixty-eight pounds of fit, pale body were topped by a head of light brown hair cut so short it was near enough shaved. There was a tiny silver ball of an earring in his right ear and it combined with the hair to make sure he didn't get stopped in the street often by nuns collecting for orphanages. What little hair that had survived the cut sat above a face with kind blue eyes, a straight, elegant nose and a wide, mischievous mouth. That open face meant that although he was adopting the demeanour of a mean guy, no one was going to mistake Josh for a member of an underground militia group. He looked kind. He couldn't help it. Nevertheless, the spirit in him that made him look the way he did was not prepared to let him stand at the counter and buy some piece of girlie shit. He shut the atlas and walked towards the restaurant.

'We got something new over here she might like.'

The woman behind the counter was smiling, her eyes lowered, looking at what she was doing and not at him. Josh cleared his throat.

'Yeah?'

Her fat fingers counted out shower vouchers in front of her like they were cards in a game.

'We got these real pretty pins. All sorts. And a machine that does her name on it while you grab a bite. Takes about ten minutes.' She indicated the contraption behind her with a small movement of her shoulder. 'You just turn that there dial to the letters you want and it gets right on doin' it. Seventeen dollars including the name. Plus tax.'

Josh was trapped. He walked slowly over and she looked up.

From behind the glass under the counter she took out a tray of cheap pewter-coloured metal brooches shaped in a bewildering variety of little objects, each with a space beneath the object for the name like the scroll on a tattoo. With his hands in his pockets Josh looked them over, grateful the store was empty.

There were tiny metal bows, a rabbit, some bees round a hive, all in a mock-antique style, and all waiting to have a woman's name scratched beneath their immobile forms. Despite his discomfort he decided they were cute and when his eyes wandered over to one made from a tiny pair of scissors cutting out a perfect metal heart, Josh knew Elizabeth would like it. The scissors were neatly appropriate.

'So you do their name on the blank bit with that machine?'

'Well I ain't doin' it. Got enough to do keepin' you guys from rippin' me off to sit here and carve your wives' names on a pin.'

Josh smiled, pointed at the one he wanted and reached for the wallet in his back pocket. 'Okay. It's Elizabeth.' He spelled it for her, watched her write it so she wouldn't make a mistake, then went to get that coffee.

'Takes ten minutes,' she reminded him to his back as she clicked the letters into something that looked like a sewing machine and with her tongue sticking out the corner of her mouth placed the brooch on a tiny vice.

3

Elizabeth was right. There was no way he could park Jezebel any-where near the store. In fact, there weren't many places in downtown Pittsburgh you could take an electric blue Peterbilt Conventional with a sixty-inch sleeper and forty-eight-foot trailer. Not unless you wanted to end up trapped like a beached whale, snared in some narrow street by four-wheelers who park like the whole world is their front drive.

Instead, Josh drove straight to Jezebel's parking lot ten miles out of town, did his paperwork, zipped up a week's worth of stinking laundry and headed home in the pick-up. He figured Elizabeth wouldn't really want to see him in the store anyhow. Not if she was busy measuring someone up as a giant tomato. Right now, he needed some sleep. He'd be more use to her wide awake, showered and ready for action.

The duplex that Josh and Elizabeth shared was nothing special, but it was on a quiet block with tiny neatly-trimmed gardens tended by peaceful neighbours. Josh owned the whole house but rented the lower half to an elderly Korean bachelor called Sim, a tiny man in his seventies who constantly complained that he was at the rim of death's abyss, usually while in the yard tending patio pots full of unpleasantly pungent spices and herbs.

Today was no different. Sim was sitting on a canvas stool against the wall of the house in the chill morning sun. A cigarette hung from his tight mouth, and he held *The National Enquirer* at a distance from his face as though he were a doctor examining an important X-ray.

Sim looked up as Josh's pick-up pulled into the yard, and by the

14

time Josh had climbed out the old man's face had changed from a lively interest in his paper to one of silent suffering.

'How it been this time, Josh?'

Josh knew the routine. He liked Sim.

'Good. Seven days, four loads. Pays the rent. How you been?'

This was how it always went.

'Oh I not got long now, you know. I had pains. Real bad. Right here.' He indicated his chest with the flat of a palm.

'Maybe you ought to give up those smokes, Sim.'

'They not problem, Josh. Living the problem. Too hard for me sometimes. Know how that is?'

Josh nodded. 'Sure do.'

He continued to nod his head gravely as though Sim had pronounced a universal truth, but by the time he was through the door and the old man had returned to reading about the secrets of Hollywood's bald stars, Josh was grinning. Life didn't look too hard for Sim. But then life wasn't too hard for him, either. Josh was thirty-two years old, and for ten of those he'd been hauling everything you could name, and some things you couldn't, from one corner of his country to another.

Now, in particular, things were pretty good. His wild years had passed when he'd driven team, swallowing anything and everything illegal to keep awake for forty or more straight hours on the road, just like all the other guys who were trying to make a living. Four years ago he'd joined the world of grown-ups, got a bank loan and bought his own rig. Josh was up to his neck in debt, with the bank's shadow looming over his house and his truck. But running his own tractor unit and trailer, even just having his name painted on the door in curly purple fairground writing, made him feel like a man who had done something useful every time he stepped up into Jezebel. It wasn't just driving any more. He worked like a dog, he had a business, and it felt okay.

The house reflected that small triumph. The kitchen he walked through from the yard door was Elizabeth's domain, full of silly calendars and photos stuck to the ice-box, dried flowers in baskets on top of the cupboards and plaid drapes swagged to the side of the windows that would never meet if anyone were bold enough to undo the huge bows that restrained them and try to draw them shut.

But in the spare bedroom that Josh had made his office, his life in the rig came back with him into the house. It was this room he headed for first, ostensibly to check if there were any faxes or messages on the answering machine, and flick through the mail that Elizabeth left in tidy piles on his desk. The truth was that the room was an airlock, a halfway stage to reacclimatize himself into a life that wasn't really his; that of wandering round shopping malls, going out for dinner, drinking beer with friends in their yard or his, or just watching TV while Elizabeth fixed their meals.

All the ordinary stuff that most people did and thought nothing of, Josh had to relearn every time he pulled on the brakes and came home. At least in this room, with its giant map of the states pinned unevenly to a cork wall, piles of correspondence, trade magazines and bits of scrap paper that related only to his driving life, he could come down gently, ease into Elizabeth's normality and try to make it his own. For a few days at a time, at least.

The fax stared back at him, insolently exposing the emptiness of its horizontal slot, and the mail was equally unrewarding. Just bills and a few late cheques from companies that paid slowly. He flicked through them with mild disappointment, the constant hope when returning home to a pile of mail that something in it would be surprising and life-altering, dashed again. Josh left the room, took a shower and crawled into their flowery linen nest for the first sleep of home. The difficult sleep. After six nights stretched out in a sleeping bag on Jezebel's sagging foam mattress behind the cab with dozens of truck engines thudding outside, finding oblivion in this big, fresh, soft and silent bed took time.

This morning it couldn't be found at all. Josh was weary, but closing his eyes brought nothing but the road rolling by on the inside of his lids. He lay in the bed, his hands behind his head, resigned to sleeplessness, content with merely resting in a state of semi-reverie until Elizabeth came home, when he hoped she would slide into the warmth and join him.

Josh remained motionless but wakeful for several hours, sufficiently relaxed to be unaware of the day as it played out its variations of light behind the closed bedroom drapes, but then he was a master of rest without sleep. Driving created a new gear for the mind, a neutral that demanded little of the body except breathing. It was almost trance-like and he'd driven in such a state plenty of times, despite the plain reckless danger of it. His enjoyment of the escape it afforded was broken by the sound of Elizabeth's key in the lock, and the slam of the screen door. He opened his eyes, surprised to have dreamed what seemed like the entire day away, then stretched and lay back with his eyes closed, waiting in delicious anticipation for her to come to him, knowing that she'd see his pick-up parked outside and realize he was in bed.

It was comforting, hearing her sounds, the clatter of domesticity, as she moved about in the kitchen, opening and closing cupboards, putting away things she must have bought on the way home, and the scrape of a chair as it was pulled out from the kitchen table. Josh waited.

There was silence.

He slid his legs reluctantly out of the warm bed, pulled on a voluminous sweatshirt and yawned. As he made for the door he remembered her gift, fished in his jeans pocket and transferred the small box into the pocket of the sweatshirt. Then he made his way through to the kitchen, scratching at his skull like a bear.

She was sitting at the table motionless, her back to him, her head turned towards the small window. Elizabeth had hair that was only marginally longer than his own, but the cut was feminine and accentuated the graceful sweep of her neck. He leaned against the door-frame and drank in the slender architecture of her shoulders.

She turned and looked up at him. Brown eyes in a pale and almost masculinely handsome face looked as if they wanted to return his heat, but they were clouded with a film of defeat.

Josh put out his arms and she stood up and moved into them. With an almost imperceptible sigh of pleasure he allowed his fingers to part the dark hair and caress her head.

'Bad?'

She nodded against him with a tiny movement.

Josh put his mouth to the top of her head and spoke into her hair.

'Hell, they just don't know what lucky is, Pittsburgh folk. The chance to zip themselves into a chicken suit, right here on their doorstep, and where are they all?'

'Fuck off.'

She mumbled it into his chest but he could tell it was said through a smile. He lifted her head and made to kiss her, but her smile died as she looked into his eyes. Then she pulled free.

Josh put his now-empty arms up in a gesture of surrender.

'Joke.'

'I know.'

She sat back at the table, where he joined her and took her hand.

'It'll pick up. Just one guy who gets his rocks off at a party dressed as a pirate and tells his friends, believe me, you'll be beating them off with shit-covered sticks.'

'You've been gone a long time.'

An accusing tone she never used. It threw him, and he withdrew the hand that had been covering hers.

'Got an extra load from Louisville. Couldn't turn it down. I told you.'

'We need the money that bad?'

'Yes.'

She looked down at the table.

'Sorry.'

His hand was still on the table top. Avoiding his eyes she slid her hand over and laid it on his. Josh reached into the sweatshirt pocket with his free hand, took out the small box and slid it towards her.

'For you. It's dumb but it's for luck.'

She looked up and met his eyes, a smile beginning to ghost in them again.

'You been screwing someone?'

'I wish.'

She opened the box, rustled the piece of tissue paper and revealed the dull metal brooch. Her name was etched clearly but unevenly on it, with the E too far from the L and the final T and H crammed so tightly together they were practically one letter, but Elizabeth took the cheap gift from the box as if it were a Fabergé egg.

'This is beautiful.'

'It's just junk. I thought you'd like it.'

'You thought I'd like junk? That's what I call romantic.'

She was smiling full on again. For Josh, the brooch had already proved hundreds of times its worth.

'You like it?'

'I love it.'

'Well wear it and things'll look better tomorrow.'

Her face clouded again and she toyed with the brooch, making a scraping sound on the table as she shifted it around.

'Maybe.'

Josh held the bridge of his nose between a finger and thumb.

'What's the deal here? I've been gone longer and you've said less.'

'I had things to talk to you about, that's all.'

'Well talk to me now.'

'It's too late.'

Josh sighed and bent his head. 'Shit, Elizabeth. You're acting like a teenager whose prom date hasn't shown. I'm kinda tired here.'

She looked at him coldly, stood up, still clutching the brooch in her hand, and walked to the sink to stare out the window.

Josh watched her face as she turned back to him, and saw some kind of battle being fought behind those brown eyes. One of the emotions eventually won and she spoke softly, as if ashamed of its victory.

'I'm pregnant.'

Josh blinked. He was aware that his heart had picked up its pace, but if that meant more blood was suddenly required and being provided, its rapid distribution seemed to be having little effect on him. It was as though his system had stalled like a smoky engine, leaving him temporarily unable to speak or move. He searched for the kick-start, and when he found it and spoke merely for the sake of speaking, realized that he should have waited.

'Is it mine?'

Elizabeth's face, already harder than he had ever seen it, darkened into the suburbs of fury.

'I'll give you one chance to take that back.'

He swallowed. 'Shit, I'm sorry . . . I mean . . . Fuck.'

She regarded him with a mixture of contempt and grief. The same eyes that only minutes ago had looked up at him like a lover were now scouring him with acid accusation.

Josh tried again. As he got up to move towards her she made him jump with a sudden violent movement, lifting her arms and waving them in front of her as if to protect herself. He backed off, hands held out in an imploring gesture, and his voice, when it came, was higher than he would have liked.

'I didn't mean that. I don't know why I said it. I'm glad. God, Elizabeth, I'm so glad.'

With those words something happened to Josh Spiller. A happiness that was beyond any he had ever experienced flooded into him and he realized that 'glad' was a weak and sickly word to describe the power of his sudden ecstasy.

Elizabeth watched the face of the father of her child as it exploded into rapture, watched his tense muscles melt into a slack, serpentine tangle of joy. Her lip trembled like a child's as she braced herself. Then she spoke quickly to interrupt the acceleration of his emotion: 'I'm not keeping it, Josh.'

His imploring arms fell.

'What?'

'I don't have a choice.'

Josh looked at her for a very long time, then turned back to the table and sat down heavily on his chair. He leaned forward and cradled his head in his hands, his hot forehead pointing straight down to the table top.

'Now hold up. This is going too fast. Talk to me.'

Elizabeth looked down at a hand which had become a fist, and when she opened it to reveal the brooch she had been clutching she could see two clear indentations that the scissors had made in her flesh. She closed her hand.

'You weren't here to talk to. I decided on my own. It's impossible, Josh.'

He looked up from the cradle of his hands.

'Why? For Christ's sake we're doing okay. Aren't we?'

She swallowed back a sob, barely able to speak.

'Nope.'

'What do you mean?'

Elizabeth moved stiffly and rejoined him at the table. She stared into the yellow pine as though the words she was speaking were printed on it.

'Commitment, Josh. That's what a baby needs. It's what I need too and I've never had it from you in any shape.'

He opened his mouth to protest but she silenced him with a sorrowful look.

'I'm not complaining. This is an accident in a relationship that's doing just fine. But it's a relationship that can't handle children.'

She was sounding rehearsed, but seven days to perfect a speech hadn't been enough to stop it sounding phoney.

'Welcome to daytime TV, folks.'

The bitterness in Josh's voice was as alien to him as it sounded to Elizabeth. Any plan she might have had evaporated, and she looked at him like a frightened child.

'Look at us, Josh. We live together but we're not married. I see you for two, maybe three days out of every ten. I've just started a new business that needs all my time and energy. There's nothing in this dumb life of ours that's stable enough to make a good job of growing another human being.'

'We love each other.'

'Then why aren't we married? Why aren't you at home?'

'Why aren't you? Is sewing fucking Batman suits better than staying home and looking after our baby?'

She looked at him coldly. 'Jesus Christ. You can take the man out of the truck but you can't take the trucker out of the man. What next, Josh? The chorus of a Red Sovine song?'

He lowered his eyes.

'I didn't know you wanted to get married.'

'You never asked.'

'What if I asked now?' His voice had an edge of desperation.

'It would mean nothing. You wouldn't be asking for the right reasons.'

There was a pause. A heavy silence that made Josh's response startling.

'FUCK!'

He slammed his fist down on the table so hard that Elizabeth leapt in her chair and caught her breath with the fright. Josh was breathing heavily, staring down at his hands, and she spoke softly when her heart had stopped pounding.

'Next week. Wednesday at three o'clock. It'll be over.'

He looked up slowly and her grief was almost uncontainable when she saw the film of tears that coated his eyes.

'Then why even tell me? Does it feel good to give me a few moments of joy and then steal them back again? Huh? Make you feel big? Feel in charge? That what you call love?'

Elizabeth started to cry. Her chest heaved and she bent her head to her chest. Josh watched, wanting instinctively to comfort her but cancelling the order from his brain before it reached his arms.

She sobbed for a few minutes in silence, wiped her arm across her eyes and nose and then faced him again.

'I told you because I was scared and lost. I always tell you everything.'

He looked at her tragic, puffy face and tried to feel the love for her he knew was there. But the imminent death of his baby, that terrifying appointment, the time already ticking away towards its execution as the baby's cells split and multiplied inside her, was blocking it like a wall. He spoke quietly and with a malice he never knew he possessed.

'You didn't tell me you were a selfish bitch.'

Elizabeth stared at him for a moment, stunned.

'Damn you to hell.' She opened her hand and with all the force a close sitting position could afford, threw the brooch at Josh's face and ran from the house.

As he sat still, listening to her car start and screech hysterically from the drive, Josh fingered the tiny scratch that his gift had inflicted above his eye. He bent to pick up the fallen weapon and closed his hand on the brooch's innocent form.

There was no question of what action to take. He would do what he always did in a crisis. Josh Spiller got up and went to call his dispatcher.

4

Time. It was at the core of everything. To buy it. To control it. To comprehend it. And yet still, this night, this eve that had been so long coming, so long anticipated, had now crept up on her like a thief.

As always, she tapped three keys on the keyboard and watched the figures scroll up the screen. She knew what she would see, but it was important to remind herself why.

This was why. The golden, glimmering, shining reason for it all. The dollars, the deutschmarks, the pounds, yen and lire, all flickering before her, lighting her face up with their green glow.

More. The knowledge and power.

But no. She closed her eyes and clenched a fist against it. That thought was forbidden. Vanity was destruction. The power was in the humble and respectful use of the knowledge. And that was why tomorrow was no more and no less than the necessary function that it had always been. The others depended on it. Their world turned on it, because God made it possible. She moved the mouse and closed the file with one diagonal sweep and click, as the sound of soft spring rain tapping at the window won the battle for her attention over the buzzing computer.

And she smiled as she looked up, imagining it soaking new buds on the blanket of trees that separated her from the dull uncomprehending mass of humanity.

It had taken the surly teenagers in the loading bay over an hour to load his trailer. And that was after a two-and-a-half-hour wait in the damp Victorian warehouse. Josh had sat in the drivers' waiting area, cradling a styrofoam cup of stewed coffee, watching the three bozos wandering around his truck like pimps on a Bronx street. One drove the fork-lift into Josh's trailer and the others hung around the doors making flipping gestures with their hands and adjusting their baseball caps as they laughed about something secret.

Normally, Josh would have gone out and kicked their butts, but this time he sat immobile behind the glass partition, watching them waste his time. It was a shitty load, Some metal packing cases for an industrial ceramics manufacturer in Alabama. No weight in them, so not much pay. But it was all he could get, and Josh would have delivered the Klan's laundry to South Central LA if he'd been asked. He would have taken anything at all just to turn off and buy his ticket away from home.

There had been two other drivers in the warehouse and, hold the front page, they had been bitching:

'So I grabs this little jerk by the collar and I says okay man, you want me to load it myself then you gonna have to tell your boss why his lifting gear got all bust up, 'cos I ain't never used it afore. 'Course I have, but he don't know that.'

The guy who'd been telling the story was about as big as his truck and the other driver listened without much interest, waiting for his chance to tell a similar triumphant story of how he showed them, and showed them good.

'Well he calls me everythin' but a white boy and then I just grabs hold of the controls and lets the whole bunch drop twenty feet onto the deck. Hee hee, did that boy load up like his dick depended on it.'

Josh had let the stream of familiar bullshit wash over him. He was numb. So numb, he'd uncharacteristically ignored both men, walked to the trailer when a nod from one of the rubber-boned kids indicated it was done, barely checked the load or how it was stacked, taken the paperwork and driven off. And now he was sitting upright, staring out of the darkened cab of Jezebel, whose bulk was untidily taking up most of the space in a southbound tourist parking lot on this Virginian interstate. He'd driven for only a couple of hours, but a lapse of concentration that nearly let him trash a guy on a Harley Davidson had made him catch his heart in his mouth and pull over.

It was two a.m. and he could hardly account for the last eight hours since Elizabeth had driven away with her, and his, precious cargo on board. He stared ahead into the dark, sitting in the driver's seat with his hands resting in his lap like a trauma patient waiting to be seen in an emergency room. Josh wasn't thinking about what to do. He wasn't even thinking about Elizabeth and where she might be right now. All that was running through his mind were the words, repeating themselves like a looped tape, 'How do I feel?'

Soft spring rain started to fall, gradually muting the intermittent roar of the traffic on the adjacent highway. He wound down his window and breathed in a mixture of mown grass, diesel fumes, and the dust raised by the rain from the parking lot's asphalt. As he tried to take a deeper breath he felt a vice tighten around his chest, a crippling tension which prevented that satisfying lungful of oxygen. The pain came not from the emptiness that was left by that brief and grotesque argument, but from the dual seed of joy and dread that was still germinating in his heart.

Wednesday the seventh of May, three o'clock.

What was it? A boy or a girl? He hadn't even asked Elizabeth how many weeks old her secret was. A bizarre omission, but more confusing was why he wanted this child so badly. Some of the things Elizabeth had said were true, he knew that. Their life wasn't exactly an episode of *The Waltons*, but until last night he'd thought it was safe and stable. It was an adult life, where two self-contained people did what they pleased and came together when they wanted. He'd never even considered how or why that might change. Never considered a third person entering the frame.

The fresh air stirred him from his miserable torpor and Josh got up, absently pulling the drapes around the inside of the windshield. He climbed back into the sleeper and lay down on the mattress with his hands behind his head.

As he lay there, staring up at the quilted velour ceiling, he allowed himself to think of her, of Elizabeth; that funny, sometimes brittle person who even in her hardest moments could be melted like butter over a stove with a kind word or gentle touch.

It was like her to carry the burden of her news silently, but it was unlike her to taunt him by telling him it was over before it began. Perhaps he didn't know Elizabeth at all. Who was that terrible mixture of defiant accusation and self-pitying grief? And who had he been, to call her what he did and withdraw the support he'd always given unthinkingly and unconditionally?

Josh screwed his eyes tight, trying fruitlessly to squeeze the scene into oblivion with the puny muscles of his eyelids.

Which coupling had done it, he wondered? Last week? The week before?

When?

Outside, a car pulled up in the lot and Josh opened his eyes to listen to the familiar human noises of a man and a woman as they left their vehicle to go and use the rest-rooms.

They chatted in low voices, in that comfortable intimate way that meant they were saying nothing in particular to each other, but were enjoying saying it. An occasional short laugh broke the flow of their small talk as they slammed their car door shut and their footsteps receded towards the rest-rooms. Josh realized he was listening to this most mundane collection of sounds with his teeth clenched and his eyes narrowed, the invisible couple's easy happiness an unbearable affront.

He lay there for a very long time, and as time ticked away, bringing neither sleep nor solution, he was aware of its swift relentless passing for probably the first time in his life.

Dawn on the first of May was less beautiful than the one Josh had tried to savour yesterday. Low clouds masked the sun's coming and a thin grey light was all that announced the day. He had lain sleeplessly in the same position all night, eyes staring up into the dark as he alternated between thinking and hurting, and now he wanted to move. The load was already late. The paperwork promised the packing cases would be in Alabama sometime tonight, but they wouldn't be.

Josh crawled from his bunk into the cab, opened the door on the new day and went to wet the wheels. As he stood, legs apart, urinating on his truck in some unconsciously atavistic ritual, he reconfirmed with himself that the best cure for any form of unhappiness was perpetual motion. Driving let him escape. It allowed him time completely on his own and freedom from responsibility. It had certainly saved his sanity when his mother died, that hellish two weeks after her funeral, when Josh knew he would never again have the chance to say the things to her he'd rehearsed so many times alone in his cab. He'd left his morose brother Dean at their empty home to go through their mother's pathetically few things, accepted a load to Seattle, and pushed the thought of his loss out with the opening of his log book.

He recalled seeing his brother's grief-torn face accusing him through the dirty upstairs window as he drove off, and it had chipped at something hard inside that Josh thought had been impermeable. Five hours later he'd put the whole thing out of his mind. Dean had never really forgiven him for that act of abandonment. But he didn't understand. No one but another trucker would.

Josh finished his task, did up his pants, then leaned forward to rest his forehead against the side of his trailer and punch its aluminium flank with the side of a fist.

'Fuck 'em all, Jez. Fuck every last one.'

5

The cloud had lifted as she stood rigid and still on the grass. That was good. She watched the thin sunlight play amongst the bare branches of the ancient tree that stood solemnly in the wide street, and as her gaze moved down to the base of its massive bole, she frowned with irritation. There were suckered branches starting to form in clumps at the base. That meant only one thing. The tree was dying.

It must have been the men laying the cables last year. They had been told to make sure the trench came nowhere near the roots, to cut a path for the thick mass of plastic tubing and wire in between those delicate arteries of soft wood rather than through them. But they were like all workmen. Lazy. And this was the result.

She ground her teeth and concentrated on fighting the irritation.

Absence of malice, absence of compassion, absence of all petty human emotion. It was essential.

In a few hours she would let her thoughts return to the vandalized tree, but not now. The workmen would never be employed by her again. And that, she decided, would be the least of their worries.

But not now. Push the thought away and leave nothing. Nothing at all.

Quarter of an hour down the highway, Josh saw a five-mile service sign and realized he was hungry. More importantly, he was approaching his thirty-sixth hour without sleep and unless he grabbed a coffee soon, bad things were going to start happening. In fact, they already had. A dull grey slowness had settled on him, making his peripheral vision busy with the hazy shifting shapes that severe fatigue specialized in manufacturing, and his limbs were beginning to feel twice their weight. But hungry as he was, he still hadn't forgotten the affront of yesterday's dawn. McDonald's might have sold ten billion, but he wasn't going to make it ten billion and one.

He thumbed the radio.

'Any you northbounds know a good place to eat off the interstate?'

The voice first to respond just laughed. 'Surely, driver. There's a little Italian place right up ahead. Violins playin' and candles on every table.'

Josh smiled.

Another driver butted in. 'No shit? Where's that at again?'

'I'm kiddin', dipshit. Burgers ain't good enough for you?'

Josh pressed his radio again, then thought better of it. What did these guys know? Channel 19 would be busy now for the next hour with bored truckers arguing about the merits of the great American burger. He was sorry he had started it.

There was an exit coming up on the right, and although the sign declared this was the exit for a bunch of ridiculously named nowhere towns, he braked and changed down. It was twenty before seven and if he didn't get that coffee soon he'd have to pull over.

The reefer tailing him came on the radio.

'Hey, Jezebel. See you signalling for exit 23.'

Josh responded. 'Ten-four, driver. That a problem?'

'Got a mighty long trailer there to get up and down them mountain roads. They're tight as a schoolmarm's ass cheeks.'

'Copy, driver. Not plannin' on goin' far. Just grab a bite and get myself back on the interstate.'

Josh was already in the exit lane as he spoke the last words, the reefer peeling away from him up the highway.

'Okay, buddy. Just hope you can turn that thing on a dollar.'

'Ten-four to that.'

'How comes she got the handle Jezebel?'

Josh grinned as he slowed down to around twenty-five, on what was indeed, and quite alarmingly so, a very narrow road. When he felt the load was secure behind him, he took his hand off the wheel to reply.

'Aw this is my second rig, and I figure she tempted me but she'll probably turn out to be no good like the last one.'

He swallowed at that, hoping the ugly thought that it had stirred back into life would go away. The other driver saved him.

'Yeah? What you drive before?'

Irritatingly, the signal was already starting to break up. Strange, since the guy was probably only two miles away, with Josh now heading south-east on this garden path of a road.

'Freightliner Conventional. Everything could go wrong did go wrong. Might be mean naming this baby like that. Hasn't let me down yet. But she's pretty, huh?'

The radio crackled in response, but Josh didn't pick up the driver's comment. It was the least of his worries. He saw what the guy meant. The road was almost a single track. If he met another truck on this route they'd both have to get out, scratch their heads and talk about how they were going to pass. Josh slowed the truck down to twenty and rolled along, squinting straight into the low morning sun that had only now emerged from the dissipating grey clouds, to look for one of the towns the sign had promised.

The interstate was well out of sight, and he was starting to regret the impulsive and irrational decision to boycott the convenience of a burger and coffee. The road was climbing now, and since the exit he hadn't seen one farm gate or cabin driveway where he could turn the Peterbilt.

He pressed on the radio again.

'Hey, any locals out there? When do you hit the first town after exit 23?'

He waited, the handset in his hand. There was silence. It was a profound silence that rarely occurred on CB. There was always something going on. Morons yelling, or guys bitching. Drivers telling other drivers the exact whereabouts on the highway of luckless females. There was debate, there was comedy, there were confidences shared and tales told. All twenty-four hours a day. Anything you wanted to hear and anything you wanted to say, was all there waiting at the press of a button.

But here, there was nothing. Josh looked up at the long spine of the hills and reckoned they must have something to do with the sudden stillness of the radio. It unnerved him. The cab of a truck was never quiet. Usually Josh had three things going at once: the CB, the local radio station, and a tape. Elizabeth had ridden with him a few times and could barely believe how through the night-marish cacophony he not only noted the local traffic report, but also hummed along to a favourite song, heard everything that was said on the CB, and was able to make a pretty good guess at which truck was saying it.

'How in hell do you do that?' she'd breathed admiringly after he'd jumped in with the sequel to some old joke someone was telling, only seconds after he'd been shouting abuse at a talk radio host who'd used the word 'negro'.

'What'd you say, honey?' he'd replied innocently, not understanding the irony when she laughed at him. She said after that, if she had anything important to tell him, she'd do it over a badly tuned radio with a heavy metal band thrashing in the background.

Except she hadn't. Had she?

It had been important, and she'd told it to him straight, her words surrounded by a proscenium arch of silence. Josh flicked his eyes to the fabric above the windshield where Elizabeth's cheap brooch was pinned. He'd stabbed it in there as a reminder that it had been bought with love but used as a spiteful missile, hoping it would harden him to the thought of her every time the pain of their argument germinated again. But it wasn't working. It just made him think of her long brown fingers fingering it with delight. Josh wished the trivial memory of her riding with him hadn't occurred to him, hadn't made him feel like his heart needed a sling to support its weight.

He leaned forward and retuned the CB as though the action could relegate his dark thoughts to another channel.

Still nothing.

Josh sat back and resigned himself to the blind drive. The next town could be two or twenty miles away, and he was just going to have to live with that. It could be worse. The road was still climbing, but at least it was a pretty ride.

Dogwood bloomed on both sides of the road and on the east verge the rising sun back-lit the impossibly large and delicate white flowers, shining through the thin petals as though the dark branches were the wires of divine lamps. Ahead, a huge billboard cut rudely into the elegance of the small trees. The sign was old and worn, with the silvery grey of weathered wood starting to show through what had once been bright green paint.

'See the world-famous sulphur caves at Carris Arm. Only 16 miles. Restaurant and tours.'

In the absence of anyone to talk to on the CB, Josh spoke to himself.

'World-famous. Yeah, sure. The Taj Mahal, the Grand Canyon and the fuckin' sulphur caves at Carris Arm.'

As if he needed it, the sign confirmed that Josh Spiller was driving around in the ass-end of nowhere, and he was far from happy. If that was the next town, then sixteen miles was way too far. He started to weigh his options. Surely there would soon be a farm gate or a clearing he could turn in. But as the truck climbed it seemed less and less likely. The mountains were a serpentine dark wall, clothed here in undisturbed forest only just starting to leaf, and neither farmland nor building broke the trees' unchallenged hold on the land. Josh had already driven at least four or five miles from the interstate and the thought of another sixteen was making him consider the possibility of backing up and turning on a soft verge, when without any warning or apparent reason, the road started to widen.

A house, set back in the trees, neat and spacious with the stars and stripes flapping listlessly on a flagpole by the porch, appeared on his right, followed by another three in a row almost identical a few hundred yards further on. No backwoods cabin these, but substantial suburban houses with trimmed gardens and decent wheels parked out front. Josh raised an eyebrow. This was what truckers called car-farmer country. The backwoods of the Appalachians were home to a thousand run-down trailers and cabins, sporting a statutory dozen cars and pick-ups half buried in their field, like the hicks who'd left them there to rot were hoping their '69 Buick would sprout seeds and grow a new one.

Even on the main routes, Josh had been glared at by enough one-eyed crazy lab-specimens lounging on porches to know that this wasn't exactly stockbroker belt. The kind of tidy affluence quietly stated by these houses was a surprise. But it was a welcome surprise to a man who needed his breakfast and wouldn't have to buy it from a drooling Jed Clampit with a shotgun raised at his chest.

So half a mile and a dozen or more smart houses later, it was with relief that Josh hit the limits of the town to which these uncharacteristic middle-class dwellings were satellites. He drove past the brief and concise metal sign with a smile.

Furnace.

The wide street was now lined on either side by houses only slightly smaller than those on the edge of town. Standard roses bobbed in the breeze and hardy azaleas and forsythia were beginning to form islands of colour in a sea of smooth lawns.

It was five before seven and although it was early, people were about and Josh was heartened by the town's potential for hot food to go. A kid rode past on a BMX, a sack of papers on his shoulder; two guys sweeping the road stood jawing against a tree, brushes in hand; a woman walking a dachsund on a ludicrously long leash stopped and waved to someone out picking up their paper from the front step. It was cosy, affluent, peaceful and ordinary. But it certainly was not what he had expected high up in this backwater of Virginia. Here, Jezebel felt ridiculously out of place, rumbling self-consciously through the street at little more than running pace, as though lack of speed could hide the bulk and noise of the Leviathan. The quiet street waking to its new day was like any other, but the affluence and suburban smugness was starting to jog a memory in Josh he didn't like.

The Tanner ice cream sign.

A dumb, irrelevant memory, and one he tried to sideswipe. But it was there.

That ice cream sign.

For Josh as a child it stood at the corner of Hove and Carnegie like a religious icon; a circular piece of tin with the advertisement painted on it, supported at two points by a bigger circle of wire on a stand that let it spin in the wind. Judging by the arthritic squeaking of its rotations, it had stood at the end of his street like that for years, that dismal street his mother had brought them up on, a strange juxtaposition of the classes that Pittsburgh boasted, where the unwashed poor lived only a block away from their bosses, separated by no more than just a strip of trees or a row of stores.

Or an ice cream sign.

The Tanner girl and boy had big rosy cheeks and were licking the same cone of ice cream, vanilla topped with chocolate sauce. But when the wind blew the sign would spin and the picture, identical on both surfaces except for the children's mouths which were closed on one side and open on the other, would animate into a frenzy of darting, licking tongues. Dean thought the sign was kind of spooky, especially when the wind was strong and the tongues went crazy. But Josh liked it. He liked it because it marked the beginning of Carnegie Lane, and more importantly, the end of Hove Avenue, an end to the crowded street that contained their tattered house. In Carnegie the houses were elegant and tall, keeping watch over their own spacious gardens with the demeanour of large wealthy women sitting on rugs at a race meeting. And unlike the regiment of dreary wooden houses that included the Spillers', every one was different. Some were brick with wide white columned porches tangled with wisteria and honeysuckle. Others had stone façades and glass conservatories, or European affectations of mock battlements and balustrades. And in addition to the neat front lawns that were uniformly green all the way to the sidewalk, each, Josh knew for sure, had generous and private back yards.

School, the stores and everything that Josh needed to service his uneventful life was at the eastern end of Hove. In other words there was no call to go west into Carnegie at all. It merely led to wealthier parts of town, parts that were decidedly not for the Spillers. But he'd lost count of the times he'd found himself strolling past the squeaking Tanner ice cream sign, stepping into Carnegie with a roll to his pre-pubescent gait that tried to say he lived there.

At least he had until one searingly hot August. Josh was eleven and the day had been long and empty. His mother's return from her job at a drug factory, moving piles of little blue and white capsules along a conveyor belt all day with a gloved hand, had been a cranky and irritable one. Particularly since she discovered that neither Dean nor Josh had made any attempt to prepare supper, but had instead been throwing stones up at the remains of an old weathervane that clung to a neighbour's roof, in a contest to free it finally from its rusting bracket.

Joyce Spiller had sat down heavily on the three car tyres piled by the back door they used as a seat, and glared at the boys, but particularly Josh, with tired, rheumy eyes. Her voice was full of sarcastic venom.

'Sure do appreciate you workin' all day long, Mom. So to thank you for that act of kindness, please accept this cool glass of lemonade and a big juicy sandwich that me an' my shit-for-manners brother have had all friggin' day to prepare.'

Dean had blinked at his boots in shame, but for some reason, looking at this woman in her short nylon workcoat, her thin brown hair tied back with a plain elastic band, and her face that looked ten years older than her numerical age, Josh had suddenly despised her. Why should he look after her, when other kids got to come home from school and be met by a Mom who'd fetch them lemonade and a sandwich? What kind of a raw deal was this, having a mother who worked all day, sometimes nights too, who was always in a foul mood and looked like shit? The absence of a father, a taboo subject in the Spiller house, was bad enough, but the fact that they lived in this shambolic house and never went on vacation was all this failure of a woman's fault.

Josh had stared back at her with contempt and then run from the yard out into the street.

He thanked God that until her dying day, his mother had taken that action for a show of shame and remorse. It was anything but. He'd seen the Tanner's ice cream sign slowly rotating in the searing hot breeze and had headed straight for the leafy calm of Carnegie, where the people lived who knew how to treat their children. Maybe if he stopped and spoke to a kid up there, they might get friendly and he'd be asked in. He'd often thought of it. That day he decided he would make it a reality. Then she'd see. She'd come home and he'd be in one of those yards drinking Coke with new friends, who had stuff like basketball nets stuck to their walls and blue plastic-walled swimming pools you climbed into from a ladder. There'd be no more kicking around in a dusty yard with nothing to do except scrap with Dean and wait for a worn-out mother to come home and cuss at them.

He ran as far as the sign, then slowed up and turned into the shimmering street with a casual step. The sign had been making a wailing forlorn sound, a kind of *whea eee, whea eee* like some forest animal's young looking for its parent. Josh strolled into the splendour of the street and walked slowly, gazing up at the grand houses, smelling the blooms from their gardens. There had been nobody about except for one man who was rooting around in the trunk of a car parked out front.

Josh got ready to say hello as he approached, but on catching sight of him the man straightened up with legs apart, putting his hands on his hips in the manner of a Marine drill sergeant expecting trouble.

He stood like that, staring directly and aggressively at Josh, never taking his eyes from the small boy until he walked by. Josh had felt his cheeks burn.

It was then that he had noticed the sounds. Just background noises at first, but with the blood already beating in his ears, they grew louder and louder until they were roaring in his head.

Lawnmowers buzzing, children shouting and laughing, garden shears snapping, an adult voice calling out, the echoing, plastic sound of a ball bouncing on a hard surface. All these sounds were being made by a ghostly and invisible army of people cruelly hidden from view. And ever present, weaving in and out of these taunting, nightmarish sounds was the *whea eee, whea eee* of the Tanner ice cream sign. Josh had been paralysed by a sense of desolation that made his bones cold in the thick heat.

The wall of expensive stone that was separating him from these invisible, comfortable, happy people was suddenly grotesque instead of glamorous, an obstacle that could never be negotiated if you were Josh Spiller from Hove Avenue. He had slapped his hands uselessly to his ears, turned and run back the way he had come, fuelling, no doubt, the fears of the man by his car that this was a Hove boy up to no good. Every hot step of the way home the ice cream sign's wail followed him like a lost spirit, as though it were an alarm he had tripped when he stepped from his world into the forbidden one of his betters.

His mother had welcomed him back with a silent supper of fries and ham, but he could tell by the softness in her eyes she was relieved to see him. Josh knew then how much he loved her. He also knew that no matter how agreeable a house he might eventually buy as an adult, how comfortable an existence he might make for himself, he would always butt up against the corner of a forbidden street, the edge of something better to which he had no access. Maybe that was why he had turned trucker. No one can judge what a man does or doesn't have if he's always on the move. The eighteen wheels you lived on were the ultimate democracy. An owner-operator might be up to his neck in debt with his one rig, or it might be one rig out of a fleet of twenty. No one knows if the guy's rich or poor and no one cares. The questions one trucker asks another are: where you going, where you from, what you hauling, how many cents per mile you get on that load?

No one would ever ask what street you lived on and give you a sidelong glance if it happened to be the wrong one. Josh hadn't thought about that dumb incident for years, but here, faced with these attractive houses in this small mountain town, he could almost hear the ice cream sign howling forlornly again. It was crazy. He'd grown into a man to whom material possessions meant little or nothing, and yet here he was being infected by that old feeling of desire and denial that he thought he'd shaken off before he'd even grown a pubic hair. And all because a town looked a little neater, a little smugger, a little more affluent than he'd expected. Okay. A lot more affluent.

Josh shook his shoulders, suppressed his discomfort at the memory as he approached the town's first set of lights, and scanned the side streets for a sign of something that might suggest food. The truck's brakes hissed, he leaned forward on the wheel and looked around.

If Furnace had a commercial centre then this was probably it. The wide street that cut across this one was lined on both sides with small shops and offices, buildings that were as well presented as those belonging to their potential customers. There was a cheerful bar on one corner, featuring long, plant-filled windows onto the street, far removed from the darkly terrifying drinking-holes a man could expect in the mountains, and an antique shop on the other that suggested Furnace did a fair piece of business from tourism. A complex metal tree of signs told him where the best Appalachian wine could be bought, provided directions to a children's farm where the animals could be petted, and reminded you that the world-famous sulphur caves were now a mere fourteen miles away. Josh conceded that bored families in camper vans might tip a few dimes into the town's economy every summer, but even if they loaded up with Appalachian wine till it broke their axles and petted the farm animals bald, it still wouldn't account for the prosperity of the town. He mused on the mystery of it, and settled with reckoning there must be a whole heap of prime farmland groaning with fat cattle hiding way back here that was keeping these people in new cars and white colonnaded porches. But if that was the case, they were keeping it well hidden. And although the mountain forest came so close to the edge of the town it made Furnace look little more than a fire-break, what the hell: it was a theory. It made Josh more comfortable to invent a logical and soil-based reason, stalling that tiny and rare niggle of envy he was feeling. He never envied farmers. Being tied to the land was just about the worst thing you could be.

Far down the road to his right, Josh could make out the entrance to a mini-mall, fronted by an open foodstore. That's where he would head and take his chance, since the parking in front of the store looked sufficiently generous to accommodate the truck.

As he gazed along the long wide road, waiting for the lights to change, the vibration of the idling engine combined with the pale early morning sun shining into his face suddenly made Josh ache to close his heavy eyes. He fought it, but his eyes won.

It must have been only seconds, but when he awoke with a neck-wrenching upward jerk of the head, the fact he'd fallen asleep made Josh pant with momentary panic. He ran a hand over his face. This wasn't like him. It had been years since he'd allowed himself to become so tired while driving that he could lose it like that. In the past, sure, he'd pushed it. But not now. Once, back in those days when he'd try anything once, he'd driven so long he'd done what every trucker dreads. He'd fallen asleep with his eyes open. After a split-second dream, something crazy about shining golden dogs, Josh had woken suddenly to find the truck already bouncing over the grass verge. He vowed then he'd never do it again. Yet here he was, thirty-six hours since sleep, still driving. He had to stop and get some rest. No question. But first he wanted to eat.

Above him, the bobbing lights had been giving their green permission for several seconds, and he shook his head vigorously to rid himself of fatigue while he turned Jezebel into the street at a stately ten miles an hour. As he straightened up and moved down the road, a car trying unsuccessfully to park pushed its backside out into the road at a crazy angle and forced him to stop. He sighed and leaned forward on the wheel again while the jerk took his time shifting back and forward as if the space was a ball-hair's width instead of being at least a car-and-a-half-length long. The old fool behind the wheel stuck an appreciative liver-spotted hand out the window to thank Josh for his patience, and continued to manoeuvre his car in and out at such ridiculously tortuous angles it was as though he was attempting to draw some complex, imaginary picture on the asphalt. Josh raised a weary hand in response and muttered through a phoney smile, 'Come on, you donkey's tit.'

He sighed and let his eye wander ahead to the foodstore, allowing himself to visualize a hot blueberry muffin and steaming coffee.

Across the street, a woman was walking towards the mall, struggling with a toddler and pushing a stroller in front of her that contained a tiny baby. It must have been only days old. Josh swallowed. He could see the little creature's bald head propped forward in the stroller, a striped canvas affair, presumably the property of its sibling and way too large for its new occupant. The baby was held level in this unsuitable vehicle with a piece of sheepskin which framed its tiny round face like some outlandish wig.

With the sight of that impossibly small creature, it was back; the longing, the hurt, the confusion that Elizabeth had detonated in him.

He found himself watching like some hungry lion from long grass as the woman kicked on the brakes of the stroller, abandoned the baby on the sunny sidewalk and dragged her toddler into the store. The tiny bundle moved like an inexpertly handled puppet in its upright canvas seat, its little arms flailing and thrashing as two stick-thin legs paddled in an invisible current. Josh ran a hand over his unshaved chin, and covered his mouth with his hand.

Would his baby be kicking like that little thing, right now, inside Elizabeth? When did all that stuff happen? A month? Two months? Six? He knew nothing about it.

Elizabeth. His mouth dried. Elizabeth, his love. Where the hell was she?

He closed his gritty eyes for a moment and the shame of what he had done overwhelmed him, making him light-headed with the sudden panic of regret. Opening his eyes again, he looked towards the infant. There was now a different woman standing behind it, both hands on the plastic grips of the stroller.

Older than the mother, possibly in her fifties, she was dressed in a garish pink linen suit that, although formal and angular in its cut, seemed designed for a far younger woman.

Her hair was red, obviously dyed, and even from this distance Josh decided she was wearing too much make-up; a red gash for a mouth, arching eyebrows drawn in above deeply-set eyes.

He had seen plenty of women like that at the big Midwest truck shows, hanging on the arm of their company-owning husbands;

women who spent money tastelessly as though the spending of it was inconvenient and tiresome but part of a dutiful bargain that had been struck.

Josh would barely have glanced at such a woman had he seen one sipping sparkling wine in a hospitality marquee, while her husband ignored her to do business with grim-faced truckers.

But here, standing outside a foodstore in this rural nowhere at seven o'clock on a spring morning, she looked remarkably out of place.

More than that. The most extraordinary thing about her was that she was staring directly and with alarming intensity at Josh. It wasn't the annoyed and studied glare of a concerned citizen, the look a middle-aged woman with nothing better to do than protect small civil liberties might throw a noisy truck.

It wasn't aimed at the truck. It was aimed at him.

In front of him, the master class in lunatic parking had ceased, the man at the wheel waving a gnarled and arthritic hand from his window again in mute thanks, and still the woman's eyes continued to bore into Josh as she stood erect and unmoving, her body unnaturally still, on guard behind the writhing baby. For one fleeting, crazy moment Josh thought he might be inventing her, that a part of his guilty and fevered mind had conjured up this stern female figure to reprimand him for his paternal inattention.

'That's right, you useless dick,' those eyes seemed to be saying. 'This is what a baby looks like. You can look but you certainly can't have. Only real men get these. Real men who stay home.'

He blinked at her, hoping that her head would turn from him and survey some other banal part of this quiet street scene, proving that her stare had been simply that of someone in a daydream, but her face never moved and the invisible rod that joined their eyes was becoming a hot solid thing.

There was no question of him stopping at that store now. Josh wanted out of there, away from that face, away from that tiny baby.

He fumbled for the shifter, starting the rig rolling clumsily by crunching his way around the gear-box as he picked up speed. A row of shiny shop windows to his left across the street bounced back a moving picture of Jezebel as she roared up through the gears. It was the clarity of that reflection as it distorted across undulating and different sized glass that gave her driver an excuse to admire the mirror-image of himself sitting at the head of his gleaming electric-blue Peterbilt, and take his eyes momentarily from the face of the woman who was still standing like a lawyer for the prosecution on the sidewalk ahead.

Had she been waiting for that irresistible weakness that is every trucker's vanity, to catch a brief glimpse of themselves on the move, and see themselves as others do? Josh would never be sure. How could he ever be sure of anything that happened that morning?

His eyes flicked back from the moving reflection down to the speedometer which showed around twenty, and then looked forward again. Back to the road and those eyes glaring at him from across the street.

She pushed the stroller like an Olympic skater, propelling it forward with a theatrically benevolent outward motion of the arms which culminated in a triumphant crucifix, palms open, shoulders high, as if waiting for a panel of judges to hold up their score cards. The timing and positioning was spectacularly accurate. She hadn't pushed until Josh had been exactly level with her, so that the front wheels of the stroller rolled at an oblique angle beneath the double back tyres of the tractor unit.

That expertly judged speed and angle let the outer tyre snag the frame and flip it on its side under the rig, giving all eight wheels the opportunity to travel directly over the stroller and its contents.

It was almost as if Josh's hysterical intake of breath was the force which pulled his right leg up and slammed his foot down on the brake. But there was little point in the action. His chair had already bounced in response to that small shuddering bump, the slight motion the truck's suspension registered as it negotiated a minor obstacle, the same motion that would indicate Jezebel had run over a pothole or a piece of lumber on the highway. Only this time it wasn't a piece of lumber. It was eight pounds of brand-new flesh, bones and blood, strapped into its flimsy shell of plastic, aluminium and canvas.

The force of the braking threw Josh forward into the steering wheel, and after he whiplashed back with a winded grunt he snapped his head round, eyes and mouth as wide open as the muscles were designed to allow, wildly scanning the view from his open window as he panted for breath. In those few seconds that felt like minutes, he noticed three things. The first was that the woman in the pink suit was gone. The second was that the reflection in the store window showed him quite clearly that there was a small mangled mass beneath the trailer, caught untidily between the back wheels of the cab. The third was that the mother was emerging slowly, as if in a dream, from the door of the store, her mouth making a dark down-turned shape that was impossibly ugly. It took a few more seconds before her screams started. First her arms twitched at her sides and her body appeared to quiver with some internal electric current, and then it was as if that current had been suddenly cut. She collapsed to her knees like a prisoner about to be executed, and her dark open mouth shaped the cry that savaged the morning air with the naked brutality of its pain.

Behind her, in the open doorway, her toddler stood howling until adult arms swept it inside.

Josh was out of his cab and scrambling desperately beneath the trailer before he had time to consider what he might find there. Had he stopped to think he would never have approached that soup of flesh, but his body was working to some private agenda that had little to do with logic or thought. It moved and acted on instinct, as if unthinking swiftness of action could somehow undo what had most certainly and irreversibly been done.

The towelling one-piece babysuit had held most of its contents together, but it had expanded when the body inside changed shape, so that now it was not so much a garment as a large, sticky, flat sack. The blood seemed so thick and black, but the worst of it was the way the main aluminium support of the stroller had embedded itself in the middle of the baby's skull, splitting the head in two in a diagonal line from one eyebrow to a tiny shoulder. It had forced both eyes from their sockets before they, too, were mashed into the glistening corpse.

Perhaps he thought the child would be unrecognizable. He was disappointed. The mess was still so obviously a baby that Josh put out a trembling hand and fingered one tiny foot that had somehow remained intact, regretting it instantly when his gentle touch made it shift slightly with a sickening slick sound. For a crazy moment, lying on his stomach beneath the trailer, he thought about those cartoons where the victim is run over by a road roller and peeled off the road in a long flat strip, and he wanted to laugh.

He wanted to shake with laughter, wanted to feel tears of mirth pour down his cheeks, and hold his sides as they ached with the effort of hilarity. But the sound he was already making, accompanying the stream of salty tears dripping from his chin, was a thin, reedy wail that came from the back of his throat. It was a sound very far away from laughter.

He lay there for a long time, then there were hands on his legs, pulling him out from under the truck. Gentle hands, squeezing him reassuringly as they tugged him back. And voices. Calm voices that sounded miles away, saying things like 'come on now, fella', 'leave it now', 'come on there'.

Josh went limp. He was pulled free of Jezebel by three pairs of hands and manhandled into a sitting position. A man wearing thick spectacles and a blue cotton coat with 'Campbell's Food Mart' stitched on the pocket, was kneeling in front of him, looking concerned.

Behind him were two lanky teenagers, one with the same coat and one in a T-shirt and low-slung jeans. The man was talking softly, as if to a wounded animal.

'S'okay. S'okay now. Weren't nothin' you could've done there, fella. Sheriff's on his way. You just sit tight.'

Josh looked at him dumbly and then turned to the sidewalk in front of the store where he had seen the mother collapse. She was sitting as he was, although being attended to by more people, but her head was thrown back and one arm reached up above her head as though trying to grab a rope. The woman, the woman in pink, that staring, crazy murderer, was nowhere to be seen. Josh realized with an accelerating panic she was not being pursued, that her absence was not an issue here. She had to be found, had to be stopped. He struggled to get to his feet.

'It wasn't no accident . . . listen . . . we have to find that woman . . . she . . .'

The bespectacled shop keeper held him down.

'Hey, hey. Come on there. You had a mighty bad shake-up. Hang on in there.'

A station-wagon ambulance was drawing up, and suddenly the hands that were pressing his shoulders down now went to his armpits and helped him to his feet.

He went meekly and sat down heavily on the edge of the sidewalk where his assistants abandoned him in favour of a split interest between the hysterical mother and the two paramedics crouching under the trailer. To Josh, the people making up this macabre tableau were moving slowly and dreamily as though they were under water. He blinked as a fat, dusty police car rolled to a halt behind the truck and watched impassively as a sheriff's deputy climbed into Jezebel and moved her to the side of the street with a shudder of badly-changed gears.

He said nothing as a square man who claimed to be the sheriff led him to the police car and gently guided him into the back seat. But as they drove off, his armour of numbness was shattered by the sight of the bereaved mother, still sitting on the sidewalk, now embraced clumsily around her thin shoulders by a rough-hewn man in paramedic's coveralls. She lifted her head as he sat in the police car, raised a trembling hand towards him and opened her mouth to speak. He waited, steeling himself for the abuse, the unimaginable but inevitable verbal wounding.

With the window shut he couldn't hear her words, but her face was so close, and she spoke so slowly he could lip-read as clearly as if she had shouted.

Josh's heart lurched as he watched her mouth say, 'I'm sorry.' Then she bowed her head and gave in to her weeping once more.

6

'No. I don't understand.'

Dr McCardie tapped his pen on the desk and looked at her without sympathy.

'It's like I said, Miss Murray.'

'Elizabeth.'

'Elizabeth.' He nodded politely but coolly, taking her point before continuing. 'I realize that a scan may be the last thing you want when you obviously have your mind set on the termination, but in order to carry that termination out without complication, we need to know how the land lies.'

'Why today? Why couldn't you do this on Wednesday when I'm anaesthetized?'

The young man looked at her with an eyebrow raised and barely suppressed a sigh. 'A scan is neither painful nor traumatic. What's worrying me here is that you seem to believe that we're just going to put everything right while you're asleep. The termination is done under a local anaesthetic. You'll be awake. But more important than your comfort, Elizabeth, you're making a decision here. You'll have to live with that decision when you get up and walk away. Do you understand what that means?'

She blinked at him.

'Yes.'

He waited a few moments until the film of tears that was forming over her eyes was re-absorbed under his professionally dispassionate glare. 'Then may we proceed?'

She looked across at the screen of the scanning machine, still showing the result of its last client, a tiny crescent blob adrift in a black universe.

Elizabeth stood up and slipped off her coat.

They tested him for alcohol, taking his blood and breath, gave him scrappy bits of food and a warm can of soda as they wrote down the fragments of his fevered statement. Then, with the comic solemnity of a man who believes himself to be of great importance, a thickset policeman led him into a small brick-lined cell. He waited until Josh sat down on the narrow bed by the wall, then nodded to him as though his prisoner had performed some act of kindness.

'Shouldn't be overlong till the test results get back. This don't mean nothin', bein' in here for now. Just procedure.'

Josh looked up at him and returned the nod. The policeman closed the door gently and locked it.

The sleep that immediately overwhelmed Josh was so deep he had no recollection of even lying down on the hard mattress. His next sentient moment after the locking of the door was the unlocking of it, and that, he discovered with a bleary glance at his watch, was at least five hours later. A different policeman was regarding him coolly, waiting for him to come round.

'It's this way,' he said, as though answering a question.

Josh stood up unsteadily and followed him out of the cell, along a corridor and into the room where the sheriff and his colleague had interviewed him hours before. He entered, sat down on one of the unsteady wooden chairs arranged around the metal table, and waited with his hands folded in front of him. The deputy pulled out a chair opposite Josh, sat down and cleared his throat.

Outside the closed door, phones were ringing in the distant office and men were talking in low voices. Not the voices of conspiracy or suppressed anger, but rather the voices of visitors to a desperately sick hospital patient. The deputy scratched at an armpit.

'Got some more stuff to ask you if that's amenable to yourself.'

Josh blinked and sat back, marginally opening his palms in acquiescence.

'While you been sleepin' we got most of the information we need 'bout what went on back there.'

Josh sat up. 'The woman? You found her?'

The man looked back at Josh with a mixture of embarrassment

and impatience. 'I'm goin' to stick to what we know here right now. You with me?'

Josh said nothing, and his silence was taken as permission to continue.

'You ain't been drinkin' or poppin' pills, an' the marks from your tyres out on the road, along with them witnesses that saw it, say you weren't speedin' unduly neither. But I guess you know you're in violation with your log book.'

Josh's mouth twitched.

'I told you where I pulled over, and for how long. I was going to fill it in when I stopped here.'

'Trucker with all them years behind a wheel knows that's against the law.'

'Sure. I know it.'

The man's demeanour was changing. Beneath his officious politeness, Josh could read a glint of malice.

'Log books ain't there for your recreation, mister. We got to know where and when you stop. In case you been doin' somethin' you shouldn't.'

The policeman waited a beat, as if hoping for some display of emotion from his interviewee, then continued. 'Like drivin' illegal hours without sleepin'.'

Josh stared back at him, his closed mouth failing to conceal a jaw that was clenching, making the tiny muscles beneath his ears protrude.

'You have a good sleep in the cell?'

'Sure. Thanks.'

'Mighty tired, huh?'

'Yeah. Been working hard lately.'

The deputy sighed, long and deeply, as though growing weary of this. 'Your stopover. It checked out. Highway patrol saw your truck there three times in the time you said you parked.'

Josh stared at him, watching him closely as he continued to see if there were a trap being set.

'Guess it was lucky you pulled over in a tourist bay instead of a truck stop, huh, Mr Spiller? Attracted attention.'

'Never thought about it.'

The deputy leaned forward, his voice menacingly conspiratorial. 'Yeah, it's real lucky. 'Cos if we thought that you'd been drivin' for more than the legal ten hours when you killed that little baby, I guess I don't know what the sheriff might do.'

Josh stared back, trying to look unmoved. The deputy hissed, 'You're gonna get a fine that'll make that shaven head of yours curl the goddamn hair it got left. You're goin' to think about how poor you are every time you open your log book.'

'It was a mistake.'

The deputy looked back at him with naked contempt. 'Sheriff needs a final statement.'

He got up and left the room. Clearly, the impromptu interview had been nothing more than a device to work out his anger at an obvious injustice. If things had been different, Josh wondered how many teeth he might be missing right now, how many broken ribs he might be nursing after having 'fallen' in his cell. There was no doubt. They had been trying their damnedest as he slept to nail him with something, and they had failed.

Josh screwed shut his eyes and clenched his teeth. Ten hours? Try thirty-six. The lie was more intolerable for being a lie that could never be uncovered. Only Josh Spiller knew he hadn't slept. Did it really matter? He hadn't killed the baby. That woman, that nightmare of a creature, had killed it. How would a night's sleep have altered that?

Unless . . .

The tiny seed of doubt that he might have fallen asleep for a split second, for that crucial life-changing, life-ending second, wormed its way back into his mind. He slammed it down. No. He knew what he'd seen. A woman, a mad evil woman, had deliberately murdered a child.

He composed himself and forced himself to concentrate on waiting. For what, he was unsure, but the process of sitting still and expectantly was surprisingly calming. It was out of his hands. Someone, some unseen witness, would have told the police about the woman in the suit and they would be out there looking for her, if indeed they hadn't already got her locked up. If they could trace Jezebel's whereabouts to the parking lot last night, surely they would already have her behind bars. Maybe she was in the next cell. He would just wait and see.

He didn't have to wait long.

The door opened and the square sheriff entered with two deputies, each carrying a cup of coffee. The sheriff carried two, one of which he put down in front of Josh.

'Coffee. Take cream?'

Josh nodded his head dumbly and cupped his hands around the warm styrofoam as the man serviced his coffee with some mini-cream cartons from his pocket.

The sheriff sat down on the chair opposite and the two other men leaned against the wall, but their presence was casual rather than threatening.

'I introduced myself earlier, Mr Spiller, but I guess you were pretty spaced out by the whole thing so let me do it again. I'm Sheriff John Pace.'

Josh looked at him expectantly, hoping by the tone of his voice that he brought not a further reprimand, but some news.

John Pace, however, looked back as though the reminder of his name was all that mattered here. When he realized that the man was going to say no more, Josh spoke:

'Did you get her?'

Pace looked down at his cup and then glanced quickly out the corner of his eye at one of the deputies. The look, unlike that of his deputy before him, was one of disappointment, of someone letting him down. He sighed before he replied.

'Who might that be, Mr Spiller?'

Josh's hands, still cupped round the coffee, changed to fists.

'The woman. The one who pushed the baby under the truck.'

The sheriff cleared his throat. 'Mr Spiller,' he hesitated, then said, 'Can I call you . . . ?' he fished Josh's licence from his top pocket and peered at it. 'Josh? That's it?'

Josh stared at him as if he were mad.

'Josh,' the sheriff continued with renewed confidence. 'I know how shook up you are, but we need to pull ourselves together here a piece. We already got statements from the witnesses. We just need yours. You know we'll have to fine you for your log book violation. There's an eight-hour shut-down goes with that. Guess you know. But since you've been out of action damn near that, I reckon once you've paid up you'll be free to go. We know you stopped where you said.' He hesitated. 'But 'fore I let you leave I need to know you're goin' to be okay. Shock makes you tired. Confused. Whole bunch of stuff. You feel better after your sleep?'

Josh searched the sheriff's face for irony and oddly found none. He fought back his guilt.

'What did they say?'

'Who?'

'The witnesses.'

John Pace leaned forward and his hand lifted slightly as if he wanted to put it on Josh's arm. He stopped himself when the look in Josh's eye warned him that he didn't want to be touched.

'No one's blaming you, son. It was an accident. You weren't speeding, you weren't drinking. Just an accident.'

Josh swallowed. He spoke quickly with panic in his voice.

'A woman pushed the baby under the truck. Deliberately.'

The sheriff was shaking his head.

'The mother left the brakes off the stroller and the wind caught it. She told us so. Saw the whole thing herself. You think she'd lie about a thing like this?'

It was Josh's turn to shake his head. Pace looked perplexed.

'Why you doin' this to yourself, fella?'

'I can describe her. In detail. I want it on my statement.'

'I'm goin' to say this again. Shock plays tricks on you.'

'I know what I saw.'

The sheriff sighed deeply and turned to one of the men leaning against the wall behind him.

'Archie?'

The man opened a notepad, pulled out another chair and joined the two men at the table. John Pace ran a hand over his short sandy hair and sat back in his chair.

'So?'

Pace gestured at him like a sultan allowing a feast to commence.

Josh took a sip of the bitter coffee in front of him, nervously coughed his throat clear and told them it all again.

He spoke slowly and deliberately, and when once more it came to describing the woman he paused, making sure that the man with the notepad had caught up with his tale. The deputy looked up expectantly, holding his pen like a high school student paying attention to a dull but insistent lecturer. Josh concentrated on his description of the woman, making it more detailed than when he'd first blurted out his hysterical, ragged tale hours ago, and as he spoke he noticed a change come about the men. The one writing glanced across at John Pace who in turn narrowed his eyes. When Josh had finished Pace sat back in his chair and looked thoughtfully across the table. He nodded to himself for a second or two, then rose slowly to his feet and made for the door. He pointed at Josh as he left the room.

'Hang on there. Got somethin' for you.'

Josh blinked at the man's back then looked quizzically at the two men left in the room. They returned his stare with the dull gazes of small-town policemen and Josh looked elsewhere to avoid those vacant eyes. They waited several minutes until Pace re-entered the room clutching a piece of paper. It had ragged fragments of Scotch tape adhering to three corners, with the fourth corner missing, and looked like it had just been ripped clumsily from a wall.

Pace sat at the table, looked down at his prize for a second, moved Josh's cup to one side then slid the paper in front of him. Josh looked down and the breath left his body.

It was her.

The photo was monochrome, but she was wearing the same suit. She was in a room that looked like a court or schoolroom, with a large flag propped in the corner behind her, and she was smiling up at Josh with even white teeth. She looked good in the picture, younger than Josh had initially guessed, and her make-up was more gentle and sophisticated. But it was her. The murderer. No doubt.

Below the picture a large caption read, *'Vote for Councillor McFarlane. You talk. She listens.'*

Underneath in smaller print the handbill informed Josh that Councillor Nelly McFarlane would be holding a question and answer session at Furnace junior school on May nineteenth.

When Josh looked back up at the sheriff's face, John Pace was registering a peculiar mixture of triumph and sympathy. But if the man was feeling smug, he concealed it well.

'This her?'

Josh nodded once, almost imperceptibly. Pace did the same.

'Like I say, shock's a crazy thing.'

'Where was this?'

'All over town.'

'You think I saw it somewhere.'

'I know you did. Hard to miss.'

One of the deputies sniggered and Pace threw him a look.

Josh slumped forward, the core of determined revenge dissolving in him, leaving his body slack and empty with misery. He let his hot head touch the back of his hand. This time, Pace allowed himself to put a hand on Josh's arm and found that it was not resisted.

'But I saw her.'

Josh's words were muffled, spoken into his own skin. Pace replied to the top of his head. 'You just had the worst day of your life, Josh. But you have to realize it weren't your fault. The mind makes up all kind of mixed-up shit to help us deal with guilt and grief. Once ran over a neighbour's dog. Couldn't sleep for weeks. God alone knows what it must be like to have killed a child. You ain't goin' mad, Josh. It happens.'

Josh raised his head and squinted at the man whose big hand was still resting on his arm. 'You're wrong. I know I saw her.'

Pace shook his head, and tightened his grip. 'Then the mother of that poor little baby girl? She gone mad?'

Josh lowered his eyes, aware of how he must seem to these solid, unimaginative men. 'Maybe.'

Pace withdrew his hand, rubbed his chin roughly and thought for a moment.

He stood up.

'I'm goin' to do somethin' outside police procedure here, Josh. But I reckon it's goin' to help things along. You want some air?'

Josh unconsciously rubbed at his arm where Pace's hand had been.

'I guess.'

Pace nodded, and opened the door for him. They left the room, re-entered the small, neat office that smelled of new carpet, and walked outside towards the car. The sheriff waved a dismissive hand above his head to the calls from his staff as he left the building.

'Shit, they'll live without me for ten minutes,' he said to no one in particular.

7

Thank God it was over. They'd made the delivery and everything was in order. Bernard Epstein didn't like his job any more than his companion did, but as he got back into the car, Harry gave him a long look.

He returned the stare and shifted the driver's seat back so that he could unzip his overalls.

'She say anythin'?'

Harry's tone was accusing.

'Like what?'

'I dunno. Like what we do next, I reckon.'

Bernard wriggled out of the top half of his suit and lifted his buttocks to slip the legs off.

'You know what we do next. Nothin'. That's what we do.'

Harry looked forward out of the windshield to the gracious sweep of the street. 'You done it before, ain't you?'

'Yeah. The once.'

'So that's all I'm askin'. Like what next?'

'It's different each time. Has to be.'

Harry looked at his hands. 'Delivery's the same.'

Bernard pulled the last of the overall from his foot and turned to look at his companion with a sigh. 'She doin' well, huh?'

Harry blinked at him.

'Huh?'

'That daughter of yours. The one you got in that fancy twenty-thousand-dollar-a-term college up in New Hampshire.'

'Yeah. She's doin' fine.'

Bernard waited a beat, his eyes never leaving Harry's, then

nodded. 'Mighty glad to hear that. Can we get back to the sawmill now? Them backs ain't gonna stack themselves.'

While Harry looked at the floor and cleared his throat, Bernard crumpled up the overall and threw it in the back seat beside the other one. The blood would come off in the wash. It had stained the green cross and half the word 'paramedic', but it would be fine with some rub-on detergent before the rinse cycle.

And anyway, they wouldn't need them again for a long time. They were woodsmen. They had their own work-wear.

Pace helped Josh into the passenger seat as though he were an elderly female relative visiting for Thanksgiving, then climbed breathily into the driver's seat and drove off slowly at policeman's speed. Josh looked across at him, waiting for an explanation. Pace kept his eyes forward.

'How were you feeling before the accident? Just when you thought you saw the woman.'

Josh's temples throbbed. He put a hand to his head. How had he been feeling? He had been feeling guilty, sad, screwed up and crazy without sleep. That's how. So crazy he even thought he might have invented the woman to chastise himself for driving away from his problems. Remember, Josh? Remember? Oh, he remembered all right, and he wrestled with the truth of it before answering.

'I felt fine. Hungry. That's all. I needed something to eat.'

What else could he have told this man? That he had fallen asleep at the traffic lights, then woken thinking about how his girlfriend was going to kill his baby? Just seconds before he killed someone else's?

Pace nodded as though that was what he wanted to hear, and steered the car carefully into a wide tree-lined avenue. Josh looked away in shame and turned his attention to their destination. If Furnace's suburbs had been impressive then this was even more so. They had arrived in the land of the seriously rich. The houses here were set far back from the road, and the maturity of the gardens, ringed with ancient oaks and high rhododendrons, told the story that they'd been here a long time. The same uncomfortable alienation that had introduced him to this town was returning. He turned back to Pace.

'What's the deal with this town? Where's the money coming from?'

Pace raised an eyebrow as if the question was not only irrelevant but also impertinent. He shrugged. 'Same as anywhere. Rich folks here got old money, poorer folks do what poor folks do. Work.'

Josh shook his head, undeterred by this oblique answer. 'No, I mean what's the bottom line? Farming? Mining? What?'

Pace looked like he was thinking hard. 'Well, I guess that's a good question. I reckon mostly it's land and timber, but we got a few people here deal mostly in money, know what I mean? Like they don't make nothing, they just sit on the phone or the fax and move money around the world. Seems to make more.'

'Up here? In the mountains?'

'You got a phone and a fax it don't matter if you're on the moon. I guess they like the mountain air.'

Josh nodded, disappointed at the mundane explanation. The easy resolution of the mystery did little to make him feel better. But then he was far from feeling good. He was feeling worse than he'd ever felt in his life. The image of that tiny foot, that thick black blood, bobbed to the surface of his consciousness like a plastic ball held under bath water and released. He swallowed hard, fighting back his horror, as Pace brought the car to a stop outside a sprawling white house. The sheriff cut the engine and sighed deeply. He tapped the wheel thoughtfully for a moment, then turned to Josh.

'This is out of order and I ain't no psychiatrist, but I reckon if you meet this lady you're goin' to realize that you made a mistake.'

Josh felt cold. My God. This was her house. John Pace was going to make him talk to her, make him look again into those eyes that had drilled him just before she . . .

'But I don't want you tellin' her why we're here, you understand? That's important. No way am I goin' to treat Councillor McFarlane like a suspect. This here visit is just so you can straighten things out in your mind and get on your way again. Can you handle that?'

Josh looked up to the dark windows of the great house and knew he had to see her. He nodded. Pace studied his face for a moment, returned the nod, then got out of the car. Josh followed him, a few steps behind.

The arrival of the police car had already made one of the drapes twitch. A child's face looked out from behind pale flowery material, and opened its mouth in naked delight that the sheriff was coming up their driveway. The drapes fell and swung as the child dived away.

Pace rang a doorbell that buzzed deep inside the house. There were voices, children's and an adult cheerfully telling them to be quiet, and then the mock-period door swung open.

She opened it. The murderer.

Councillor Nelly McFarlane was wiping her hands on an apron that hung loosely around the waist of a plain denim knee-length dress. Her red hair was tied back in a knot and her open friendly face was without make-up. Clinging to her skirt was a girl of about nine or ten, and in the background a younger boy and a slightly older girl hopped around with open curiosity.

Nelly McFarlane looked at them both and smiled, showing those fine white teeth that graced her campaign handbill.

'John! Hi! Come in.'

She motioned to the men to enter, but looking questioningly at Josh. He was aware that he looked like a criminal. Take a trucker from his truck and he always does. He was well used to being followed round factory outlet malls by store detectives who fixed on his clothes and haircut like pointer dogs on a duck. But right now, he was more aware that he was looking *at* a criminal. A first-degree murderer. Pace put a hand behind Josh to push him gently forward, speaking to the woman as he did so.

'I want you to meet Josh Spiller. He's a trucker from Pittsburgh.'

She widened her smile and raised her eyebrows. Josh was grateful that she didn't offer a hand to shake. He was barely in control, but to have been forced to touch the flesh that had launched the baby into oblivion . . .

The children scuttled away inside and vanished, satisfied that the police visit was to be a dull social one.

Josh hesitated, his heart racing in his chest. The space between his shoulderblades told him that he was about to be clubbed from behind with a baseball bat, but his eyes, his logic, his head told him he was the unannounced guest of a bewildered and respectable Furnace citizen. He stepped into the large, cool hall. In the spacious living room to which she led them, a television was blaring cartoons to a room now vacated by children. Nelly McFarlane moved to a low mahogany coffee table, picked up the channel changer and silenced the noise.

Josh flicked his eyes to it just in time to see a coyote being pursued on a dusty road by a huge rolling rock before the picture fizzled away to black. He looked away quickly, a hot, sick feeling returning to his head. She sat down on a long sofa and motioned for the men to do the same on an identical one on the opposite side of the coffee table. They sat, and Pace clasped his hands on his knee.

'Sorry to trouble you, Nelly, but there's been a real bad accident.'

Josh watched her face carefully as a line of fear and confusion passed over its undoubtedly handsome structure. She was much younger than he'd thought. In her late forties maybe. It was hard to tell. But she looked good. He held his breath. He was confused and light-headed. Pace saw what she was thinking and hurried along to halt it.

'Alice Nevin's baby was killed this morning.'

Her hand went to her mouth. 'Oh sweet Lord. Alice? Berry Nevin's girl?'

Pace nodded.

'How?'

Her voice was croaky.

'It was out the front of the mall. Maybe you saw some of the commotion if you were in town early?'

He looked at her carefully, but if there was to be any flicker of guilt or duplicity it was not going to register on this woman's sympathetically open face.

She shook her head slowly, her hand now at her neck.

'We haven't been out yet, John. What happened?'

'Stroller rolled right out into the street. I'm here to tell you 'cos I know that's a big piece of your campaign, Nelly. To get them metal barriers up in front of the store.'

She was shaking her head in disbelief now, and Josh watched her, seeing only a woman in genuine distress at an appalling tragedy. Pace was continuing.

'Mr Spiller here, well, he was the real unfortunate one who just happened to be passing by slowly in his truck. Just shows you, you were right about an accident waitin' to happen. He was way under the speed limit, braked an' everythin', but there was nothin' he could do. Little Amy rolled right under there. Didn't stand a chance.'

She silently mouthed the words 'little Amy' to herself, then turned her eyes on Josh. There was a fleeting second, no, less than that; a fraction of a second, in which a cold wind blew across his heart and he imagined he saw the same cold reptilian eyes that had stared him down at seven o'clock this morning, light years away.

And then his bruised mind allowed him to see what was really in front of him. Two eyes that were already glazing with tears and regarding him with an expression of horror that the killer, albeit an unwitting one, was here in her house, which was being replaced with some obvious effort by a sympathy that seemed so warm and genuine he felt tears prick his own eyes again.

John Pace looked concerned. 'You okay, Nelly?'

She swallowed and waved a hand at him. When she spoke, she was still visibly wrestling with revulsion and compassion. 'I don't know what to say. You poor man.'

Pace looked at his feet.

'Like I say, Nelly, if those barriers had been up like you've been shoutin' for, this'd never have happened. I just wanted Mr Spiller here to know that it ain't never goin' to happen again. Kind of put a bit of his mind at ease.'

Josh stared at her, his mind spinning. How did he get here? A few hours ago he was on the interstate trying to find his breakfast, and now he was in a living nightmare that he was never going to wake from. Nothing would ever be the same again. *He* had killed a child. Not her. Not this middle-class, bland and ordinary woman who spent her life campaigning for tiny small-town victories. Him. He had been sleepless and crazy. Seeing things. He had seen some dumb poster on a wall and his mixed-up, fucked-up brain had concocted that stuff. It was no one else but him. He was the killer.

She got to her feet. Her face told the story that she was still unsure of him, almost as though she were reading his guilty mind, and as she spoke her next hospitable words, her eyes suggested she was thinking of running to get a gun.

'Can I fetch you something, Mr Spiller? A coffee? A cold drink?'

Josh shook his head. 'No. Thank you.'

She paused, staring at him with an expression that was difficult to read, then spoke gently. 'Well let me give you this. Please.'

She went to a drawer in an elegant sideboard, took out a small yellow pamphlet, crossed the room and handed it to him.

Josh took it and looked down at its cover. It showed a poor drawing of a family, a mother and father straight out of the Brady Bunch, all big collars and bad seventies haircuts, and two apple-cheeked children encircled by their parents' arms. At the back of the family, the figure of Christ was holding his shepherd's crook out and beaming great rays of light over them. Large seriphed type declared, *Jesus, the head of the family of man. His love heals all.*'

He looked up at Nelly McFarlane in dismay. She had almost lost all trace of uncertainty and dismay, but now adopted the brain-damaged expression of the born-again Christian, beaming at him as though she had given him some delightful gift.

'Are you a believer, Mr Spiller?'

He looked at the pamphlet again to avoid her eyes. 'No. I'm afraid not.'

'Please read it anyway. It might help you. Jesus wants to help the unbeliever not only to be at peace, to be healed, but also to come to Him and embrace the word of God.'

Pace was looking at the table, his hands still clasped, and it was impossible for Josh to see if it was out of embarrassment or piety. The woman turned her attention back to the silent sheriff.

'Should I go round there, do you think, John?'

'She's been taken to the clinic, Nelly. She's pretty shook up. I reckon you should wait a piece.'

She nodded, then turned back to Josh.

'May I pray for you, Mr Spiller?'

Josh felt awkward and silly. 'Sure. Thank you.'

'Then I will. I'll pray very hard. You must be in terrible pain.'

He nodded and then looked to Pace, telegraphing that he was desperate to leave. The sheriff read the face of his companion and stood up. Josh did likewise.

'Anyhows, Nelly, I'm real sorry to intrude, but like I say I thought you should know. Hope it's helped Mr Spiller here, too, knowing that it's something that's goin' to get fixed.'

Nelly McFarlane stood up, moved quickly round the table and grasped Josh's arm. He recoiled, but her touch was not the horror he had dreaded. Her hand was warm and soft.

'You can be sure of that, Mr Spiller. Barriers are going up on that sidewalk if I have to build them myself. But for the moment, while the pain of this is still crippling you, try and let Christ into your life. He can help too.'

Josh nodded dumbly and shifted his feet. She scanned his face for a few more moments then led them into the hall. At the door Josh unzipped his jacket pocket to put away the pamphlet, and as he did so the handbill that Pace had given him poked out of the corner. She saw it, smiled and pointed with a slender finger, clipped clean nails without varnish. The finger of a neat, God-fearing mother. Not the painted nails of a terrifying harpy.

'Guess you hoped I'd be a slice more glamorous if you saw that picture before we met, Mr Spiller. Sorry you caught me in Grandma mode.'

Josh managed a weak smile.

'You look just fine.'

She responded with the coquettish grin of a woman flattered. 'Well I just throw that old pink suit on when I need to look like I mean business. This is me really.' She lifted the sides of her denim skirt like a little girl.

Josh gave an embarrassed upward nod of acknowledgement. The sheriff shook her hand, asked to be remembered to Jim, and they walked back to the car. She watched them go then quietly pushed the door shut.

Josh was silent for the first few minutes of the return journey, gazing out at the passing houses and their uniform blankets of velvet gardens. Pace broke the silence.

'Well?'

Josh remained quiet, thinking. Agonizing.

Pace looked sideways at him.

'That your murderer?'

Josh hesitated. It was still so real. But of course it couldn't be. That woman, that ordinary woman wasn't capable of anything more than boring the nuts off you at a church social. There was no other explanation. He was ill. He hadn't slept. He'd made it up.

'I guess not.' Josh continued to stare out of the car, then turned to his driver. 'Why are you being so kind?'

'You think I'm being kind?'

'Yeah. I do. I reckon some of your deputies would be mighty pleased to see me strung up.'

Pace drummed the wheel with a finger, his eyes still forward.

'You made a mistake forgettin' to log, Josh, but we both know the accident weren't your fault. Now there's already one person dead. We can't change that. But I'm damned if I want you freakin' out on the highway out there and have me come and scrape up some more mess. I seen men confused and lost about a lot less than you been through.'

Pace sighed through his nose and then spoke again wearily as though this kind of bizarre incident happened on a daily basis.

'Now. Want to change your statement?'

Josh chewed at a fingernail. 'That necessary?'

When Pace replied, his tone was one of irritation. The concerned policeman was disappearing: he sounded like a man who had proved a point and needed to get about his business.

'Sure it's necessary. You change your mind about what happened, you have to change your statement.'

Josh said nothing, but they drove back to the sheriff's office in the silent understanding that the favour was over and it was time to clean up. The problem was he had no idea what he would say in a new statement. How could he say the stroller rolled with the wind, when he didn't see that? He'd seen it being pushed. He had. He closed his eyes and the picture was still there.

Suddenly Josh wanted Elizabeth very badly. He wanted to be held in her arms, have her run her hands over the shaved nape of his neck the way she did, and smell the clean, sweet smell of her body. He needed her to tell him it was going to be okay. Only it wasn't okay. A baby was dead and he was losing his mind. Panic rose in his throat again, and he turned his attention to the sanitized land-scape of Furnace's tidy houses to help battle it back.

Moments later he was back in the small room they had left less than half an hour ago, walking with his eyes fixed firmly on the man's back to avoid even the tiny task of thinking about where to take his next step.

He was lost and dazed and the emotions were so alien to him that he reeled from them. Once, lounging on the sofa at home, he and Elizabeth had been watching that dumb TV game-show where the glazed-eyed contestants begin by describing their own charac-ters. She'd laughed and made him do the same. He recalled pulling a serious face and adopting a joke manly voice to say,

'Hi. I'm Josh Spiller and I get things done. I take control.' Would he say that today and still expect her to laugh? The truth wouldn't make either of them laugh. Try 'Hi. I'm Josh Spiller. Things happen. I run away.' Right now he was seriously out of control and there was nowhere to run. He sat back in the shaky wooden chair and let his arms flop heavily onto the table.

The deputy who'd taken the statement returned, bringing with him a pile of paperwork, arranged himself at the table and looked to the sheriff for instruction. Pace nodded and the man smoothed a new piece of paper with his hand, held his pen expectantly and looked to Josh.

'You want me to read you back your first statement and amend it, or just start from new?'

Josh looked at him with dull eyes, still unsure what he could say that would replace the one he'd given. He stalled for time.

'Can I hear it back?'

The man straightened his shoulders and started to read haltingly like a shy child standing up in class.

Josh listened, his mind playing the movie that went with the words, fighting to make himself believe that his clear and accurate account was the product of a temporarily fevered brain. As the deputy reached the description of the woman, Josh slid the crumpled handbill picture of Nelly McFarlane out of his pocket and onto the table in front of him. He gazed down at the woman's open, friendly face as the man's voice droned in the air like some monotonous tour guide in a national monument.

'. . . hard to tell her age, but older than the mother, wearing a little too much make-up, and a tailored pink suit. Her hair . . .'

Josh looked up.

'Wait.'

Pace, who had been picking at his thumbnail, apparently bored and barely seeming to listen, looked up at Josh.

Josh was excited, his eyes flashing with impatience. He spoke quickly, turning to Pace to make his point.

'Pink. You hear? I said it was a *pink* suit.'

Pace put his wide hands out palms up, and raised his eyebrows in a silent question. Josh stabbed at the handbill with a finger.

'You heard her as we left, sheriff. She mentioned this pink suit, the one in this picture.'

Pace was still looking quizzical, but Josh could detect falsehood in that expression, could see the conclusion to his observation being born behind the sheriff's narrowed eyes before Josh spoke it.

'If this is what I saw, how could I have known the suit was pink? This picture is black and white.'

John Pace looked across at his deputy and then back at Josh, who was breathing more quickly now. The deputy's mouth remained slightly open, as though he wished to continue his reading aloud. Pace spoke slowly.

'Well now, that's a fair point. A fair point.'

He turned to the deputy, his voice casual and light.

'Archie. Any of these posters around town in colour?'

The man with his mouth still open closed it, and scanned Pace's face carefully before speaking.

'Eh, I can't rightly say.'

Pace rubbed his chin. 'I guess the only explanation is that there must be.'

Josh's heart raced. 'But it's something you can find out.'

'For sure.'

'And if there aren't any in colour then where does that leave our theory about how I'd seen her before?'

There was a pause. A long pause, and then Sheriff John Pace clasped his hands together in front of him and looked Josh straight in the eye.

'Up shit creek, Josh.'

Josh sat back in the chair and almost smiled. But there was very little to smile about.

'Then I stick by my statement. Until you find out about the poster.'

Pace paused again for an awkward length of time, then unclasped his hands and wagged a finger like he was scolding an invisible dog.

'Okay. We're gonna get right on that. But after you've paid your fine for that dumb stunt with your log book, there ain't no reason to keep you here any more. You feel up to drivin'?'

Josh nodded, unsure how the atmosphere in the room had changed, but certain it had.

'Sure. I kinda feel better already knowing I might not be crazy.'

This time, Pace snorted. 'Yeah? You saw Nelly. Even if a decent woman like that could have slipped in and out of town in broad daylight to do the deed unseen by anyone but you, what motive would she have for doin' somethin' as wicked as happened?'

'How should I know? Jesus freaks are always missin' a few floorboards upstairs.'

As soon as he'd said it, Josh knew he shouldn't have. Archie made a blowing motion with his mouth and Pace's voice dropped an octave and darkened to the same degree as his face.

'Now I reckon you ought to keep that smartass truckin' talk to yourself. Specially when you're referrin' to good folks who choose to follow the Lord's path.'

Archie said a quiet 'Amen' and they both looked at Josh with matching contempt. Josh ran his hand over the stubble of his hair and looked from one man's face to the other.

'Sorry. No offence.'

Pace's face told him that offence had indeed been taken. He stood, pulled Josh's licence from his pocket, dropped it on the table and waved a hand at the paper in front of Archie.

'Sign your original statement, take a copy. When you've paid your fine, Deputy'll give you back the truck keys.'

Josh opened his mouth to speak and was silenced by a fat finger held up and pointed rather too directly at his face.

'We'll be in touch if we got anythin' to tell you.'

Pace turned to leave the room, speaking as he went with his back to Josh.

'Drive careful.'

The two men were left in the room, facing each other over the table. Archie Cameron turned the statement towards Josh. It had been neatly typed, presumably when they were out on their less than social visit. He read it through then held out his hand for Archie's pen. It was given with bad grace, and retrieved with the same.

'You wait here. I'll have this photocopied and you get to keep one.'

The deputy left the room. Josh rocked back on the legs of his chair and exhaled deeply. His mind was racing with more than his embarrassing error. The sheriff had almost convinced him he'd seen McFarlane's poster and subconsciously dropped her into his mad and confused recollection. Now he didn't know whether to be pleased or dismayed that the theory wouldn't wash. His mind was working like an abacus, clicking possibilities, fantasy and realities together like wooden balls on a wire. Except nothing was adding up.

The baby's mother slid uncomfortably back into those thoughts. Why would she, the most important and relevant witness of all, say it was an accident? He let the chair bump forward again and ended up with his head in his hands, elbows on the table. Josh looked miserably through his wrists at the papers in front of him, a pile of official-looking forms, mostly handwritten. He glanced up at the door, then put a hesitant hand out and rotated the papers towards him. The top sheet was a scrawl of notes and observations on the position of the truck and the time of the incident, but the next two pages had a hastily-written list of witnesses' names and addresses. He scanned it quickly, found Alice Nevin, and before understanding why he was doing it memorized the address and turned the papers back to face the empty chair in front of him.

The deputy's return was abrupt, but he was formal to the point of a lawyer serving a summons in making sure Josh took his copy of the statement. 'This here is yours. You take that now.' He held out a brown business envelope with the neatly folded paper protruding slightly from the open end.

Josh took it from the deputy's hand and was observed carefully as he pressed it into the inside pocket of his jacket.

'And you get these back.'

From another larger brown envelope the man brought out a plastic bag of Josh's personal belongings that had been removed from his pockets when they put him in the cell.

He watched Josh as he removed the items and started putting them back in his jacket. When it came to the wallet the deputy smiled unkindly.

'Guess you're gonna need that all right. I'll get Deputy Busby to bring in the paperwork for your ticket.'

He walked to the door, opened it and called down the corridor. As Josh suspected, the man who answered the call was the angry policeman who had led him from the cell. He was holding a pad of tickets, a credit card swipe machine, and he was grinning.

Archie Cameron left the room with a long look at Josh and Deputy Busby took a chair.

'You take a copy of your statement to keep?'

Josh nodded numbly, trying hard not to think of the horror contained in the words that were tucked so neatly inside his jacket.

'Yeah.'

'Yeah? Well here's another souvenir from Furnace, Virginia.' He slid the square of paper towards Josh.

'One thousand bucks.'

Josh stared at him, his eyes narrowing. 'The maximum? Even though my stopover checked out?'

'Mister, if I were you I'd be pretty thankful for walkin' outta here at all after what you done. Looked in your wallet and I guess those hundred and forty-five dollars ain't goin' to cover it. Pleased to tell you we take Master Card.'

Josh was about to protest further, but the policeman's face told him it was useless. Part of Josh wanted to pay a fine. A huge fine. But no amount of money would undo his deed.

The transaction was performed in an uncomfortable silence until the deputy folded up the credit card receipt and a copy of the ticket into an envelope and handed it to Josh. He watched Josh's face as he took it.

'You keep hold of that now.'

Josh looked at him suspiciously, since the man's tone was of a dishonest merchant who has successfully swindled a fool. The deputy read his face and added with a glare of indignation, 'In case anyone needs to check up on you. Believe me. I'm goin' to make damned sure they do.'

Only when the envelope was safely away, did Deputy Busby hand Josh the keys to Jezebel and the licence that he'd scooped up from the table.

'You need a ride back to the truck? I'm supposed to ask.'

Josh shook his head. 'It's only a few blocks. I need the walk.'

'Good. Cause you ain't gettin' a ride.'

Josh stood up and pocketed his keys. He looked long and hard at the man's face, but any aggression he might have been able to muster before today was dissipated by the knowledge of his own inner guilt. He broke the stare first, turned and left the room.

John Pace was gone from the main office and Josh was oddly disappointed he hadn't stayed to say goodbye. He'd heard enough horror stories from other drivers about the consequences of committing a violation in backwater towns, to know that by the sheriff, at least, he'd been treated fairly and with respect. But even though the law had decided he'd done nothing wrong, as he walked down the concrete steps to the clean sidewalk, he felt like a man being released from prison.

The air smelled sweetly of catkins and sap, and a gentle breeze moved the young chestnuts that lined the street. Josh walked slowly at first, then picked up speed as the fresh air revived and invigorated him.

Alice Nevin. The woman who started today with two children and ended up with one. Thanks to him. He knew she wouldn't be home. He could almost see her now, lying on a hospital bed somewhere, her pupils dilated with tranquillizers and her thin arms lying immobile by her sides. But maybe something . . . anything . . .

Josh had no idea what he was going to do. He just wanted to go to her house. There was a drugstore at the end of the block. He pushed open its glass door and walked to the empty counter. A pretty but dull-eyed girl stopped stacking packets of sanitary towels, walked slowly over and filled the space behind the cash register.

'Yeah?'

'You know where Strachan Boulevard is from here?'

She looked at him. He knew she'd be weighing up the hair, the clothes, the earring. But he moulded his face into contours of friendly expectation and she broke into a half smile as she decided to co-operate.

'Okay. You want to make a right here, then take a left into Frobisher Place and then two blocks down you're there.'

'Thank you.'

'You're welcome.'

As he turned to go Josh's gaze swept past a telephone on the wall. His heart lurched. Elizabeth. He should phone Elizabeth. He felt in his pocket for his wallet and found his phone card. He could feel the girl's eyes burning into his back and knew that although this call, of all the calls in the history of time, should be made in private, he couldn't wait any more.

He punched in the complex code, waited for that monotonous and irritating voice to tell him how much time he had and then at last heard the long ring of his own phone. There was a click then the heart-sinking hiss that meant the answering machine had kicked in. His own voice.

'Hi. You've guessed. We're out. Try the numbers that follow, call back or leave a message. Here we go, the shop number is . . .'

He hung up. He hadn't left the answering machine on, so at least that meant she'd come home and been there to switch it on. So she was safe. Cold comfort. She wasn't answering.

He stood for a moment and let his heart slow down. What would he have said if she'd picked up the phone? This was new territory. Josh Spiller was a man, and a man who drove forty tons of truck around America. Yet right now, he wanted to put his forehead against this wall and weep. For a moment he saw himself reflected in the shiny chrome of the telephone, saw himself as he knew the girl behind the counter was seeing him; a haggard, haunted face that belonged to someone he barely recognized.

He dug his fingernails into his palm, took a breath and walked quickly out of the store. Movement. As always, it was the only cure.

8

Sim was worried about his lemon balm. The leaves were turning brown around the edges and there were aphid casts on the new shoots. He bent over the big terracotta pot and poked pointlessly at the sick plant with a gnarled finger. Herbs were tricky. You had to know when they came indoors to avoid the frost and when they should go out again to harden off. He reckoned this time he'd got it wrong, underestimating once again the bitter spring winds that chilled Pittsburgh, and he tutted as one of the leaves fell off with his touch.

Inside the house, Josh and Elizabeth's phone rang. The old man straightened up and shuffled towards the open window. Sim liked it when they had their answering machine on. He could hear all their messages clearly through the window, whether open or shut, and it made him feel part of their lives that he knew what was going on, often before they did. Sometimes it was just messages from Josh's work, and sometimes it was Elizabeth's family. But he always listened in the hope of hearing something secret and exciting. And there was something else.

Sim had a pointless but amusing little gift. Mostly, although occasionally he got it wrong, he could tell who was phoning while it was still ringing.

He had no idea how he knew, but he did. He liked to play the game with himself as the phone rang its four short peals before the answering machine intercepted.

'Dispatcher,' he would say out loud on the second ring, and then slap his thigh when the familiar voice came on, droning, 'Josh? Got a pretty high-paying load with your name on it. Call me, would you?'

Or he would mouth, 'Oh oh, Elizabeth's brother,' and then look delighted when the sulky sibling's voice left its disgruntled message. If he were ever forced to explain the process, and he knew he never would, Sim would have to say that he could see not so much the person, but the essence of the person as the phone rang, and the times he got it wrong he believed were simply the times when he just wasn't concentrating hard enough.

Of course he never mentioned any of this to Josh or Elizabeth. Sim thought they probably knew he listened to their messages but said nothing. They were so kind. They knew no one ever phoned Sim, and he guessed Elizabeth left the window of the office open purposely so he could hear. Maybe one day he would show her what he could do. He would like that, to see her pretty face light up in delight as he performed the trick for her. Only it wasn't strictly speaking a trick. It was real. He just *knew* who was on the line.

Today, however, it was habit rather than design that made him move to the window. Sim wasn't sure he wanted to hear the message after the fight he'd heard yesterday. He'd heard Elizabeth's car screech away after Josh had come home, and last night her crying had kept him awake, wondering whether he should go upstairs and comfort her or just leave her alone. He'd opted for the latter, so hysterical and forlorn were her wails. How could anything an old man would say heal that kind of wound? Things must be bad, he thought, for such good people to hurt each other so badly. He waited by the window as the four short phone rings completed and the answering machine clicked in.

'Josh,' Sim said to himself, supporting himself against the wall with an outstretched hand.

An eavesdropper couldn't hear the outgoing message, only wait patiently for the caller to start speaking. Sim waited to hear Josh's voice, but the caller hung up.

'Josh,' he confirmed with himself, nodding as he shuffled back to his herbs.

A cold wind eddied around the edge of the house and stirred the lemon balm. Two more leaves dropped from the stem and Sim cursed in Korean. He bent down again and resumed fussing with the plant.

'Josh,' he repeated to the herb. It ignored him, and dropped another leaf.

* * *

By Furnace standards, Alice Nevin's house was pretty ordinary. By anywhere else's yardstick, it was an expensive and desirable property. But unlike a Bostonian or Beverly Hills house where the lawn is God, here the front garden was littered with toys. Two plastic pedal cars lay on their sides as if there had been a collision. A ragged fun-fur horse was splayed over the porch steps and an odd assortment of tiny plastic figures were distributed so evenly around the property it was as though they had been placed there to serve some kind of gardening function. Josh stood across the street and stared up at its long white wooden porch and colonial dormer windows, wondering what he was going to do next.

She wasn't here. Why was he?

A figure came to the downstairs window. A man. He had a crying child in his arms that looked about a year old and small heads moved about at his hips betraying the presence of more children. The man was trying to make the baby look out into the garden, pointing at things and jogging it up and down in his arms in a vain effort to comfort it. It was only a matter of seconds until he saw Josh, and when he did, he stopped moving. He stared at him for a moment, then moved away from the window.

Thinking was getting in the way. So Josh stopped thinking and walked swiftly across the street, picking his way through the toys to mount the steps and ring the doorbell. A distant dog barked, as though shut in a room, accompanied by a variety of screams and shouts that reinforced his belief that he'd seen several children. The door opened wide and aggressively fast. The man, wearing a sweat-stained T-shirt, cheap stone-washed jeans, and holding his tearful burden, stared at Josh. At this close range Josh could see that the man had eyes almost as red and puffy as his baby's. He had been crying.

'Need somethin'?'

It was a challenge rather than a question, a voice and demeanour Josh might have expected in a pool hall if he'd knocked a guy's pile of dimes off the table. It was way out of place in the doorway of an elegant house. Josh felt colour come to his neck and cheeks. This was all wrong, but there was no going back.

'Mr Nevin?'

The man's face crinkled from aggression to suspicious aggression. 'Who the fuck are you?'

A child screamed from the core of the house. Josh looked past the man at the sound, but it screamed on ignored.

'I just need to know if you're Mr Nevin.'

'There ain't no Mr fuckin' Nevin. And I asked you a question.'

Josh remembered. Berry Nevin's girl. That's what McFarlane had said. That would mean either that Alice Nevin had kept her maiden name in an unlikely modern fashion for this small mountain town, or quite simply that she wasn't married. The baby in the man's arms started a high-pitched whine again and was swayed from side to side by the man in an unconscious act of comforting. It was the action of someone used to holding kids.

Josh lowered his voice and spoke quietly, never taking his eyes off those of the man opposite him. He was glad he was burdened with the child. It would be harder for him to hit Josh when he heard what was coming.

'My name is Josh Spiller.' He paused, and when he spoke again Josh's shame was apparent in his voice. At least to him. 'Are you Amy's father?'

Some things happened to his face. Strange things, as if a dial had been implanted in the man's that could be turned to a variety of different emotions, and someone was spinning it. His eyes were a mixed carousel of grief, confusion, anger, and most perplexingly, fear.

'Yeah.'

There was no rise in the intonation of the word that would have made it a question. Inexplicably, Josh wanted to touch the man, wanted to reach out his hand and hold his arm, to tell him it was okay and he understood. Instead he savaged him with his words.

'I was driving the truck.'

The eyes that had registered that abnormal mix of emotions now became cold, opaque and unreadable.

'What you want?'

Josh looked at the baby and then back up at that hard face.

'To say sorry.'

The man took a step back into his house, shaking his head like Josh had drawn a gun.

'You git off. You fuckin' git off now. Right now.'

Josh lowered his eyes and stood still almost as though he were going to pray. In truth he was wondering feverishly why he was here.

What lunacy was gripping him, making him behave so irrationally?

He could hear the man panting as he turned and made to leave. A babble burst from the figure in the doorway and Josh turned back towards him.

'It was her fault for fuck's sakes. The kid was seven days old. You hear that? Seven fuckin' days old. I says to her to watch it, I says to her, but shit, she never listen to nothin', that dumb bitch. Never listen. And it ain't goin' to be okay. I knows it ain't.'

He started to cry. A horrible sound, all high and whining like his child.

'She was so beautiful, my little darlin'. I sees her bein' born. I ain't done that with the other six. But I sees Amy come right here into the world and I tells her that everythin's goin' to be okay. But it ain't. I couldn't do what I had to do. Couldn't do it. Maybe I'm not man enough, maybe I'm too much of a man. I just couldn't. She was so little, know how I mean? I don't know what she was thinkin'. She knows it ain't goin' to be safe. I don't know nothin' no more.'

He let his whining develop naturally into full-scale weeping, while Josh watched, horrified and baffled. The man was senseless, and the babbling insanity of his outburst was far more terrifying than the violent retribution that Josh had anticipated, and perhaps secretly desired. Still facing him, Josh breathed that he was sorry again, although this time it was more an expression of sympathy with the man's hysterical condition than remorse for his actions. He backed off down the steps and walked crab-like over the lawn. The sideways walk became a canter, and as he turned his head away from the crying, ranting man at the door Josh broke into a loping run.

He kept running until he was three blocks away, where he stopped, bent over and put his hands on his thighs to regain his breath. The purpose of the visit had been unclear to Josh, an order that was impossible to disobey from some despotic part of his subconscious. But if its secret agenda was to free his head from the maze of craziness, then it had failed spectacularly.

What had he learned? Nothing. At least nothing except a heap more stuff that didn't make sense. The baby was from a big family. The parents weren't married. They looked poor and undereducated but they lived in a house a surgeon or a lawyer might be proud of. And the father. The father didn't blame Josh the way any redneck mountain-bred man would, regardless of circumstance. He blamed the mother of his children.

Josh was sweating from his ludicrous, panicking run and he wiped his face with the sleeve of his jacket. Reality. Familiarity. Normality. There was only one place where those precious things resided. He had to get back to Jezebel.

9

She'd taken the call calmly, although there was a suppressed fury in her voice that seldom surfaced, a fury the man on the other end of the line recognized and silently prayed would be contained. But there was no time for displays of personal anger. There was work to be done.

A 10A scalpel blade had always been her favourite. Straight edge and not too short. She turned it over in her hand for a moment, feeling its weight, the coolness of the handle, and then positioned it delicately between thumb and forefinger ready to cut. As the blade pierced the skin, the subtle drag on the metal parting those tiny cells told her how sharp this instrument was. She sighed.

The waste. The infernal waste. The potency was not inexhaustible, and to remove a part now for such an unnecessary task was shambolic in the extreme. She used her left hand to steady the rest of the tiny corpse as she made the second incision. Too much. The blade had gone too far. She put the scalpel down carefully and picked up the engraved copper rule. It confirmed her mistake. The second incision was a fraction over seven inches. No matter. The two short cuts that would complete the skinny rectangle would redress the inaccuracy.

Seven inches by seven sixteenths exactly. It would dry smaller, but it had to be cut precisely. She picked up the scalpel and held it alongside the rule, running the blade down the straight edge, and with a steady hand made the final two cuts. This was where the 10a held its own.

A curved blade was useless at prising the skin from the flesh, but with the accuracy of such a straight point she could easily slice away the precious shell from its red fruit without tearing.

At last she allowed herself a smile. It was perfect. It would need washing and drying of course, but she had already prepared the solution. In only a few hours it would be completely ready.

The thud of a ball hitting the back yard wall near her window made her look up and stay still like a thing hunted. She waited on her side of the closed venetian blinds, senses keen and on standby for action. The children's voices were full of laughter and sunshine.

'Oh my God. The window. You nearly hit the window.'

'Get the ball, you jerk.'

'Get it yourself.'

She waited. They were laughing, those young high-pitched yelps, growing faint as they receded to some distant part of the yard where their game was in progress, and mentally she ticked off the faces she knew matched the voices, counting how many there were, listening for the tiny dangers of playful curiosity or insubordination.

Then, certain it was safe, she put down her tools and lifted the strip of skin to the light. The light shone through its pinkness and she smoothed it between her fingers, assessing how much time it would take to dry. They didn't have long. Maybe these few hours were not enough.

She took a deep breath at that alarming thought, then walked to the high table and began the ritual. She pulled the skin over the stone, pinning it at either end with the copper pins, and lit the candles. It was a time to concentrate, not to concern herself about the tasks of others, and so she closed her eyes and pressed a thumb to her forehead.

As she practised the words inside her head before they were spoken and could never be corrected or retracted, a fly circled the room clumsily and came to rest on its target.

Once there, with the only person in the room who would shoo it away deep in meditation, it crawled freely over the remains of a terry towelling babysuit stiffened with blood, and made ready to feast on the shining new rectangular strip of exposed flesh.

It took only five minutes to walk back to the truck, during which time he worked hard to get that sad mixed-up man's face out of his mind.

She was still there, parked at a tortuous angle outside the store and his heart leapt at the thought of the simple pleasure of climbing into his own private space, the place that smelled of him, that housed the detritus of his driving life, and starting her up. But as he came closer, Josh remembered the consistency of what had been under those wheels, and his pace slowed to a crawl. Would they have cleaned it up? Would anyone have been under there since they slid beneath the trailer and scooped out what was left of Amy Nevin? The saliva dried in his mouth. He approached the trailer from the back and walked slowly along its flank towards the cab.

There was nothing to see. The wheels were just wheels.

A darker patch of asphalt under the whole cab was the only sinister suggestion that maybe someone had taken a hose to it, and it made him look towards the store. There were people in the window of Campbell's Food Mart peering out at him.

He could see their heads and shoulders turned towards him, watching silently over a display of cans and giant bags of nachos as if waiting for something to happen, and for a moment he thought of going in, asking them what they saw. But the face of Amy Nevin's father came back. That twisted, weeping, mad face. He wanted no more of this. Either everyone here was blind and insane or he was, and right now he didn't care to work out which.

Driving would help him think. It always did. With eyes boring into him, he unlocked the cab, climbed in and sat down heavily in his seat, which bounced in happy response. There was a brief moment of paralysis as Josh started the engine and waited for it to warm up. He listened to the familiar throaty throbbing, feeling it vibrate up his spine, and for a fraction of a second he thought he might never drive again. There had been plenty of fur and feathers beneath those wheels, but never soft white skin and tiny bones. He'd never even clipped anyone, despite cretins stepping out of car doors into his path and kids playing chicken on city streets. He stared at the gas pedal as though it had grown teeth, then took a breath, dug deep into what was left of his tattered resolve, and won.

Josh Spiller wanted out of Furnace.

The street was not sufficiently wide to turn in, so Josh drove ahead looking for a side street that would take him back the way he'd come. The opportunity came at the end of the block where a sign told him that the interstate was seventeen miles away down the route to his right. It was a different route from the one he'd come in by, and longer, but it was heading south so he would make up the mileage when he rejoined the interstate. And from here it looked like a better road.

There was little pleasure in driving, but as he increased his speed past the last of those heavenly suburban houses, and a small sign said *Leaving Furnace*, the vice around his heart loosened a notch.

The road was heading back down the mountains again, but this time it did so in a more generous and less winding fashion. Lacy budding forest still formed an impenetrable cloak on either side, but only a few miles out of the town normal Appalachian life started to appear. Here and there the odd tatty cabin poked a roof or porch from the trees, and an unpleasant-looking general store even boasted a roadside location with the comforting sight of abandoned rusty cars growing from the sumachs in the rough field behind.

Josh was numb now. He was back on automatic and he drove without thinking, letting the moving landscape roll in front of him. Five miles on and a huge clearing to his left revealed a long low restaurant called Mister Jim's. It looked modern and clean, but more importantly the parking lot was big enough to take Jezebel. Josh started to brake and pull in.

He couldn't be defeated by an answering machine. There was no question that he had to hear her voice, that just to hear Elizabeth's mouth working its way around words, whether angry, hurt, loving or indifferent, would be his only salvation. The shop. He could call her there. He had to call her.

There were only two other vehicles in the parking lot, a crumbling Dodge Ram pick-up, and a blue and cream van that had the logo of the restaurant painted inexpertly on the back doors. Josh pulled the rig into the side, parallel to a regimented line of sapling trees tied to stakes that suggested Mister Jim wanted his restaurant to rival an urban fast-food lot. He left the rig running to heat up, climbed out and locked the door behind him, casting an affectionate eye at the few bold birds, who, undeterred by the growling of the engine, were flying at the radiator grill to feast on the insect life that was killed and stored there.

In Mister Jim's at least, the class system had restored itself. White trash wasn't at home mowing a smooth thousand-dollar lawn. It was watching TV behind the counter.

The girl was overweight and the hair that framed her pasty face had plainly been several colours before arriving at this dry thatch of yellow. She popped a membrane of gum and turned towards Josh as the swing door creaked slowly shut behind him.

'Seat yourself. Be right with you.'

She turned back to the television set which was showing a children's programme, suggesting that her last promise was unlikely to be honoured.

There was plenty of choice of seating. Only one other diner, undoubtedly the owner of the Dodge Ram, sat nursing a beer with his back leaning against the window and his legs up on the long, red, plastic-cushioned bench.

Josh didn't need a seat.

'Where 'bouts is the phone?'

She continued to watch the screen. 'Gotta eat to use the phones. Otherwise there's a booth at the store ups the hill.'

'I'm planning on eating. Where is it?'

She turned to him and took a notepad and a portion of a pencil from her greasy pocket. 'Yeah? What'll you have?'

Josh looked up at the TV, clenched his fists and ran a tongue over his dry lips. When he looked back down, the waitress's face was all but obscured by the expanding gum sphere. It popped.

'A coffee and a Danish.'

'No Danish. Got donuts.'

'Okay, a donut.'

She nodded and wrote it down as if it needed remembering, then looked lazily back up at him. 'Phone's out by the washroom.' She indicated with her head.

The other diner watched Josh without interest as he walked quickly in the direction of the indifferent nod, then got back to rubbing the neck of his beer bottle with a thumb.

10

She was perfectly still and he watched her from the corner of an eye, careful not to let her see him staring. He waited quietly, trying to be equally still until she spoke.

'Well, there it is.'

'Yes, mam.'

She ran a hand thoughtfully over the dash of the police car and sighed. 'Are you frightened of me, deputy?'

The man felt his pulse quicken. 'No, mam.'

She laughed, a crisp brittle sound. 'Really? That's good.'

She turned to him, watching him squirm for a second, then her tone changed quickly into a business-like chirp. 'How long has he been in there?'

''Bout ten minutes.'

She nodded, then ran her hands over her legs. 'Okay. Let's get to it.'

The man returned the nod and was rewarded with the dazzle of her smile.

Deciding that anything would be preferable to remaining under the searing insincerity of that grin, Deputy Cameron shifted the gear stick clumsily and moved off.

'Come on . . . come on . . . for Christ's sake.'

Josh gritted his teeth as the calling card voice went through her brain-dead speech before connecting him. Then, at last, the sound of a phone ringing.

'Hi. All Dressed Up.'

He closed his eyes and breathed out through clenched teeth, speaking his word in a hiss with the last of that breath.

'Nesta?'

'Yeah. Who's this?'

His eyes flicked open.

'Casper the friendly ghost. Who the fuck do you think it is? Let me speak to Elizabeth.'

There was a silence, a muffled silence, as though a hand had been put over the receiver for a moment, then Nesta's voice was back, but this time it had been dipped in acid.

'Cute, Josh. Real cute. And to think I said, naw you're wrong, the guy's okay. Nice language.'

'Look, Nesta, just put her on.'

'She's not here.'

'Sure she's there. I can see you making dumb faces and flapping your hands at her from here.'

'Yeah? Can you see this?'

'What?'

'My middle finger, smartass. You can spin on it.'

Josh put a hand to his brow. He took a deep breath and tried to sound calm. 'Okay, Nesta. I'm sorry. Okay?'

There was a huffy silence.

'Okay?' he repeated.

Nothing except the background noise of voices, dull thuds and clanking. Shop noises.

'I just need to talk to her. I know she's there. Please. Look. Just tell her I love her. I'm sorry and I love her.'

'She doesn't want to speak to you.'

'Tell her for Christ's sake.'

The hand went over the telephone again. Josh listened to that thick silence, his heart increasing its pace in anticipation of who might speak to him next. But the next voice was not the one he'd expected. It was a woman okay, but it was that robot of a woman on the phone card.

'You have one minute left on Driveline.'

'Shit. Nesta! Can you hear me! Nesta. I only got a minute left on this card!' The silence continued. For a long time. Josh raked in his pocket for dimes. It was long distance from here. He'd need a lot of dimes. As it was, he had none.

And then the hand was lifted and her tearful voice suddenly caressed him.

'Josh? Where are you?'

He closed his eyes again, and exhaled like a man winded. 'Oh babe. Shit. It doesn't matter. I'm coming home.'

'No. Don't.'

Her voice had gone flat and dead again, the voice of someone who wanted him to know the bitterness was still there. This would take time. He didn't have it. The line went dead. Josh screamed at the phone, slammed it down on the hook and ran back into the restaurant. The girl was still watching the TV show where big furry green birds were now dancing frenetically.

'Give me some change for the phone. Quick. Please.'

Her eyes stayed on the TV.

'It don't take coins. Slot's broke.'

He gawped at her, considering how good it would feel to rabbit-punch the back of her thick fleshy neck, then turned, ran back to the phone and instead punched in one zero zero.

'AT&T operator. How may I help you?'

This woman was real, but her voice was as flat and miserable as the recorded one on Driveline.

'Yeah. Collect call. Pittsburgh.'

'Number.'

He ran through them.

'Calling who?'

'Elizabeth.'

The name. It was making his eyes film over with tears.

'Your name?'

'Josh.'

'Tosh?'

'Josh.'

'I can't hear you. Jaws?'

'JOSH! Fucking Josh!'

The line went quiet and he thought his temper had blown it, meaning he'd have to call again. But then . . . ringing, and a distant pick-up, sounding as far away as the moon.

'This is the AT&T operator. I have Josh? . . .' she paused and then went on, '. . . for Elizabeth calling from McNab County, Virginia. Will you collect?'

There was a pause, a muffled conference, then Nesta spoke.

'No. Sorry.'

She hung up.

Josh stared at the wall, his fingers clenched around the phone.

'I'm sorry, caller. I'm unable to connect you.'

He put the phone gently back on its hook and stood looking at it for a moment. Then the door to the restaurant opened and his only fellow diner pushed past on the way to the washroom, letting loose a belch like an old bear. Josh glared at him, and the man glared back.

'Got a problem?'

Still looking at him, Josh folded his laminated calling card in two, in four, then let it drop on the floor.

'War, incurable disease, and the national debt of Ecuador. How 'bout you?'

The man looked back at him like Josh was a simpleton, belched again deliberately and open-mouthed, then catching the look in Josh's eye, quickly entered the washroom. Josh, after all, still looked like Josh.

This time when Josh pushed open the restaurant door there was a new diner. A girl was sitting sullenly in the corner booth finishing off an orange juice and a sandwich, her only companion a giant overstuffed rucksack propped against the window. As Josh looked at her, wondering about the speed with which she must have been seated and served by the sullen waitress, a movement outside caught his eye. Pulling out of the parking lot, almost obscured by his truck and the young trees, but visible for this one brief moment as it turned, was a police car.

It glided and bounced silently out of his vision, leaving Josh staring out of the window. The girl lifted her head to him like a meerkat, misinterpreting the direction of his gaze and offering a challenge. His eyes slid a fraction to the side, refocused and met with hers. They were the intense, silly eyes of the young, the innocence of childhood gone and not yet replaced with the wisdom of adulthood. But green irises, heavy dark lashes and eyebrows made them beautiful.

He looked away quickly, turned and sat down in a booth near the door. The waitress was absent from her post, and three puppet dogs blared out a Brechtian atonal song about the letter D at the two people in the empty room. Josh clasped his hands in front of him and gazed out of the long window.

He could have talked to her, made her understand why he was hurting as well as convincing her he was truly sorry. He knew it. Could hear it in her voice. Fuck that delay. It had made her change her mind, strengthened her resolve. But a lot had happened to Josh too. He knew Elizabeth wanted him to orbit around her pain like some healing satellite, apologizing and gesturing until she let him land, but he'd needed her too, today more than ever in his life, and she'd let him down. Badly.

Of course she was going through it, but how about him? Josh could feel his need for her, his remorse, starting to sour back into resentment.

A white ceramic mug was slammed down in front of him, spilling some of its cooked black contents on the Formica table top.

'Creamer?'

Josh didn't even look up.

'Cream. Yeah.'

'It's creamer. We ain't got cream.'

He raised his head to look at her. She was holding a fan of brown rectangular packets of powdered creamer between her thumb and forefinger as though they were the prize money on a game-show, and her bored eyes were already starting to swivel towards the dogs and their song.

'I'll take milk then.'

Her head was now completely turned in the direction of the television screen as she answered him in a drawl. 'You only get creamer with coffee.'

Josh looked at the side of her pasty face, noting with distaste a tide-mark of grey grime that ran the circumference of her collar.

'What if I ordered a glass of milk?'

Something in his tone this time made her turn back to him. She looked at him to assess whether this was the beginning of an argument. There was a glint in her eye that suggested that she might look forward to that.

'You'd get milk.'

Something was building in Josh. A release of tension, guilt, fear, resentment and loneliness. And it was being released without his permission. He could feel the confrontation in his low voice, could feel himself seething where he would normally shrug and laugh. He couldn't stop it. It was too late.

'Then why don't you pour some of that available milk into a container and bring it here so I can put it in my coffee?'

'You want a glass of milk, mister, I can bring you one, but I have to charge you for it. You get creamer with coffee.'

The girl at the other end of the room was looking at Josh from behind her rucksack, her head cocked and her eyebrows slightly raised as though she too thought he looked like a trouble-maker. Josh's gaze was steady.

'You don't get off on being a waitress much, do you?'

Her eyes hardened. 'I like it fine.'

'Yeah? Well I'm not getting off on being your customer.'

'That's your problem, mister.'

Still looking at her, Josh slowly reached out his hand and knocked over the mug of coffee. It swilled over the table in a great dark wave, and splashed its way to the floor via the cushions of the bench opposite him.

'Looks like that's your problem.' He smiled at her without mirth, then let the smile die abruptly. The girl held her ground, never taking her eyes from him. Her drawl, when she spoke, was soft with an undercurrent of menace.

'Now I'm goin' over back there to get a cloth. And when I come back, you're goin' to clean that up. You hear?'

Josh stared back, unmoved.

She turned, walked with a measured pace to the counter and disappeared through a doorway. Josh closed his eyes in shame. A slow hand clap started from the other side of the room. The girl with the rucksack was glaring at him as she performed the ironic act of appreciation.

'Big tough guy, huh?'

He ignored her, but her scorn merely highlighted what he already felt about his behaviour. He'd lost his temper with a dumb little waitress, and he felt like a shit.

For something to do, he turned his attention to the TV and then to the man returning from the washroom, whom he followed with his gaze as he left the restaurant and climbed into his pick-up. The man leaving reminded Josh that he didn't need to stay and wait for further confrontation. Still watching him through the window Josh started to slide his legs from under the table, but before he could stand, the girl was at the end of his table, rucksack on shoulders, ready to leave. Her voice was pitched high with indignation.

'All you need to know, Mr Dick Brain, is that she probably gets the kind of weekly wage you spend daily on deodorant to keep you from stinking like the sexist pig you are. That might be why she's not too anxious about treating you like you're the master of the fucking universe.'

'She was rude,' Josh said unconvincingly.

'No. She's just bored and exploited. *This* is what being rude's like: go fuck yourself, you sad old cock-sucker.'

Josh nodded, and for the first time on this dark and terrible first day of May, he fought to keep a smile at bay.

'Thanks. I'll know it now when I hear it.'

She frowned, tried to look threatening and failed.

'I'm wasting my time, and missing a ride.'

She tossed her head, although there was not much hair to respond, walked defiantly to the door and exited. The man in the pick-up was starting the engine and she broke into a run to reach him before he pulled away.

As Josh watched, bemused but nevertheless shamed by the girl's attack, the waitress reappeared, predictably with a large-bellied man in a dirty apron. Josh held both hands up to them in surrender before they reached him.

'I'm sorry. I really am. Forgive me.' He was saying it a lot today. There was a lot to be sorry about.

The pasty-faced girl looked disappointed. Despite the admirable feminist defence from her sister of the cervix, the waitress still looked to him like a poisonous vixen who was looking forward to a fight.

'I don't care to be treated like that. There weren't no call for it neither.'

The man said nothing, but crossed his arms menacingly. Josh nodded once.

'I know.'

'You'll wipe it up good and pay for that coffee.'

'Sure.'

She dropped a stinking cloth onto the table and made an ugly and satisfied smirk, which faded when she looked across to where the girl had been. 'Shit, Jim. That girl ain't paid me.'

They both twitched like pointer dogs and lunged in readiness to pursue the hitch-hiker, but Josh stood and held out his hands.

'Whoa. I'm picking up her tab.'

They looked at him suspiciously, but the waitress stood back and nodded, a sly grin playing at the corner of her mouth again.

'Fifteen dollars. Includin' yours.'

He was about to protest at the obvious extortion, then decided that fifteen dollars wasn't that much in the scheme of things if it got him the hell out here. He fished out his wallet, took out a twenty and handed it to her. 'Keep it.'

The waitress took the bill and folded it into her pocket. Mister Jim decided it was safe to speak.

'Get the fuck outta here, you stinkin' low-life truckin' shit-hole.'

A day ago perhaps, in what felt like another century, his temper at such an unprovoked insult might have left Mister Jim with a physical souvenir of Josh's visit, something facial for the big ugly man to bathe in Dettol. But not today. Today Josh had already done damage that would last him a lifetime and beyond. He met their gaze with steady eyes, then left quietly, making sure the door didn't bang behind him, climbed into Jezebel and roared out of the empty parking lot.

The trees that lined the road arched and thrashed in the wind of the truck's wake, as Josh accelerated down the mountain towards the interstate.

What to do? He had fully intended, regardless of his load, to drive home to Elizabeth. But now he was stinging with her rejection, stirring a bitter broth in his heart that had transformed guilt into a sense of betrayal and abandonment. He wasn't going home. Not yet.

The CB crackled for the first time since he'd left the interstate that morning, and as the truck slowed approaching a crossroads, Josh leaned forward and tried channel 19 again.

'. . . aw, shit, I said you can pay the niggers that, but I ain't haulin' for that kind of money. Know what I'm sayin'?'

'Yeah? That so, driver? Think you're the fuckin' master race? Huh? I bet you're the big fat piece of scum I passed playin' with himself 'bout a mile back. Sure was impressed.'

'There ain't no call for profanity. You guys are so damn smart you can't even talk your garbage without profanity.'

'Smarter than you, you old asshole.'

'That why you're drivin' truck, you dumb fucker, instead of runnin' the country?'

'Whoooooeee! Now if that ain't profane? What's got up your butthole?'

Josh turned the volume down, his initial delight at being back in radio contact diminishing with the reminder that the highway was still teeming with bored jerks. He brought the truck to a stop at the junction and checked the side roads. There was a community billboard at the corner, a rustic affair with vines creeping up the wooden supports and a small wooden tiled roof tacked along the top, keeping the rain off the assortment of fluttering notices for yard sales and barn dances. As he looked left, checking the road, Josh's eye roamed over its tattered display.

His heart lurched.

It was bigger, pasted inexpertly onto the wood at a slight angle, but it was the same photograph, the same slogan. And it was in colour.

He stared at Nelly McFarlane's smiling face, beaming out at him from above her lurid pink suit, and his head began to swim. The lead weight that pulled his heart to his boots was back, and this time the weight had a name written on it.

Elizabeth. It was all her fault. She had made him so crazy that his sense had gone.

There it was in full colour. The proof that Josh's mind was on some Loony Tunes vacation when the accident happened, transposing an innocent photograph of an equally innocent woman he'd seen and not registered into an empty picture of a baby being blown by a fatal wind.

Without warning a bulbous tear formed, rolled down his cheek and dissipated into the forest of rough stubble on his chin. The bottled grief for the dead child, the horror of his own temporary sleep-deprived madness, released itself and left him empty.

He was utterly defeated. If he could hallucinate so clearly and convincingly at that point, at a moment when all his wits and sanity had been required, when might it happen again? Would he be sleepless and confused from now on? What had Elizabeth done to him, with the selfish, blind countdown to her abortion?

He wiped his nose on his sleeve, shifted into first and drove on, away from that crookedly hung picture that told the world Josh Spiller was going crazy. As the dust from the wheels spiralled up in the disturbed air and Jezebel disappeared into the Appalachian late afternoon, the corner of Nelly McFarlane's poster lifted and curled, and from under the paper a small trickle of new and runny paste slithered down the wood and dripped onto the dirt.

11

'I think you shoulda talked to him that time.'

Elizabeth looked up at Nesta. It was dark back here in amongst the rails of costumes, and she was crouching beneath the comforting heavy cloth curtain made by long Jacobean skirts, her arms circling her knees.

Nesta crossed her arms and took her weight on one foot. 'You hearing me, Liz? You can't go on avoiding each other.'

'He ran out on me.'

A customer called from the front of the shop. 'Hey! Anyone back there?'

Nesta hollered back: 'Sure. Be right with you.'

She looked back at her friend and partner. Liz was pretending to sort through costume jewellery but Nesta could see she was huddled on the floor like a traumatized child. She bent down to be level with her face.

'Look, I don't know what this is about but it must be real bad. If you don't want to tell me, then fine. But if you do, you know I'm here.'

Elizabeth nodded.

Nesta returned the nod solemnly, stood up and went to deal with what might be their only customer of the day.

'Nesta . . . Did he sound . . . you know . . . sorry?'

Nesta leaned against a shelf holding pantomime horse heads for a moment, her expression full of sympathy. 'Yeah. He sounded totally broke up.'

Elizabeth looked at the floor again.

As Nesta left, to flatter and joke with the man out front who wanted to look like Mel Gibson in *Braveheart*, but never would in this life, Elizabeth ran her hand through her hair and sniffed.

She slid her hand into the deep pocket of her fleece top and slowly pulled out the square of thin paper. Just a black blob. A tiny photo of a black blob inside her, growing and living. Elizabeth stared at it for a long time then gently replaced it in her pocket.

She would take his next call. She wished now she had taken the last one. But next time. Next time they would talk.

Josh saw her standing by her rucksack on the left of the narrow road. She'd seen him first, of course. It was hard to miss a truck. By her body language it was clear she wasn't sure whether it was worth sticking out a thumb. As rides went, the one with the pick-up driver must have been the shortest in hitch-hiking history. She'd been dropped a good five miles away from the interstate junction and it didn't look like she was pleased. Before he knew why, Josh was slowing up.

The girl glared up at him as he stopped level with her, watching him wrestling with similar indecision. Josh looked back at her for a moment through his closed window, then slowly wound it down.

'You make him apologize once too often for being born a man?'

She tried to set her mouth into a hard thin line, but Josh saw a movement play at the edges that suggested a seed of mirth.

'He was only going this far.' She indicated a rough track between the trees behind her with a slim shoulder, never taking her eyes from his.

'Where you heading?'

She looked back steadily. 'Anywhere. Away from here.'

Josh turned and looked through the windshield for a moment, his fingers drumming the wheel thoughtfully. If the girl imagined his musing was merely a decision about carrying her she was wrong. Josh was deciding about a whole lot more. He turned back to her and his voice was low, almost sad.

'I'm going south.'

She looked at him and then her face ignited with a smile that gave her a new identity. It was a young and lovely face and it lit up unexpected parts of the darkness that wrapped Josh.

'Neat. I've never been in a truck.'

With a twitch of the head he motioned to her to get in. She

picked up the rucksack, skipping around to the passenger door as though her sizeable luggage weighed nothing. Josh stretched over and opened the door for her as she struggled to climb up. She tossed the rucksack onto the seat and then as Josh reached out with the intention of moving the large pack, she took his hand and pulled herself into the cab.

The fingers were slender and warm, and as they curled into Josh's palm he frowned, shamed by the heat her hand was generating in another unrelated part of his body.

She grinned at him as she withdrew her hand, wrestled the rucksack behind the chair into the darkened cabin and sat down with a bounce. The petulant feminist had been replaced by an excited child.

'Wow. This is amazing. You sleep back there?'

'Yeah.'

'Wow.'

She ran her hands over the sides of her chair and bounced up and down on it a couple of times. 'Hey. This moves around.'

'Counteracts the rough ride you get when we're all loaded up. You can make it stop if you want. There's a lever under there.'

'Naw. I think it's cool.' She bounced again and then looked across at him. 'I'm Griffin.'

Josh raised an eyebrow and smiled. 'Griffin?'

'Yes. Griffin.'

'Yeah? See now why you're kinda angry with the world.'

'Get me a doctor, I'm busting my guts laughing. You got a name or will I just call you sir?'

'What happened to sad old cock-sucker?'

She held his gaze unflinchingly, still waiting for a reply. He gave in.

'Josh. It's written on the door. Put your seatbelt on.'

Josh watched until she had clicked it home before moving off. As they drove without speaking, he watched Griffin from the corner of his eye as she hugged her knees in delight, occasionally fingering the dash or the door as though the truck were some clever illusion to be exposed. He leaned forward and turned up the CB. Griffin slapped her thighs with glee.

'Aw, too much. CB radio!'

Josh swiftly searched her face for irony, and when he saw none he shook his head and gave a small laugh. He lifted the handset and pressed talk.

'Hey northbounds, what's it lookin' like down south there?'

He waited a moment and then there was a reply.

'Eh, it's lookin' good southbound. There's a state bear 'bout a mile before exit 27. Reckon he's only huntin' four-wheelers though.'

'Ten-four to that driver. Have a good one.'

'Goin' good so far.'

Griffin was staring at Josh as though he had just spoken in tongues. 'Shit. You really say all that seventies stuff.'

'What stuff?'

'Ten-four good buddy, smoky bear and everything. You know. Looks like we got a convoy.'

'Aw come on, gimme a break.'

'Cool.'

The road was straightening up, getting ready to merge with the now visible interstate, and Josh let himself look at his passenger for a little longer this time. She was still twitching with some inner delight as she gazed out her window, and Josh let himself take in her long legs encased in baggy jeans, both knees ripped open to reveal honey-coloured flesh, brown feet in Teva sandals and a thick hooded sweatshirt that, although it was pulled over an equally shapeless long T-shirt, did little to hide the fullness of her breasts. She had short dark hair like Elizabeth, but was probably ten years Elizabeth's junior, a fact that was obvious from the inner glow and elasticity of her golden skin. She turned back to him suddenly, catching his look. Josh felt obliged to speak.

'What age are you, Griffin?'

'Why?'

'In case I'm drivin' a runaway, that's why.'

'I look that young?'

'I can't tell. Kids all look the same age and sex.'

She laughed. 'Old old old. You talk like you're fifty.'

'I'm thirty-two.'

'Yeah, that's old.'

'Come on, smartass. I'm not going to guess.'

'I'm twenty-one.'

'Sure.'

'I got ID says so.'

Josh smiled. 'I got a bumper sticker says my other car's a Porsche.'

'And it isn't?'

'Maybe if I started haulin' smack instead of steel.'

She shrugged and looked back out of the window again. Up ahead there was a parking lot just before the merge to the interstate. Maybe it was the talk of lies that did it, but Josh suddenly remembered that, despite everything, his speedy departure from Furnace still hadn't included completing his errant log. He started to pull over.

'Christ. Where's my head at?'

They rolled to a stop and Josh pulled on the brakes, whose ear-splitting hiss made Griffin jump.

'Shit, that's loud.'

He ignored her. 'Pass me that book under your seat.'

She fumbled beneath the seat and found the black plastic folder that with the help of three rubber bands contained his paperwork, and held it slightly away from him with a coquettish grin.

'Say please.'

Josh rubbed at an eye. 'You best listen, kid, 'cos I'm only goin' to say this once. I already bailed you out by pickin' up your tab after you did a runner, though Christ knows why. I ain't doin' it again, and I sure as hell ain't takin' any more smart-assed shit from that big mouth of yours. I mean it.'

Her face fell, and for a moment a look of alarm flitted across her reddening cheeks. Then she passed him the book silently and looked out the windshield.

Josh smoothed out the blue log sheet with his hand, gazing at the week stretching out on it day by day, and his eye wandered unasked to Wednesday the seventh of May. Knots of muscle at the back of his jaw tightened. The log book had the hours of the day neatly divided in black ink. He looked at three o'clock.

What would he be writing in the space marked 'remarks' while his child was being killed? Stopped for a burger? Pulled over for gas?

He breathed sharply in through his nose and rubbed his fore-head. Griffin was still staring ahead quietly, smarting from her rebuke. He spoke to her without looking up.

'If you want a leak better take it now. Ain't stoppin' till Nashville.'

She shook her head and said nothing.

Josh filled in all the blanks, fabricating the times and places he'd stopped to suit the trip like every other truck driver in America, although this time he had no choice but to state the reason for his stop in Furnace.

Any state bear with half a brain could catch him out on that one if they took his timetable apart. He wrote 'accident' shakily in the space, wrote out the rest about weight and mileage, then slapped the folder shut.

'How much was it?'

Josh looked across at the girl, puzzled. 'How much was what?'

'The check. For my sandwich.'

'Don't matter. Here. Put this back.'

She took the folder obediently this time and carefully stashed it where it came from.

'It does matter. I owe you.'

Josh threw the truck into gear and pulled out. 'Couldn't say. Your buddy overcharged me.'

Griffin arched her back and fished around in a back pocket. She took out a tightly-folded five-dollar bill and held it out to him. 'Here. It was more, but this is all I can manage right now.'

Josh waved a limp hand. 'Keep it. I don't need it.'

'You have to take it. I don't like being in debt.'

'What about bein' in debt to the restaurant. You're a thief, remember?'

'That's different.'

'How?'

'They're scumbags in there. Deserve to be ripped off.'

Josh laughed out loud and slapped the wheel. 'Jesus, you change your goddamn mind by the minute, girlie. I thought the waitress was a noble slave needin' her fuckin' chains broken. She become a scumbag the moment she asks you to pay for what you ate?'

Griffin was unmoved, the little square of five dollars still held out. 'Take it.'

Josh glanced sideways at her and his smile increased at the childishly indignant rage he saw on her face.

He put out his hand and took the folded bill. As his fingers closed on the greasy paper Josh experienced a faint but hot wave of nausea. He pushed the money into a pocket already crammed with his wallet and the various envelopes and paper he'd gathered from the sheriff's office, and then rubbed at his forehead. It passed as quickly as it had come.

'There,' she said with great solemnity. 'We're even now.'

'If you say so.'

The road finally joined the interstate and as if to celebrate Josh turned up the CB, switched on the radio above his head and pushed a cassette into the tape deck.

Jezebel took her place at a steady fifty in the line of trucks on the nearside lane and her two occupants sat passively, cocooned by the kind of noise that would drive the fainthearted insane.

12

Dividing. Dividing again and growing.

There is heat in the darkness, and as it grows the darkness is its delight. It is deep and black and hot. It remains unseen but growing, and the growth is unstoppable. It stretches and moves. It is unaware of who has summoned it into being, but it knows instinctively now who carries it, understands their essence, recognizes who will bring it through from this dark hot place into the world of light and coolness. To lose the carrier would be death. Nothing must touch the carrier until it rips and bloodies its host as it moves from this world to the next. The carrier is its gateway. The carrier is everything. And the carrier must be made aware that it is there. It moves again. Kicks and struggles. Turns and flexes what limbs are formed. Then it sleeps again and dreams of heat and blackness.

They had passed Lexington by the time Josh spoke again, and when he did it was to himself rather than to the passenger he had all but forgotten.

'Jesus. I don't believe it.'

He turned the CB's volume up and Griffin, who had nearly been asleep, looked across at him with heavy eyes.

They were in the right lane, sitting close behind a gleaming refrigerated trailer that blocked out any view except a reflection of themselves in the fading light.

Josh was grinning, staring ahead and listening intently to the crackling babble on the radio that Griffin had blocked out hours ago, unable to decipher the accents or the jargon. She sat up and tried to listen to what was exciting her driver. It sounded the same as it had been all the way, a collection of anonymous guys insulting each other from the privacy of their cabs. But Josh, unusually, was now listening intently.

'How do I know your wife's a cheap whore? 'Cos she don't take American Express, that's how. I got to pay that bitch in cash every fuckin' time.'

'Hardy har.'

'Get off the radio, asshole.'

'Yeah? Well that ain't the worst of it. Your daughter won't give no local tax receipts. Not even for a blow job.'

Josh snatched up his handset, and Griffin raised an eyebrow as he affected a corny southern drawl.

'Well I ain't surprised you got to pay for it, driver, if your face is as ugly as your rig.'

There was a succession of whooping from at least two other disembodied voices, but Josh stared ahead, still holding the handset, waiting. There was a pause and then the voice that had been cheerful came back irritated.

'Now that must've came from one of you asswipes at my tail, and unless my mirror is tellin' lies, you are one bunch of hog-ugly motherfuckers to be handin' out insults to a workin' man's truck.'

Josh punched the air in triumph with his fist full of the handset. He pressed talk again, and moulded his face into the shape he seemed to require to fake his ridiculous southern accent.

'That right? Well maybe I'll just bring this baby on round and let you eat my dust with that shit-caked rust-bucket you draggin' down the highway.'

'Uh-huh, driver? What you got there then?'

'Some of us calls it a truck. But then you wouldn't know much about that would you, Eddie?'

'Sheeeit!'

The voice on the radio guffawed with laughter, and Josh's face seemed lit from within as he beamed ahead listening to it.

Griffin watched him, puzzled.

The voice calmed itself and managed some words.

'If it ain't Sperm Spiller! What the fuck are you drivin', man?'

Another voice cut in before Josh could press talk again.

'If you faggots are goin' to start kissin' why don't you get off the fuckin' radio an' do it someplace else.'

Josh looked ahead expectantly, mouth slightly open, waiting for Eddie to come back on. He did.

'Surely, driver. Thank you kindly for the invite. Just tell us where you're at an' me an' my good buddy'll be right round there to add another lane to your ol' Hershey highway.'

Josh was sniggering like a teenager. He got to the talk button before the irate driver could get back.

'Come on, Eddie. Alzheimer's set in or you still remember the channel?'

'Sure.'

'See you there.'

Josh put out his hand and retuned the CB. He waited, still apparently oblivious to Griffin's presence, and just as she was about to break the silence and ask him a question, the radio burst back into life.

'Yoo-hoo! I'm home, honey!'

Josh smiled. 'So. Sneakin' back towards the east without givin' us a call. What happened to our marriage?'

'Shit, Josh, you went to bed too many times without a strict facial cleansin' and moisturizin' routine, that's what. I'll tell you about it. Where you at?'

'Just cruisin' past that big fireworks factory on the right. Don't know what exit.'

'Man, you're further back there than I thought. I'm about eight miles up front.'

Griffin was watching sullenly from the corner of the cab. Her body language spoke volumes about her exclusion from this conversation.

'You stoppin'?'

'Naw. I'm late on this one. I gotta lose this garbage in Arkansas by morning. Time penalty.'

'Shit, Eddie. Ten minutes for a coffee.'

'Christ, I'm here, Spiller. What a piece of pussy you turned into. Buy yourself a speedin' ticket and come on in behind me. Where you headin' anyway?'

'Callin' it quits in Music City tonight. Then Alabama.'

'Well we got nearly five hours till then. That ain't long enough for you? What you done with your life in the last two years that's gonna take that long to tell, huh?'

Josh looked sideways at Griffin then ahead into the darkening evening.

'I got a passenger.'

A small silence, then Eddie came back. 'Elizabeth ridin' with you?'

Josh clenched his back teeth.

'Nope. Hitcher. A girl.'

'And she's from the fuckin' CIA?'

'Guess not.'

'Then what's the problem?'

Griffin noticed that Josh's fist was clenching and unclenching around the radio handset. He thought for a moment. 'Let me catch up with you. I'll talk to you when I'm up your ass.'

'Sure. I'll stay on this channel. I'm kinda tired of being the cabaret on 19.'

'Yeah. They'll miss you like I miss shittin' my diaper.'

'You miss that too? Thought it was just me.'

' 'Bye, Eddie.'

Josh hung up the handset and stared ahead. Griffin looked quizzically at the side of his face, until her steady gaze made him turn to her for a second. 'I drove team with him for three years.'

'What's that mean?'

'It means you spend your whole life with someone in a cab like this. You drive, they sleep. They drive, you sleep. The truck never stops. You can make a lot of money.'

'Did you?'

Josh laughed again. It was a nice sound.

'Naw. We were kids. We messed around too much.'

Griffin sat upright and ran her hands over imaginary creases in her jeans. 'Look, I know you want to talk to your buddy in private and everything. You can drop me anywhere here. I'll hitch another ride.'

Josh shook his head. 'I'll take you to Nashville. That was the deal.'

'So what you want me to do?'

'You got a Walkman?'

'Sure.'

'You can go back there and lie down if you want and listen to it. That'll give me plenty enough privacy.'

Griffin nodded, but kept looking at Josh. He looked like he

wanted to say something else. She waited, and her stillness made him clear his throat.

'I had a pretty bad day today. I need to talk to someone.'

Griffin smiled like a sitcom wife confronted with her office-weary husband. 'Yeah? How bad could that be?'

Josh looked across at her briefly, then back out at the road, and her smile faded as she caught the thunder behind his eyes.

'I killed a child. This morning.'

Griffin kept her widened eyes on the side of his face. She could see his jaw clenching under his ears. He stared ahead for a moment then spoke again.

'A baby. It was . . . it rolled under the truck from the sidewalk.'

Griffin's body stiffened.

'Jesus Christ. Where?'

'Furnace.'

There was a pause.

'My town?'

Josh looked back at her. 'You came from Furnace?'

She was nodding, mouth open, a cocktail of fright and uncertainty in her green eyes.

Josh shifted in his seat, then ran a hand over the bristles of his head. 'Baby's name was Amy Nevin. You know them?'

Without looking directly at her, he could see her nodding. He could also see her hands going to her face, covering her open mouth in horror.

'Jesus Christ,' she repeated from behind a shield of fingers.

They drove on in silence for an uncomfortably long time.

Griffin stared ahead and her hands dropped back in her lap, writhing together now as though washing with invisible soap. 'I always knew I had to leave that place. It was only ever a question of when.'

Josh frowned, unsure as to why his dark admission had caused this unsolicited confession. His reply, partly prompted by a relief that she seemed to be taking his story no further, sounded fatuous and shallow.

'It's a comfortable town. You could do worse.'

Griffin snorted and wheeled round to look at him again. 'Yeah? Well that's all you know.'

Josh stroked the wheel with open palms and tried unsuccessfully to shift his attention from his own extraordinary sorrow to his passenger's selfish and quite ordinary rebellious angst. He tried, but he failed, and the question that had been born on his tongue, to ask why she hated her home so much, was killed and replaced with one he really wanted an answer to.

'How well you know the Nevins?'

Griffin glared at him, annoyed that he was not catching the line she wanted to throw him. 'Not that well. I see Alice's man in town sometimes. He used to work for my Dad.'

'Doing what?'

'Stuff. Handyman stuff, you know.'

'He's got a pretty neat house for a handyman.'

She shrugged, then bit at a fingernail, watching him from the corner of her eyes. 'Did Alice see it happen . . . you know . . . ?'

Josh was irritated but unsurprised by her dodging of his question. But then why should a young girl know or care about the economic ratios of job to living standards? This was clearly a privileged young girl whose Dad would pick her up in his car from a variety of expensive leisure pursuits, whose Mom would surf the malls with her picking out clothes, who would run away from home for a while, and return triumphant and defiant to settle down with some wealthy neighbourhood boy whom she would always consider not good enough for her. Girls like Griffin thought of themselves as enigmatic and mysterious. Josh knew they were easier to read than one of Sim's tabloids, and considerably less interesting. He bit his lip and remembered the shape Alice Nevin made with her mouth as her child had the life crushed out of it by rubber as unforgiving as stone.

'Yeah. She saw it.'

'Oh my God.'

Josh was tired of this. He wanted to talk to Eddie, to another adult who shared his past, who knew Elizabeth, and who could understand this nightmare without having the emotions spelled out on a billboard.

'You want to go back there now and listen to some music?' Griffin looked at him, and for the first time it occurred to Josh that she was weighing up how safe it was to be in his company. He could see it in her eyes, which were narrower now, scanning his face for clues.

'Sure.'

She unclipped her belt, climbed back into the sleeper and fumbled around in her pack. After a few moments she found the sleeper cabin light, and Josh heard the hissing rhythmic buzz that was escaping from her headphones. A glance in the mirror confirmed that Griffin had settled herself on his bed as comfortably as a cat finding a patch of sunshine, the Walkman and one spare cassette clutched in her fist. He brought his shoulders up to his ears to release the tension that made them ache, then changed down and stepped on the gas. Eddie was somewhere up ahead, and even the sight of his tail-lights would go a long way to help soothe the loneliness that had overwhelmed him once again.

Jezebel responded to her master's command, and as she roared southwards, the delicate spring grasses that her headlights picked out along the highway's edge bent and swayed in her wake like fearful worshippers of some great powerful beast.

13

John Pace flicked on his desk lamp and fingered the pile of mundane papers on his desk. He hated taking work home. In the kitchen he could hear his wife scolding the youngest boy and he ran a hand over his tired face in anticipation of his inevitable involvement.

A bitch of a day. He was weary, sure, but more than that. He was afraid. He knew it would be sorted by now. Well, as good as. But what about his part? Did they think he'd messed up?

He was a good policeman. He cared. But right now, as the commotion from the kitchen worked its way along the hall towards the closed door of his study, he knew that sometimes caring wasn't the same as protecting. And despite the approaching raucous cries of his son, he loved him as he loved them all, and knew that he should have thought a whole lot harder about protection when he'd had the chance.

The door burst open and the tear-stained face of a six-year-old boy squinted up at him.

'It was my Spiderman, Daddy, and Noah took it.'

'Well I guess you just have to learn to share, don't you, Ethan?'

The little boy opened his mouth and let out a wail once more, turned and ran back to the kitchen, leaving Pace's door wide open. He watched his wife's arms reach out into the hall from the kitchen and scoop up the boy in a firm but loving embrace, and as he stood up and quietly pushed his own door to block the image, he closed his eyes and put a hand over his mouth.

Sharing. Even if it could, if the world could somehow be made able to understand, Furnace would never share what it had. Never.

*   *   *

By the time their two trucks peeled away from each other, Eddie Shanklin had already decided that he would drop his load quicker than a chilli diarrhoea, relocate his friend and shadow him up the interstate. Screw getting a decent load back north. They had talked for nearly four hours straight and Eddie knew Josh was in trouble. He wouldn't be hard to find. The dispatcher who gave Josh his next load would tell Eddie where he was bound on the way back through Nashville and he'd take it from there. The most important thing was that Josh had someone to talk to. Sounded like he was going through it.

When Jezebel had sneaked up on Eddie's Kenworth, a half hour after they'd first made contact, Eddie had practically hugged himself that his buddy had tucked himself in at his tail. He was so ready to laugh, itching to drag out some of the running gags they'd shared for years and dust them off. But in the first hour, an hour in which Eddie had barely spoken except for the occasional 'shit, man!' or 'no way!', it became clear to him that laughter was not on the menu.

It had often struck him how much the dark interior of a moving truck was like a confessional box, but never more so than tonight. If Josh had said the things he'd told Eddie on the radio face to face, they would have both been embarrassed.

There was a liberation of expression that outstripped even alcohol in the simple act of staring ahead, mesmerized by the darkness and the lights that pierced it, speaking into a small square of black plastic in your hand that had no eyes to accuse you.

It broke Eddie up to think of Josh suffering like he was. Eddie liked Elizabeth. In fact he liked her a lot. If Josh hadn't gotten in there first, well, who knows what might have happened that day they'd met her, watched her hollering for some dead-beat boyfriend competing in a drag race near Cleveland.

They'd followed her like beggars all day, finally charming her sufficiently with some terrible gags at the hot-dog stall, to read the doubt about her circumstances written in her eyes. She'd liked them both, and yeah, maybe it could have been Eddie who'd won. At least he liked to fool himself that way. But he knew the truth was that, in any competition for women, Josh's boyish white grin and his body that looked like it was worked out at a five-thousand-dollar-a-year health club instead of getting the way it was just by pulling on tarp ropes, would knock Eddie out of the game before it started.

Eddie made up for it with a wicked mouth and a preponderance for instant action in any situation that made even the most politically-correct women recognize some unhealthy atavistic desire to be protected. And he had a woman that he wanted to protect right now.

She was waiting for him in Indiana, with an emerald engagement ring on her finger so big Eddie thought it looked like she'd wiped her mouth with the back of her hand and got some spinach caught there. But she thought it was the best thing she'd seen, and she was going to be his wife.

Looked like Elizabeth wasn't so simple to please. Eddie hadn't known what to say about the whole mess. About the accident with the kid, that could be dealt with. He understood. Happened sometimes, and you just had to ride with it. He'd heard worse, even though he reckoned Josh's story about the woman he'd thought had pushed it was the damnedest shit, and most likely and tragically a sleep-at-the-wheel dream. He'd caught Josh's tone though, when he'd started to suggest it, and backed right off.

If that's what Josh said happened, then maybe it did. Who was he to say different? But about Josh's own baby? That stank like old fish. Eddie wanted time to think some more, which was why he was going to shadow him. He could tell that even though Josh had said his hitcher was up the back listening to music, he'd been reluctant about some details, holding back just a little. Well next time they talked she would be gone, and by then Eddie would have figured out what best to say.

Yeah. He would think of something to say. It might not be right. But it would be something.

The lights of Nashville were dismal through a drizzling rain that had started fifty miles back and hadn't let up. Josh gazed at the orange and white twinkling pinpoints of light, watched vacantly as the rain on the windshield blurred them to ragged, ill-defined spheres, until the wipers made them sharp again with a jerky half circuit. Despite the depressing effect the rain was having on the home of country music, Josh felt better just for having spoken to Eddie. Not healed, but relieved temporarily of the unspeakable loneliness that had overwhelmed him when Elizabeth refused to take his call. Eddie had saved him for now. Otherwise, Nashville might have finished him off.

The route to the downtown truck stop was a melancholy journey through tangled intersections lined with crummy billboards. Some music company had taken space above Josh's exit to inform him that Ellis Freedman had a new album out called *Lovin'*.

Ellis Freedman looked pretty pleased about it and pointed at Josh with a four-foot-long finger as he leaned on a cherry-red guitar. The rest of Nashville surrounding the billboard looked a little less pleased.

As Josh pulled Jezebel up at the lights, halting them at the bottom of the exit ramp, he turned his head to look for the first time at his recumbent passenger. Griffin was lying with her back to him, arms huddled to her chest, the Walkman earphones knocked askew as she'd turned in her sleep. As he watched she began to stir, woken either by the first real absence of motion, or perhaps by the unconscious knowledge that eyes were roaming over her sleeping form. She arched her back, lifted her arms above her head and stretched with a feline fluidity. Josh watched until she sat up and turned sleepily to face him, rubbing her hands in her hair like she was washing it.

'Where are we?'

'Nashville. Nearly at the truck stop.'

She blinked, crossed her legs and put her hands on her hips. 'Shit. I must have been asleep for hours.'

Josh continued to look at her until she unhooked the earphones from her neck and smiled. 'I think those lights are trying to tell you something.'

Josh looked ahead at the green light, threw the truck into gear and moved off. He'd barely reached fourth when Griffin climbed forward and took her seat with a satisfied bounce.

'Did you talk to your friend?'

'Yeah.'

'It's important to talk sometimes, huh?'

'I guess.'

'Josh?'

He looked across at her, surprised at the intimacy which using his name bestowed on her voice.

'Yeah?'

Griffin was staring at her lap, fiddling with the white knots of cotton that protruded from her drawstring sweatshirt. 'I'm really sorry I was so mean to you, you know in the restaurant. Guess I was edgy about leaving town and everything. I didn't know that . . . well I mean, you'd had a rough time and I didn't know . . .'

'It's okay. I was out of line.'

Griffin nodded, brushed at her lap in an embarrassed way, then sat upright and rubbed at her head again. 'Is this a real truck stop you're heading for?'

'How do you mean?'

'Well I know some people say "truck stop" and it's like, just a McDonald's where there's maybe a truck or two but mostly regular people in cars, families with kids and shit . . .'

Josh laughed, turning to her with a wide grin that made her stop mid-sentence with the brilliance of it.

'And you want a bunch of mean hairy-assed truckers instead.'

She returned his laugh. 'Well, it'd just be kinda neat to say I'd been in one, you know?'

Josh looked back out at the miserable night. 'It's a real truck stop. I think you might be disappointed.'

'Can I get a bus from there or something?'

Josh nodded. 'Sure. But it's three a.m. I ain't lettin' you go off by yourself until the town gets goin' with normal folk.'

He threw her a mischievous look.

'It's them I'm thinkin' of. If there's more of them about they can defend themselves.'

Griffin tried to look offended, but she settled down into her seat with a half smile and said nothing.

The downtown TA in Nashville was a big one. As they roared into the lot and drove slowly between row after row of growling trucks, Griffin sat forward and peered out of the window with her hands on the dash. Everything was scaled up here. The parking bays were gigantic diagonal slashes on a prairie of asphalt, the trucks man-oeuvring between them like grazing dinosaurs, and as Josh inched Jezebel forward searching for a space, the CB was busier than at any time on the road. Even through the closed windows of the cab, the noise of hundreds of idling diesel engines was tremendous, and Griffin stared at it all as though they had landed on Mars.

'Wow!'

'Yeah. Wow is right. Looks like all the good spaces are gone. Let me guess. Another night parked next to a reefer.'

'What's a reefer? Is it bad?'

'It's a refrigerated trailer, and the engine has to be kept on all night. Get the picture?'

'Noisy.'

'You get used to it. Think of the poor guy who's haulin' it.' Josh tutted a couple of times when what looked like a space turned out to be just a truck parked a few feet back from the other noses, until he spotted an empty bay, predictably between two reefers, did a job of backing up that he knew was impressing his passenger, and brought the rig to a halt with a hiss of the brakes.

'Pass me the book.' He indicated the black folder, and this time it was passed without comment or protest.

Josh scratched at his paperwork as Griffin waited silently beside him, staring out at the forest of trucks that glinted in the rain, reflecting what little light there was in the badly-illuminated lot. Josh could tell she was nervous, and for the first time since their peculiar meeting he felt a pang of protectiveness for this inexperienced girl, on the run most probably from some imagined family slight which would be repaired by a hasty home-coming the first time her trip got difficult.

He spoke to her with his head down, still busy writing. 'I'll finish this and then we can get somethin' to eat.'

She perked up, but her voice was higher, indicating a certain nervousness. Still, she was young, she'd never been in a truck stop before. She was a girl.

'Sure. Great.'

Josh scribbled a few more lines, fussed about with some bits of rogue paper, then snapped the book shut, passed it back to her and stood up.

'Okay. Let's hit the Hilton.'

'There's a Hilton here?'

Josh looked at her, saw she was serious, shook his head and then laughed. She laughed too, although in her laughter there was a mix of embarrassment, anxiety and something else. It was the something else that stayed with Josh as he led her from the truck towards the restaurant, feeling her trotting at his heel as he walked along the line of trucks, unable to keep up with his stride.

*　　*　　*

Josh was reading the weather page at the back of *USA Today* when Griffin spoke conspiratorially through a mouthful of potato. 'Do they think I'm . . . you know?'

He looked up at her, then across at the men she was indicating with a twitch of her head. Across the smoky restaurant, its air thick with the smell of grease and diesel, two bored truckers, identically bearded and dressed, their bellies pressing against the table as though they were protective air bags, sat in a booth gazing absently at Josh and Griffin. When Josh looked up, one of them nodded in acknowledgement and gazed gloomily down at his coffee. Josh looked back at Griffin.

'Naw.'

He got back to his paper. Griffin continued to chew, and looked around her like a spy in a comedy movie. There wasn't much to look at. She'd acted scared when she first came in, skirting too obviously around some young black drivers who were hanging around the entrance smoking, wearing long thick oilskins like firemen. They threw Griffin and Josh a long look that was interrupted and diffused by that look being returned by Josh. Griffin had stepped closer to Josh and stayed at his shoulder while he bought some stuff. For a few moments he'd hovered around a machine that sold telephone cards, looking like he was making up his mind about something, until finally, to Griffin's relief, he'd made a decision, bought a twenty-dollar card followed by a newspaper which he read as they walked into the restaurant. There were only a half dozen truckers eating, and far from being threatening, the scene was heartbreaking. The men looked eroded, worn down like river pebbles. None of them looked like bums – they were neat and relatively clean – but it looked like there had once been more to them all than this, that something bigger had been ground away, almost imperceptibly, until they were down to their last layer.

There were phones in every booth by the wall but only one person was using them, a man sitting in the corner, his posture as upright as if he were a general taking a call from the president. Griffin watched him for a while as he spoke an occasional quiet word without any change in expression, until he hung up, curled a finger around his coffee mug and stared ahead. No one was laughing or even talking cheerfully. The only sounds of life came occasionally from the kitchen, when the diners looked up expectantly to see if the joke would spill out into the restaurant and involve them. When it didn't they returned to their meals and the job of contemplating the road ahead, gazing out of the dark rain-stained windows.

Griffin's surveillance was broken by a waitress sauntering up to Josh's elbow with a jug of coffee.

'Need a top up, honey?'

'Yeah, go on.'

She poured the hot liquid into his mug and as Griffin touched her own mug in anticipation the waitress smiled and walked off.

'Shit. How come I don't get any?'

Josh smiled and emptied some cream theatrically into his mug. 'They do that. They don't like women in here. Pisses off the women truckers something fierce.'

Griffin raised her dark, prettily arched eyebrows. 'You get women truckers?'

'Sure. Plenty husband and wife teams too.'

Josh swallowed after he said it, a wave of something sad breaking at his shore again. Husband and wife. Sounded nice.

'What do they look like?'

'They look like truckers.'

'What? Like those guys over there?'

'Well some don't have beards.'

'Do I look like a trucker?'

Josh put his paper down and sighed. 'No. You don't.'

'Why don't I?' She sounded mildly offended.

'You just don't look like one. Okay? You can tell.'

'Shit. Then they probably do think I'm a hooker.'

Josh smiled. 'I doubt it.'

'Well of course they must.'

'I don't think you'd do much business if you were.'

'And what exactly is that supposed to mean?'

She was genuinely annoyed now. Josh's smile was widening.

'You're not dressed for it.'

She stared at him for a moment, then her face broke into a smile of unparalleled loveliness. Josh felt his pulse quicken and he looked back down at the lurid map of America on the paper.

'What do they wear then?'

Josh found himself reddening slightly. He picked up the coffee and obscured his face with it for a moment until the sensation subsided. 'What do you think? Shitty cheap things. Short tight skirts. Sparkly stuff. High shoes.'

'Where do they do it? In the cabs?'

'Naw. They lean up against the pumps while you fuel up and try and get you to come before the tank's full.'

It was Griffin's turn to redden. The mischief had been replaced by genuine adolescent horror.

'What? Out in the open there? With everyone watching?'

'Don't be dumb. Of course they do it in the cabs.'

She looked hurt, and Josh relented. 'We call 'em lot-lizards, and if you don't want to get bugged by them some guys put a sticker on their sleeper door with a lizard on, and a line going through it. You know, like a no-smoking sign?'

'Do you have one?'

Josh shook his head and smiled. 'Nope.'

'Then you get bugged by them.'

'Haven't so far.'

'Does that mean you're waiting to be?'

Josh sighed and pulled at the skin on his throat. 'Finish up. I want some sleep.'

He stood up and fished in his pocket for money. His hand found the five dollars that Griffin had given him nestling beside his wallet. He looked down at her, hurriedly gulping at the remains of her coffee in case she got left behind, and he felt that tenderness come over him again. He took the bill and pushed it back into his wallet as he took out a twenty and dropped it on the table. Then they were out of the restaurant and into the lot, Josh once again pursued by the trotting of a companion who tried to match his stride through the gloomy corridors of throbbing metal as though her life depended on it.

14

'Jesus. What a mess.'

Elizabeth gave a half smile across the table and shrugged at her friend. 'Could be worse, Nesta.'

'How?'

'I dunno. Lots of ways. I'll think of some.'

Nesta took a greedy gulp from her wine glass, and pushed out an arm as the waiter passed by. 'Hey, Tony. Two more here, huh?'

The young man looked to Elizabeth for confirmation as he gathered the two glasses.

'Hey, not for me. Thanks.'

Nesta raised an eyebrow. 'What does it matter? You know, if . . .'

Elizabeth shot her a warning look that had thunder in it. 'Yeah, okay. One more white wine and . . . ?'

'A Coke.'

'Yeah. A Coke.'

Tony put his hand on a hip. 'Diet or Classic?'

Elizabeth sighed. 'Shit, Tony. Do I look like I'm on a diet?'

'Jeez. You crabby women. Who needs ya?'

He minced off to fetch their drinks.

'No one,' answered Elizabeth softly to his back.

Nesta put her hand across the table and touched her friend's. 'That ain't true. He'll be back. Christ, you just freaked me out with this baby stuff. How'd you think he must have felt?'

'I know how he felt. Betrayed.'

'What about you?'

'Confused.'

113

Nesta put her other hand over Elizabeth's and lowered both her head and her voice. 'You want it. Don't you?'

Elizabeth stared back into her friend's face, and as her eyes filled with tears Nesta nodded and sat back.

'Thought so.'

There wasn't much room in the Peterbilt's sleeper. Josh had seen the rig advertised in a trade magazine and wanted it straight off. But although the guy who sold it to him moved around in the sleeper as he told Josh what a golden baby she was, holding his short chubby arms out like a man trying to fly, there was no getting away from the fact that it was fine for one, but tight for two.

Elizabeth had only been on a handful of trips in Jezebel, and on every single one she'd banged her head on something. The inevitability of the accidents made Josh laugh, even when one injury had drawn blood after she'd caught her temple on the edge of the shelf that held the microwave. She'd hit him in a temper then, and after that they'd fallen onto the skinny mattress, and that had been that for an hour or more while they'd made amends.

Now, with Griffin crouching and fussing around over her rucksack, Josh realized that this was the first time he'd had a stranger sleep in his cab. It made him feel peculiar. He sensed strongly somewhere deep and almost unreachable that there was someone in his cab that most definitely shouldn't be there. And it was made all the more strange by the fact that his conscious mind was thinking exactly the opposite.

He sat in his driver's seat and watched Griffin in the rear view mirror as she moved around delicately, like a small animal preparing a nest, and admired the fact that as yet she hadn't bumped her head once. When she spoke as she dug around in the bottom of her pack, it was with the intimate tone a wife might use to a husband on a camping trip.

'I don't know if you need to go to sleep right now, but I've got something in here you might like.'

'Yeah? You got the pay check from the dispatcher in Georgia who ain't paid me?'

She smiled into the pack as he watched and then pulled out a pear-shaped bottle. She held it up as he swung around to look at her.

'Ta-ra!'

'What is it?'

Griffin clambered forward and sat in the passenger seat, the bottle held around the neck by her slim brown hand. 'Appalachian brandy. A bottle of the finest.'

Josh shook his head. 'I don't drink when I'm on the road.'

'But you're not on the road now. You've stopped over.'

'Not for long. I got to drop this load in Alabama today. That means gettin' movin' in around six or seven hours.'

Griffin held the bottle up and looked lovingly at the label.

'It's ten years old.'

'No shit? Older than you?'

Griffin rolled her eyes and slapped the bottle down in her lap. 'Jesus. If you absolutely have to know, I'm twenty-one years old. Okay? Just turned it on the twenty-fourth of April.' She counted on pretty fingers. 'I got a pair of binoculars, two computer games, a mountain bike and heaps of cards. The only non-legit thing about me is that I swiped this from my Dad's cabinet before I left. Now is that such a crime?'

Josh was interested. 'They know you're gone?'

She looked at the bottle to avoid his eyes. 'They'll know by now.'

'So why'd you leave?'

'Wrong colour mountain bike.'

'I'm serious.'

She sighed and looked out through the windshield, which was running with water as the rain streamed down it unimpeded by the immobile wipers.

'Furnace is a bad place.'

'Yeah?'

'Yeah.'

'Bad full stop, or bad for you?'

'Both.'

'It sure wasn't great for me. But as towns go it looked a pretty decent place to grow up.'

Griffin turned to Josh and regarded him with an intense stare. In the dim light cast by the single lamp above the rear view mirror she suddenly looked a lot older than twenty-one. The shadows were harsh. She stared at him for a few moments before speaking, and when she did it was in a low voice, like that of a psychiatrist to a patient. 'Pretty decent place? You telling me you don't regret the day, the hour, the very second when you decided to turn off that interstate and crossed into McNab County? And that you won't live with that regret of having ever set foot in Furnace until the very last breath of your dying day?'

Josh's heart started to beat a little faster. Her tone was unsettling, and his head swam with the memory of it all. He ran a hand over his hot forehead, trying to push that towelling sleep-suit and its contents to the blackest, deepest well in his head he could find.

'Ten years old?'

Griffin registered surprise, as if broken from a daydream.

'What?'

'The brandy.'

She smiled like a shy child, looking awkward at having shared her feelings with him, and lifted the bottle again. Her cheerfulness was forced, but Josh was grateful for it.

'Yeah. People laugh at Appalachian wine and brandy. But speaking as a woman whose entire bitching family are of Scottish descent and never shut the fuck up about it, I reckon it beats even the finest Scotch single malt.'

Josh reached behind him and fished about in a velour pocket stitched onto the wall. He retrieved two cups, one a white china mug with the logo of the Owner Operators' Association on it, the other an opaque red plastic tumbler covered in fragmented cracks from being mistakenly loaded in a hot dishwasher.

Josh put them down in the cup-holders between them, then leant forward and pulled the drapes round the windshield. Griffin smiled wickedly at him as she uncorked the bottle.

'Cute. Drapes in a truck.'

'You keen on seein' the hairs on some fat trucker's ass?'

She laughed and poured the brandy carefully into the containers, passed him the mug then held the tumbler up and touched it to his drink.

'Slange.'

Josh raised a quizzical eyebrow as he froze the mug a little distance from his lips.

'It's Gaelic. For good health. You know, cheers.'

He inclined his head in acknowledgement, touched her tumbler with his own mug again, and took a large mouthful. It burned his cheeks momentarily then slipped over his throat. He let it warm him for a second with his lips tightly pressed together, then let out a satisfied exhalation. Griffin had a point. It was top-notch liquor. Its anaesthetic qualities were almost instantaneous and he was grateful for the subtle physical suggestion that the sharp part of him still slicing away inside was beginning to go numb.

She threw hers back like a labourer and placed the tumbler back in its plastic hole. 'Any music? Can I look at your tapes?'

Josh pointed at the shelf above the dash. 'Sure.'

She clattered around, fishing out tapes and discarding them until she found one she liked.

'Hey, this'll work. Del Amitri. Scottish, so of course they must be good.'

'Yeah?'

'Yeah. You like British bands?'

'Yeah. Kind of. Not especially. It's Elizabeth's brother. He's into that kind of stuff.'

As soon as he'd said it, Josh regretted it. Why did he have to speak her name? Of all the things in the world, she was the last subject he wanted to discuss. He flicked his eyes at Griffin.

She was fishing the cassette out of its box, spending a long time looking at the photograph of the band on the cover. He waited for the inevitable question. It never came.

'Can you put this on?'

Josh took the cassette and slid it into the player. As always he hadn't rewound the tape, and it came on in the middle of a track. The guy was singing a line about driving with the brakes on. Another sad one, about breaking up with someone, about not being able to say you loved a person. Or something like that anyway. He never could work it out. But although he liked this track a lot, he was still anxious, waiting to be grilled about Elizabeth by this keen-eyed, curious passenger. Griffin said nothing, but sang along in a high-pitched, whiny voice as she opened the brandy and poured them both another large measure. Josh was going to put his hand out and stop her, but the numbing effect that the alcohol was having on his pain was too good to ignore. He let her pour, and they sat drinking in silence, staring at the grey velour drapes as the melancholy music competed for their attention with the drumming of the rain on the cab, and the thrumming of the reefer that was parked hard up against them.

It must have been three or four minutes before Griffin nodded towards the padded strip above Josh's head.

'That hers?'

Josh looked at what had caught her attention. It was the scissors brooch, still pinned to the fabric, boldly declaring her name with its uneven etching. So she hadn't missed a thing. She'd been weighing it all up.

'Nope. It's mine.'

She nodded as if it was all she wanted to hear. 'It's pretty. Elizabeth's my grandmother's name.'

Josh looked at her for a moment and then a madness came over him. 'Do you want it?'

She turned to him with a half smile as though he might be joking, and when she saw no humour, but a very deep solemnity, she took another sip of brandy and wiped her mouth.

'For real?'

'I'm not plannin' on wearin' it.'

She examined him closely again, and then lit up into one of her gorgeous smiles. 'Thanks.'

He stretched up and unpinned it. 'It's just cheap tin junk. Probably make whatever you pin it to go black.'

He handed it to her, and his heart sunk when he watched her turn it over in her hands in almost exactly the same way that Elizabeth had. He looked away. She sensed his discomfort and neatly pocketed the brooch.

There was an awkward pause, then she jumped in her seat. 'Aw shit. This is my favourite. Listen to this guy's voice. Oh man. Turn it up. Turn it up, will you?'

He leaned forward and turned up the music, and continued to look away as she swayed in the seat next to him as though at a gig, reminding him again of the difference in their years.

Josh swallowed his brandy and willed it to do what only eighty per cent proof could.

The worst thing was that it took so little. Josh was by no means drunk, only mildly loosened by the brandy when he first touched her. He hadn't meant to, but when he'd leaned across to her window to pull the drape the full way round and his hand had brushed the back of her neck, he knew it had been on the agenda since he'd picked her up.

He knew too, that the decision to be unfaithful for the first and only time in his relationship with Elizabeth had been made in retributive anger at that roadside, looking down at Griffin's young sullen but willing face, not here in the gloom of the warm cab, with the rain beating a rhythm on the roof. The deed had already been done in his mind; now it was time for his body to catch up.

Her shoulders had tightened at his touch and instead of pulling his hand away, he'd let it linger, the backs of his fingers gently brushing soft warm skin. She'd turned to him, his face now so close he could smell her sweet brandy breath from slightly open lips, then she'd closed her eyes.

It hadn't been clumsy or difficult getting from there into the back. It had just happened. Only once as she kissed his neck and he lay staring into the ceiling had he thought of Elizabeth. He conjured up a picture of her at the shop, imagined her standing behind Nesta as he phoned, smug that she hadn't taken his call, and for that moment he made the effort to hate her. He tried to hold fast to that emotion, but even as he struggled to do so, he wondered momentarily, in the hazy dream-like state of arousal, why he was committing this unprecedented act of betrayal. Then he'd felt Griffin's hand sliding beneath his shirt, running over his nipples like syrup, and his own hands had found her large, firm breasts. Josh put Elizabeth from his mind completely and gave himself up to the explosive relief that the joining of their bodies was affording almost every part of him.

Afterwards, they lay like lovers rather than spent and embarrassed strangers, Griffin's head in the hollow beneath Josh's shoulder, his hand toying with the short strands of her hair.

When she spoke, Josh mused dreamily on the fact that they had both used the pleasure not merely to escape from something, but perhaps also to hurt someone. He could hear it in her voice.

'I want you to promise me you'll never go back there.'

'Hmm?'

'Furnace, Josh. Don't ever go back.'

He tried to look at her, pressing his chin into his neck, but her face was buried in his chest.

'Why would I go back?'

'I don't know. If you have to for an inquest or something. I don't know.'

He thought about it. 'Well I would only go back, I reckon, if they dug up evidence about . . .' He paused. He hadn't told Griffin about the woman. About the murderer. He certainly didn't want to now.

'Evidence about what?'

She sat up a little, pushing herself up on one elbow.

'I don't know. I'm talkin' garbage.'

She looked at him, searching his face, then kissed him softly and resumed her place beneath his shoulder. She spoke into his skin, her words muffled and slow. 'I thought I could fit in, you know. Be like everybody always wants you to be? But I guess I want more.'

'Sure. We all want more.'

'What do you want, Josh?'

He let his free arm flop out on the mattress, and his hand played with the grimy corner of his comforter. 'A family. Life.'

It was so slight that he might have imagined it, but he felt Griffin stiffen in his embrace. She was silent for a long time and then she rolled over and tucked into him like a spoon, still holding onto his hand.

He felt her body jerk slightly and then her breathing became regular and deep. Josh lay awake for a time, thinking about what he had said, and then closed his eyes and gave in to sleep.

He saw it spinning in the wind. The children were licking at the ice cream cone, and the dust was blowing in miniature twisters around the base of the sign. But the noise. It was loud, piercing like a scream of pain, and the combination of its volume and pitch of distress was unbearable. He put his hands to his ears, but the Tanner ice cream sign was revolving faster now, the tortured screeching approaching the level of white noise. *Wheeea. Wheeea. Wheeea.*

And worse. The picture was changing on that disc. As it spun in the infernal wind, the children's faces were changing. Changing into one face. A mashed and ruined face. The face of a baby that was no longer a baby.

Wheeea. Wheeea. WHEEEA!

Josh sat upright with a shout, and as he blinked, measuring his surroundings, he realized that the noise had not quite stopped with his waking. He blinked twice, slapped the heels of his palms to his eyes, and only then was there silence. Josh breathed out heavily and groaned. Bad dreams that persisted even seconds past the waking moment were very bad dreams indeed.

He straightened up and looked to his right. Griffin was gone. A thin line of yellow daylight sliced through the windshield drapes. He leaned forward to read the digital clock on the dash, which told him in tiny green numerals that it was nine-thirty.

Josh lay back down on the bed and put one arm behind his head. Part of him wasn't surprised she'd gone, but he remembered how freaked she'd been by the truck stop and he wondered how she would fare, a country girl trying to find transport in this decidedly seedy part of a large city.

Although there was relief in the neatness of her departure, the difficulty of facing their deed now avoided, Josh was disappointed. Even the guiltiest part of his mind had to admit that the sex had been exquisite. Just thinking about it now was making him hard again, making him want more. He closed his eyes and thought about her firm young body, her sweet pink tongue and those slim, brown, elegant hands. Somewhere inside, as his hand slid down to his crotch, some chastising puritanical brain cell slyly replaced those brown hands in his memory with Elizabeth's, making him remember how they too could smooth away his pain, make him forget everything except her while they worked. But more, it made him remember that when Elizabeth caressed him it was with more than desire. It was with love. Trivial things, things a million light years away from sex, started to nudge the lust from his head; the horrible socks she bought him constantly, the way she watched TV lying full length on the sofa with her knees hooked over the back, the way she looked out for Sim without the old man knowing she was doing it.

Josh's eyes opened and started to moisten with remorse.

He lay for an age, wallowing in his sin, then sat up, sniffed back the unwelcome emotions, and swung his legs over the edge of the small bed. He had a load to deliver and he was going to do it. It was already late. He dressed quickly and clumsily, started the truck up, and with only a small gesture to what had happened, a quick smoothing of the bed with a hesitant hand, left the warmth of the cab to go and take a leak.

15

The drive to Carris Arm was more ritual than necessity. But wasn't that the case with most of it now? She knew they had done it properly, respectfully, the first time, one hundred and nineteen years ago, walking, robed and with the copper vessels ready to receive the sulphur. Why bother when you could just drive there and pick the stuff up? Or better, have them bring it to you? That would be going too far. She needed to make the short journey if only to remind herself of the ones who originally negotiated this mountain ridge, strangers in a new world, longing for their distant country where their own people feared and despised them, determined as they walked that they would never be exiled again.

And they had come this way, they or their descendants, sixteen times before. This was the seventeenth, and it would not be the last. What would they think of her now, cruising along this narrow mountain road in a seven series BMW, her instruments lying beside her on a leather seat instead of tied with leather around her waist?

She smiled. They would think she was admirable. She had kept it going. Taken it to its logical and modern conclusion.

The morning was crisp and sunny, the warmth only beginning to get to work on the wet roads and dripping trees, and the dark metallic blue car made a thick swishing sound as it glided through the puddles on the road.

The next tight bend revealed an RV crawling ahead at fifteen or twenty miles an hour, an obstacle now impossible to pass for at least the next five miles of winding road. She braked and inched the car near enough to study the licence plate. New York. Nothing suspicious. Early-rising suburban nobodies taking their family on a mundane Appalachian adventure.

But since that camper van and its three non-vacationing occupants from Washington DC three years ago, she had every right to be wary. You never knew when they were on to you, and no one could afford to relax.

And she hadn't.

Even now, she checked the site in the woods regularly to make sure the growth pattern of the new trees wouldn't reveal the buried van from the air. Helicopters saw a lot more than the uninitiated imagined.

The memory gave her an idea. Did she still have enough power? Probably not, but it was worth a try, and it would be delicious to be able to get past this pile of junk.

She took a breath and in a low voice began to recite the words that were so important and equally of no importance. Words so ancient and almost unpronounceable that they had ceased to have any meaning at all, other than the raw power of meaninglessness itself.

Yes. There was still some energy left in them. She was surprised, and her delight made her green eyes shine with pleasure. As her voice grew stronger, she felt her vision rise, her sight increase in that familiar giddy way as she started to see the car she drove from above. Higher, just a little higher and she would be able to see the road ahead from the air, see if it was clear to pass.

But she was bellowing now, the strain of retaining both her real vision and the aerial one starting to become intolerable. Veins stood out on the side of her neck and her brow began to moisten with sweat.

Not enough. She couldn't get up enough height. She exhaled with a shout, letting the power go and tumbling back into her body with a jolt. A curse, ancient and guttural, left her lips and she pulled the car back a yard.

So she was stuck. No matter. In only a few days it would begin again. And maybe if her work could be completed soon, this time it would last longer than just those short ever-diminishing seven years.

She settled down to her slow journey and contented herself as much as anyone could, faced with a back window full of swinging cuddly toys adhering to the glass with suckered feet.

Maybe he had adultery written all over his face, or maybe this truck stop had just gotten unfriendlier while he slept. Either way, Josh noticed something when he went to pay for a coffee and a mushy croissant he'd heated in the store's microwave. He'd waited as the girl behind the counter serving two guys before him did so with a smile and a wisecrack. They'd passed on laughing, leaving her pointing at them with an outstretched arm and a grin that split her face.

And that grin had still been in place when he'd put his food on the counter and she'd turned to give him her full attention. Josh had returned the smile and then watched her face as a curious transformation came over it.

She looked, he thought, as though he'd sneaked up behind her and hollered 'boo'. For a fraction of a second the girl appeared startled, and as quickly, that startled expression was replaced with one of mild confusion and distaste. Josh scrutinized her face to see if he could read his unwitting crime in her eyes.

'That all?' she said as he examined her, and she began to ring up the coffee and croissant, no longer looking at him.

'Yup. That'll get me started.'

Josh's attempt at standard truck-driving nicety was ignored and she mumbled the price, took his money and returned the change without a word or a glance in his direction. Josh gathered up his breakfast and as he reached the swing doors out of the store cast her a brief backward glance. She was staring at him, that expression of confusion still in place but being overridden by one of suspicion. Josh smiled and she looked away quickly. He shook his head, raised his eyebrows in mock-offended resignation, then pushed open the door with his hip and walked outside.

The rain had stopped and the warm southern sun was already drying things up. It made Josh feel good, the intermittent heat on his face as the sun darted behind the rows of trucks while he walked, like someone playing hide and seek. He found pleasure in the way the climate gradually changed as he drove around the country, enjoyed spotting new plants, animals and birds that started to appear as he crossed from one state to another. Already here, this morning, he was noticing the difference in the birds that were clinging to every radiator grille, working away at the dead and dying insects laid out for them like a buffet.

Some he recognized, but others, the smaller ones, brightly coloured and dainty as they fed, were alien southern birds and he watched them with interest, making a mental note to look them up and name them when he got home.

When he got home.

He took a deep breath and let it out slowly. When was he going home? He would have to face it soon. Decide what he was going to do. Would he just stay away until she'd done it? He could. He could easily drive for another week. Then he could come home and carry on, making no mention of it ever again. Or maybe he could deliver his load and drive straight back, take her in his arms and try to persuade her that they should have the child, that everything would be okay, that he loved her and cared for her and . . .

He blinked as the low sun hit the side of his face again from behind the long corridor of trailers, and this time it seemed harsh and too bright, hardening a crust around his heart. He'd had an accident. The worst accident in the whole world. So bad he'd thought in his feverish sleepless brain that it had been no accident at all. He'd killed a child. And how had his life companion helped him through that? She hadn't listened to him, hadn't even given him the chance when he needed to talk, that's how.

Well fuck her. He wasn't going home.

He walked past the last few trucks before Jezebel, then stopped in front of her shiny chrome nose. There were birds fluttering and pecking away on the grilles of the reefers both sides of Jezebel, despite the engines vibrating noisily just like his. But on Jezebel's grille, which boasted every kind of juicy moth, fly, bee and more, there was not one single bird.

He squinted at his empty radiator for a second before unlocking the door and climbing in. It seemed that neither he nor Jezebel were very popular this morning.

He drove over to the fuel pumps and filled up, drinking his coffee and stuffing the sad croissant down while the tank filled, the fumes of reeking diesel winning the battle of taste over the soggy pastry, then strolled to the pay window and handed the guy his card. It was dealt with swiftly and without conversation, but Josh had already decided he didn't need small talk and was glad that the man hardly even looked at him. He pocketed his receipt and two free shower tickets they gave with diesel at this truck stop, then walked through the sunlit puddles of water and oil back to the security of his truck.

It would take him two hours at least from here to reach the drop-off point for his load, and he had to get his paperwork done. Josh was late, but for once in his driving life, it was the very least of his worries. He rolled slowly out of the fuel stop, drove a few hundred yards on and pulled into the side. This was not a time to leave his log book until later. He didn't put it past the county deputy in Furnace that he would send out some kind of alert to the state bears. In fact he was surprised he hadn't been pulled over last night. But even if he was just being paranoid and no one was going to single him out, Josh didn't relish the thought of explaining his movements over the last forty-eight hours to anyone. And failure to fill in a log would mean just that.

He got up and leaned across to the black folder pushed beneath the passenger dash, manoeuvred it out and sat back heavily in his chair with a sigh.

Gazing dreamily out the windshield, he snapped the elastic bands off, thinking involuntarily for a moment of Griffin, wondering where she was, remembering her mouth on his body and unconsciously moistening his lips as, without his permission, his mind gave that memory all the air-time it needed.

He wrapped the elastic band around his wrist as he always did, and opened the folder over the wheel as he continued to gaze into space. It was the noise that made him look down. The noise of shredded paper fluttering onto the floor with a dry rustle.

On his lap was a pile of blue confetti – confetti that used to be his log sheets. He stared at it, uncomprehending for a moment, then cautiously put out a hand and touched the tiny bits of paper.

There had been a month's worth of log sheets in the folder, stuck together in pad form and now most of it had been torn and ripped into ragged paper shrapnel. Most, but not all. There were three surviving sheets.

Josh picked them up and stared at them, as though by their survival he somehow held them responsible for the violent destruction of the rest. The last one had the corner neatly turned over, the way someone might mark a half-read book. He lifted the two top sheets cautiously and peered at the third.

Written across the space headed 'remarks' was a scrawl so deeply embedded in the paper it had broken through in two places, revealing that it had been written on the cushion of the other sheets before they were so savagely torn off. Josh's mouth opened slightly, trying to make sense of it, mouthing it silently to himself as though that would make it clearer.

In black ink it read,

'Three days alive permitted.'

He closed his fist around the mess of paper and squeezed it. His heart was racing and he licked his lips again, though this time it was not through the memory of sexual excitement, but because they were dry with a mounting panic.

The panic was that Josh quite simply could not understand what he was looking at. He recognized it. Not the bizarre threatening sentence, or what it meant. No. Not that. That was completely and utterly baffling to him. What he recognized, even in the terrifyingly manic state in which it had been scrawled, was the handwriting.

It was his own.

16

Elizabeth had dreamed again last night. It had been a dreadful dream, full of fire and screams, and when she woke it had been like almost every morning these days, with her hands clutched across her belly as though to protect her unborn child from whatever hot and terrible thing had been pursuing her through the darkness. She took a moment to understand it was morning in her own bed, then she wept like a child, not caring that Sim would hear. Her emotions were her master since she'd become pregnant, and she grieved now that she hadn't kept them in check when she'd first told Josh her news. But how could she? She didn't know how she felt from one moment to the next. All she really needed from Josh was . . .

What? What did she need? A husband? A business? A last-minute reason to let her baby live? What, in God's name? Maybe just a phone call from him. That would be a start. Another chance to try to put things right. She thought that he might call last night, but he hadn't. She'd stared at the silent phone again most of the evening like some heartbroken teenager, trying to imagine where he might be, what he might be feeling, and somehow, for no logical reason, she'd hoped that wherever he was, he was all right.

The hideous foreboding, the overwhelming feeling that the person you loved was in terrible danger, it was all a natural part of pregnancy. Her mother had once told her that. She'd laughed about her own time, when she'd carried Elizabeth. Her memory was that whenever Elizabeth's father went out the door her mother was sure it was the last time she'd see him.

The story had been rounded off with a roll of the eyes and 'if only', but Elizabeth knew that at the time it had been real and miserable for her. Now she understood. She was scared for Josh. Irrationally scared, but scared for sure. She pulled her hands up to her face and covered it. Right now, all she really wanted was to go to sleep again and never wake up.

Tennessee had turned into Alabama before he had calmed sufficiently to work it out. She must have done it. Of course she must. But how? He couldn't recall leaving Griffin alone in the cab for even a minute. Had she performed the bizarre act while he slept this morning? Josh didn't think so. To sleep through someone gently getting their belongings together, silently dressing and leaving with a quiet click of a door was one thing. To sleep through a frenzy of paper being shredded was quite another.

The only way Josh believed she could have pulled it off would have been to take the folder with her into the truck stop restaurant and do the damage while she was out of sight in the women's rest-room. He thought back to what she was carrying. Nothing. She'd left her only luggage, that big rucksack, back in the rig. But that didn't mean she couldn't have hidden it under her sweatshirt. It was baggy enough to conceal the book if she'd stuck it down the back of her jeans. The handwriting she must have copied from any one of the numerous documents in the folder that Josh had scribbled on over the course of his last long trip. But hell, she was one brilliant forger.

When he'd first looked at that scrawl his heart had just about stopped. It was so damned accurate, the way the Ts were crossed and the backward slant of all the uprights on the letters. And it was genius to make it recognizable as his while scrawling it in such a demented fury. How long must she have practised to get it so right? But if that was how she did it, the worst question was still hanging there waiting to be answered.

Why?

Maybe after the unluckiest day of his life, Josh Spiller had just spent the luckiest night of his life. If he really had slept with a major A1 psycho, then he could thank his guardian angel that all that had come of it were two memorable orgasms and a log book that looked like rabid polecats had fought over it. But it didn't make sense, and more importantly, it just didn't feel right.

She'd seemed in no way disturbed, and at no point even remotely pissed off at him. Quite the contrary. In fact for a one-night thrash with a total stranger, Josh had experienced a surprising quantity of tenderness in their sex. He was no shrink, but he had encountered enough mad people on the road to spot the signs. You had to in his game. This was a big crazy country, and from coast to coast there were barking lunatics just waiting for some luckless truck driver to pick them up.

He'd seen plenty. There was that time that he and Eddie had given a ride to a guy up in Oregon who'd flagged them down by a bust car. He'd told them gratefully that he was a professor of languages, on his way back home after teaching some disadvantaged kids in Portland how to speak Spanish. Sounded so weird it should have been true, but both of them knew straight off in the first five minutes, by the way he was talking too fast and the way his hands kept touching his face, that he was out of it.

Eddie had the gun he carried under the seat pointed in that guy's side before they'd even made ten miles, which was just as well since the screwball pulled his own piece out at fifteen.

They'd left him standing at the roadside, nose slightly bloodied and his gun thrown out of the cab three miles back but otherwise intact, hollering about the fact that he was the rightful Spanish King and would claim back his throne without their help.

As far as Josh knew, Eddie, like a lot of truckers, still carried a gun illegally in the cab, and sometimes he wished he had the balls to do the same.

But Griffin hadn't given any hints, however subtle, of being the kind of basket-case to pull a stunt like this. Why would she do it? Why, for Christ's sake?

He stared ahead and concentrated on that question as he drove. He concentrated very hard indeed. For at the back of his mind, somewhere so scary he didn't care to look, was the ghost of another possibility. But it was a possibility too dark and dangerous to consider.

No. There was nothing wrong with his mind whatsoever. Things had been going wrong, true. Things had been going very wrong. But he was sane and together and everything was going to be just fine.

All that was really wrong was that he had a load of packing cases

behind him, that someone fifty miles south of here was pulling out their hair to receive. He focused on that thought and just drove.

'I'll bet you got some real good reason. Yeah?'

Josh narrowed his eyes at the obese man who was holding the documents he needed in order to get paid for this shitty job. His bald head had a smear of dirt on it that ran comically from the crown all the way down behind his left ear, and in order to keep him from losing his temper at the lard-ball, Josh concentrated hard on how he might have acquired such a mark.

'Yeah. Real good.'

'Let's have it.'

Josh shifted his weight and looked at the mark more closely. Grease from the fork-lift, he decided. Smeared when the guy had scratched at an itch with a mucky finger.

'You got the cases.'

'Yeah. An' I got the delivery receipt right here. Guess I might just make a note on it that you was late so they hold your pay-off. Unless I get to know what made you a whole friggin' day late.'

Behind them, Jezebel was being unloaded by a small wiry man in a fork-lift who whistled tunelessly as he drove at a leisurely pace back and forth on the dock, watched sullenly by two factory hands and another driver waiting to unload his covered wagon. Josh ran a hand over his hair.

'Same old story. Abducted by aliens. Hate it when that happens.'

The man waved the thin paper. 'Yeah? Well whistle for it, boy. You be lucky to see a cent a mile for this one. You be payin' me after I talk to your people.'

He officiously snapped shut his pen and rammed it in the top pocket of his overall, a pocket stitched with the name Leonard, where Josh noticed a small dark patch which indicated the pen had been leaking. Unconsciously echoing Josh's gesture, the man ran the hand that had pocketed the pen over the top of his head and left another mark.

Josh smiled as the man waddled away to deal with the other driver, but his smile faded quickly, and he sat down heavily on the edge of a pallet and watched the rest of the cases coming out of Jezebel's tail. Across the loading bay, on the wall beside a picture of a beaver with a hard hat on telling you ten ways to stay safe at work, was a pay phone. He'd been trying not to look at it since he got here, but now his gaze drifted back. Jesus, he was blowing hot and cold about her. One minute she was the cause of everything bad in his life right now. The next, he wanted Elizabeth so badly he ached.

He rubbed at his stomach and tried to deal with the hot worm of guilt that was starting to writhe in his guts again. Killer. Adulterer. Where did failure to phone home come in that roll-call? He glanced across again. The beaver was still lecturing him about safety, and the phone was still free. He stood up and walked across, followed by the small eyes of the fat man, who watched him with contempt as Josh stood beside the phone and contemplated it. Josh took out his Driveline card, flicked it over in his fingers like a card sharp and bit his top lip. Twenty dollars' worth of talk-time. But would she talk? He leaned forward against the wall on outstretched straight arms, his head down looking at his boots while he tried to sort it out.

Someone was looking at him.

He could feel their eyes, their intense gaze burning into his back. Josh stayed in the same position while he wrestled with how he might know that, then slowly straightened up and turned around. Across the loading bay the men he'd just left were still there. The fat guy was standing with one hand on his hip, watching a new truck roll slowly up to the dock, and the rest of them stood in an angular work-shy huddle round the pallets. But no one was looking his way. He scanned the factory floor for the eyes that he felt even more keenly now had been watching his back, and saw nothing.

The only view offered was one of stacked and tightly wrapped aluminium, forming corridors which boasted their length and height by displaying perspectives that nearly came to a point in the distance.

He remained motionless for a moment, barely breathing as he tried to rationalize why he still felt observed, and then equally, as his eyes roamed across those long dark avenues, why he just as suddenly felt the watcher had gone. Josh rubbed a hand over the back of his neck as if those unseen eyes had scalded his skin, then slipped his phone card back into his wallet.

The fat man looked across and raised an eyebrow as Josh walked slowly away from the wall, waiting for him to come closer, when he would hit him with a remark that would make that fresh driver think again about smart-mouthing him. But when Josh turned and looked straight through him, the man saw something in his eyes and thought again. Shrugging brusquely towards the guy's truck to indicate it was finished unloading, he kept his silence.

Leonard liked to have the last word in any situation and he'd been looking forward to this one. But the truth was ... well, he couldn't quite put a finger on it. Whatever it was, it was giving him a bad feeling between his shoulderblades. Hell, it was crazy.

Not only did that trucker look like he kept real bad company, but somehow Leonard felt he'd only just avoided meeting it.

He shivered once and against his better judgment, turned his back on Josh and walked away.

A series of minor roads snaked through ramshackle towns that led to the dispatch office, and Josh gazed out at the untidy buildings occasionally brightened by Alabama's taste for ostentatious signs. He watched them catch the light – red and blue glitter-discs strung together to advertise a hair salon or a gun store twinkling as they moved in the warm southern spring breeze.

That breeze was becoming more than warm. It was making the inside of the cab uncomfortably hot, but then the southern states were a meteorological mystery at this time of year. He'd shivered out here in a quilted parka in April, and had just as sure been sweltering in eighty degrees in March. Today had obviously decided it was going to be a hot one, even though oddly, it hadn't given any indication of it earlier. For the first time in months he reached for the air conditioner and flicked it on. Josh didn't like using the AC. He preferred to ride with the window down, an arm resting on the sill, feeling the breath of whatever part of the country he was in blow on his cheeks with its own special mixture of tell-tale odours. Mown hay in Virginia, ripe apples in PA, diesel mixed with cooking in the small pull-off to nowhere towns along almost any interstate you could name. It helped him know he was travelling, reminded him he was the one who was moving through the landscape, instead of sitting in a stationary box where pictures moved silently in front of him like the windshield was a movie screen. But he was too hot and he wanted to get cool. He moved forward to unstick his clammy back from the seat as he waited for the AC to do its work.

He waited a long time. The cab, if anything, was growing hotter.

And worse. There was a smell, faint at first, but growing with the increasing heat, and it was stomach-turning.

At the first wrinkle of his nose, Josh's senses registered something that approximated sewage, and his brain automatically apportioned the blame to the shabby town that Jezebel was rumbling through in line behind a motley procession of beat-up Alabama traffic.

But if the odour was genuinely emanating from the waste dropped from the collective backsides of this town's residents, then Josh thought they should get some medical help.

The stench was revolting. It was more than just a broth of fermenting faeces. It had an undertone of rotting flesh, a sweet, cloying, almost solid quality that was starting to make Josh gag. He coughed dryly, his throat threatening to rise with bile, and reached out for the controls. His fingers found the air-recycle switch and snapped it on, and as the atmosphere shifted around his face he held his breath for a moment, allowing time for the hot foetid air to depart.

It wasn't enough time. When he next inhaled, the odour now being recirculated was so strong he felt it bite at his chest. With streaming eyes and a retching cough he clutched at the window handle and jerked it open.

Gradually something approximating oxygen started to replenish his bursting lungs, and Josh gulped at the fresh air like a goldfish tipped out on the carpet.

As he wiped at his eyes and shook his head, he made a strong mental note never to organize a cook-out in Alabama.

Groves' Dispatch and Haulage was housed twenty miles south of Scottsboro, in a temporary building in the centre of an enormous clearing of scrub oak and alder. There were already two rigs abandoned seemingly at random on a huge gravel area outside the building that could happily serve as a parking lot for a battleship, when Josh pulled Jezebel in and tucked her alongside one of the trucks.

He kept her running and climbed down out of the cab. As Josh walked towards the office, stretching his stiff limbs as he went, the noise of his boots on gravel and the drone of Jezebel's engine were undercut by a thin, scrabbling, metallic sound. He stopped and looked back to the truck, then smiled as his eyes quickly identified the source of the sound. Hopping across the front of his radiator grille was a large, black bird. A very large bird indeed. As he watched, Josh's relief that Jezebel's radiator was back in favour for snacking gave way to a nervous curiosity as to the species of creature that was moving across the chrome grille with disturbingly humanoid movements.

He put his hands on his hips and peered at it, and although he was some distance away from the truck, and too far to be able to examine it closely, he narrowed his eyes and put a hand to his forehead to shield them from the sun.

Almost as though the creature realized it was being observed, it turned a misshapen head and with alarming speed flipped upside down and scrambled over the radiator to the darkness beneath the truck.

Josh let his hand fall from his face and stared stupidly at the empty grille. It had only been a glimpse, and a glimpse from a distance, but the impressions it left were disquieting.

It couldn't have been a bird. It had seemed more like a cross between a small animal and an oversized bat. Its wings were leathery and stunted and attached to long scrawny arms.

But worse. When it had turned, Josh could have sworn that two almost-human red eyes glared back at him from a deformed face.

He wiped his hand across his tired eyes, then crouched down to see if he could spot the animal beneath the truck. The familiar darkened underbelly of an eighteen-wheeler was all that Josh could make out. Of course there were a hundred nooks and crannies for something that size to squeeze itself into, but somehow Josh didn't think a wild animal would be too happy to nestle in between growling, vibrating machinery.

Standing up, he ran his hand over the back of his head. He was tired and he was in the south. It could have been anything. They had all kinds of crazy animals down here, and if Josh had to look up the birds he saw, he was even worse with animals. He could barely tell a racoon from a rabbit. He looked towards the truck for a beat, still unsure of what he'd seen, then dismissed it, turned and walked towards Groves'.

Behind the window of the main office, Sandi Englehart lifted her head from a telephone conversation and looked out at Jezebel. She recognized the rig and waved a hand in greeting as she bent her head again. It was only Josh Spiller, and he only dropped by when he needed a quick load back home. Groves' didn't pay as much as the company Josh was leased to in Pittsburgh, but they always had something going north and she guessed that was why he was here. Good. She could use him today. She drilled a pencil into the desk top and carried on talking as Josh crossed the vast acres between his truck and the office.

'You're darn right we mean it, darlin'. We need you to pick it up in the next two hours or the job's gone.'

She smiled as the person on the other end protested, then looked up again as Josh entered the office and stood waiting by a large and unhappy pot plant by the door.

'Well now, Thomas, if I wasn't a lady I guess I'd know what that meant, but since I am I can only take a stab at it and figure it's a no?' She laughed and tapped her pencil some more. 'Yeah? Okay you got it. Sure. I got all the paperwork you'll ever need right here, darlin'.'

She hung up and looked up at Josh with the grin she always gave drivers. Josh returned it and walked towards the desk, but his grin subsided as he saw the smile fade on Sandi's face.

Burning. That was the only way Sandi could rationalize the sudden panic she was feeling. But it was more than that. It was the smell when something is singeing, just before it bursts into flame. That was it. Josh Spiller smelled like he was going to burn.

'What?'

Josh put his hands out, searching her face for whatever was causing her concern.

She crushed it and pulled back half a smile. 'You been drivin' through a forest fire or somethin'?'

'What you talkin' about, Sandi?'

'You smell, kinda . . . I don't know . . . smoky.'

Josh looked puzzled and sniffed unconvincingly at his shoulder. 'Yeah? Last town I came through smelled like every goddamn man, woman and child had shit themselves and hung their assholes out to dry in the wind.' He grinned down at her, and tried to coax her full smile back with one of his own. 'But I guess that smells like Chanel No. 5 to a southerner, huh?'

Sandi's smile remained incomplete and she wagged a finger. 'Boy, you northern drivers sure know a lot about assholes, huh? Guess that's 'cos you talk out of 'em most the time.'

Josh made a face that winced in mock pain, and she licked a finger to mark one on an imaginary scoreboard in the air.

But her unease was sneaking back. There was something more than a weird odour about Josh that made her not want him in the office. Then Bob Taylor walked through, the usual handful of paper clutched in his fist. He looked up and nodded at Josh, before disappearing into his portion of the long pre-fab. Sandi couldn't help noticing through the glass partition that separated them, that Bob's head was up, instead of bent over the crap he kept his nose in all day long, and he was continuing to look at Josh from behind his desk.

Josh watched Sandi's face. 'I still smell?'

She shrugged and shuffled some papers of her own. This was dumb.

'Aw shoot, honey. I have no idea what I'm talkin' about this afternoon. I know you want a load goin' north though. How's about that for mind-readin'?'

Josh rubbed at an arm. 'Yeah.'

'Don't even need to tap into my Mac, sweetheart. There's a whole stack of aluminium needs pickin' up from Scottsboro right now, goin' all the way to your front door.'

'Piss money?'

'Uh-huh.'

'Okay.'

She smiled at him and motioned to the seats by the pot plant.

'You must want home awful bad, Mr Joshua Spiller. Never had you not argue the price with me before.'

'Yeah. I do want home bad. Real bad.'

As Sandi Englehart picked up the phone to call and book the load she thought that she and Josh were a lot alike right then.

She wanted him home real bad too. In fact just out of the office and as far from her as he could manage would do just fine.

17

Why was this state of growing, of being born, so mysterious to man? To that which was becoming ready to be born, it was a natural state of grace. That it could sample the outside world through its carrier was part of that simplicity.

If there was mystery, it was in why that which was waiting to be born could remember where it had been, where it had come from, only while it waited to meet the light. Afterwards, there would be no memory. Only the urge to live, the cry as it came through, the knowledge of the suffering its carrier would endure in its passage.

But for now, as it grew and changed, it could remember everything, and it floated in its dark hot place, thinking of the deeper darkness it was leaving.

Eddie Shanklin was singing. It was toneless and horrible, but it made him feel good.

'. . . maybeeee I didn't hold yoooo . . .'

He sang in a high, whining voice, a grin remaining constant as he contorted the muscles of his pale, bearded face to reach the high notes. For the first half hour after it was free of a load, the rig felt like a formula one racing car, and even though running empty meant he was burning a hole in his wallet, Eddie had sat back and enjoyed the feeling. But that was hours ago, and even though the truck had lost that first sensation of being loosed from its shackles, Eddie was still high.

They were going to have themselves some fun, he and Josh. In under an hour they'd be stepping out of their rigs and into the parking lot of a motel just outside Chattanooga, checking in and letting loose.

He could hardly wait. Even hearing the surprise in Josh's voice over the radio when Eddie had ambushed him outside Martintown had left him grinning for about five miles. Yeah, Eddie was pleased with himself.

After they'd parted last time, he'd guessed the four possible dispatchers that Josh could have used in the area near his drop-off, and had got lucky on call number two. Sandi at Groves' told him that Josh had left for the smelter about two hours ago. That meant that given time loading, weighing and general shitting about, Eddie figured he'd be able to intercept him on the one and only route back to the interstate. And he had.

Now, he and his buddy needed some serious rest and recreation, and the unconvincing fight Josh had put up, whining about not being able to take the time out, had taken Eddie about ten minutes on the CB to break down.

He missed Josh. He tried to figure why he hadn't called him, hadn't even sent a postcard. Nothing. Not since they spent a weekend getting wrecked at the truck show in Louisville a whole two years ago.

It just seemed like he didn't need to. He knew that the next time he saw Josh it would be just like it always was. You didn't have to call each other like teenage girls planning a pyjama party to stay friends. He'd figured the next time they'd meet would be at the wedding – whenever Mabel made her frigging mind up about when that was going to be – and he'd never questioned that his friendship was intact hundreds of miles away, secure in its silence.

Now he knew he was right. There was no embarrassment in rekindling its fire. Only comfort. And he sensed after that grim conversation they'd had through the night that it was well-timed comfort.

As he stepped on the gas, he screwed up his eyes and threw his head back again, trying hard to reach an impossible falsetto. And if Elvis was really dead, even though Eddie knew he wasn't, he would have shifted uncomfortably in his grave.

If Eddie hadn't gotten there first, maybe Josh would have just turned around and kept driving. But there was no escape. There he was, leaning smoking against a Kenworth that walked a thin line between attracting the disbelieving stares of children and making decent folks shoo those children away while they called the authorities.

It was more sculpture than truck. Everything that could be chrome was, and that included a lot of things that shouldn't be. A double row of orange lights framed the radiator grille and topped the windshield like eyebrows, and, clinging to the exhaust pipe with one arm while it beat its chest in silent rage, was a two-and-a-half foot plastic gorilla. Mounted over the sleeper roof on a long board in front of the model ape were light-refracting rainbow letters that unnecessarily picked out the words 'King Kong'.

Eddie grinned as he watched Jezebel roll into the parking lot, flicked away the cigarette and stood to attention.

When he'd parked and climbed down, Josh waited by the open door, his hands on his hips, and smiled at the man walking towards him. Eddie was a big guy, but he looked like he was made of butter, filling his denim jacket and overalls the way a steamed pudding fills muslin. The only purpose served by the shoulder length sandy hair pulled in a ponytail behind his grimy baseball cap, was to foil a long, darker beard and moustache by failing to match it. Eddie stopped in front of Josh, and echoed his stance by placing his hands on his own hips.

'Toss for it?'

Josh nodded.

'Heads.'

Eddie took a coin from the pockets of his overalls, looked his friend in the eye and flicked it in the air. He caught it deftly in his palm and showed it to Josh.

'Shit, Eddie. That coin weighted?'

'Nope. Lady fate just ain't kind to you, Spiller.'

'That's for sure.'

'You'll check in?'

'I'll check in.'

'I need your credit card and I need to see trucker's ID for your driver's rate.'

The girl behind reception barely looked at Josh as he complied. He could feel Eddie hovering behind him, waiting. The girl crossed her arms and scratched at her upper arm with long pink plastic fingernails as Josh slid his card and licence across the desk. She took them with a small clacking noise of nails on wood, like a racoon foraging on a tiled floor behind an ice-box.

Josh cleared his throat. 'Mam? Eh, my colleague and I here were wondering . . . well, eh, we were wondering if you're someone who could help us get hard.'

The woman looked up, her expression darkening and her mouth slightly open in indignation as she looked from Josh's innocent face to Eddie's impassive one. Josh took a breath. Timing was everything now. He had kept his own mouth open after the last word. That was always important. He left her for a few beats more and cut in as though he'd been taking time to think, just as he saw her lips about to form a word.

'. . . hard copies of our overnight accounts. You know? Not just the credit card total. Need more than one itemized copy, you see. Accountants never do believe we only eat, sleep and drive . . .'

Still unsure, she closed her mouth and searched Josh's face very hard for even the ghost of a smile. There was none. There couldn't be. Ten dollars and the first round of drinks always rested on it.

She made a pursing movement with her glossed lips and looked him straight in the eye, although there was something in her own that suggested she was finding that uncomfortable. 'Sure. You just ask here tomorrow when you check out.'

Josh nodded politely. 'Thank you, mam. 'Preciate it.'

Their business was concluded in silence and Josh took the plastic room keycards from her taloned hand, listening sagely to her monotone directions to the elevator. She followed them with a sullen gaze as they walked casually back out the glass doors to the parking lot, wanting to glare at them with female menace but finding herself curiously uncomfortable and unable to look directly at the handsomer of the two. But if they imagined she didn't witness them double up and punch at each other in glee as soon as they hit the fresh air, then they were wrong.

'Hey, Cherie,' drawled the receptionist to a bored-looking companion as she tapped her computer keyboard with the tips of her nails. 'I'm shutting off the adult pay channel in Beavis and Butthead's rooms. If they want to watch some porn they're gonna have to call down here and beg.'

*   *   *

'They're actors.'

'They ain't actors. They're just regular people that got asked to do it.'

'I need to know what makes you think that, Eddie. I mean how can you think that?' Josh took a deep swig from his beer bottle and shook his head in exaggerated disbelief.

'I'll tell you how, right? You say to an actor, look buddy, we need you to look like a regular Joe that stacks shelves in a store, and then when I say "action" you tuck your arms in and wave your elbows about, makin' like you're a fuckin' chicken, and then sing "I feel like chicken tonight". It ain't gonna happen with a genuine smile is it?'

''Course it is. That's what actors do.'

'Yeah, but they never look like real folks. They'd look like actors. These are real people. Morons maybe. But real morons. You can tell.'

'Look, Eddie. You give an actor money and you tell him to stick his own dick in his mouth, he's gonna do it with a smile and make it look as natural as you want. These are not real people in that commercial.'

'How d'you know?'

'Jesus, man, they look too good. You stack shelves you probably don't have health insurance. You got bad teeth and zits. Sure, you might feel like chicken tonight, but you ain't goin' to get any.'

He paused thoughtfully.

'That's what real people look like.'

Josh indicated the ugly mass of flesh and patterned nylon on the dance floor. 'Look kinda like you, Eddie.'

'Yeah yeah. Eat my meat, Spiller.'

Josh lifted his beer to his mouth and as he tried to drink from it Eddie nudged his elbow, sending a stream of liquid down his chin and over his shirt.

As Josh spluttered through a wet laugh, a pant-suit-clad family at the next table eyed them both with naked disdain. Eddie noted the mother avoiding his gaze by urging her youngest son to finish up his soda, while the small ferret-like father attempted to look protective and manly with only a mixer drink as an unlikely prop.

Josh and Eddie were neither out of place nor at home in this cavernous motel lounge bar, a room that smelled of sour carpets and the chlorine that had drifted in from the indoor swimming pool down the corridor.

As with most of the motels that welcomed drivers, someone had given the huge carpeted, mirrored, split-level barn a name, trying to pretend, but fooling no one, that it had character and a local clientele. This time it was called 'Poppers'. Crude stick-on pictures of champagne bottles popping their corks were glued at angles on the mirrors round the room, and a three-man band played some dismal soft rock covers backed by a mural depicting two giant champagne glasses clinking together. When Josh and Eddie had first come in around six-thirty, it had been practically empty. But now, hours later, their fellow motel guests had showered, eaten and changed, and it was filling up.

The collection of fat people in shiny clothes that Josh had cited in evidence, were stepping their way through the alley-cat on the dance floor, and while the singer was smiling at them, the bass guitarist was watching them the way a child might watch a parent burn their collection of baseball cards.

Eddie and Josh sat in silence for a while, gazing vacantly at the dancers, until Eddie looked down at the table and toyed with the paper drip-mat that ringed the stem of his redundant glass.

'How you feel?'

'Bad.'

Eddie nodded, still not looking at his friend. 'I ain't got much to say that'll help that.'

Josh continued to gaze at the dance floor, and Eddie leaned back into the cushioned booth, resting his beer bottle on one knee.

'I figure some things though.'

Josh turned to look at him and Eddie lifted his bottle to his lips and met Josh's eyes over its glass neck. He emptied the bottle's contents and wiped his mouth.

'I reckon you can't change what happened to that kid. You can't change the fact you humped a basket-case of a hitcher. But you still got a chance to put things right between you and Elizabeth.'

'Maybe.'

'You gonna try?'

'Maybe.'

Eddie sighed and leaned forward on his knees. 'Man, this ain't like you. You been through shit before. Always came out the end stinkin' of it but smilin'.'

'I don't reckon I'll get out the end of this one.'

'Why? What's the fuckin' deal? You had an accident that weren't your doin'. Live with it and forget it.'

Josh touched the hoop in his ear. 'Want another beer?'

Eddie softened his voice as much as his pride would allow. 'Come on, man. Talk to me.'

It was Josh's turn to sigh. He remained silent for a long time, aware that Eddie was looking at him, then bit at a knuckle as he spoke. 'Am I actin' weird, Eddie?'

'Yeah. You're actin' like a fuckin' fruit.'

'I mean it. Like actin' in a way that would make people I don't know want to cross the street?'

'How you mean?'

'I don't know. That's why I'm askin' you, dick brain.'

Eddie shook his head. 'You're leavin' me behind here, man.'

Josh was finding it hard to meet Eddie's gaze. In fact he was finding it hard to say this at all. 'I'm startin' to imagine bad things, Eddie.'

'Like what? Roseanne Barr naked?'

Josh continued without catching the smile Eddie threw him.

All sorts of stuff. Worst one is I feel like I'm being watched.' He lowered his voice, his turn to feel an unmanly shame. 'In fact I'm feeling it right now.'

Eddie blinked at him, then slowly turned his head and scanned the room. He wiped his mouth again, then turned back to face Josh. 'Well maybe one of them lard-balls in the K-Mart party frocks got the hots for you. Any of 'em might be eyeballin' you right now. Don't mean much.'

Josh looked around. There was no one taking any notice of them at all in their dark booth. But what he'd told Eddie was true. He could feel that inexplicable sensation of an unseen watcher, heightened by the sensation that whoever or whatever possessed those eyes was not looking kindly on him.

'Yeah? Well how about this, then. You need another beer, right?'

'Right.'

'How many we had so far?'

'Shit. I don't know. Six. Maybe seven?'

'Seven. Want to know how many times out of those seven orders I managed to get the waitress to come over?'

'You got me.'

'None. Zero. You grabbed her every time. She won't even look at me.'

Eddie looked at Josh for a moment with a hint of panic in his eye, then he poked a finger in Josh's shoulder and laughed. 'Is that what this is about? You runnin' scared that you don't make them go wet no more?'

Josh didn't return the laughter. He turned around and regarded him with a mixture of desperation and anger that immediately cancelled the grin on Eddie's face.

'Watch.'

Josh searched for the waitress who'd been serving their booth all night, and spotted her wiping a table. He glanced once at Eddie, making sure he had his full attention, then sat forward, adopting the universal body language of straightened back and stillness of head that means someone wants a drink.

Eddie turned from his friend to watch the waitress. She finished wiping the table, balanced three glasses on her tray then straightened up. As she turned, she saw Josh as he raised his hand and waved at her. Her eyes met his, and he used the moment to yell, ''Scuse me. Miss?' across the room.

As Eddie watched, the girl's eyes registered a fleeting hint of confusion before she turned away, pretending she hadn't seen him. Josh slumped back in his seat.

'Now you try. Just like you been doin' all night.'

Eddie licked his lips. She had moved back to the bar, a mile away from their table. But she would be back. They waited in silence, a tension between them that Eddie found hard to interpret. When she returned to serve someone four tables away, Eddie caught her eye as she waited to be paid, and raised his finger.

She raised a hand back, and as she pocketed the money wandered over to them and scooped up their empties.

'Same again?'

'Yeah. Don't need glasses.'

Josh was right. She didn't look at him at all. Eddie watched her as she made the long journey back to the bar, then leaned back heavily and stared ahead as Josh spoke quietly, almost to himself.

'You see, the weird thing is, she don't even know she's doin' that. Know what I mean? It's like she hasn't figured why she don't want to look at me.'

They sat quietly for a moment, then Eddie nudged his shoulders playfully up against Josh.

'Come on. Don't mean nothin' if one waitress don't get off on you.'

Josh turned to look at him. 'You feel it too. Don't you, Eddie?'

Eddie Shanklin felt his heart alter its rhythm by half a beat. He moistened his lips beneath their thatch of rough hair and tried to buy himself time to think. He'd been dreading that question. Ever since Josh had raised the issue, it had opened up a dark crack he'd been trying to seal ever since he greeted him in the parking lot.

Yes. He did feel something was wrong with Josh, from the moment they faced each other and touched. And it was something badly wrong. Something that made Eddie instinctively not want to be around him, just in case . . .

In case of what?

He had no fucking idea what. All he knew was that it had been troubling him for hours, a curious sensation of apprehension and at its most extreme, a tiny trace of fear. And he knew long before Josh had raised it that the waitress was feeling it too. But it was nothing he could define or understand. This was a friend, who, if he were man enough to be honest with himself, he loved. So quite simply, he'd ignored it.

Until now.

Eddie moved a few inches away, giving himself room to turn and meet Josh's gaze. 'I feel how strung out you are. You act like someone clipped jump leads on your balls. But I ain't blamin' you none. Not after what you been through.'

'Nothin' more?'

Eddie looked away. That way, Josh wouldn't see his eyes. 'You know what the real problem is?'

Josh waited.

'Man, you said it yourself a minute ago.'

Josh made a questioning grunt.

Eddie slapped the edge of the table with one finger. 'Seven beers.

146

That's the fuckin' problem. I can't believe we only drank seven lousy beers each in three hours.'

He could feel, rather than see, Josh smiling at his elbow.

'Time we stopped drinkin' like old ladies.'

18

'At least he made sure the kids didn't see nothin'.'

Pace looked up from the mess of brain, blood and skull and stared at his deputy. Archie Cameron swallowed and gesticulated vaguely towards the expensively draped window.

'He dumped them off at the neighbours.'

Pace looked back at the corpse of Bobby Hendry. The thirty-eight calibre was half concealed under his body, where the kick-back force of the shot to his own head had whipped his arm back and pinned it bizarrely behind him as though a bouncer had ejected him from a club. Pace pinched his nose thoughtfully and spoke softly as if to himself.

'Alice Nevin's sure havin' a good week.'

Cameron looked at him as though he was missing the point.

'Was never exactly goin' to be parade day, was it?'

Pace's face darkened, and he looked back at the younger man with narrowed eyes. 'Think she expected this?'

'I don't rightly know what she expected. We ain't never been chosen.'

John Pace examined his deputy's face. His expression was pious with a trace of resentment. It was a stupid look and it made Pace want to hit the man, but he watched with some satisfaction as that stupidity turned to naked fear when Cameron read the anger in his senior's features. Then Pace turned to leave the room, addressing his parting shot to the wall.

'May you thank your God for that as long as you live.'

*   *   *

'What my friend is trying to say, is that he thinks outta all the states he's driven, he thinks Iowa is definitely the most interesting.'

Josh nodded and swayed slightly to regain his balance after the effort.

The woman took a long sip from a glass that contained numerous cocktail umbrellas and cherries, leaving little room for liquid.

'Yeah?'

'Straight up. Where exactly in Iowa you girls from?'

The plumper of the three women sitting in a row, all of whom had ceased being girls more than a decade ago, answered politely, as though questioned by a new school teacher.

'I'm from Algona, and Linda and Kerry are originally from Titonka, though they don't live there no more.'

Eddie raised his eyebrows in mock interest. 'Tit . . . onka. Huh?'

The gap between the first syllable and the remaining two was so long, Josh closed his eyes in embarrassment. He opened them again sharply as his head started to spin.

'You been to Tit . . . onka?'

The question was aimed at Josh, who struggled to focus on Eddie's face. 'Can't recall. Maybe I have.'

The woman with the cocktail sighed. 'You want to leave now?'

'Aw come on . . . Kerry?'

The plump woman answered again, using a fat finger to indicate each of her friends. 'Naw, she's Linda. This is Kerry. And I'm Olive.'

'Well, Olive. I'm real glad to make your acquaintance. I'm Igo Chasbeaver, and this here is my friend Jesus.'

Olive looked slightly shocked.

'His Mama's Mexican,' added Eddie.

All the women looked at Josh, and just as quickly looked away again. Eddie used the moment. 'May we buy you girls a drink?'

Olive spoke for them all again. 'No, thank you kindly, Igo. We were just about to call it a night.'

'You passin' through Chattanooga?'

'No. We're attending ourselves a conference here.'

Eddie sat down, unasked, leaving Josh to sway behind him, holding onto the back of his chair.

'That so? Well that's real interestin'. What might the subject be?'

The woman with the cocktail spoke again, this time addressing her comments to her companion in the middle who so far had said nothing. 'Well if it were about fuckwits, I guess these guys could hold a mornin' session.'

Olive raised a disapproving eyebrow, while her two companions brayed with laughter and after a beat Eddie joined them.

Josh had to sit down. He pulled up a chair beside Eddie and fell into it.

'Now that ain't very polite. A man's just tryin' to make conversation here.'

Kerry and Linda looked bored, their eyes wandering constantly to the far-off bar, an island of curved plastic on a horizon of patterned carpet. Olive was more in the mood for conversation. Eddie could see why. Her two companions were dressed in casual clothes without style, but they had neat, well-kept bodies for women in their early forties.

Olive was bespectacled and round, and the long-sleeved T-shirt she was wearing boasted a gruesome sequined motif of a peacock, horribly misshapen from being stretched over large, sagging breasts. But they were the only women sitting alone in the whole bar and that was good enough for Eddie. She pushed her spectacles back up her nose.

'Oh she don't mean nothin' by it. Actually, it ain't exactly us attending the conference. Well not even me.'

She giggled. Eddie laughed with her.

'I just got asked along 'cos I never been to Tennessee and I'm real friendly with Kerry's sister June, and she couldn't go on account of her leg and everythin'. An' anyway what the Jiminy do dah do I know about keepin' America white?'

She had used her fat fingers to parenthesize the last three words, and Eddie blinked at her. Even Josh, reeling as he was from the Wild Turkey that had all but replaced his blood, looked up at the woman quizzically.

Eddie cleared his throat.

'You're goin' to a conference called Keep America White?'

Olive pushed her spectacles up again and lifted her glass of Coke. 'Is it called that, Linda? Or is that just what it's about?'

Linda was smiling, and nodded towards the bar. 'I don't rightly know, sweetheart. You can ask Douane and Bill. They're the ones who's goin'. We're just here to spend their money.'

The women laughed again.

Eddie licked his lips. He didn't need to turn round. He'd seen them at the bar all night. Two guys with necks so thick their shirt collars pinched the skin like string around pork. Eddie had thought at first they were drivers. This motel was, after all, on the trucker's discount list. But they looked like mean fuckers, and not only were they too clean to be on the road, they had military haircuts and creases down the front of their jeans.

He stood up and took Josh's arm as he did so. 'Well I hope you girls enjoy yourselves here in the south. Have to bid you goodnight now.'

Eddie guided Josh towards the exit, and as he left he heard Olive shouting over the band, who had resumed murdering some old favourites, 'Maybe catch you at the buffet breakfast, Igo!'

'Shit. I musta left that fuckin' plastic card thing on the table.'

Eddie let go of Josh's arm temporarily while he used both hands to check all his pockets. Josh slumped against the wall next to Eddie's door and slid down it.

Eddie bent down and spoke into his face. 'I'm just goin' down to get the key, Spiller. You stay right here and don't throw up till I get back.'

Josh nodded.

Eddie ran along the acres of corridor back to the elevator and pressed the button. Josh thought how tiny he looked so far away like that, and watched in fascination as the *ting* of an equally faraway bell ushered his friend away and out of sight.

He hadn't meant to get as wrecked as this. But once he started drinking the enormous whiskeys that Eddie had kept on coming, he couldn't stop. It felt too good to be completely numb. And it had been fun. Eddie had made him laugh like a kid, doing all the old dumb stuff, making the front desk continually page Josh Spiller, representative from Friends of the Beaver every time he left to go to the bathroom.

And best of all, now he felt nothing. No eyes watching him. No fear. No crazy stuff at all. Except he was smashed and might even up chuck like a teenage drunk if he didn't concentrate.

Josh narrowed his eyes and tried to focus on the massive runway of carpet he was sitting on. He looked to his right, to where the corridor ended in a square black window, its uneven glass distorting the reflection of the wall-mounted lights. To his left was the majority of the corridor. Dozens of doors lined up like sentries guarding their few square feet of soft sidewalk, stretching away into the distance without a break. It was disconcerting and depressing looking at it, so Josh let his head slump back onto his chest and looked instead at his hands.

The elevator went *ting*.

Josh raised his head slowly and prepared to greet Eddie. But it wasn't Eddie. Two bulky men, one clothed in a tartan shirt, the other wearing one of plain green linen, were walking purposefully towards him. Neither looked as though they were searching for their room number. Josh twitched and scrambled to his feet. The men increased their pace.

He swayed unsteadily and started feeling in his own pockets for his room key.

The men started to jog. Josh turned and stumbled towards the black window. Maybe the fire exit would be down there. He ran a few paces and then fell. As he sat up, pushing himself into a sitting position with straight arms, the men stopped a few yards away. Josh raised his head to look at them. They relaxed, and the larger of the two crossed his arms over the well-pressed plaid of his shirt as he spoke, while his companion splayed his legs apart and let his arms hang by their sides.

'God's gift to women and the ugly fuck can't even stand.'

Josh took a deep breath and with all his concentration pushed himself up and stood to face them. He tried and failed to focus, but gave it a beat and their faces swam into some kind of definition.

The man spoke again, this time with less comic contempt and considerably more menace in his thick voice.

'Well that's real impressive, boy. An' just how was it you were plannin' to stick your faggot dick in our wives when seems to me you ain't even up to findin' your fuckin' zipper?'

Josh felt vomit rising in his gorge. The air around his head was becoming hot, pouring into his mouth and nostrils, smothering him like a pillow. He fought back nausea, panting for sweeter air.

The other man spoke for the first time, taking a step forward. 'Maybe you want to answer my friend here? He's a-talkin' to you.'

Josh took a stumbling step back towards the dead end of the window. The man in the green shirt matched the gesture, closing the distance. As he did so, Josh felt another wave of hot air move around his face. He raised his heavy head and tried to speak, slurring his words, as he put his hands out in a gesture of conciliation.

'Aw come on, guys. This is crazy.'

Josh squinted at them, trying to make two of them instead of the four that were constantly moving, crossing over each other's images like Venn diagrams. They were only marginally bigger than him, but there were two of them, and right now, they were in considerably better shape. Maybe sober, Josh would have given it a square go and come out grinning, but as it was he didn't stand a chance. In a few moments he was going to be mincemeat.

Green Shirt turned his head back to Tartan and put his hands out in an imitation of Josh, and he started to repeat the words Josh had spoken, using a theatrical girl's voice, but he stopped mid-performance as he saw his friend's face.

The man in the tartan shirt was staring ahead as though he'd been knifed in the shoulderblades. His mouth was hanging open, his jaw working slightly at some silent purpose, and both deep-set eyes were showing as much white as their eyelids would ever allow. He had uncrossed his arms, and now held his clenched hands up in front of his chest like a baby on its back.

'What the fuck, Douane?'

The man in the green shirt stared at Douane's stricken face for a second then swung around, following the direction of those fear-mad eyes with his own. Josh tried to steady himself. All his concentration was being spent on trying to see straight, but no matter how many times he narrowed his eyes, blinked and refocused, there were still only shifting blurs where he knew his attackers stood. The most important thing in his mind right now was not survival or flight. It was trying to breathe in the oppressively hot air that was so solid and tangible he could feel it searing his skin. He clenched his fists and gulped in a lungful of what was available, gasping as it did nothing to relieve the pressure in his bursting chest. The two men were now staring ahead, not at Josh, but at the space behind and above him. They were looking towards the window.

Josh fell to his knees again, his hot head bent low, nearly touching the carpet. He coughed once and raised his head sufficiently to see the men's legs from the knees down. They were backing away slowly from him, and one of the owners of those legs was muttering in a high, childlike voice: 'It ain't so. It ain't so. Sweet Jesus it ain't.'

The legs stumbled back a few more paces, then turned and ran. Josh put a hand to his face, wiped his eyes and tried to follow the frantic progress of those retreating legs.

He could make out the distant running figures of the men as they skidded to a halt at the fire door beyond the elevators, tore it open and disappeared from his indistinct view.

Josh shut his eyes and let his head fall again. There was a double relief in the men's inexplicable exit, the air seemed to be growing cooler and he could feel the painful constriction of his chest beginning to loosen.

With an effort of will more than body, he pushed himself upright and made his way unsteadily to his feet. The corridor was empty. Josh leaned against the wall for a moment, enjoying the taste of breathable air in his open mouth, then turned his head and looked towards the corridor's only window.

It seemed his eyes were still not obeying his brain. In the uneven undulations of the glass something was moving; huge, and darker than the black night that pressed up against the window.

He gritted his teeth, put his fingers to his temples, shut his eyes and opened them again to squint hard at the square of inky glass. It steadied in his vision long enough to report back its contents. An infinity of lights, a smashed trucker leaning against a wall, a highway of carpet, and nothing else. He slid down the wall and sat there, breathing heavily and shaking his head in a drunk's despair.

And when only a few minutes later Eddie returned triumphant from the bar with his square of computerized plastic, there was no one conscious to greet him. Josh Spiller was fast asleep on the carpet.

19

The copper rod touched the globes of quicksilver gently, and she watched, eternally fascinated, as the globes divided and re-formed in their own perfect, but multiplied image. The double trace of blood that circled the metals had been completed by her two middle fingers, and its route resembled some macabre race trail left by gory snails.

Already, the air around her was busy with servants from the other side, eager to be called, desperate to be unleashed. She inhaled the sulphur and closed her eyes, pulling a sharp thumbnail down between her breasts where it left an angry red weal.

In the corner, the eerie green light from the computer screen flickered over the top of several stacked crates, the dancing shapes picking out a dull reflection from the lumps of grey metal within like some corrupt open fire. And as she opened her mouth to speak, the machine's low buzzing heightened the silence in the small room.

She started normally, each word spoken in a voice without intonation, but at a speed that would still count as language. And then the velocity increased. It increased until the beating, thrumming sound that emanated from her tongue was little more than a hideous single note.

Behind her, the computer screen changed, silently updating its information to tell the back of this woman's quivering head that the franc had fallen two points.

'Man. Look at this guy.'

Eddie let out a guffaw and slapped the back of Josh's head twice, receiving a groan in response. At the foot of the bed, a television was showing a man in a waterproof jacket printed with 'Team Drey-fus', talking his way through his hot-saw improvements to an announcer with a hand mike.

'Fuck me. Would you listen to that dipshit?'

Josh groaned again and curled further into the foetal position he had adopted to avoid any more unwelcome physical contact with his friend.

Eddie looked down at Josh and realized his recommendation to view was being ignored. He slapped him again, this time on the back.

'Come on, Spiller. Sit up and drink the goddamn coffee.'

There was no response. Eddie leaned over and hooked his arms under Josh, hauling him into a sitting position against the padded headboard.

'Gimme a break.'

'One hour per unit of alcohol. That's how long it takes even a crocked out ol' body like yours to get rid of the stuff. Science says you should be sober now. So I say you're just bein' a lazy fucker.'

Josh groaned again, less convincingly this time, and opened his eyes. Eddie handed him a cup of instant coffee and pointed at the screen again. 'See what you've been missin'? National hot-saw championships. This saddo just cut up a log in thirty-four seconds and instead of telling him to go get a life, they're congratulating him.'

'What's the time?'

Josh took a mouthful of coffee. It tasted good.

'Twenty after ten.'

'Aw shit, Eddie. Why didn't you wake me?'

'I just did. Drink up and shut up.'

Josh took another gulp of coffee and swung his legs over the edge of the huge bed. Sleeping in the clothes he'd had on last night had left him dishevelled like a beggar. His head hurt and his mouth was dry, and as he rubbed his face his eyeballs ached at the back of their sockets. Eddie punched him unhelpfully in the back.

'Go take a shower. You stink.'

Josh lashed out belatedly with an arm to ward off the blow. 'Quit that, would you?'

Eddie punched him again and laughed, making Josh curse as he got up off the bed and shuffled through to the bathroom. He took a long leak, then leaned on the sink and grimaced at himself in the mirror. Two and a half days of stubble was turning into a beard and his eyes were bloodshot and bagged. He pulled the thin plastic curtain across the bath, turned on the shower, then fished in Eddie's washbag for his razor and foam and started to shave. Almost as if touching his possessions triggered an automatic response, Eddie hollered from the bedroom.

'You are not goin' to believe this. This guy tuned his chainsaw. Tuned it, y'hear? Like it was a hot-rod? Fuckin' far out.'

Josh smiled and ran the razor under the hot water tap. He felt good and bad at the same time. Bad, because his head was thumping and his body felt like it had been poisoned. Good, because talking to Eddie about everything crazy that had happened had made him feel sane again.

The stuff last night. There was an explanation for it all right. And if he'd been sober he'd have known what that explanation was. Maybe it was the very fact he'd been totally rat-assed that had saved him. Maybe he just dreamed it all in his alcoholic stupor. In a minute he'd tell Eddie what went down and they'd laugh, but right now he had to try and look human again. The steam from the shower was misting the mirror and he wiped an arc clean with the heel of his palm. Peering at the fuzzy reflection, he continued to shave.

'Aw, Spiller. Get this. The lulu's got a fuckin' name for his saw.'

Josh shouted back, regretting it instantly as the volume made by his own voice hurt both his throat and head. 'We got names for our trucks. What's the difference?'

'What's the difference? We live in our trucks, man. This is a fuckin' saw we're talking about. You got a name for your tyre pressure-gauge?'

Josh grinned through the shaving foam. He slid the razor from under his ear towards the corner of that grin, and as he did so a line of red blossomed in its wake.

'Shit.'

Before the curse had left his lips, the bathroom began to stir. It stirred violently and precisely at the moment the first dark bead of blood oozed from Josh's wound, and it was that stirring, not the careless laceration, that made Josh stand rigidly still and hold his breath.

The movement of air is rarely visible. Sometimes it's witnessed through shafts of sunlight in the smoke of woodland fires or betrays its frantic contortions amongst the snowflakes of a blizzard. But the most common observation of something invisible becoming visible, even the minor disturbance of a person having passed through that air and left their trail, is in the steam of a bathroom. And the steam from the shower that had been shifting lazily behind Josh in the mirror was now thrashing wildly.

He dropped the razor into the sink and spun around. The clouds of water particles were spiralling and boiling in front of him, driven by some imperceptible tempest that Josh widened his eyes to find and failed.

'EDDIE!'

Josh screamed like a child, pressing back into the edge of the sink as though escape was possible through the Formica. The speed with which Eddie got to the bathroom meant there had been no mistaking the hysterical pitch of Josh's cry.

He ran through the door, bringing his own air currents that stirred the steam into mini twisters then settled back into the peaceful mist it had been only moments ago.

'What the fuck?'

Eddie quickly scanned the tiny room for the source of the panic, and seeing none, faced Josh. His face was bleeding from the razor cut, but it was Josh's eyes that gave Eddie cause for concern. They were wide with fear and searching the empty room wildly for something that quite obviously was not there. Eddie put his hands on Josh's shoulders, attempting to recapture his attention by blocking his friend's view of the empty bathroom with his own face.

'Come on, man. You're scarin' me.'

Josh refocused on the face only inches from his, closed his eyes in despair and groaned.

Eddie stepped back and lifted his arms out in a gesture of exasperation. 'You want to tell me?'

Josh opened his eyes again and looked at Eddie in defeat.

Eddie gestured again like some Jewish matriarch. 'The toilet paper weren't folded at the corners. That it?'

The absence of embarrassment or even bewilderment in Josh's voice when he replied, unnerved Eddie more than the cry he had responded to from the bedroom. His voice was a croak, full of a mystifying air of doomed resignation.

'Thought I saw somethin'.'

'Saw what?'

'I don't know. Somethin'.'

Eddie let his arms drop and propped his hands on his ample hips. He looked at Josh for an uncomfortable length of time as though waiting for him to laugh, and when it was plain that wasn't going to happen, he left the bathroom shaking his head. The steam swirled in his wake and settled again. Josh stood motionless for a moment, then raised a hand to his cut face. He looked at the blood on his fingers, and then across the empty steam-filled room to the shower spraying the wall.

The crummy music of a soap opera from next door told him that Eddie had gotten bored with hot-saw champions and switched channels. Josh mouthed the word again to himself and absently rubbed his blood into his palm.

'Somethin'.'

20

It had only three shoots, but it was healthy enough. It would do. Sim looked down at his hand clutching the tiny plastic pot of chervil, and got ready to knock. She was home, that much was for sure. But whether she would answer or not was another matter.

He curled his gnarled finger and rapped it lightly against Elizabeth's door. Three gentle taps. After a few silent moments he rapped again, louder, and deep in the house he heard the noise of her approach.

Sim supposed she might be haggard, weary from lack of sleep and grey from unhappiness. But Elizabeth was creamy and glowing from a bath when she pulled open the door and smiled at him.

'Hey, Sim.'

She towelled her hair with one hand as she beamed at him.

Sim melted under her smile, and although he'd planned a concerned fatherly expression when she greeted him, it gave way to the coy delighted grin of a schoolboy. 'Hi. I just call to bring you this. Taken from the mother plant, but you feed it good, it grow as big as you like.'

Elizabeth tossed the towel over one shoulder and held her hand out for the pot. 'God, Sim, you're so sweet, but you're out of your mind if you think I'll do any better with this one.'

'This one not die. You see.'

She pushed the door open wide and turned to go back inside. 'Come on in and show me where to put the damn thing. You said it was positioning that massacred the basil.'

Sim grinned even wider and followed her in, shutting the door behind him gently.

She shouted from the kitchen before he even got there. 'I don't even know what this is. What the hell is it?'

He waited until he was in the room and then waved a hand towards the window. 'Chervil. Good for meat and fish. You put it right there. Beside that thing.'

She turned and made a mock scowl. 'It's an indoor hydrangea. Don't get fresh about my plants.'

'You no eat it, it stinks.'

Elizabeth took a sniff at the chervil and gave him a look. He laughed, a dry wheezing old sound that seldom left his body. She laughed too and Sim could tell by her visible enjoyment of the sound that right now it was almost as rare in her life as his.

'You want some herbal tea?'

'Thank you. Yes.'

Elizabeth pointed at a chair and got busy. Sim sat down slowly, knowing the next bit would be harder. There was silence for a long time and then he spoke first.

'Josh away right now?'

She had her back to him, filling the kettle at the sink. 'Yup.'

'Where he at this time?'

'Dunno exactly. South I guess.'

He nodded, though he knew she wasn't looking.

'Shop going good?'

She plugged in the kettle and turned with a smile a child could tell was phoney. 'Yeah. Pretty good, you know? Taking the morning off to catch up with a pile of paperwork and let Nesta deal with the ugly hordes.'

Sim nodded again and looked at her kindly but very directly. Elizabeth looked back into his narrow gimlet eyes and wondered if he could read the truth.

The truth.

She wasn't in the shop because she couldn't face it. She'd been sick most of the morning. She kept crying. She had no idea what was going on with Josh or what she was going to do about it.

Yes. He could read the truth. She could see it in his eyes as surely as he could read hers. Elizabeth knew Sim must have heard her wailing, and since he watched their movements like a concierge he'd have to have been blind, deaf and dumb to have missed both Josh's and Elizabeth's exits after their argument. Sure he knew.

That's why he was here. And it was the relief of that knowledge that made the tears well up and spill out over her cheek, even as she continued to wear her smile.

'Sit down, Elizabeth. Tea can wait.'

She did as she was told and sat facing him, letting the tears fall unhindered.

'He phone?'

She shook her head, and then changed her mind, altering the nod into a clumsy rotation of the head, which she accompanied by holding up a finger.

'Once. To the shop.'

'He say where he at?'

She shrugged, shoulders starting to heave a little now with the pressure of containing her sobs, then let her head fall forward and rest in her hands. 'I don't know, Sim. I don't know. I've been acting crazy. I wouldn't even speak to him, and he sounded so . . .'

She shooed away the rest of the sentence with a limp hand. Sim wanted to reach out to her, but it wasn't part of his character to touch. He stayed still in his seat and nodded again at the top of her head as she sobbed.

'He come home soon. I know it.'

Elizabeth drew her breath and sat up, wiping her face with both hands. 'Yeah. I know. Sorry.'

'You want I make the tea?'

'Okay.'

Sim knew where everything was and performed his task slowly, moving objects around with an old person's geisha-like delicacy. He was spooning neat piles of camomile tea into a cheerful blue teapot, when the phone rang. Elizabeth sat up at the sound like a deer in long grass, and then as quickly looked to Sim. On the first trilling of the phone he had tipped the tea from his spoon onto the counter where it fanned out in a complicated mess.

Elizabeth ignored Sim's uncharacteristic accident and stood up cautiously but hopefully. 'That might be him,' she said in a small voice.

Sim's hands were shaking. He stared at her as though she were about to attack him and then started to shake his head violently.

'Not Josh. It not Josh. No. No. It not him.'

Elizabeth gawped at him, and then glanced towards the hall where the phone was still sounding its innocent chirping. Sim had dropped the spoon and stood waving his hands at her like a madman. She wanted to go across and pacify him, but the desperation to answer the phone was stronger. She made a calming movement with her own outstretched hands and backed towards the phone. 'It's okay, Sim. It's okay. Calm down. You might be right. Maybe it isn't him. Just stay cool and sit down for a minute, okay? I'll be right back.'

Their roles had changed so swiftly, she now the comforter, he now the distraught hysteric, that Elizabeth could make no sense of it.

But all that mattered right now was who was calling.

Elizabeth's hand hovered over the phone for a moment, as though she were feeling a heat from it, then she picked it up and held it to her ear.

'Hello?'

A storm of static raged at the other end of the line. There were distant sounds and cries, all masked by an infernal crackling white noise, the chaos of a weak radio transmission.

'Hello? Josh. Is that you?'

Elizabeth strained to make out the background noise babbling beneath the electric fog. Was it voices? It almost sounded like animals. She looked up at the door to the kitchen where Sim stood, his fists clenched and his mouth slightly open. She spoke to him kindly, trying to affect a casual smile.

'I think it's a mobile. I can't hear.'

Sim started to shake his head again and lifted his thin arms in a manic gesture towards the phone. 'No. Not Josh. You hang up. Not Josh.'

Elizabeth kept her eyes on Sim, but she spoke once more into the phone, this time as if to a stupid child. 'Hello? Josh? If that's you I can't hear you. It's a terrible line. If you can hear me, hang up and try again. Okay? Hear me? I'm going to hang up, and you try again.' She replaced the receiver on its cradle and moved towards Sim. 'It's okay, Sim. It was just a bad line. A mobile or something.'

Sim was still shaking his head. She put a hand out and touched his arm.

'What's wrong?'

The phone was wrong. That's what. The moment it rang Sim knew it wasn't Josh. Oh Josh was there somewhere all right. He could sense it the way he always could. But it wasn't really Josh on the other end. There was something else trying to speak. Something he didn't want to think about, because to think about it, to give any room in his heart or mind to the feeling when it came slithering through the phone line into this house, would be the way to madness. He said nothing, but looked into Elizabeth's eyes with an expression of feral panic, as she guided him gently back into the kitchen and sat him at the table.

Sim could tell by the way Elizabeth was moving, the way she was glancing at him as she prepared the forgotten tea, that she thought he was a mad old man. Maybe she was thinking he wouldn't be living with them much longer if he was going to go crazy. Maybe.

He didn't care. Right now, try as he might to leave it alone, he cared about what had been on the telephone. And the more he thought about it the more he knew.

It was Hell calling.

'Crock of fuckin' shit.'

Josh slammed the phone down and punched the wall. A few yards away in the foyer, Eddie watched from behind a carousel of postcards. Josh composed himself and then walked across to join him. Eddie's moustache moved sufficiently to tell Josh there was a cheerful grin beneath it. It was a phoney grin, but it would match the phoney camaraderie in his voice.

'Need a scenic panorama of the lovely Chickamauga lake in spring's mantle? Fold-out wallet of ten views only five dollars fifty.'

Josh put one hand on his hip and rubbed his face. Eddie stopped spinning the card stand.

'Big guess. She didn't pick up.'

'She's at the shop. I just wanted to leave a message on the answering machine at home.'

'And it weren't on.'

'Naw. Damn phone's bust. It answered, but it sounds like the line's down.'

'Well call the phone company.'

'Yeah.'

'Or call the shop.'

Josh looked at the ground. 'Guess I couldn't stand it if she didn't take the call. That's why I wanted to leave a message. You know? Least she'd have to listen.'

Eddie nodded and looked at the cards again. 'Send her a post-card. Dear Elizabeth. Killed a baby. Fucked a psycho. Met Eddie. Got ball-brained and fell over. Our room marked on picture with a cross.'

Josh rubbed at his skull. 'I'll be home before it gets there. I'm gonna hit the road now, Eddie.'

The two men looked at each other in silence for a moment, addressing the awkwardness that had grown since Josh had yelled in the bathroom, and increased when he told Eddie what had happened the night before. He wished he hadn't. It had sounded dumb.

Josh made the first attempt to break through. 'Still think I'm crazy, huh?'

'And ugly.'

'I mean it.'

Eddie sighed and pushed the cap back on his head.

'Your head was soup, man, as my wallet can testify. Doubles of whiskey don't come cheap in this shed.'

'You're not bein' straight with me. You don't believe me, do you?'

'What can I say? I weren't fuckin' there.'

'So it follows you reckon I'm on the ga-ga express.'

Eddie looked into Josh's eyes and spoke in a quiet voice, embarrassed as a lover trying to suppress a public row. 'Spiller, man. Cut yourself some slack here. I ain't never had the kind of two days you just had. Maybe if I had, I'd be seein' Martians givin' Elvis a shoe-shine.'

Despite the fact that Eddie's comparison answered Josh's question in the affirmative, he found himself smiling and raising an eyebrow. Eddie caught the smile with relief, put out his hands and smiled back. 'Not that seein' the King would be loopy or nothin'.'

Josh nodded, his anxiety giving way against his will to the comfort of familiar mirth. 'No. 'Cos he ain't dead, is he?'

'Nope. Gas-pump attendant in Wickenburg, Arizona saw him only last week.'

'I got to go, Eddie.'

Eddie nodded once. 'Yeah.'

Josh started to walk towards the front doors, expecting him to follow. When he realized that he was alone he turned and stopped. Eddie indicated the phones.

'Need to make some calls.'

Josh walked back, and Eddie looked at the carpet. 'Eddie?'

'Mmm?'

'I'll call you.'

'Sure.'

'I mean it. And thanks.'

'Fuck off.'

Josh grinned and left, and as he walked to the truck he felt his heart lift at the stupidity of the whole damned thing.

Eddie was right. Stress and booze were bad bedfellows. He was heading home and things were going to be fine.

His friend watched him go and thought differently. Things were far from fine, and his worry wasn't just that someone he cared about had indeed boarded the ga-ga express. As far as Eddie could tell, Josh Spiller had bought himself a season ticket.

21

He smiled and turned the volume up.

'Hey hey hey. Can I stop you there, Pete? Where are you calling from?'

'Maryville.'

'And you're telling me there are no children whatsoever in your town doing drugs.'

'That's what I'm sayin'.'

'How do you know that?'

'Pardon me?'

'I'm saying how can you possibly know whether there are or not?'

' 'Cos I got eyes in ma head, that's how, Brendan. There ain't no blacks hangin' round school gates givin' the stuff away. There ain't no kind of stuff that you get in the big cities. Like you see on TV, you know?'

Josh shook his head at the radio speakers, signalled and moved out to pass a flat-bed hauling a kit house.

'And what's your point, Pete? Like I care.'

'Well you should care. 'Cos my point is just that all the stuff you been talkin' hogwash about, like it was a real bad problem, only applies to them foreigners in the cities. They's the ones who's pushin' the stuff. There ain't none of it down here. Us people here still know how to live like Americans.'

'WWPBAL comin' at you on the Brendan Earl Holler Hour. That's Pete from Maryville. Pete? Whatever you're on, buddy, I wouldn't mind a sniff or a smoke if it made me believe the crap you're coming out with. Could someone with a brain please call me? Back with more after this.'

Josh stepped on the gas and pulled past the flat-bed. As the driver signalled that he had room to pull back in, Josh adjusted the volumes on his two radios, the CB winning the battle over a musical commercial for weed killer.

'Come on back in, Jezebel.'

'I'm there, big truck.'

'Chicken-house 'bout five miles ahead is open, driver. In case you haulin' somethin' you shouldn't.'

'Naw. I'm way below weight. 'Preciate the information all the same.'

'No problem.'

The irritation that Josh felt, knowing he'd have to pull over, made him realize just how eager he was to get home. There was a fine if you didn't stop to be weighed when a station was open, and even though it would be a detour costing him only about five minutes, and that was supposing there was a queue, it still rankled. He sighed and turned the local radio station back up.

'You can call us crazy, you can call us bananas, you can call us anything you like. But we're still offering two, yes two whole years to pay on our best ever selection of pine kitchen and dining-room furniture, right here at Sit an' Eat, Western Avenue, Knoxville. Okay. You're right. We've lost it. We're insane.'

With six rolls of aluminium sheet in the back, Jezebel was topping out at sixty-eight thousand pounds, a good twelve thousand pounds short on the legal limit. This was a cheapskate job. Since there were at least a dozen rigs all moving the same consignment, he was nowhere near fully loaded and he wasn't getting the rate even if he had been. But like the lady said, it was going home to Pittsburgh. And being light meant a straight run through the chicken-house.

He ticked over in line behind a shiny reefer and avoided looking at his own image in the reflective doors by fumbling around in the dash tidying things up. The light hanging from a wire above the weigh-station office turned green and the reefer moved up. Josh pushed the gear stick and followed.

The reefer crawled over the metal plate sunk in the asphalt and as it pulled away the light stayed green. Josh was next. Jezebel inched forward onto the plate and the light went red. The guy in the booth pointed to the holding area and used the loudhailer.

'Pull over to the right, Peterbilt. To the right, please.'

Josh held his arms out to the guy. 'What, for Chrissakes?'

The guy pointed again. Josh sighed, and pulled into the big lot behind the booth. He shut her down with an exhalation of breath that almost matched Jezebel's brake hiss.

This was now more than an irritating delay. It was serious. If you weren't overweight then they wanted to look at something else. Through the window of the office, a state trooper was now visible putting his hat on and gesturing towards the truck with a clipboard. The guy he was talking to was gesturing too, almost with a shrug, but even watching them closely, Josh couldn't interpret the body language of their conversation.

He pulled out his black folder with a frown, already dreading having to discuss the hell of the last few days, and plucked at the rubber bands in irritation.

The truck shuddered. Josh knew that vibration as well as he knew the beat of his own pulse. It was the movement that every trucker knew and automatically registered even in their sleep. It was the shudder a vehicle's suspension made when someone was climbing on or off. Josh glanced quickly at the mirrors, saw nothing, then opened the door and stepped down. He walked cautiously down the length of the trailer, scanning the top for any signs of movement, and, moving like a man expecting attack, made a complete circuit of the rig.

There was nothing.

Josh shook his head, exasperated that his nerves were on such fine tuning that a gust of wind could have made him believe Jezebel's security had been breached. Sighing, he reached up into the cab and pulled out his folder. Josh waited at the door of the truck for a few moments, breathing in the fumes from the long line of trucks, watching jealously as they inched unchallenged over the scales and headed back onto the interstate. It took the men three or four minutes to emerge from the booth, but when they did, the state bear and his sidekick were still deep in conversation. Josh greeted them, a hand on his hip.

'What's the problem? I weighed at the factory. She's only hauling sixty-eight thou.'

The bear stood with his legs apart and echoed Josh's posture. 'Want to know what we got?'

'Let's have it.'

The two men looked at each other, and Josh saw something in the policeman's eyes. The same something that had been in the waitresses' eyes at the motel. The trooper looked away quickly and nodded for the smaller man to speak, like a proud father urging his son to recite a poem.

'We make it five hundred and fifty thousand pounds.'

Josh stared at him to see if he was joking. He wasn't. Josh laughed mirthlessly, and the man gave another apologetic shrug. The silent discussion witnessed through the glass now made more sense.

'We all know that's impossible.'

'We sure do. Them scales only measure to a hundred and fifty.'

'So?'

The trooper spoke again, his eyes roaming over Jezebel. Anywhere but Josh's face. 'So while we call for Mulder and Scully maybe we better take a look anyhow.'

Josh shook his head in disbelief. 'How in God's name you think anythin' on wheels could carry half a million pounds of weight?'

'I know it can't. Scales must've gone apeshit, but I'd like to see if anything you got in there helped them go that way, before we weigh you again.'

Josh blew out of pursed lips, shook his head a couple more times, put his folder down on the running board and went to open her up. He found the trailer keys on a ring already barnacled with dozens of others and snapped open the padlock.

'What you haulin' here?' The trooper talked to Josh's back while he unbolted the doors.

'Aluminium.'

'Going to?'

'Pittsburgh.'

'I guess if the door ain't lyin' you'd be Josh Spiller.'

'Yup.'

'Okay, Mr Spiller. You want to crack some ID and paperwork for me while I step in here and have a look?'

The doors swung open and the three men looked inside. Six innocent rolls of aluminium sheeting sat in two rows in the airy space of the trailer.

Josh turned, but the trooper continued to stare at the aluminium, making no move to climb up and inside. The weigh-station official was looking down at the clipboard that he had retrieved from the policeman, flicking over the top sheet as if deeply interested in what lay beneath. Josh scratched the back of his head.

'You need a hand to get up there?'

The trooper fumbled for a pen in his breast pocket. 'Just get the paperwork.'

Josh searched the policeman's face curiously, trying to decipher his agenda, then walked back to his door and fetched the folder, cursing as he picked it up.

This was bad luck. No one ever got pulled over without being given the full works. Now they would go over the paperwork, and every nut, bolt and axle of the truck like ants on syrup.

The men were still standing at the open doors when Josh walked back the full length of the trailer. He handed the folder to the policeman and waited to see what their plan was. The trooper flicked the black plastic cover open and fumbled hurriedly through the log sheets and delivery bills. It was obvious he wasn't looking at them at all.

'Okay. This sure as hell can't be overweight. We need you to drive over the scales again and then that's it.'

Josh nodded, astonished, and took back the folder that was being pushed at him without eye contact. 'Sure. I'll just check the load's still secure.'

'Drive it round the back of the office and rejoin the line.'

Both men walked away quickly, leaving Josh staring after them in astonishment. The moment they'd stopped him, he'd mentally written off a couple of hours, the time it would take to grill him. It had happened plenty in the past. The more eager you were to get back on the road, the slower they would search you.

But not today. Today, it seemed they wanted him gone.

'You see, Eddie? I ain't imagining it,' he said under his breath to the men's backs.

He watched them until they re-entered the office, then laid the folder on the edge of the trailer floor and climbed up.

He felt it as soon as he stood up.

The heat.

Josh stayed still, balancing on the balls of his feet at the edge of the trailer opening. It felt like wafts of warmth from a radiator, and the cooler air that was coming in the open door was mixing with it, shifting it around his face. Josh swallowed and walked forward. The trailer creaked beneath his weight and he paused. The air was hotter now, and the ticking noises from the metal structure that broke the silence confirmed the fact that it too was registering the abnormal temperature. But there was nothing to see. Each roll of metal was three feet in diameter and stood only five feet high on its pallet, giving Josh a clear view of the acres of space between.

He moved forward again, licking his lips, every sense on alert, until he reached the first load. Slowly, he reached out a hand to touch it. It was warm. Josh withdrew his hand and scanned the rest of the trailer. The rolls of metal remained impassive. With a glance behind him he moved forward between the rolls until he was half way up the aisle.

There, the heat was more intense, mixing with the diesel and metal to make a smell like the aftermath of a scrapyard fire.

Something dropped on Josh's shoulder. A tiny shard of metal. Josh looked up at the ceiling and blinked.

Running from the middle of the trailer's ceiling almost all the way to the back wall in two uneven sets of three were six long, ragged gashes. He stared up at them, his head tipped back on his shoulders, his mouth slightly open, and stepped back a pace. The gouges were each about a half inch wide, cut deep and violently into the thin metal ceiling, and whatever tool had made them must not only have been sharper than an axe, but would have required an inconceivable force to have left their trail so destructively. He took another step back and his heel came up against the corner of a wooden pallet, causing Josh to lose his balance. He put out a steadying hand behind him and touched another aluminium roll, warm as skin. Josh spun round, and putting his other hand up, felt the heat radiating from it.

He stared wildly about him, then stumbled towards the open door, panting, a profound and bubbling fear brewing in his guts.

Jumping from the trailer doors, he kicked his folder to the ground and slammed the doors shut. As he stood, gasping, trying to regain his breath and his sense, he remembered they could see him from the office.

He stood up and took a deep breath. In the seconds that followed Josh Spiller asked himself some difficult questions. The first was why he didn't run to the office for help, to make them come and see his inexplicable find, to make them help him make sense of it. The second was why he somehow felt guilty, responsible for something he could neither identify nor articulate.

But the third and most pressing question was the worst. He shut his eyes against it as he bent down to pick up the folder, aware he was being watched from the booth, and trying to keep his movements casual after the suspicious haste of his exit from the trailer.

Walking back along to the cab, he kept his pace steady and his shaking hands safely at his chest.

But the question was still there.

Oh there was an answer to a bit of it, but it didn't help. The answer was that it had only recently departed Jezebel's trailer.

But the question?

What the fuck was it?

22

'Son of a bitch.'

She leapt back and threw her arms out. The splash from the puddle had completely soaked the front of her sweatshirt, and she looked down with rage at the muddy mess. Then her green eyes flicked back up and followed the back of the retreating Chevy Suburban that had unwittingly done the damage.

'Damned four-wheelers,' she muttered under her breath, letting a smile twitch at the sides of her mouth as she realized she was aping Josh.

Griffin held the base of her sweatshirt in two hands and wrung it out. Muddy brown water dripped onto the asphalt of the parking lot, and she sighed as she let the soggy material fall back against her body and walked back across to the rucksack she had left leaning up against a fence.

Hitching wasn't quite as easy as she'd planned. A ride from a trucker in the TA in Nashville had only taken her thirty miles until he kicked her out, and now she was all but stranded in this out-of-town mall parking lot in the ass-end of nowhere. Not that she'd been sorry to get out the truck. The guy had been nothing like Josh. He'd weighed in at about two hundred and eighty pounds and had smelled like a Salvation Army hostel. But worse. He'd eyeballed her as she climbed into the smelly cab, and only Mother Teresa might have believed his lascivious leer was well-intentioned.

Thirty miles was plenty, both for Griffin to endure the smell of the dumb brute's armpits and for the driver to realize his passenger wasn't going to put out. They'd parted without a grunt of farewell.

And so she'd tried car drivers, but thus far without luck. She sat down heavily on her rucksack and rolled up the sleeves of her ruined sweatshirt. The sun was playing tricks, appearing intermittently from behind thick cloud to dry up rain that kept falling in violent sheets. It was steamy and growing hot, and Griffin was getting annoyed.

She looked down at the brooch, pinned at an angle to the thick material, and fingered it, making its dull metal glint in the sunshine. The driver might have been a cretin but he could read, and if he wanted to think she was called Elizabeth, then that was fine by her. It hadn't occurred to her that it would be useful in that respect, but now it had become a tool of anonymity.

'You should be a whole lot prettier,' she said to the cheap grey metal and ran a well-manicured nail over its uneven surface.

The thought made her smile again, and her smile was still in place as the roar of a truck entering the lot made her look up. Of course she could just give in and make one call and someone would pick her up in a matter of hours. But that wasn't how it was going to be. Not if she could help it. Another ride from a truck driver wasn't an attractive prospect, but it was better than no ride at all. She kept her smile fixed, stood up, pulled on her rucksack and walked regally through the puddles towards the vehicle.

'Peterbilt? Unless you're dead on the road you'd best get your ass out from behind them Schneider eggs, 'cos there's a bear sniffin' around northbound at my tail 'bout nine miles.'

Josh stared at the back of the passing reefer that had called him and out of habit lifted a hand to pick up the CB handset in response. He stopped midway through the action, unable to move.

Jezebel was sitting on the wrong side of some orange-and-white traffic barrels pulled over at an angle beside the road construction vehicles that unlike her had every right to be there. Josh didn't care. He'd had to stop. The thought of Griffin tearing at his log book like an animal had been unsettling and horrible. The thought, after he'd driven away from the weigh-station, that maybe she hadn't, that maybe someone or something else had, was nothing more than the mouth of madness. But was he mad? The traffic roared past him on the left, and he watched it with glazed eyes. Everything looked the same as it always had done. The cars hadn't grown arms and legs, the trucks weren't made of Jell-O, and the highway was still a highway. John Pace's voice spoke quietly in his head.

'I'm goin' to say this again. Shock plays tricks on you.'

Neat tricks. Really neat. He played it all back. Bit by bit. Everything from the accident to this. And still Josh Spiller could not accept that he was losing his mind.

He knew what it was like to be out of your box. He and Eddie, the stuff they'd done made it miraculous neither had ever done time marking days with a penknife on the wall of some county jail. He stirred that one around for a second, grasping hopefully at it, until a helpful word surfaced. Acid. Yeah, acid. That might be it.

He'd heard somewhere that even one tab, taken years ago, meant that you could have a trip again at any time in your life. So they said.

But then they always said crazy shit to try and keep kids off drugs. In his experience it had the opposite effect. You could tow a banner behind a plane saying 'Hash makes your balls shrivel up and drop off', and folks would likely just appreciate the reminder that they hadn't had a blow for a few days. As for bad trips that recurred decades after the event, he certainly hadn't ever met anyone it had happened to. But then again . . .

He leaned forward on the wheel and thought of all the dumb crazy stuff he'd done in his bad days. Like driving his turn all the way from Denver to Salt Lake City after dropping a tab that Eddie had lovingly laid out on the dash for him with a Rolling Rock to wash it down. But even that hadn't been particularly crazy. Eddie used to see all kinds of things on acid, shouting at Josh to watch out for bottomless holes in the road and insisting with great solemnity that if Josh tied a rope to the back of the trailer Eddie could fly by holding on. But he remembered being disappointed that all he'd felt was mildly disorientated and more acutely aware of colours and shapes. It was so unremarkable that he'd never tried it again, and stuck to the odd line of coke to help him stay awake when he could raise the cash. Which is why Josh thought the chances of that stupid pointless little experience coming back ten years later to haunt him with this crazy shit was remote. But if not that, then what?

'You okay in there, big truck? Come on?'

The CB was talking to him again. A double trailer this time. He sat up and took a deep breath, but his hand was still shaky as he lifted the handset and pressed.

'Eh, sure. Thanks there, doubler. Had to pull over. Thought I'd lost a back axle there.'

'Shoot, buddy. That bad dream come true?'

Josh's throat tightened again. Bad dream. Oh Lord, what now? His eyes were frozen on the retreating trailer as he pressed talk, praying that there would be no more insanity. He spoke in a hoarse half whisper.

'Come again?'

He closed his eyes dreading what might come from the speakers mounted on the dash. He waited, and as he did the passing seconds seemed like minutes. When the driver came back, Josh held his breath.

'The axle? Had it left for Texas?'

Josh laughed then. Just bowed his head to his chest, let his breath go and laughed. He smiled up at the traffic. 'Naw. False alarm, buddy. 'Preciate the concern.'

'No sweat. Have a good one.'

Josh kept hold of his smile. It felt good. He rubbed his face and reached for the gear stick. He was good at working things out. It was only a matter of time before he would work out what was going on here, and then he would look back at how spooked he'd got and blush to his navel. Maybe now, he should just drive and let the facts work themselves out slowly in the part of his brain he didn't seem able to use right now.

Back north. Despite everything, the thought made him feel warm. Sure, he was going back to what he had left and that would still be a mess. Nothing had changed. And worse, he was carrying home two new kinds of guilty baggage. One he could discuss and one he couldn't. But Jesus, the thought of home suddenly seemed the cure for the world's ills.

And as a contribution to those ills, Jezebel deftly knocked out two traffic barrels with her tail end as she pulled back onto the highway, almost like she meant to.

23

He'd thought it had been enough when Samuel died. Thus far and no further. He'd mouthed those very words under his breath when the body had been carefully wrapped and carried to the funeral parlour as though Sam had died innocently in his sleep. He remembered watching limply, impotent like some prurient by-stander at a street shooting.

But he had gone further, hadn't he? He'd gone all the way with it until now. After all, Samuel had had his throat cut open like a gutted fish exactly twenty-one years ago, and that was a pretty long time to still be making up your mind. Three opportunities since then to stop taking part in this madness, and every one rejected. And for what? Security? Money? New homes for both his mother and Rachel's parents in North Carolina? Or was it the secret hope and prayer that it was somehow right, somehow good?

John Pace opened the top of a set of four office drawers with a small silver key, and lifting some papers aside, slid out a postcard. He expelled a breath he'd held too long, and held up the card to look at the picture.

It was a glossy black-and-white gallery postcard, a detail from an engraving from a Dutch museum.

His eye roamed over the picture, then he placed it gently on the desk top, running a finger around its edges as though trying to define its shape.

The typed caption was on the plain side of the postcard, printed discreetly along the top lefthand corner, leaving space for the purchaser's message. But John Pace didn't need to turn the card over to remind himself of that. He knew it well enough. It would tell him it was by a fifteenth-century German engraver called Israhel van Meckenem, and the subject matter was the Temptation of St Anthony.

The picture showed the saint being borne in the air by a collection of terrifying demons, monstrosities that defied nature with their grotesquely deformed bodies, their gaping, fang-filled mouths screaming as they tore and clawed at the weary man caught in their talons.

Pace's finger lightly traced a demon's hooked beak and spined head before he turned the card over and looked at the elegant handwriting on the back.

It was addressed to him at the sheriff's office where a lot of eyes could read it before it ended up on his desk, and it had been sent seven years ago. The last time he had doubts. The time he thought those Government men shouldn't have died. Not the way they did. He closed his eyes briefly, as he remembered their screams, then swallowed as he looked again, turning the card to read the words he'd read a hundred times before.

'John,' it began, in a cheerful open hand of blue ink. 'Knowing your interest in such things I thought you might find this fascinating. The extraordinary thing is I become more and more convinced that van Meckenem, like Brueghel the Elder and Bosch after him, was such a master draughtsman he can only have been drawing from life. What do you think?'

The signature was a scrawl, but its familiarity was such he would have recognized it had only a tiny portion of its flourish been visible. Truth was, such a message left no need for a signature at all.

He turned the card back over and continued to look at the picture until a subconscious registering of absence of movement through the glass door to the outer office made him aware he was being watched.

Archie Cameron was looking at him. Sheriff Pace held his deputy's stare until the younger man broke it off and bowed his head to his computer keyboard, then, as gently as he had fetched it out, he put the card back in the drawer and got on with the work he was paid to do.

She had calmed him and taken him back to his part of the house. But despite his assurances that he was perfectly fine now, Sim's bizarre attack had unnerved Elizabeth. She'd never seen the old man like that before. He'd gone completely crazy and now she looked at him sitting uncomfortably in his upright high-backed chair, and wondered when it might happen again.

'You sure you don't need me? I can stay and fix something to eat.'

Sim shook his head almost imperceptibly. There was shame etched into his lined face and Elizabeth's heart grew heavy at the thought of what might be ahead of the sad lonely man if Sim really was losing the plot.

'Okay, Sim. But I'm just upstairs if you want anything. You hear that? Anything at all.'

She touched the arm of his chair once, almost like a child playing tag, and turned to leave.

'Elizabeth.'

She stopped and turned. His face was crinkled with a mixture of his humiliation and something like the fear she'd watched consume him when that phone had started to ring.

'Yeah?'

'When he call again . . .' He gulped a mouthful of saliva. '. . . talk to him with your thoughts.'

He tapped the side of his head in case she might have trouble knowing where they might be found. Elizabeth nodded kindly.

'Sure.'

She left the room and Sim listened as she closed his front door, then to her soft footfall as she went back upstairs.

'He just maybe hear you. Just maybe,' he said to the empty room, then let welcome sleep overcome him as his head fell forward onto his thin chest.

The shop. It was worth a try. Even if she wouldn't talk, at least he could tell Nesta to report the fault to the phone company. And he could tell her he was coming home. Tell her he'd tried to leave messages on the answering machine but that technology was stopping him.

He took a breath, punched in the card exchange number and from his exposed phone booth looked around the forecourt of the gas station as he waited for the dumb girl's voice to run through her crap. Maybe this wasn't the best place in the world to have a

reconciliation by phone. It was noisy and public, and rain was starting to sheet down, spiralling in rivulets through the holed canopy
over the gas pumps and dripping onto his head and shoulders. But
now he'd started, Josh's heart was already beating faster with the
anticipation of hearing her voice.

'Thank you for calling Driveline . . .'

Josh closed his eyes in irritation. She had all that stuff to get
through and then the recorded messages would join up, leaving
that ridiculous gap between her droning 'you have . . .' and then a
second later '. . . twenty dollars left on Driveline' in a completely
different voice. Sure, they could put a man on the moon but they
couldn't find a way of stopping telephone recordings sounding like
they'd all been done discount at the local loony bin.

'. . . on the America network. All calls will be . . .'

'Yeah. Yeah. Get on with it, you dozy fruit.'

'. . . long distance or local. You have . . .'

Josh looked in boredom at the rain splashing round his boot
while she worked it out.

'. . . two days alive permitted.'

He stayed staring at his boot, his head down and his heart thumping blood in his ear.

She had said it in the same droning voice she'd said all the other
stuff. But no mistake. She'd said it. She'd said it and now she was
carrying on as though she hadn't.

'Please dial your number now.'

He croaked softly into the phone, his hand a knot of muscle
around the plastic. 'Hello?'

It was ridiculous. He was talking to the ether. Her message was
on a tape and there was no one there. But she had said those
words. She had. There was silence on the line while the computer
at Driveline waited for its caller from Virginia to dial his number
and get on with the business of making them money.

Instead, the caller slammed the phone back on the hook like it
had burned him and backed away from it with wide eyes. He walked
backwards like that for nearly ten feet until his body came into
contact with the bulk of a fat black guy, filling the tank of a beat-up
Maserati.

'Hey, watch it, man.'

Josh stumbled and put his hands out for balance, gripping the big man's shirt sleeve as he turned. But if the car owner had any ideas about taking his annoyance further as he shook off the stranger's grip, Josh's eyes stopped him. The man held up his own hand in silent forgiveness and watched Josh stagger slowly back to his truck then glanced across at a woman who'd been watching while fuelling up a space cruiser full of kids. He wanted to make that sign with his finger to his head that the trucker was nuts, but she looked away quickly, and when he thought about it, he realized he didn't much want to look anywhere either, except down at the nozzle pumping gas into that round black hole. He didn't want to do what would have come naturally, namely to stare insolently and aggressively at the guy's truck, and he sure as hell didn't want to look into those eyes again.

As the cab door slammed in the blue Peterbilt, he shifted his weight and leaned towards the pay booth, joining everyone else in looking the other way.

Josh fumbled with his wallet on the seat, breathing deeply and trying to keep calm. His hands were shaking so much he couldn't get the phone card back into any of the empty leather credit card slots, and he clenched his fists for a second, waiting for the trembling to stop.

Rain pelted the windshield and even though water was splashing in through the passenger window, open by a couple of inches, Josh was unable to muster sufficient will-power to lean across and close it. He sat numbly for a few moments, feeling the splashes on his hands and cheek, until he felt a thread of strength return to his arms.

There was no reasoning away what he just heard, except the explanation that he didn't really hear it at all. And that, of course, would mean he was mad. He picked up his wallet and phone card, tried to put it away again and failed. In a frenzy of temper Josh closed his fingers over the whole fat messy contents of his wallet, receipts, crumpled dollar bills, photos and old tickets, and pulled them violently out onto the floor.

The debris scattered around his feet and he clenched his fists again and brought them down hard on the steering wheel.

'Christ.'

He let his head fall forward onto his clenched fists and stayed hunched like a gargoyle for an age until an unfamiliar fluttering noise made him snap his head up and look round. The wind coming through the open window was toying with the mess from his wallet, and flapping around his feet was a thin strip of paper, like a super-market check.

His eyes followed it mutely as it tumbled over itself and rotated towards the passenger side as though being sucked instead of blown, and although it was clearly nothing more than a scrap of paper, Josh felt his mouth drying as he watched its contortions, the way it writhed like a worm on a hook.

He stretched out an arm to catch it as it cartwheeled along the rubber matting on the floor, but as his hand came within an inch of it, a gust of wind lifted the paper high into the cab and sent it slapping flat up against the open passenger window. A glance at his feet told Josh that none of the other contents of the wallet were in any way affected by this freak breeze, and he looked back to the thin strip with dread in his heart as it fluttered and inched its way up the glass towards the two-inch gap at the top that would give it its freedom.

Suddenly, it became important to him that this small piece of paper never reach the outside world, and with a speed that surprised him he leapt towards the window. His fingers closed around the strip just as it rolled once and tipped through the gap, leaving Josh holding it delicately like a streamer in the wind. The paper fluttered like a captured bird, rattling and burring wildly as Josh pulled it in, and then with his free hand wound the window up.

Almost instantly, the paper ceased its wild contortions and slumped back into the inanimate thing it had been.

He sat back down and examined his prize. It was no receipt. The paper was thin and brittle, like an ancient piece of map mildewed in the attic. It had a buttery hue and the marks on it were an unpleasant reddish brown colour. Marks were the only loose description Josh could find to explain what he was looking at. They were neither figures nor letters, but something between the two, and even trying to make sense of them was causing his head to spin. He rubbed at his temple and looked out the windshield.

The rain was lashing straight down on the glass, huge droplets bouncing back up and colliding with those still falling. It was a typical Virginian spring rain. Sheets of water and not a breath of wind. Not even a breeze.

Narrowing his eyes, he smoothed the paper over his leg and bent down to gather up the rest of his wallet's contents, his hands now surprisingly steady. Josh Spiller had no idea where the paper had come from, but as he folded it twice and stuck it deep and safely into the zipping part of his wallet, he vowed it wasn't going anywhere else until he found out.

24

Father? Father? There was no concept of either in this warm blackness. Only sometimes, when there was threat, or the opportunity to see and hear, could that which was growing stretch out and almost taste the freedom that the light would bring. It was like a dream. In this dream it could act as it would when the time came to be. It had mobility. It had substance. It had purpose. But it was becoming difficult to separate the dreams from reality. The smell of its host was so strong, so delicious, and yet sometimes the dreams let it stand outside. They let it act as though the time had come and it was born and could greet its host the way only it knew how. The way thousands had greeted their hosts before it in the long history of man's world.

It felt a dream beginning again, and it shifted and stretched and twitched in its warm cocoon. As it did so, it felt the pain and the fear of its unwilling host. And it was glad.

'Tell you what. Ifin I weren't drivin' this company cow with a tachograph that tells my boss when I fart out my breakfast, I'd pick her up for sure and show her some hospitality.'

'Get a life, you sad bastard.'

A woman's voice. A four-wheeler by the sounds of it. Josh barely registered the crap coming out of the radio, but somewhere in his confused and anxious mind, some brain cells had been assigned to listening.

'Hey, thermos. Where you say this hitcher is?'

'Where you at, come on?'

'Eh, I'm just cruisin' past them signs for caves an' stuff, 'bout a mile from exit 176.'

A new voice.

'You guys talkin' north- or southbound there?'

It was ignored.

'Okay, ifin you already passed them signs, then she's standin' waitin' on you gettin' her tasty ass soaked in the tourist pull-off three exits on. You got that?'

'Sure do.'

'She got a big backpack and big tits to balance it.'

The listening brain cells sounded an alarm in Josh's head. He sat up, his heart racing, and thumbed the radio. Someone beat him to it.

'Repeat. That north- or southbound, you shits?'

'Northbound, asswipe. Pay attention or git off the damned radio.'

Josh let his thumb relax. It couldn't be her then. Why would Griffin be hitching back north? On his left, through the driving rain, he glimpsed the signs for the mineral caves and he swallowed. But what if she'd given up her adolescent adventure and was heading home? He pressed talk again and this time got through.

'How you know so much 'bout this girl if you didn't give her a lift there, thermos?'

The woman four-wheeler's voice again. 'How you guys know how to tie your fuckin' shoelaces?'

Josh tutted with irritation. This was no time for political correctness. He wanted answers. He waited.

'Well ain't we all gettin' interested all of a sudden? Matter of fact my buddy just dropped her off. Happy?'

'You sure she's headin' north?'

'Well if she ain't, she's standin' on the wrong side of the road.'

Josh hung his handset back on its hook and pressed on the gas. If the other driver only just passed the cave signs, then it was probably that covered wagon three trucks ahead. It was hellish driving through this torrential rain, but if he stepped on it, maybe Josh could get to the rest area first.

Maybe.

This was worse than before. She was soaking now, and in this small strip of parking there was no shelter whatsoever, unless she chose to run to the scrub trees at the edge of the highway and crouch like an animal. But what was the point? Her clothes were wet through to her skin: what she needed now was to get a ride and get somewhere to dry.

Griffin glared at the cheery sign nailed to a post at the end of the rest area.

'Adopt a highway. Barras County Lion Cubs Boys Team.'

As she read it, cursing the jerks who thought picking up litter was recreation, water dripped from her nose and disappeared into the sponge that had become her sweatshirt. Even if there had been a waterproof in her pack, she doubted it would have been effective in this downpour.

But she hadn't thought to pack one. Not in the rush to leave. She had, after all, been heading south. Surely it didn't rain like this in the south.

The stream of traffic was relentless, throwing up spray that made the tailing vehicles practically invisible, and Griffin had long since given up even putting her thumb out. The only hope was that a car or truck would stop in the bay and she could approach them personally and beg a ride. It had worked in the mall lot, but like last time the ride only took her a meagre fifty miles before the guy announced he had to make a west turn onto 64 at Lexington. So she made him drop her here, and now she was sorry. Maybe going west would've been good.

She sat and mulled that one over for a moment, and as she imagined what the sun might feel like on her face a roar of spray and thunder pulled into the rest area alongside her. Griffin jumped back as the great truck squealed to a halt, and in case the driver had time to think about driving off again, she bent down to snatch up her pack and ran along the trailer to the driver's window.

He watched her coming in the mirror, studied her face and body as she started to recognize the rig and hesitate. Josh didn't give her the opportunity to change her mind. He opened the door, stepped down into the rain, and stood facing her.

Griffin's short hair was matted to her face, and as she blinked at him through the water, blowing a drip from her nose, Josh's heart leapt at the creamy beauty of her angular face. They stood looking at each other for a moment, and as they stared silently, letting the rain soak them, their intense gaze was broken by the swish and roar of another truck entering the bay.

Griffin twisted her head round, glanced quickly at the Mack that had pulled up hard behind Jezebel, then flicked her green eyes back to Josh.

' 'Bye.'

Before she could turn to leave, Josh's hand was around her wrist. She tried to pull away, but his grasp was strong and insistent, only a fraction away from pain. Griffin opened her mouth a little and stepped back. Behind her, Josh could see the driver of the Mack watching from his seat. His heart raced a little more. From up there, this must look bad. Griffin's voice was as low as it could be over the roar of two truck engines and a stream of spray-washed interstate traffic.

'I suggest you let go.'

'I just want to talk to you.'

Griffin tried and failed again to pull her wrist away, more obviously this time, with a glance over her shoulder to the other driver. He was getting out of his cab. Griffin turned back to Josh.

'We don't need to talk.'

Josh looked deep into her heavily-lashed eyes. His own were pleading.

'Please.'

The man was walking through the rain towards them. He looked mean and not a little pissed off. Josh let Griffin's wrist go and she rubbed at it with her other hand. It hurt.

'This fucker botherin' you?'

Josh stood up straight and wiped the dripping rain from his eyes. Griffin had turned away from the man, and was looking directly into Josh's face. He stared back and saw a number of things. Her eyes were soft, but they betrayed pleasure in the childish power she had over him at this moment. Behind that there was something he had grown accustomed to in the last two days. Fear. Not the fear the other driver might have expected a young girl to feel when a man twice her size grabbed her by the wrist in a wet rest area. But fear of something else. The man shouted this time.

'You hear me?'

Josh looked up at him. 'She hears you. What's your problem?'

The man put his hands on his hips, shook his head and let out a hollow laugh. 'Apart from your pervert ass cuttin' me up on that highway like you was on fire? Yeah? That sound like you? Well besides that, I got a real big problem with you jumpin' this lady here, that's what.'

Josh looked back into Griffin's eyes. She was wrestling with something Josh couldn't fathom and she masked the fear Josh had glimpsed as she turned slowly to the man and wiped the rain from her face with a wet sleeve.

'It's okay. I know him.'

The driver and Josh looked at each other through the slashing rain, until, shaking his head again, the man turned and walked back to his rumbling cab. As he stepped up onto the running board he pointed a finger at Josh.

'I got the time, the place, the date of this, you hear? There even a sniff of trouble I'm onto the state bears like you wouldn't believe, mister.'

Josh stared him out and both he and Griffin stood perfectly still, like animals waiting for a turn at a watering hole, watching the Mack crash some gears as it pulled back onto the highway.

He looked down at her.

'Want to dry off?'

She looked at her feet, and he could see she was breathing very fast, her chest rising and falling as though she had been running, and when she spoke she did so to the puddle they were standing in.

'Sure.'

He held out an arm in invitation and she walked in front of him to the truck like she was going to the electric chair.

25

'Yeah? If you don't like it then step on the gas, jerk-off.'

Eddie muttered into his beard as he watched the pick-up in his spot mirror peek out from behind the cloud of spray at his tail again. He was keeping King Kong at crawling pace in the righthand lane, and it was pissing off a lot of drivers. But he had no choice. If Josh had pulled over ahead, Eddie didn't want to pass him. He'd stayed about three miles behind for the last sixty, and now was no time for Josh to realize he was being tailed by a friend concerned for his sanity. But there had been nowhere to pull off the highway and maintain the gap. He'd listened to the CB and knew instantly that it had been Josh asking about the hitcher, and whether it turned out to be the loony tunes log-book-ripper or not, he also knew that Josh wouldn't pass up a chance to find out.

The difficulty was, he was gaining rapidly on the rest area that the thermos driver had described, and if Josh was still there it would be hard for him to miss Eddie's truck rolling by, even in this downpour.

He braked some more and received a horn blast from the pick-up. Eddie raised a hand, palm up to the sky. 'Aw, get to fuck, you pussy.'

He shook his head and sucked at a rogue hair that was curling into his mouth. He was no good at this spying shit. It made him nervous. Made him feel bad. In fact, Eddie Shanklin was feeling bad about the whole damn thing right now, and he didn't like it. He glanced in the mirror and saw the heavily loaded pick-up about to make its play to pass. As it started to draw level with King Kong's sleeper, Eddie smiled for the first time in an age.

'Aw, what the heck.'

He stepped on the gas.

They sat staring ahead through the windshield, as the whir of the cab heater at full blast competed with the engine and the beating rain. Griffin was the first to break the motionless tableau by lifting her arm and running a hand through the wet strands of her hair. Josh turned to her.

'Goin' home, huh?'

She looked out her passenger window, face turned from him. 'No.'

'No? Well south's that way. You just follow the sun.'

Although she wasn't watching, Josh made a gesture over his shoulder with his head. She turned to him and her eyes flashed momentarily with childish indignation.

'I got a bum ride, okay? I wanted to go west and this is where I ended up.'

Josh nodded and looked out front again. He cleared his throat.

Griffin shook her head and blew an exasperated whistle out of pursed lips. 'You guys been talking about me on the CB? That how you found me?'

'You surprised?'

'After the rides I've had nothing would surprise me about truckers. Jesus. Missing link? It's on the highways.'

'I wasn't lookin'. I just heard you were here.'

'And you raced that ape.'

'Yeah.'

Her voice was smaller now. 'Yeah? Well I guess I wouldn't have enjoyed his company much.'

He cleared his throat again. 'Griffin. I'm sorry about what happened. I didn't plan it.'

He could feel her eyes boring into him, and he turned to meet them as she answered in a voice of surprising tenderness. 'I'm not sorry. I enjoyed it.'

'You left kind of sudden.'

'It was tricky. I couldn't think of anything to say.'

Josh moistened his lips. 'So you left a callin' card instead?'

Griffin ran her hand through her hair again and narrowed her eyes quizzically, catching the hardening of his voice. 'What do you mean?'

He held her gaze. 'The creative knifework.'

She was studying his face for clues, and as her eyes searched and her mouth opened fractionally, Josh knew instantly she had no idea what he was talking about. He closed his eyes and let his head fall back against the seat. He covered his face with his hands and let out a groan of despair. A hand touched his arm gently.

'Hey.'

He shook his head beneath his fingers and she withdrew her hand. It took him a long time to compose himself and let his hands drop to his lap, but when he did, Griffin was looking at him with a mixture of confused concern and wariness. Josh blinked at her. Her returned gaze was unfaltering.

'What is this about?'

'You didn't touch my log book, did you?'

She shook her head slowly, her eyes still uncomprehending.

Josh's voice was low, almost resigned. 'No. I guess you didn't.'

Griffin shifted in her seat, stirring the smell of wet hair and warming damp cotton. She picked nervously at a fingernail. 'I'm not understanding this, Josh.'

'There's no reason you should. I don't understand it either.'

'Are you going to stop talking in riddles and tell me what I'm supposed to have done?'

Josh massaged his mouth and chin with a hand and looked out front again. 'I'm sorry. None of this has got anything to do with you. I guess I'm clutching at straws.'

'Can I hear about it?'

'You'll think I'm crazy.'

'I already think that.'

He looked at her and nearly smiled. Nearly, but not quite. 'Sure you want to?'

'Yeah.'

'I think somethin's followin' me.'

Griffin widened her eyes. 'Some "thing"? What do you mean?'

'I don't know. It's invisible.'

Griffin opened her mouth to match her eyes, but now her eyebrows were also raised and her face, started to register the first hint of mirth. 'Invisible?'

'That's right.'

'Then how exactly do you know this "thing" is there?'

'I can feel it. Sometimes I can see where it's been.'

This time, Griffin laughed out loud, a staccato bark of derision. She held up a slim hand. 'Whoa. Is this a joke?'

Josh shook his head once, and his expression reinforced the answer.

'It ripped my log book up and left a message.'

Griffin stared at him, and although the mocking smile was still curving her open lips, Josh saw something change in her eyes. Something like the reluctant beginning of fear.

'What message?'

'A scrawl. In my own handwriting.'

'Saying what?' She sounded impatient.

Josh swallowed. Her sudden interest was making him more uncomfortable than her contempt. He watched her face carefully as he spoke. 'It said I had three days alive permitted.'

The muscles around Griffin's eyes twitched almost imperceptibly and her smile faded. She looked away, rubbing at her nose in an amateurish attempt to conceal her feelings. Josh watched the side of her face as he continued.

'And I found this.'

He pulled his wallet out from under the wheel, unzipped the small ticket compartment, and teased out the strip of paper with a careful thumb and forefinger. Griffin turned her head slowly, first looking into his eyes and then letting her gaze drift down to what he held in his hand.

The violence of her reaction made Josh jump in his seat. She slammed herself against the passenger door with a throaty scream, her arms held in front of her face and her legs pushing uselessly at the cab floor as though their continued pressure would help her body dissolve through the door.

Josh gaped and clumsily held out his hands to her, his right one still clutching the paper.

Her eyes widened further with terror and she screamed at him, pointing at it. 'Jesus. Jesus. Jesus! Put it away. Get that fucking thing away!'

Josh patted the air gently, trying to reassure her, and slowly folded the strip and placed it back in the zipper compartment of his wallet. 'It's gone. Calm down. It's okay. See? It's okay.'

She was breathing heavily, still pressed up against the door, watching him with a wild look in her eye, as though she were cornered by some beast making ready to strike.

Josh held up his empty hands again. 'Griffin. It's okay.'

She brought an arm up and wiped at her nose with a wet sleeve. Her eyes moved from his face to his wallet and back again, and to Josh's relief they slowly started to lose the quality of hunted animal. She blinked at him, her voice shaky.

'Where did you get that?'

Josh tried to sound as calm as he could. She was still scared, and her bizarre reaction had unnerved him. 'I don't know. I found it in my wallet.'

Her eyes darted around the cab as though the answer would be floating in space, and then suddenly, catching sight of Josh's astonished face, she became aware for the first time of how she was behaving. He watched her body relax and she took her arm from her face and slumped back into the seat. She wiped her mouth and brow and stared at him.

'Shit.'

Josh stared back at her for a second and felt like laughing. Her performance had been astonishing. He'd shown her a piece of paper and she'd acted like he'd pulled out a rattlesnake. He waited until the colour started to bloom back in her cheeks, then he put a hand out towards her to touch her arm. She withdrew it as though he meant to burn her.

Josh recoiled in mirror response. 'What the fuck is this, Griffin?'

She held the arm he'd aimed for with her other hand, cradling it as though it had just escaped injury, and studied his face. She was thinking hard, and if she was trying to conceal the process then she needed more practice.

'I don't know.'

'Oh sure.'

'I mean I don't know . . . exactly.'

She squinted and gritted her teeth, mentally correcting herself, trying hard to verbalize the thoughts that were so nakedly computing behind her eyes.

'I mean . . . shit. This is my turn to seem crazy.'

Josh's voice was gentle. 'Thank fuck for that. It was gettin' lonely.'

She looked at him with a seriousness that he knew was a reprimand for the lightness of his tone, then bit at her lip before speaking. 'I think you're in big trouble, Josh.'

'Because I've got a bit of paper in my wallet?'

'Because you took it willingly yet unknowingly.'

'Want to start talking English?'

She was thinking hard again, eyes unfocused on the rivulets of rain on the windshield. 'I don't know if it would do any good.'

Josh sighed and bent his head. 'Oh, man. I'm going out of my mind here.'

Griffin continued to stare at the streaming wet glass and after an acre of silence spoke almost in a whisper.

'That might be for the best.'

Josh looked up slowly, and as he turned to face Griffin he watched a tear roll down her cheek and slide beneath her jawbone. 'What?'

She swallowed and brought her hand up to cover her mouth, as though the words had escaped. Griffin shook her head and her eyes continued to brim.

Josh Spiller felt the blood draining from his head. Three days ago he might have nudged her in the ribs and laughed. But three days ago was another lifetime. He became aware of his hands feeling light and starting to tremble, and he clasped them together like a priest as he composed himself to speak. It gave him the physical demeanour of a man taking confession, and his voice took its cue from his body, acting as sombre frontman for the chaos of panic that raged in his heart.

'Even if you're as crazy as I am, I need to know what you know.'

Griffin sobbed behind her hand. 'Jesus Christ. I don't want anything to do with this. Don't you understand? I left to get away from all this.'

Josh took a shallow breath. 'Left Furnace?'

She nodded violently, eyes screwed shut against her tears.

'This piece of paper has to do with Furnace?'

Her reply was swallowed. 'It's more than a piece of paper.'

'Yeah. You kinda hinted at that.'

Turning to him, she wiped her face with a sleeve, then stared deep into Josh's eyes, looking from one to the other, and for the first time her body was angled towards him as she sat rigidly forward in her seat.

She stayed like that for nearly half a minute, chewing at her lip, as Josh watched some secret decision being debated behind her green irises. He waited like a condemned man for her to announce the result.

'Josh.'

He said nothing and she hesitated. Her words when they came were no longer tearful, but confident and unhurried.

'Someone has passed you the runes.'

'The runes.'

Josh's tone qualified the sentence rather than questioned it, but the edge in his voice was fear, not sarcasm.

'It's a parchment. The marks are runic symbols. It . . .' She faltered again, but only momentarily.

'It calls something.'

'What do you mean, calls?'

'When you took it, something started to come . . . from somewhere else. It grows. Well not really. Shit. How to say this? It gets here, gets to the last carrier of the parchment, when the time is up on the runes.'

Josh kept his gaze fixed firmly on hers, and in those earnest eyes he could see no trace of deception or mockery. If this was insanity, then they were insane together.

'What's comin', Griffin?' he croaked.

She broke his gaze to look at her lap and think, then as quickly met it again. 'Have you felt either very cold or very hot in the last two days? Like at strange times.'

He thought about the trailer at the weigh-station. The gust of air in the motel corridor.

'Hot. Sick and hot.'

She lowered her eyes. 'Shit, Josh. You must have pissed them off bad.'

'Stop talkin' to me like a child.'

Griffin looked him in the eye and there was a hardness there. Whether it was indignation at the bark of his rebuke, or merely a defence to what she was about to say, Josh couldn't divine. He noted it and it chilled him. But not as much as her words.

'It's a hot elemental.'

'Talk sense.'

His irritation didn't sound convincing and it did nothing to soften her voice.

'Okay. If you want to use the language of Dark Age ignorance. It's a fire demon.'

He pause a second, mouth open, then let out a snort. Inside, some part of him was screaming. But the part he liked to think of as Josh Spiller, trucker, was seeing himself in this damp cab, listening to some kid talking a heap of bullshit big enough to bury Jezebel.

It was plainly ridiculous, and with an effort he tried to pull himself back to the land of reality: the place where fear was a jack-knife in the fast lane, where mystery was how you fitted the fax roll, and where nightmares were dreams that truck stops started charging to crap in the john. He turned from her and rubbed at his chin as he stared out front.

'Yeah? That so? Well you know I figured it was something like that. Soon as I found that paper I thought, this is either a fancy receipt for them jockey shorts I bought in a factory outlet, or else it's a parchment calling up a fire demon. Shoot. Never can tell one from the other.'

'Have you seen it yet?'

It was as though he hadn't spoken.

Josh closed his eyes and gave in. He shook his head, and then, hesitating, made an uncertain shrug.

'But you've felt it?'

A nod.

'Listen to me, Josh. Did anyone give you anything in Furnace? Anything at all?'

He swallowed and wiped his mouth, eyes still closed.

'Try to think.'

He screwed up his face, doing as he was told. 'No. Yes. Well bits of stuff. Nothing really.'

'What stuff? Come on, Josh.'

He opened his eyes and looked at her, his face a maze of emotion. 'What does it matter, for Christ's sake?'

'Because you have one day left. Don't you understand? You can still pass them back if you can find out who passed them to you.' Griffin's voice was shrill, excited and exasperated. She watched him sinking deeper and then sighed. 'No. Of course you don't understand. I'm not making much sense, am I?'

He wished she was making less sense, but didn't say so. Griffin sat further forward, as though she could advance his understanding by proximity.

'I'm going to explain what I know and I want you to listen real careful. Even if you think I'm a screwball I want to know you listened. That's important to me right now. You hear?'

Josh nodded dumbly, incredulous that the tables should be turned in forty-eight hours, in which this novice pupil of life had suddenly become his teacher.

'Whatever happened to you in Furnace, and believe me I don't want to know any more than I do, is something they don't want anybody else hearing about.'

Josh held up a weak hand. 'Who's "they"?'

It was Griffin's turn to snort. 'Whoever you goddamn met. Whoever you spoke to, bought from, touched, passed in the street.'

'I see.'

'No, you don't. Just listen.'

He winced.

'Somehow they passed the runes. They could have been in anything. A parking ticket, a rolled up newspaper, a book, anything. You have to get back there before your time is up, find out who gave them to you and give them back. But this is important.'

She made upturned claws of her hands to stress the point.

'You have to give them back the same way. Understand? They have to take them willingly and unknowingly.'

Her face was a picture of intensity. She held that expression of pleading instruction as Josh tried to assimilate the bizarre information, at the same time as a bubble of hysterical laughter threatened to erupt from his throat.

'I nearly lost them.'

That hardness again in her face. 'But you didn't.'

'No.'

'Lucky. Whoever cast them must have rushed it. They don't usually survive to give you the chance to return them.'

'What would happen if they'd gone?'

Griffin relaxed her body and slumped a little. 'Then you'd have had two choices.' Her eyes started to well again. 'I'd take the first,' she whispered.

'Which is?'

'Suicide.'

Josh tried to sound amused. 'Nice choice. And the other one?'

She looked at him and let a bulbous tear spill through her lashes. 'Wait. And greet your guest.'

They looked at each other for a moment, then his laughter won. He held the side of his head and guffawed, tears of his own forming as his stomach muscles contracted with the spasm. 'Aw shit. This is fuckin' rich. What are we talking about here?'

'A death horrible beyond imagining.'

Josh stopped laughing abruptly and looked at Griffin with anger. His voice was calm and quiet. 'Who the fuck are you?'

'Someone who should have taken a different ride out of McNab County.'

She looked at him with eyes that pleaded before they shifted to her feet, as she added, 'A long time ago.'

The passion of her regret cut the anger from Josh. He put out a hand to her arm but was once again rejected.

'Griffin. What the hell's goin' on in Furnace?'

Her feet remained her fascination. 'I don't know it all. What I know is bad enough.'

'Are you trying to tell me it's like some crummy *Twilight Zone* thing? Like the mayor dances around with the librarian, naked except for antlers and a satin cape?'

She flushed him a warning glare. 'Don't be stupid.'

'Then you'll forgive me if I choose to dismiss this as hog piss.'

As if to etch in action what his words had implied, Josh switched on the wipers and let the blades sweep an arc in the opaque mat of water.

'The baby. The one you killed. Was it an accident?'

Josh's mouth dried. 'Yes.'

'But you got sympathy when you called home. Right?'

Josh's cheeks were blanching. He turned slowly to her and saw the gleam of righteous anger in her face. 'I couldn't reach anyone.'

'Because the phones were out, huh?'

'That's right.'

'And somehow people who used to like you don't want to be around you much?'

He was light-headed now as his blood went somewhere other than his face. 'Griffin.'

'You see, Josh? The runes. They come with some pretty standard witchcraft. You get isolated. You can't contact anyone. Tricks make you think you're going mad. They want you to take that easy way out. It's tidier. A lot less mess. Easier to explain than what's left behind the other way. And the best way to help you in that task is to isolate you. Make you crazy.'

He put his hands out on the wheel and spoke quietly to its centre. 'What can I do?'

Her voice was adult and serious. Someone in charge solving a problem.

'How far are we from Furnace?'

''Bout five hours.'

'And when did you find the message in the log book?'

'The mornin' after . . . you know . . . when you left.'

Griffin bit her lip again. 'Then you've got until sunrise.'

He looked at her again, aware his heart was beating in his ears. 'How do you know so much if you're not part of all this?'

She shaped a bitter smile that contained neither warmth nor humour. 'I know how they play football but I've never been a quarterback.'

'And what kind of game they playin' in Furnace?'

She replied in a small and lost voice. 'I don't know, Josh. I just know I don't want to find out and end up being destroyed by it. Please don't ask me.'

The wiper blades, on intermittent, swept across the windshield and squealed. The rain had stopped as suddenly as it had started and already the late afternoon sun was pushing from behind the clouds, like an understudy actor eager to steal the stage. Josh turned off the wipers and touched his open palms against the sides of the steering wheel, as though measuring a variety of imaginary fish.

There was no longer any point in questioning this. What Griffin had told him was insane, but in a world that had turned demented for Josh since his eyes had first connected with the woman in Furnace, Griffin's bizarre instructions seemed almost logical. How else could she know the tortuous details of the last few days?

He became aware of the silence between them now that the rain had ceased. The heater still blew and the engine grumbled, but over it all Josh could hear Griffin breathing.

'How will I know who gave me the runes?'

'You won't. You have to remember which people gave you what and work it out.'

'And if I get it wrong? Say I pass them back to someone who didn't give them to me?'

'Then it'll be like you lost them. The runic device stays with you.'

He stared at her, and she read his need to have that qualified.

'You'll be fucked, Josh.'

His expression told her he believed that part already. She softened her eyes, if not her voice. 'It's not going to be easy. You can't let the rune-caster know what you're doing. Do you understand? Whoever cast them won't let you within a mile of them.'

'Then what's the point?'

'The point is it's your only hope. Even if it's a slim one.'

Josh started to shake his head. He groped for mental balance. This was all wrong. He was going home. Home to Elizabeth and the very real problem of their baby, not back to that smug mountain town where he was sure of nothing. Not even sure what had happened there.

'Christ, they'll think I'm crazy if I go back and walk around trying to sneak a concealed strip of paper into strangers' hands.'

Griffin looked down. 'Oh no. They won't think you're crazy at all.'

She paused before her next words.

'They'll just wonder how you knew.'

He licked his lower lip. For the first time since they had started this lunatic conversation, Josh realized this involved her too. He looked at her and saw what he had first seen in the restaurant. A young girl, a cocktail of arrogance and innocence, rebellion and a desperation to conform; a beauty that she was both aware of and indifferent to.

But all those contradictions were common in adolescents. What was uncommon about Griffin was that in under ten minutes she'd convinced a thirty-two-year-old truck driver who'd seen just about everything life could spit up, that there was another world he hadn't even guessed existed. And it was a dark world that, through no fault or design of her own other than a geographical accident of birth, she seemed to know intimately. He realized he cared.

'What'll happen to you if they work it out?'

'I'll be long gone.'

'And distance works?'

'In my case, yes.'

'But your family . . .'

'Believe me. They'll be fine.'

He put a fist to his forehead. 'Then help me, Griffin. I'm dyin', for Christ's sake. Gimme a fuckin' lead here.'

She sat awkwardly for a moment, touched by his terror, then pulled her knees up to her chest. Then she spoke softly from behind her barrier of limbs.

'Do you want me to come with you?'

He tried to read her and failed. The answer was yes, but his heart spoke for him. 'No. Shit no. Just tell me where to start lookin'.'

She bent her head and buried her face in her knees, and when she emerged her eyes were puffy with tears. 'I don't know, Josh. I wish I did. Just retrace your steps. Every one of them.'

She sniffed, straightened up and reached for the door-handle. Outside the truck on the wet asphalt, her pack sat dripping where she'd left it. Griffin looked at it through the window, then turned to Josh, tears filling her eyes. She blinked and let them take their uneven course over her high, sculpted cheeks.

'If you can't find that person, if you can't give them back . . .' She hesitated, looking down before she met his gaze again. '. . . promise me you'll keep the first option in mind.'

Josh said nothing, but as he watched her face his heart stood still, for he saw in her eyes the pity for a dead man.

'Sure. Good tip.'

Griffin closed her eyes in exasperation, took a deep breath and got out. She walked round the front of the truck and rejoined her forlorn rain-darkened backpack. Josh wound down his window.

'You be okay?'

She nodded. 'I'm heading west.'

He let his eyes roam over her once more, then pushed the truck into first.

'Josh!'

He braked and looked back down at her.

'The runes.'

He waited while she fidgeted for the rest of her sentence.

'They're not written on paper.'

Josh looked at her until she turned from him and walked back down through the puddles of the rest area. He watched her go in the mirror, then signalled and pulled back out onto the highway, his hands automatically and unthinkingly priming the comfort of his cab, turning up the CB and turning down the heater.

'Yesssir! Northbounds! Just passed what looked like a chickadee sniffin' for cock in that rest area north of 176. Hurry hurry while stocks last.'

The guy in Radio Shack who sold Josh the twin Blaupunkt CB speakers didn't do them justice. Even he couldn't have predicted the miracle, that one of them would withstand a punch from a fist that had the force of primal fury behind it.

26

As he walked, Sheriff Pace listened to his shoes squeaking on the shiny linoleum floor of the corridor. Apart from the muffled buzz of machines in side rooms, a telephone warbling behind a desk and the occasional cough from a distant bed, it was the loudest sound in the clinic. Deputy Caroline Spencer had done the deed and Alice Nevin was still under sedation after the visit. He wondered if what she'd been told had even got through the mince they'd made of her brain with those drugs, but something behind her big dilated pupils when she'd looked up at him from the pillow suggested that it had.

Now she was more than just one child short. She was one man down.

John Pace hadn't liked Bobby Hendry. He was a whole lot of trouble when he drank and the memory Pace had of him would always be of his wide, crumpled face waking up on a bench in the cells after a binge.

But he'd been a good enough man, and he'd almost been a good father. Then again, 'almost' wasn't enough to save your child. Not in Furnace.

He thought about that for a moment. What if things had been different? If he'd had daughters instead of two strong sons? Would *he* have been that good a father? Would he have been any more able than Hendry to do the thing that would keep them safe?

The metronomic squeaking of his shoes was interrupted by an arrhythmic clicking, and he raised his eyes to the two shiny black patent woman's shoes coming towards him.

'John. How is she?'

Pace straightened up, took off the hat he'd replaced on his head after leaving Alice Nevin's room and held it in front of his chest. 'Not so good, councillor. They got her on pills for her nerves.'

Nelly McFarlane tutted and looked past John Pace to the distant open door of the patient's room. She lowered her voice to a conspiratorial stage whisper. 'I'm no doctor, sheriff, but it seems to me people ought to have the proper time to grieve. Suffering is what makes us strong. Don't you agree?'

Pace looked at the woman's neatly made-up face, creased with concern and lit with a motherly warmth that illuminated her eyes. He nodded. 'I guess. Maybe everyone got a different way of grievin.'

The woman smoothed her skirt with an elegant hand and turned back to him as though he hadn't replied. 'And you? How are you and your staff dealing with this tragedy?'

'We seen worse, Nelly. You know that.'

She looked into his eyes, searching for something, and if she found it, nothing of its discovery registered in her own face. 'Yes. I know that, John. I never envy the job of a policeman.'

He shrugged politely and she smiled at him with affection. 'I hope everyone in this town realizes how lucky we are to have men like you at the helm of our little ship.'

Pace shifted his weight onto another leg and looked down at his hat. 'I do my job. Ain't no call for applause.'

'Sure there is. You leave it to us folks to tell you when you're doing swell. There's been a Sheriff Pace here now for nearly a hundred years, and not one of your family has ever let us down. Your Daddy was a fine man, and so was his Daddy before him. And I'll bet either little Noah or Ethan is going to make us proud one day.'

Pace looked back up at her a little too quickly. She raised an eyebrow at his expression and put a hand out like a mime artist touching an invisible wall. 'That is, assuming they want to follow you into the law enforcement profession.'

Pace coughed into a fist. 'Well I won't influence them unduly either way, Nelly. I guess we'll just let them be what they want to be.'

'Of course. After all, you've always done what you wanted. Haven't you?'

Her eyes were half moons, crinkling as they smiled at him, and try as he might, John Pace couldn't stop his narrowing in response.

'Sure.'

Her smile broadened. 'That's all the Lord asks, John. Contentment with our lot.'

They looked at each other for a second, until Nelly McFarlane lifted a finger and pointed up the corridor. 'Is it appropriate for me to visit, do you think?'

Pace pulled at his mouth. 'I reckon. She might not know you.'

'Well maybe if I sit with her a while, she'll remember.'

He nodded, replaced his hat and walked away. After six steps he realized that the squeaking of his shoes was once more the only sound. John Pace didn't need to look round to know that Councillor McFarlane was standing still in the same spot he'd left her. Nor did he need to turn round to know which way she was looking.

If there had been enough of a gap between the cars the endless line of red tail-lights would have reflected on the wet road like a carnival. But there wasn't an inch between bumpers. The traffic was solid, petrified by the simple need to funnel two lanes into one. As he stared into the night, viewing the endless frozen river of metal in front of him, Josh sat so far forward in his seat that his right knee nearly touched the dash.

The CB was going crazy, a cacophony of voices butting in and out.

'Man, oh man, northbounds. Best settle down and start yourselves a family in that there line, 'cos the kids goin' to be old enough to go to college by the time you reach Harrisonburg.'

'Yeah. Real helpful, southbound. How 'bout a location when this shit ends?'

'Hey, come on, covered wagon. Let me get my goddamn nose in there, would ya?'

'Bears up the inside in case you guys gonna try and side-step this.'

'Well, northbound, reckon you got about two miles of Schneider eggs an' caterpillars 'fore you even see the road agin.'

'Peterbilt? You want in this outside lane here I'm ready to hold back these four-wheelers for ya? Come on.'

Josh scanned the lane ahead to see who was offering him an escape from the static line of cars. The traffic on the left was crawling, but at least it was moving. He looked along the conveyor belt of assorted vehicles until he saw a shiny tanker about ten cars ahead, stopped with a gap in front. He thumbed his radio.

''Preciate it, thermos. My lane ain't shiftin' none though.'

'Hey, you guys think you own the fuckin' road?'

'Shut the fuck up, you four-wheelin' scum. Man, who sells these jerk-offs their radios?'

'Eh, Jezebel? Don't worry none 'bout that. Your lane's gettin' ready to move. You want me to sit here and wait?'

Josh pressed talk again like he was detonating a grenade.

'Yeah. Yeah. Real nice of you. I'm right there, buddy.'

'Ten-four, Peterbilt.'

Sunrise. That's what she said. Three hours had disappeared driving north in a fearful trance and one had gone just sitting in this line of traffic. Josh took a couple of deep breaths to stop from screaming and gripped the wheel.

His invisible companion.

It was watching him. He could feel it. Only half an hour after leaving Griffin he'd started to question the whole damned thing. It had been the normality of it all. With the light fading and the rush-hour traffic building up just like it always did everything had seemed so comforting and familiar. Josh Spiller had found it difficult to keep hold of Griffin's words. He was sick, he'd decided. He'd see a doctor when he got home. Maybe a shrink.

That sheriff. He'd said it straight, remember? Shock can play tricks on you. Yes, it surely can. He'd almost made himself believe that again, and then, hours later, as he pulled out to pass a dump-truck, he felt it.

Those eyes locking onto him. And he knew it was real.

Did it have eyes? Could it see? The sweat had started to bead on his forehead as soon as he felt that prickling between his shoulderblades. Josh had pulled back into the slow lane and looked slowly around the darkened interior of his cab, more afraid than he'd ever been in his life that his eyes would settle on something that justified his alarm. But there had been nothing. At least nothing to see.

He could feel the air in the cab growing warmer but blocked out the information he now held about the cause, choosing instead merely to treat the symptom by opening the window.

It was harder to deny the fact that he could sense a malignant gaze.

He believed Griffin. He believed her against his will and his reason, and he was heading back to Furnace to try and save himself from a horror he neither understood nor fully accepted.

But now there was a new problem. The traffic.

Sunrise. He tried not to let hot panic stop his breath, tried to use the time wasting away to do what Griffin told him and retrace his steps.

As his lane started to inch forward Josh thought about the sheriff's office. Had they given him anything? Sure they had. A copy of the statement. A ticket. A form to say he'd got all his belongings back. The belongings themselves, including his wallet. He ticked them off mentally, trying to recall the moments when they were handed to him and by whom, as his gaze drifted to his right, and the twinkling lights of distant farmhouses and cabins on the darkened rise of the foothills. The car in front moved forward a few feet and Jezebel nosed after it almost as though Josh were a passenger. At the edge of the left lane tall halogen lights illuminated the roadworks, bathing the near-static vehicles in a cruel light. In its harsh beams the tanker stood still only a few car-lengths away, reflecting back the slow-moving lane of cars from its ovoid steel drum as it waited for Josh to catch up and pull over in front.

Although he'd done the same thing dozens of times for other drivers, tonight Josh's gratitude for the courtesy was immeasurable. Time had never been so important. He wiped the sweat from his upper lip as the truck crawled forward, turning the CB down a notch against the abusive protests from some four-wheeler stuck behind the stationary tanker.

The heat in the cab was more than noticeable now. It was becoming uncomfortable. Josh wound his window the full way down and propped an elbow on the sill, but the cool early spring evening air he anticipated was a disappointing reek of diesel and carbon monoxide.

He coughed and inched the truck forward a few more feet. The tanker driver was faint on the CB now that he'd turned down the volume, but Josh still registered he was being spoken to.

'Keep her comin', driver.'

He turned the volume back up and replied, 'Surely will.'

Jezebel's nose was coming level with the tail of the tanker and Josh made ready to pull in front. The long cylinder of burnished stainless steel danced with light from the stream of headlamps and tail-lights, and Josh turned his head to look at the curious elongated reflection of Jezebel that would join them as he passed it. Even though a brief vain glance at his own image had proved disastrous in Furnace, it was impossible not to look at the truck in the moving mirror that was a tanker. On a sunny day it made the rig impossibly glamorous as it passed; blue sky and stretched clouds forming a backdrop to the flattened strip of its image. But at night, as now, it was even better. Every orange light on Jezebel's nose would be stretched to a coloured rope, sandwiched between the gleaming bulk of the truck's silhouette like side-show lamps reflected in the crazy mirrors of a funfair.

Josh wiped more sweat from his forehead and let his arm dangle out the window as he looked.

As always, you had to figure out which bits of the truck you were seeing. It was a visual puzzle until you had it, and then it was easy.

This time it took Josh a little longer. His cab was already half way along the tanker's side and he still blinked at his own reflection, unable to decipher its complexities. The electric blue of Jezebel's paint work was illuminated by the halogen lamps which painted a long familiar dash of colour in the polished steel. But something about the shape wasn't making sense. He narrowed his eyes, trying to work out what he was seeing. There were the lights at the front, and there was the exhaust pipe, shiny and squat.

But there was something else. It was indistinct at first. No more than an irregular dark shape on the roof of the trailer. But as Jezebel progressed along the side of the tanker, Josh blinked at the dark hump as it slid into view, and his pulse began to beat in his neck. Whatever it was, it was moving. It was impossible to define its nature from the stretched reflection, but its glistening undulations and steady progress along the top of the truck made Josh's soul freeze. Like the reflection of the truck itself, the thing moving swiftly and fluidly over its top was stretched into a ribbon of black.

It was only when the CB barked that Josh realized his foot had left the gas pedal and Jezebel was coming to a standstill alongside the tanker.

'What ya doin' there, big truck? Get on up here. Them four-wheelers are bitin' my ass to get in.'

Josh had no voice to reply. He stared at the image in the curve of the thermos, watching as the reflection of the glistening form loped along the trailer and, with one supine movement, jumped onto the roof of the cab. Heat had already dried his mouth, and now fear was stalling his breath.

His widened eyes swung to the velour-padded ceiling of the cab. The heavy thump above him that had ripped his gaze from the reflected horror was now accompanied by an excruciating scratching and scraping of metal. Josh knew a scream was being born at the back of his throat, but as his eyes slowly followed the grating noise along the roof and down onto the edge of the windshield, the next sound aborted the cry by removing what breath he had left, making him slap his hands over his face to block it out.

Wheeah. Wheeeea.

Not possible. The Tanner ice cream sign, that forlorn, squealing messenger of his inadequacy, was a million years away from this. It lived in another lifetime, in his dreams. Not here, in this waking nightmare on a packed interstate.

Even through the red-black of his screwed-shut lids, he could see those Tanner children and their painted faces. Their tongues, licking in and out. Sharp, blood-red, pointy tongues, darting between rows of white teeth, that even as he struggled to banish the image, were becoming as pointed as those little wet triangles of flesh.

Josh pressed his palms into his face and groaned.

'No. Jesus. No.'

But the sound persisted, screaming above the raised voices of channel 19, above the noise of Jezebel's idling engine, above the muffled reverberation of the static traffic. *Wheeea. Wheeeaaa. Wheeeeaaa.*

He let his hands fall from his face and opened his eyes. Moving across the glass at the top of his windshield were two long, curved objects. It was the way they were scraping against the transparent barrier between them and Josh that was producing the heart-stopping noise. Josh's mouth moved silently as he tried to make sense of what he was seeing. Each object was around four inches long, the thickness of a palm frond, smoking slightly as though about to combust and ending in a curved point that narrowed to a razor edge. They moved slowly against the windshield, the bony fingers to which they were attached showing long strands of matted, coarse hair, the cartilage shining black and horny in the halogen light, and they left a sticky trail on the glass as they scraped. As he watched in terror, another started to appear from the opposite top corner of the windshield.

Josh knew what they were. Yes, he did. He could read a road sign. He could recognize a friend in the street. He could tell a ship on the horizon from an island. Why should he choose now to deny what his eyes told him? They were talons scraping against the glass. Long, scabbed, diseased talons, searching for a hold on the roof of his cab.

His head took control of his paralysed body, and before he could cry out, Josh let out the clutch and slammed his foot on the gas.

The rig leapt forward as though it had been hit from behind, and the claws scrabbled wildly for an instant before disappearing back over the roof. Josh threw Jezebel into first, punishing the engine with revs that pushed the needle into the red. The rig roared ahead, and as he steered for the clear patch in front of the tanker Josh cast one quick glance at the reflection as he passed. It had been thrown backwards, but only a little. As the truck built speed it was already lowering its massive body against the trailer roof and trying to move forward again. Josh swung the truck into the outside lane, then swung it again, crashing through the line of traffic barrels into the closed works lane. He straightened her up and stamped on the gas like he was trying to kill a bug.

'Jesus fuckin' H. Christ. What you doin', Peterbilt?'

The tanker driver was yelling over the radio. He was joined by a Greek chorus.

'Man, are you fuckin' crazy?'

'All trucks. There's a lunatic screamin' up the closed lane. Repeat. He's comin' up fast.'

'Sheeit! Would ya look at that?'

'Whoa! That's fuckin' cool.'

Josh was breathing fast through a wide open mouth. Over the roar of Jezebel's tortured engine he could just make out the noise of claws on metal, and a whimpering sound escaped from the back of his throat as he pressed his leg harder to the floor.

In front of him the pool of halogen light ended, and the way ahead was a strip of darkness, bound on the righthand side by two lines of slowly-moving red tail-lights. He was already doing forty, and he had no intention of touching the brake. The speedometer rose steadily, and Josh held his breath as he gripped the wheel with white fists.

In amongst the cars forming the two solid lines ahead, trucks were starting to sound their horns.

Josh's head was reeling. He had acted on instinct and now his head was catching up. Surely this audience knew what he was doing? They must have seen it plainer than he had. Must still be able to see it. The nightmare had materialized and was clinging to his roof. Not in some dark alley or shadowy forest. But here, in front of hundreds of witnesses, able to watch him try to escape something unspeakable, from the warmth of their vehicles like some drive-in movie. Why were people not running screaming from their cars, pulling off the road or driving for their lives up this closed lane like him? Surely anyone catching a glimpse of what he carried on his roof would not only forfeit sleep for a very long time, but risk everything as he was doing just to be free of the sight of it.

But if that were so, his fellow truckers, at least, were paying more attention to Josh's eccentric driving than to his dark stowaway.

'Yeeha! Go for it, big truck.'

'Man, hope your rig's got wings, fella. 'Cos unless you take off pretty soon you're gonna meet some hard-hat hardware square on.'

Almost as soon as Josh heard it, Jezebel's lights picked out the bucket of a digger lying at an angle across the lane ahead. The right lane was still solid with traffic, but he judged there was a gap of around twelve feet between the digger and the row of traffic barrels confining the line of cars. To brake now would mean jack-knifing for sure, if not turning turtle over the cars on his right. There was no choice. He would have to keep his speed and try to squeeze through the gap.

Harvey Walker, the driver of the Saturn that was inching its way forward to draw level with the abandoned digger, did not have the benefit of CB radio. He and his family were listening to a taped version of *Aladdin* for the eighth time in a row, and although it was still keeping the two-year-old passenger quiet, it had worn the driver's nerves down to a thread.

'The lamp! Give me the lamp, you fool.'

Harvey sighed and drummed the wheel. 'Yeah. Give Jafar the goddamn lamp and we can cut the shit down by fifteen minutes.'

His wife shot him a look. 'Hey. Enough.'

He held his hands up in surrender without looking at her, as a satisfied chuckle in the back reminded him why they were listening to this garbage. Harvey rolled the window down and stuck an arm out into the cooler night air.

'Mind Elroy's not in a draught.'

He looked at his wife this time. 'You think I can make a draught happen in a car that's doing no miles per hour?'

'Well I can feel one.'

Harvey rolled his eyes and looked forward, then paused. 'Hey. Listen to those guys.'

The droning of truck-horns drifted in, mercifully drowning out Aladdin's eighth discourse with the genie.

His wife wrinkled a nose. 'I guess truckers think it's beneath them to wait in line like everybody else. Though what good hooting is going to do, I don't know.'

Harvey was about to reply in defence of truckers, just for the spice of an argument, when his wing mirror filled with light.

In the four seconds he had to do anything, Harvey did two things. The first was to pull his arm in the window, and the second was to yell his son's name. But as Jezebel ploughed along the side of the car at fifty miles an hour, slicing off the wing mirror with the bumper, then ripping both doors from the chassis with the tarp hooks on the trailer, his wife burst a blood vessel in her throat with her scream.

There was a silence then, as the car left spinning in the truck's wake came to rest with a bump against the central grass verge.

In the few seconds of silence that followed the accident, Harvey Walker felt the cold air around him and knew he was alive. He held his breath and in those few moments he heard the sweetest sounds of his life. Elroy Walker said, 'Daddy?' and Mavis Walker started to sob.

Harvey blinked out of the empty space that used to be a door and watched as the tail-lights of the truck careered off a closed exit ramp and disappeared behind a cover of trees.

From the speaker hanging by a wire from the dash, Princess Jasmine spoke to him in a breathy voice.

'Oh Aladdin. Is it really you? I thought you were dead.'

Harvey cupped his hand over his mouth and started to laugh.

27

'What's the longest he's ever gone without calling?'

Nesta's face was a study in adult calm, quickly ruined by the beer she'd just opened frothing over the top and spilling over her hand. Elizabeth passed her a magazine to catch the foam.

'In all these years? Two nights.'

Nesta slurped at the top of the bottle to stop the flow of rogue beer.

'No shit? He calls every night?'

'Pretty much.'

'It must have been some row.'

Elizabeth looked at the wall. 'I wanted to hurt him, Nesta. Guess I did a good job.'

Nesta sat back in the low sofa and sighed. Only an hour ago she'd wrestled with whether it would be intrusive to drop by and check on her friend and partner, but now she was glad she had. Seemed that Sim downstairs had lost a few more brain cells, and a loco lodger was the last thing Elizabeth needed right now. What she needed was that special someone they both knew. The someone who'd forgotten how a phone worked.

'That's the bit I don't get. Why did you want to hurt a guy like Josh? They ain't makin' them like that any more.'

Elizabeth looked back at her friend and smiled without warmth. 'Because I could.'

'Oh well, that explains everything.'

Nesta took a contemptuous swig of beer and Elizabeth looked at the floor.

'What I mean is, I was so hurt myself. Hurt that he was just going about his business, getting on with his life, taking me for granted. I couldn't believe it when I found I was pregnant, and I was so angry he wasn't here to talk to about it. To share the problem.'

'But honey, he wasn't AWOL. He's long-haul. He's never here.'

'I know. I was way off beam.' Her cheeks reddened. 'Way off,' she repeated softly.

Nesta softened her voice. 'How you feeling? You know . . .'

'Weird. Want to know something?'

'I want to know everything.'

Elizabeth smiled again, this time at her lap. A sad smile, but not a bitter one. 'I'm fourteen weeks gone.'

Nesta opened her mouth in theatrical surprise.

'What?'

Elizabeth looked up, and Nesta thought something like joy was fighting for space behind her eyes.

'I know. I had no idea it was so advanced. I just found out with the scan.'

'But are you showing?'

'Sort of. It's hard to tell.'

'Like you never weigh yourself?'

Elizabeth looked away dreamily, ignoring the question. 'The strangest thing is, and I know it's impossible, but I can sometimes almost feel it moving.'

'You're right. That's not possible. It's the size of a jelly bean.'

'Well maybe I dream it. I don't know. The feeling's so strong sometimes.'

Nesta softened her gaze and her voice. 'You've done it, haven't you?'

Elizabeth looked at her. 'Done what?'

'Cancelled the appointment.'

Elizabeth nodded, and this time there were tears in her eyes. Nesta sat forward and put a hand out to her arm.

'Good.'

'He was right, Nesta. We can work it out. All I need to do is talk to him. Tell him it's going to be okay.'

Nesta sat back again as if everything had been sorted with that admission. 'So if he's not calling 'cos he's mad at you, then I guess it's up to you. How we goin' to get in touch with him then?'

Elizabeth rubbed at her wrist. 'I guess we could call his dispatcher.'

'So let's call.'

The phone trilled from the hall as though roused by the suggestion, and Elizabeth looked to Nesta in panic.

Nesta held out her arms and shrugged. 'Answer it, for Christ's sake.'

As she walked to the hall Elizabeth realized that Sim's madness had affected her. She was already planning how she would think her love down the line to Josh if he couldn't hear her. She would think at him so hard, no beat-up mobile line in the world could fail to carry her message of remorse and her ache for him. Nesta slid into view at the door and watched as Elizabeth picked up the handset.

'Hello?'

Elizabeth closed her eyes and bit her lip. Nesta's hand went to her neck.

'No, Rudy. That's okay. Sure I'll tape it for you.'

Nesta shook her head and went back to her beer.

Had he done it again? Had he killed? Josh was shaking, his jaw trembling as though he were suffering extreme cold, though his face was slick with sweat. He'd brought the truck to a stop about two miles along the country road that led from the interstate exit, and he sat now in terror, not knowing if his fear was for what he might have done to the occupants of the car, or because every nerve in his body was waiting for the sound of claws on metal. Far away beyond the trees, the immobile line of red and white lights of the interstate glittered between the branches as though they were party lanterns hung for a home-coming. It was only a matter of time before they would be joined by flashing blue and red lights, and then the bears would come after him.

Jezebel's headlights made a fan of white in the tunnel of black wood ahead, and Josh stared into it as though a play were about to begin. They were still talking about him on the radio. There was a lot of shouting and cursing, but the mood was almost jubilant. The consensus seemed to be that someone had gone apeshit with the traffic line and broken loose. Some truckers thought that was cool, others thought it was a case for the electric chair. But that was it. No one was screaming about the unholy thing on his trailer. No one was trying to call the national guard or praying for deliverance to their God over the airwaves.

Josh knew then, with a sickness that invaded him to the core, that its appearance had been a private view. The air in the cab was considerably cooler and he let his eyes leave the road ahead and swivel up to the innocent velour padding of the interior roof. He could hear nothing except the reassuring rumble of the engine. It was gone. For now.

The voices on the radio were talking about the car he'd hit. He looked forward again and fumbled for the volume.

'Jeez, did those guys ever have a lucky one walkin' away an' all.'

'Ten-four to that. You see the doors, man? Clean off. An' that little kid, lookin' like he won a prize, 'nstead of nearly havin' his head pulped.'

Josh slumped forward and buried his head in his hands. The rest of the voices washed over him unheard. They were all right. The people in the car were all right.

He exhaled into his hands, his shoulders rising and falling between the spasms of his faltering breath. How long did he have now? Ten hours? Twelve? It would have him. He knew that now, and his bowels shifted with the reality of what that might mean.

And where the fuck was he? He'd been about an hour from the Furnace exit when he'd hit the traffic, and now he was simply off the interstate in some Godforsaken Appalachian forest.

Josh sniffed, raised his head, and wiped his eyes. The wall of trees on either side of the road shifted like the fur of an animal in the light wind, receding into blackness beyond the limits of Jezebel's headlamps. He let himself muse on where his stowaway might be now. Was it watching him from the darkness ahead? Waiting? Josh searched the dark bands of wood for movement other than the unwelcoming shivering of branches.

His roving eye was rewarded, but not from the view ahead. A sudden movement in the rear view mirror, just within his peripheral vision, made his ribs seem flimsy tools to contain his heart. Josh held his breath and focused on the mirror. Within that rectangle of silvered glass was a reflected portion of the darkened sleeper behind him, and as he watched, the movement that had attracted his unwilling eye was repeated.

Something was flapping at his back. Slowly Josh turned his head, his ears now confirming the disturbance, registering the unmistakable rustle of agitated material. In the dark box that contained his bed, his thin quilted comforter was rising from the mattress, making a shape that implied the writhing bulk beneath it was slightly bigger than a man.

Josh pressed back against the dash and opened his mouth to scream, but before he could give voice to the cry, the comforter's contours lit up with weak shards of flashing blue and red. Then like a silk handkerchief emptied of its rabbit by a magician, the square of fabric stopped its thrashing and settled gently back down onto the mattress. He gaped at it, trying to make sense of what he was seeing, until logic penetrated his panic and made him tear his eyes from the quiet bed to the possible source of the lights . . .

The trees ahead were brushed with the same hues. Blue lights danced in the branches and from a side turning in the trees a police car swung onto the road in front of Josh. He watched it come, unable to react.

The car passed the truck, bounced to a halt on the road behind Jezebel, and two policemen stepped out, putting their hats on as they closed the doors. Josh watched them come in the mirror, took one more look at the innocent passivity of his comforter, and with trembling fingers turned on his interior light.

Lighting the cab was habitual truckers' etiquette when stopped at night by the bears, to let them see they weren't dealing with a maniac with a knife between his teeth. But Josh wasn't being polite. After all, they were here to arrest him. He just wanted light on his bed.

The first cop stopped at the footplate, and looked up at him through Josh's open window.

'Got a problem here, mister?'

They didn't know. Jesus. These were county bears, not state ones. Did these guys not have radios? Josh thought fast, praying his dishevelled state was less visible from four feet down. He clenched his hands into fists, cleared his throat, and hoped his voice wouldn't betray the tremble that was in his limbs.

His fear of being caught for the insane highway detour had been substantially eclipsed by the fear of what had been moving beneath his cheap comforter. Part of him, a big part of him, was pleased to see human flesh.

'Temperature gauge was goin' spacey. Reckoned if I sat here here a moment, she'd cool off.'

The cop nodded sagely, scratching at an armpit. His companion was already walking around the trailer, sniffing for petty violations.

'See your licences, please?'

'Sure.'

Josh leaned across and fumbled for his black folder. Oblivious to the fact that he'd dived out of view, the policeman continued to talk to the empty window.

'Where you headed, mister?'

Josh sat back up into back into view, and looked directly down into the man's face as he replied, trying his best not to throw a glance back into the sleeper that could be interpreted as guilt.

'Furnace, Virginia.'

If it meant anything to the man he hid it well. He neither nodded nor inquired further, but merely held his hand out, waiting for Josh to fill it with some ID.

Josh opened the folder and sifted through its contents until he found his licences. As he pulled them from their plastic wallets, the other man joined his companion and stood reading Josh's door.

Josh held out his documents and stretched down towards the policeman. Like a frog's tongue catching a fly, the second man's arm shot out and grabbed his colleague's wrist, only just preventing it from grasping the papers. The first man looked at him with anger, until he read the panic on the other's face. Josh heard only a portion of what was hissed between them.

'Spiller . . . damn it, look.'

The papers were still there in Josh's hand, held out to be taken, but now the policeman who had demanded them was staring at Josh's outstretched hand as though it held a gun. He backed away a pace and put his hands up at his shoulders, not so much in surrender, but in horror at something disgusting, nearly but not quite touched.

Both men were regarding the truck as though it would burn them. Josh rubbed the back of his head with the hand still in the cab, and shook the papers like a play-enticement to a kitten.

'Here you go.'

The man was shaking his head.

'That's okay, Mr Spiller. Ain't no call for it. Sure everythin's in order. Hope your oil stays cool now.'

Both men backed towards their car instead of turning and walking, leaving Josh with his arm stuck ridiculously from the window like an Arab bartering lazily from a bazaar stall. The police car revved like a hot rod and pulled back out in front of Jezebel. With his arm still hanging from the window Josh watched it pass, only just glimpsing the words written above the badge on the side.

He read them aloud to try and calm his racing heart.

'McNab County.'

Withdrawing his arm, he rested his body on the wheel, then swallowed and turned his head to the softly illuminated quiet of the sleeper.

Nothing.

He put a fist to his forehead and closed his eyes, speaking aloud again, but in a voice weary with fright.

'Not far to go, Jez. And I guess now they know we're comin'.'

28

Had it been born before? The query kept forming in its unformed mind, although there was not yet sufficient reasoning power to answer even the simplest of questions. There was such familiarity in this black dark nothingness, and yet also a familiarity in everything its carrier felt and saw and smelled and touched. It had writhed in pleasure at its carrier's fear when it made itself known, although again, the method by which it announced itself was still ineffable. But now its carrier knew it was there, and while that was the true way, the only way, there was danger in it. To be aborted before it had grown sufficiently to see the light, to taste the air, to bathe in the sweet blood of its birth, that would be unthinkable.

And yet was it not its nature to strike fear into the heart of him who carried it? Hadn't countless numbers before it done the same, and as a result been terminated before they could quash the fear of the carrier forever?

It could only be what it would be, and it was not long now until it would know what that was.

She'd stared ahead, unmoving, almost unblinking, at the headlights on the interstate for at least an hour before fatigue started to overcome her. There was no necessity to fight it. The driver who'd picked her up from the rest area was silent and morose, but she knew instinctively he was harmless, and Griffin was grateful for the peace as he drove them through the night.

Her mind had been racing since Josh had gone. She'd had to close her eyes against the horror, the nightmare of seeing those scrawled symbols again, and offered up a rapid, ragged prayer that she would never see them in circumstances like that again.

Where was Josh now? And more importantly, how long did he have? Griffin's hand went to the brooch she'd pinned back on her sweatshirt. She ran a finger across its crudely moulded surface. She liked it a lot better now she'd shined it up some. As she touched it gently with the tip of her middle finger, she saw Josh's face, the way it had looked down at her in the warmth of his tiny bed, and a shard of something hot touched her heart and crotch simultaneously. She looked down at the brooch.

What was Elizabeth like, she wondered? Would she cry for Josh when he didn't come home? Griffin felt she knew her. Of course she'd listened to Josh pour his heart out over the radio to his friend, had pushed her Walkman headphones a little to the side of her ears just in case Josh looked round. And now she knew just about all there was to know about Josh Spiller and the woman he loved back home. What would that be like, she wondered, to have Josh love her the way he loved Elizabeth? What if Griffin were carrying a wanted child, the child he so badly craved? Her eyes drifted to the digital clock on the dash of the truck and her mouth dried at the seconds of Josh's life clicking past.

But she needed to rest, and although she knew her sleep would be full of hot and dark horrors, there was nothing more she could do now except ride this truck as far away from Furnace as it was possible to get. She gave in and closed her eyes.

Ten minutes later her driver saw the exit sign, cast a glance at his passenger and noted the regularity of her breathing. Checking his mirror, he indicated and made ready to pull onto the ramp. It was impossible to do a U-turn on this westbound interstate, but any exit would lead to a town that was as good a place as any to double back and head north again.

What did he expect? Peasants with pitchforks? A gunslinger in the middle of the street? He'd expected something, and there was nothing. He'd found the route he recognized after a few miles of errors in the forest roads. It had made him approach Furnace the way he'd left it, and as he'd passed Mister Jim's restaurant he felt a selfish pang of longing, wishing Griffin were here with him. In fact any human company would have soothed him, but company who knew the facts about what he might face was the company he wanted.

The CB had fallen silent at exactly the same point as last time, and Josh had never felt so alone in his life. Except that he wasn't alone. Not completely.

He had at least stopped holding up the bizarre and horrific events of the last few days in comparison to his real life. There was simply no relationship any more, no points of reference from which to take a sane bearing. He was on a trip through Hell with a demon on his trail, and the only sense he had left was that there might still be time to escape it.

But if the town knew he was coming to try to effect that escape, then it didn't much care. It was half past ten at night when he guided Jezebel slowly down the main street, his heart a sick weight in his chest at the memory of what had happened here beneath his wheels. He swallowed at the sight of Campbell's Food Mart, lit up and still open, with the usual ugly band of small-town teenagers hanging round its doors looking for trouble. A tall gangly boy with a bottle of beer in a bag whistled at the truck and gave him the finger.

Josh glared back at him through the window, and the boy's mobled insolence dissolved instantly at what he saw in those two haunted eyes.

He drove on towards the sheriff's office, watching, waiting for something but not knowing what. A man and woman kissed by a car before the woman got in and drove off. Two men stood looking at a shiny motorbike parked under a streetlamp, hands in pockets, nodding alternately at each other's comments. An elderly woman and a young girl emerged from the porch of a house, packages under their arms, and waving to the two figures in the front-room window.

It was hardly the stuff of nightmares, but Josh's senses were on a hair trigger. Where could he start? If Griffin was right, and after the lunacy of the last few hours he no longer even questioned that she was, then he had until sunrise tomorrow. To return to John Pace's office was the only plan he had right now, but it was a plan that stopped there. What would he say?

What could he do? Judging by his encounter with the county bears on the forest road, no one was going to be that keen to take anything from his hand.

And how would he know to which hand he should try to return

the ridiculous piece of paper that was folded snugly in the zipper compartment of his wallet?

It's not paper.

That's what she had said. Josh grabbed at his mouth and mashed his lips. What the fuck was that supposed to mean? Did it matter if those hellish marks were made on marzipan or marble? The thing that mattered was that, in a language he didn't understand, they spelled his death. He believed it.

There were two lights on outside the sheriff's, and one behind the blinds in the office at the front. As Jezebel hissed to a standstill across the street behind a solitary parked police car, two fingers penetrated the blinds and made a gap. Josh watched from the darkness of his cab as the fingers withdrew and the blinds swung slightly in response. He took out his wallet and balanced it on one thigh.

Almost everything Griffin said was crazy, but its logic was the logic of what he saw and felt and knew to be true. New laws of physics for a new universe. But she'd stated one thing that had tortured him since they'd parted, and he wrestled with it now as he started to open the leather wallet on his leg.

You must have pissed them off pretty badly.

Obviously. But how? What had he done? And to who? The police were the ones so keen to convince him it had been an accident. If someone was so mad at him for killing the child that they would set this monstrous hound on him, then why didn't they just deal with him then? He leaned forward, elbows on his legs, his right one cushioned by the fatness of his wallet, and held his aching head.

Maybe that was the way. To try once more to convince them what he'd seen was true. That it wasn't his fault. That somewhere in their midst was a murderer so cold and calculating that they should search for her until they dropped.

As if his body didn't believe him any more than the Furnace police, Josh sat up, opened the wallet and found the strip of runes. Even its touch was repugnant, like thin, mouldy leather, but Josh gripped it hard, with great care, and examined it. The marks were fainter than he'd last noticed, like they'd been faded in the sun. He looked around the cab and his eyes rested on a pile of road atlases, dog-eared and stained from years of use. He leaned across and picked up the most battered, and with the delicacy of a surgeon inserted the runes between two pages near the centre.

'Sorry, Kansas. Nothin' personal.'

He closed the atlas tightly, held it securely under his arm, and leaving the engine running got out of the cab.

Archie Cameron ran a finger round the inside of his collar and looked over at Lena as he heard the footfall on the wooden steps of the office. She toyed with the state-of-the-art phone headset around her neck and looked back at her computerized switchboard to avoid his eyes.

'My shift ends in a quarter hour, Archie.'

'Then I guess we're here together for another fifteen minutes.'

She stabbed at something on her keyboard and flushed red. The door opened and although he knew who would enter, Archie turned to look.

'Help you?'

'Yeah. Josh Spiller. You remember me from a couple of days back?'

Deputy Cameron leaned forward and made an unconvincing remembering face.

'I ran down Alice Nevin's baby.'

Lena shot Cameron a look, which was ignored.

'Sure. Kinda hard to forget. What brings you back, Mr Spiller?'

Josh scanned the room. 'I need to talk to you some more.'

'What about?'

'About the accident.'

Archie Cameron cleared his throat and leaned back in his chair. 'Well I guess the sheriff would be happy to hear anythin' you got to say, but he ain't here right now, an' in case you didn't notice, it's crackin' on eleven o'clock. You want to come back sometime tomorrow?'

Josh was watching the man's face. For what, he didn't know, but he watched it anyway. 'I can't do that.'

'Why's that?'

Josh knew his upper lip was starting to bloom with sweat. He fought his own body, willing it to play poker. 'Just passin' through. Got a load to deliver.'

As casually as if she were alone in this sleepy office, Lena tapped in some numbers on her keyboard and a flashing code on the screen told her the number was being dialled.

There were four words on a loop in Josh's mind, and they were screaming at him.

How will I know?

He had no idea how, but he was going to try and find out. This man had given him a copy of the statement. It had been a thin thing. Two photocopied sheets, and yes, he'd taken it from its envelope and folded it into his crammed wallet along with everything else in the whole damned world. But if he passed the runes to this deputy and he wasn't the one ... what had she said? It would be like they'd been lost or destroyed.

Sunrise. And then it wouldn't matter any more.

Josh swallowed a mouthful of bitter saliva.

The deputy was rubbing his chin. 'It need seein' to right now?'

'I'd appreciate it.'

Cameron stood up and walked slowly to the hatch in the window, his every step watched by Lena. He arrived in front of Josh and placed both hands on the teak counter that separated them.

'Shoot.'

Josh was lost. 'It wasn't an accident. You have to believe me.'

Archie Cameron groaned and bowed his head. 'I thought we'd bin through this like ten thousand times or somethin'.' Josh hesitated. He was groping for clues. 'Was passin' through. Just wanted to make the point again.'

'Well you made it. Anythin' else?'

Josh looked deep into Deputy Cameron's eyes. They were opaque. There was no hint of fear, no triumph of victory.

'Yeah. I got kinda lost last time.' He held up the atlas. 'Point me at the best route outta here to the northbound interstate?'

Cameron examined Josh's face for a beat, then sighed and made a gesture with his hand. 'Sure.'

Josh's hand was trembling as he lifted the atlas to the counter and started to slide it towards Cameron's waiting hand. It was about an inch from the man's fingers when Josh stopped pushing it, slammed his hand over the ragged cover and barked, 'No.'

The deputy jumped. 'Hey! What's your problem?'

The problem, as Josh had just realized, was that Archie Cameron was going to take the runes. Willingly yes, unknowingly, maybe not. But they were going to be taken by the wrong man. Josh had known at that moment that Cameron had no fear of whatever Josh had to give him. If there was fear in the man's demeanour at all, it was merely fear of Josh himself. Or perhaps what was accompanying him.

Josh's heart was thumping at the nearness of his loss. He would have passed them, and they would have been destroyed.

Josh pulled the atlas back over the counter towards himself, picked it up and cradled it against his chest, panting with panic. He licked the sweat from his upper lip with a dry tongue. 'I just remembered. I know the way.'

The policeman nodded slowly, humouring a lunatic, and stood his ground, hand on hips. Josh looked to the woman by the telephones, nodded to Cameron and turned to the door. He was watched carefully by two sets of passive and inscrutable eyes, and he stopped and looked back.

'I might just stay the night. I'd like to see Sheriff Pace.'

Josh won a prize. Archie Cameron's eyes flashed with the first sign of discomfort. He glanced quickly at his female colleague and back again at Josh, clearing his throat once more for no good reason.

'Sheriff ain't around tomorrow.'

Josh had his hand on the door-handle. 'No? Where is he?'

'On leave.'

Josh looked from one face to the other and knew they were lying. He nodded once, gripped his atlas tightly in his fist and left the building.

'Call her,' said Cameron to the door.

'Already did,' said Lena to her keyboard.

29

She didn't mind the drugs. In fact she didn't mind being in hospital. How long was it since she was here before? A week? Sure, but before that. Not the time Amy was born, but the time that Amy was made. Nine months. That was it. That was how long it took.

Alice Nevin rolled her head on the soft pillow and let the even softer cushion of diamorphine fold itself around her head. Funny how the injections could make her think about all that stuff without crying any more. She closed her eyes and smiled. Bobby's face, when she told him they wanted his spunk in a tube. It was a picture. What did he say again?

I hit a bull's-eye six times afore. What makes them think I can't do it a seventh?

Oh, but he was mad. Took her hours to tell him that it wasn't like that. That it had to be done on exactly the right day. And the people at the hospital were going to take her egg and his sperm and make their baby in a tube before they put it right back in there where it belongs to grow. There was nothing wrong with that, was there?

Nothing. Except that Amy wasn't here any more. Nor, for that matter, was Bobby. No more bull's-eyes. For a second, a sharp edge of grief pierced the layer of chemical padding around her heart, and her mouth started to turn down at the edges and tremble. She brought her thin arms up to her face, and the plastic wristband with her name scrawled in blue ink caught her chin. She choked back the sob, and then another delicious wave of calm broke over her.

What day was it? Had Councillor McFarlane been here? It was like a dream. Alice tried to remember if it was real or not, then decided she felt so peaceful right now it didn't matter. But she remembered her sitting in that seat beside the bed, she surely did. She'd been speaking in a low motherly voice, a beautiful voice, holding Alice's hand, telling her all sorts of things. Telling her how everyone was proud of her, that she'd done so well. That she was real sorry about Bobby and who could have known, but he was going to do a bad thing to Amy and no one could let that happen, could they?

Amy shifted under the covers, and stroked her arm.

Was he? He'd sure been acting strange a couple of days after Amy was born. Had gotten all jumpy, like a bird being chased by a cat. Made him kind of bad to be around. The kids noticed it. Hell, even the dog noticed it. But what would he have done to Amy? Bobby loved his kids. The kids. Who had the kids?

Councillor McFarlane had said who had them. Who was it again? Didn't matter. She'd talked about the fancy colleges they were going to go to. That was nice. That was real nice. Maybe she would just snuggle down and think about that. About big white buildings with Virginia creeper growing up the front, where her kids would get the kind of education she never had.

The councillor was a good person. Look how she'd changed their lives. There was Alice living in that shack in the mountains with her brother with no wits to speak of, and a daddy beating ten kinds of shit out of her daily. No, Alice had no hope for anything better in life. And then the councillor came. And she and Bobby had got that beautiful house with all those rich folks in Furnace. And all Bobby had to do was a few odd jobs for the councillor's husband and all Alice had to do was have kids.

That made Alice real happy, but it made the councillor happy too. Yes, she was a good person. People like that didn't happen by every day. She was such a smart lady. And she knew what it was like to be a mother too. Seven kids. Or was it six since the boy who died years ago? And God alone knows how many grandkids. That's how many little ones Councillor McFarlane had. Seven. Just like her and Bobby.

The boat she was sailing in hit rocks again and Alice felt her breath burn in her throat. No. Nelly had six and she had six. Amy was dead. Crushed like a little doll by that truck. Alice Nevin opened her mouth, crammed a balled-up fist of sheet into it and wailed. In response, the corridor outside clicked with heels and in only a very short time Alice Nevin was sailing a golden ocean once more.

Eddie bowed his head, closed his eyes and hit the wheel with the edge of a fist. There could be no doubt it was him. As soon as he heard those dicks whooping about the blue Peterbilt like they were sports commentators, he knew it was Josh who'd flipped out. And what could he do now? If Josh had taken the exit they were all sniggering about, then Eddie was at least three miles back from the action. Stuck, same as everyone else, in the line of traffic that had made Josh bail out of his box. Or had it been the traffic? Eddie wasn't so sure. His buddy was in a bad way, seeing stuff, going paranoid. But would the Josh Spiller he knew really go spit-dribbling bonko over a bit of a tailback?

Sure, maybe he'd curse and get on some four-wheeler's case by sounding the horn, but he would never take a suicide route up the hard-hat highway. So something else must have got to him. If Eddie was going to find out what, he had to make sure he didn't lose him. But even as he thought it, Eddie thought he could guess where Josh was headed.

He glanced across at his sleeping passenger. She was out of it. Her mouth was hanging open and her head was slumped on her chest like a drunk. But even in the unladylike pose, Eddie could see what made Josh take a dip. Who knows, if it had been on offer, and he wasn't a man condemned to the altar, maybe he might have been tempted himself. Then his eye caught that brooch on her shirt and he reminded himself his cargo was not just a psycho but a thieving psycho.

That brooch with Elizabeth's name on it must have cost Josh at least a month's pay. As two heavy chains around his wrist and neck bore testimony, Eddie was pretty partial to gold himself, and there certainly was no mistaking twenty-two carats when you saw them. Well, Josh was going to get it back. He would see to it. If he really had run back up some shit-caked mountain roads to get to that dumb town he was so obsessed by, then Eddie would wait a little further up the interstate and catch him on the way out.

He'd already cast an eye on the Rand McNally, and if Josh planned on heading home to Pittsburgh, there was no way out of that mountain garbage except this highway. There was a quiet tourist stop a mile after the most northerly exit from those nowhere towns, and Eddie decided that it would do just fine to sit there and wait until Josh came by.

The only problem would be how Missy Lightfingers was going to react when she woke up and found herself within spitting distance of her home town instead of watching the sun come up over the Colorado Rockies.

Well she'd just have to live with it. Because she wasn't going anywhere until she handed that brooch back to its owner and explained herself. She had a lot of explaining to do, and if Eddie decided she'd stay put and do it, then nothing in the world would change that plan. Nothing.

He walked this time. It was the only other place he knew to go, and from what he could remember of its leafy location, an eighteen-wheeler at eleven-thirty at night might cause a drape or two to twitch. But as Josh walked towards Nelly McFarlane's house he wondered why that should bother him. There were already eyes on him. Malicious, inhumane, hungry eyes that had locked onto him about a minute after he'd left Jezebel's cab. And now he had seen an image, albeit a distorted image, of what those eyes belonged to, Josh thought the fear in his belly might drive him mad. He could barely walk with the weight of it. His hands were trembling at his sides and what breath he had was trapped in a burning knot in his throat.

The worst thing was knowing. Somehow, before Griffin had told him what his feral senses suspected, there had been comfort in his confusion, an escape route from a reality that was too bizarre to accept, an exit door marked simply *insanity*. Even now, he struggled to regain that bewildered disbelief. But it was gone. Josh Spiller was not mad and there was little point, now that his time was nearly at hand, in denying what his primitive senses had been telling him throughout the age of this nightmare.

And so he walked, accepting at last that something others could sense, but only he for the moment could see, was walking with him.

The old chestnuts swaying above him were only just in leaf. He could smell their sap rising, hear the soft rustle of new foliage.

And he could smell something else beneath it, the first wafting tendrils of the same stench that had nearly made him vomit in Alabama.

And it was growing stronger, more pungent, with every step he took. Josh's head reeled with the image of sewers flowing with a mixture of excrement and bloated, rotting flesh. Closing his eyes he concentrated, willing himself to taste only the sweet night breath of the trees.

But it was growing worse. Burning flesh. The smell of entrails sizzling with heat and disease. Skin peeling back from bubbling fat and ulcerous muscle.

His gorge was rising and his walking slowed to a shuffle as he gasped for breath, trying desperately to stop the acidic flow of saliva to his cheeks that he knew meant that bile was on its way. As he bent at the waist, hands on his stomach, using what tiny reserve of will-power remained at his disposal to halt his dry retching, a sound to his left made him widen his streaming eyes and keep his body as still as a thudding heart would allow.

It was a thick sound, like a clumsily-slaughtered animal's death-rattle, rasped through a syrup of mucus. And yet despite the distortion and the effort that was plain in its making, the sound was unmistakable.

It was trying to say his name.

Josh straightened up slowly, turning his head in the direction of the unbearable noise. But before his darting eyes could register the source, the noise came again, and this time whatever was making it did a better job of working its hellish mouth around the single syllable. There was an intelligence in the sound, a mocking, insolent imitation of human language that communicated centuries of unfathomable hatred.

Almost as if the sound of his name had been a trigger, Josh found himself crouching like defensive prey.

The street was wide and dark and empty, the houses unlit and sleeping at a luxuriously long distance from the sidewalk. Josh wiped his mouth and looked ahead. Her street was the next on the left. He was almost sure.

He peered up at the biggest tree in the line of closely-planted chestnuts and took an unconscious sideways step away. Like most elderly chestnuts, the tightly-packed branches made its night-time shape black and complex, but the more he stared unblinking at it, the more its branches appeared to have a random motion other than the gentle stirring of breeze.

He watched as that shape, the shape that should have merely been the snarl of old wood, untangled itself slowly. There was a glimpse, no more, of details. Black matted hair on skin that glistened, sharp-angled limbs from which smoke curled like steam from a pie, a flash of something that could have been outsized yellowed teeth or claws.

And then with a speed that was fluid and reptilian, it began to descend. The branches rustled heavily in protest and Josh started to run. He stuck his jaw forward, willing his body to keep pace with it as his legs slammed onto the sidewalk and his arms pummelled the air at his sides. He ran until his eyes had stopped rolling like those of a frightened horse and his lungs felt as if they were going to burst like balloons in his chest.

Loping to a stop at the T-junction, Josh bent forward again, fighting for breath, fighting for the courage just to stand upright. Because right now, he wanted to huddle like a foetus on the sidewalk and lie there until Judgment Day.

And as he stared at the ground with eyes still wide and his breathing still agony, he suddenly found something, if not courage, then its close relation, anger, growing from the very heart of him.

Standing up and turning to the dark and empty street behind him, Josh Spiller filled his lungs and bellowed with a shout to wake the dead.

'Sunrise! You fucking bastard! You don't feed until sunrise! You hear me?'

If the shape in the trees, now no longer visible, was insensible to the shout, then the residents of Muir Avenue were not. Like the end credits of *The Flintstones*, lights began to come on behind windows in a random patchwork along the street. Josh stood panting, his arms hanging limply at his sides, and then slowly looked around as if he had arrived in this place from another planet. For a moment he thought he had. It was familiar. The street, the feeling, the weight on his heart. He was outside again. Outside and alone again, in a prosperous avenue of big silent houses. Behind those lit windows were people who didn't want him there. Wiping his mouth, he turned away, increasing his stride as if strength of purpose gave him immunity from madness.

Wheeeaaa. Wheeeea. He stopped dead, and from his lips a small helpless plea piped thinly into the night air. 'No.'

It was spinning slowly in the cold breeze and the air was full of the unlubricated labours of its revolutions.

There was no doubt that it was the sign. It stood in almost exactly the same spot on Nelly McFarlane's street as it had on that uncrossable boundary to Carnegie. But this time there were no shouts of children, no sounds of mowers and invisible picnics. This time there was only the dry rustling of the trees and the sound of metal grinding on metal. He was frozen to the spot, staring dumbly and with terror at nothing more than a circular piece of tin selling ice cream. It was directly under the streetlamp, and the faces of the children were illuminated clear and fresh as though it had been painted yesterday.

But there was no Tanner's ice cream any more.

So he wasn't seeing it. That was the explanation. It quite simply wasn't there. He started to move forward. He would walk past it and keep walking to her house, and the sign would just have to join this week's long list of things that couldn't, shouldn't, be happening.

Josh kept walking, and the sign kept turning. The children's tongues were licking their cones, and their half-moon eyes registered the pleasure of it. In and out, the tiny tongues, darting over tiny teeth. Sunny smiles that, as the sign seemed to gather speed, were growing wider. Saliva trickled down the back of Josh's throat reminding him to swallow or breathe. He did both.

The mouths of the boy and girl were starting to stretch into grotesque wide slashes, splitting their faces in two, and as he watched, those tiny white teeth were growing into something else. Their eyes were alive with malice, not pleasure, and they stared out at him like unworldly beasts from their tin circle.

Could he shout at this? Was he sure that this was merely a sick illusion to feed the fire of his terror? He was sure of nothing any more. His world was a dark and hateful maze of fear, in which every dark passage led only to the centre of something unmapped and inescapable.

The tongues had now changed. Impossibly elongated, livid, red forked membranes slithering across long, reeking teeth. And they seemed to be able to leave the confines of the sign. Josh was no longer looking at a picture. The faces were standing proud of the tin, the tongues darting out over the sidewalk, unquestionably looking to find contact with Josh.

He stumbled more than ran, and as he fell forward in a series of swaying dives, he whimpered like a child, saliva leaking from the corners of his lips. Red darts flew at him as he fell past, and above the screaming of the spinning sign he could hear a reptilian hiss of irritation as the tongues failed to meet their target. Falling to his knees, he crawled for a few feet until he found the balance to stand. The hissing was louder, with a growing undercurrent of vibrating resonance that suggested something larger was emerging from the three-dimensional horror than those two small, pointed faces. Unable even to make the sounds of fear now, he merely gasped as he pushed himself up. Lifting his head he saw a figure two houses away standing on the lawn, hands on hips, legs apart. Josh wanted to raise an arm and call for help, but there was too much that was familiar about that stance. His legs gave way and he crumpled onto the ground like a broken puppet.

There were voices now. He could hear a man and a woman talking. And then footsteps, clicking along the sidewalk towards him. There was no strength in him to resist. He lifted his head and looked up like a puppy at the two people walking towards him. The woman's voice spoke first. Quietly, and with great concern.

'Mr Spiller? Is that you?'

The man bent to Josh's level and took him by the shoulder. 'Can you stand?'

Josh didn't reply, but he found himself being helped to his feet. He blinked at the faces swimming in front of him, and when Nelly McFarlane said softly, 'I think you'd better come inside,' he went like a lamb.

30

Sim's bed was no more than a narrow series of wooden slats, topped with a thin horsehair mattress. But mostly it afforded him great comfort. He liked to lie in it on his back, his face turned to the peach-painted ceiling that was Josh's study floor. He'd worked long hours all his life, from the first day he'd arrived in this country that was as hard to live in as it was easy, and to Sim the chance to lie in bed with nothing pressing on his time was a luxury he felt justified in savouring. Tonight, however, he lay in bed on his side, his face towards the door, thin knees drawn up to his waist.

Elizabeth thought him mad, and perhaps he was. The images that had filled his head when the phone rang had been so terrible, so beyond anything the sane mind could conjure, that he felt sick at their memory. And now, in the dark of the night, still they wouldn't depart. He could force his fists into his face, and there, moving behind his tightly-closed lids as though his eyes were open to a bright flame, were sights and sensations of such grotesque evil he wondered how long he could bear it.

It was the hunger that was the worst of it. That thing that was all around Josh was so very hungry. And Josh. He'd been there all right, shouting as one would over a storm, without knowing that the dreadful thing was blocking his contact and revelling in his isolation.

How could such things exist? He had lived the best part of seventy years and only once, as a child, had he experienced any hint that there was anything in the world more harmful than men.

A neighbour, a man called Nringar who had been openly stealing from Sim's father, had terrified him one day by revealing what he called his 'other faces'. Sim was cleverer than the rest of the stupid villagers, the man had told him. He would be able to see them if he looked. He'd concentrated, as instructed, flattered by the compliment, and what he'd seen made him unable to sleep soundly or walk alone for the rest of his time in the village.

Of course as the years passed, and a modern American life replaced the Korean one he'd left, he had passed it off as childish fantasy, no more than the infectious disease of superstition that affected all those who lived as they had, in isolated jungle villages.

Now, he was no longer sure. His gift for guessing the identity of callers he'd regarded as no more than a parlour trick. If it was, then he was a madman, conjuring up things from a dark crack in his soul that no civilized man would comprehend. And if it was more than a trick, a real gift that let him know more than a man should, then he was wrong about most things in his life. Man was a known quantity; dangerous and evil, arrogant and foolish; destructive beyond his own ability to repair, full of vengeance and powerful with malice. But the terrors of mankind at its worst were nothing as compared to the unholy predatory force that Sim had sensed guarding Josh.

Sim bunched his fists tighter. That was it. The nightmare had been guarding him. Not in the sense of protecting Josh, but the very opposite. Guarding its prey, the way a cat plays with a mouse.

He curled tighter in his hard little bed. When, he wondered, would the cat lift its paw and open its mouth?

Ethan and Noah. Even forming those sweet, simple syllables in his mind made Sheriff John Pace ache with the love of them. He sat on the long porch of his eight-bedroomed house, feeling the cold night air rasp at his skin, and wondered why it had taken him this long to address their future. He wanted to believe it was because everything had been so easy, like being in a dream, that he had neglected the reality. But it wasn't true. It hadn't been easy. It had been getting more difficult with every passing day. Maybe it had been different for his father, but somehow Pace didn't think so. He'd watched him grow prematurely old with the strain of it all, and for what? For this? A big fancy house and three cars? Were his family really such under-achievers that they were forced to stoop to . . .

His eye caught the stars and stripes, stuck into an earthenware pot on the patio, blowing gently in the breeze, and the word 'murder' fluttered like a trapped insect in his heart as though to echo the flapping silk.

Those two men had only been serving that flag. And he; what had he been serving when he'd handed those men, guilty of nothing more than the poor pretence of being tourists, the booklets on 'Camper Safety in the Appalachians', with two strips of potent dried flesh hidden between their pages?

Pace closed his eyes and let his head fall back against the cushioned headrest of the porch chair. Only three years old, and yet Ethan Pace had taken the hand of his big brother Noah a week ago and asked his father if the bad things Mrs McKlintoch talked about at school, the things that came and took away boys and girls who strayed from Jesus, would ever get them. Noah, being five, had tried to look as if it was nonsense, but his eyes were pleading for his father to confirm they were safe.

Were they? Could their father promise that? He gripped the arms of his beechwood chair as the memory of what he'd seen pushed its way past the honeyed image of his children's faces.

'Don't be there, John.'

It was said so simply and solicitously.

'Nobody needs to be there. It's better. In fact that's the whole point, don't you see? And what's more, until their time, it's still dangerous for you.'

But he had been there. He'd followed them during their last hour, watching their speeding camper-van swing erratically around the road as they tried to escape the inescapable. Had he hoped he could reverse what he'd taken part in? No. That wasn't it. The truth of admitting it was hideous, but he forced himself to face it. John Pace had simply been curious.

And though she could have done, McFarlane hadn't stopped him. Because there was no better warning to the curious than to let them have that curiosity sated.

They had run from the van, the taller of the two men with his gun drawn, waving it wildly in the air at nothing. At least nothing Pace could see. The other man followed, panting, falling into the woods as though the tightly-packed oaks would protect them from what was coming. The men ran as far as five or six trees deep, and he thought he would lose sight of them. Just as his hand reached reluctantly for the door-handle he saw something, deeper in the woods than the men had penetrated, and it made him take his hand from the door and sink lower back into his seat. The dawn was bright, the rays of the sun just appearing over the top of a thick blanket of scarlet leaves. But even so, the interior of the forest was as dark as twilight. And from it a sickly light was growing, flickering like a guttering candle, making a new forest of dancing shadows amongst the tree trunks. In its light, Pace could see the silhouettes of the two men, and as he watched, his eyes only just above the rim of the car window, both figures dropped to their knees before the light, as though being summoned by an executioner. Even now, although the picture he saw was burned into his brain like a brand, he was unable fully to comprehend the hideous shapes it had made in the trees.

The speed. That anything could move as swiftly and effortlessly through such thick undergrowth was unthinkable. But it had come at the two figures with an almost mechanical velocity. And the animalistic choreography of its slaughter. Dear God, that had been the worst. Slick, fluid yet random movements. Sometimes tearing and ripping, sometimes pulling and tossing. But not an animal. No. Not even close to an animal. The concentration of its gait and posture almost suggested an elegance of human toil, a master slaughterer excelling at its work, comprehending, savouring and analysing the destruction in a way no animal ever could.

As the last of the screams died, screams that had caused a hot sheet of urine to soak the car seat beneath him, he glimpsed the face of the creature through the tendrils of smoke that curled from its flesh, its muscular, pulsating body crouching as it turned to look at him through the gaps in the trees.

From such a distance he could barely make out its features, and yet he had no doubt that the two crimson slits of hatred and cunning that served as its eyes were boring into him and had known of his presence all along. Even from the cowed position in his car, he had read them. It was longing for him, aching to consume him as it had consumed the two Washington men, but Pace knew in his frozen heart that it was unable to, and he closed his eyes against the horror of it.

He'd stayed like that for God knows how long, huddled, wet and terrified, until a numbness in his joints made him shift and dare to open his eyes.

The woods were still and gloomy, and slowly he'd slid up in his seat and started to scan the undergrowth for movement. There was none.

He should have driven away, but he couldn't. The self-loathing and disbelief at what he'd participated in was stronger at that moment than his fear, and in a numb trance he'd opened the car door and started to walk towards the woods.

There was silence. No birdsong or distant deer broke the still-hot air, and as he walked between the first two oaks, the noise of his feet on the dry twigs of the forest floor was like firecrackers going off.

Sheriff Pace had attended the scene of almost every kind of human carnage you could name; car crashes that looked like an explosion in a butcher's shop window; a knifing in one of the backwood cabins that had left the victim alive and twitching, but without ears, nose or lips; and a sawmill accident that had taken off a man's head and shoulders. He expected worse here. He had seen many acts of violence, and he steeled himself.

A perfect murder. There was nothing. No pieces of flesh or tattered cloth. No burnt remains or blood-soaked earth. Only smells. And the first smell that hit him would have been almost delicious, the same smell that firemen know, but never discuss when collecting burnt bodies, that can make a hungry man think of chicken with herbs. But the secondary odour lingering in the trees was stronger than burnt human flesh. It was an unspeakable concoction of rot and disease, of faecal matter and bile. He'd turned and walked to his car, chewing at the insides of vomit-coated cheeks to prevent his scream.

Pace couldn't remember how he'd got back to Furnace. He must have driven, but his recollection stopped after getting into his car and quietly closing the door.

Ethan and Noah.

He opened his eyes again and breathed the night air in through flaring nostrils. Bobby Hendry had strayed away from Jesus. He must have. But he'd been a cheat. He'd blown his brains out before the thing that Mrs McKlintoch was warning his children about could come and take him away.

John Pace suddenly knew, with a certainty that was as strong as his love for his family, that the only way to be a real father, a real man, was not to provide a house and cars, deluxe health treatment or riding lessons. It was to be able to look his sons in the eyes and tell them with sure and certain knowledge, that nothing would ever come loping through the trees looking for them. Never.

Now all he had to figure out was how a man in a town like this could keep a promise like that.

'Better?'

Jim McFarlane left off holding the back of Josh's neck as he took the glass of water from his lips and straightened up. Josh looked up at him and licked his wet lips.

'Yeah. Better. Thanks.'

The door to the sitting room opened and Jim McFarlane moved across to make sure it stayed that way for his wife, as she entered with a tray. It had three steaming mugs balanced on it and she set it down on the low table in front of Josh with a matronly smile.

'Herbal tea.' She held up a hand in protest to Josh, though he had said nothing. 'Now don't say no till you try it. Calms the nerves. Soothes the spirit.'

After having lain on it for nearly five minutes, Josh was at least now sitting upright on Nelly McFarlane's long, low sofa. He ran a hand over his mouth and looked at the mugs for somewhere to rest his eyes other than upon his hosts' anxious faces. Nelly sat down beside him.

'I'll let you drink before you tell us what's up. We heard someone shouting. I guess it was you?'

Josh picked up a cup and sipped the hot liquid. It was revolting, but he sipped again, to avoid her question. Nelly looked up at her husband.

'Was that Herm crying?'

The big simple-looking man cocked an ear. 'Could be. I'll check.' He paused. 'Grandkids,' he said to Josh with an indulgent smile, then left the room through another door, closing it with a finality that Josh knew meant he wouldn't return.

Nelly adjusted her dressing-gown, pulling the satin tighter over her breasts.

'We didn't expect to see you back, Mr Spiller.'

Josh sipped again and put down his mug. He looked at her to see what she meant and saw nothing except a small-town busybody, pleased with herself for taking an active part in a small-town drama.

'Didn't reckon on it either.'

Now there was something else in her face. A desire he could see, burning brighter perhaps than she planned to show, to know what exactly he was doing here.

'Did someone attack you out there? As I say, we heard a shout.'

Josh shook his head, his eyes never leaving hers. 'Nope. Just came over dizzy on the sidewalk there.'

She returned his gaze steadily. 'Sounds like you ought to get that checked out.'

'For sure.'

She was silent for a few beats, then she smiled. 'I presume you were making your way here, when you came over all dizzy.'

There was the first hint of sarcasm in her last four words and Josh's senses stepped up their alert.

'Yes, mam. I was.'

'Well. Now you're here, and feeling a bit better, what can I do for you at nearly a quarter to midnight?'

Josh sat forward, awkward that she was beside him. 'I needed to see the sheriff about somethin' and they tell me he's on leave.'

'Well if they tell you that then I guess it must be so.'

'Could you tell me where he lives?'

Nelly McFarlane looked at him for a moment, then stood up and smoothed her expensive and uncreased gown.

'Now, Mr Spiller. What would you do if a stranger you hardly know, and only know at all in fact as being the unlucky participant in a terrible accident, turned up at your door near midnight, looking like he'd been in a fight, and asked for confidential information?'

'It's confidential, where the sheriff lives?'

'Did you ask at his office?'

Josh looked down, and there was a cold smile on her face when he looked back up. 'No. Because they wouldn't have told you, would they?'

Josh stood up. 'I guess not. Thanks for the tea.'

'Where are you going now?'

'You're right. It's late. I'm sorry, I hadn't realized.'

Nelly made a small movement in his way. 'What did you need to see Sheriff Pace about exactly?'

It was Josh's turn to wear a cold smile. 'That's confidential.'

'Maybe I can help you, Mr Spiller. After all as councillor in this town I work very closely indeed with our law enforcement agency.'

'Thanks. But I need to speak to him.'

Josh stepped aside and walked to the door. As he reached it he stopped and turned. 'Oh, I forgot. I was going to return this to you. Thanks for the thought.'

In his right hand he held out the pamphlet helping him to find Jesus.

Nelly McFarlane looked down at the cheap little book, then, with eyes that were filling with something other than housewifely concern for his immortal soul, she began to walk slowly towards him.

She kept her eyes on his and lifted her hand to the book. Josh watched her like a rabbit fixed by a weasel, and as her hand opened to receive it she spoke quietly. 'Thank you.'

Her fingers closed on the pamphlet and she held it there in her hand, never taking her eyes from his. Josh tried not to swallow and failed.

'Did you have time to read it?'

He felt the heat in his neck and face and turned from her to leave.

When she spoke again, it was in a voice so different from the one he'd been addressed in so far, it made his skin crawl like a current over a circuit board.

'Mr Spiller?'

He turned and looked at the woman who had been just a housewife, and was no longer. She spoke softly, but the power behind her voice was a force so immense he felt like backing against the wall just to escape her words.

'Who told you?'

31

He was eating nachos when she woke. Griffin's hand went to her aching neck and rubbed it hard, moving her head from side to side in an effort to relieve the pain. She yawned and spoke through it as she kept up the massage.

'Christ, that's sore. Where are we?'

Eddie fed another handful of nachos into the invisible mouth beneath his moustache and indicated the tourist stop with his head.

'A four-wheeler stop'n'shit.'

Griffin looked sleepily to her left. They were in an empty parking lot outside a low wooden building divided in two by a central glass box. The two wooden wings of the building were obviously male and female rest-rooms, and the glasshouse dividing them boasted nothing more than a stand filled with dozens of tourist flyers.

She yawned again and scratched at her head. 'Mind if I use it?'

Eddie shrugged and lifted his chin. 'That's what it's for.'

She cast him a grumpy glance, straightened her crumpled clothing and climbed out the cab. The engine of the truck was still throbbing, and maybe she'd have been nervous the guy would drive off with her pack and leave her stranded if it hadn't been that Josh always left his running, even when they went to eat.

Josh. She shivered as the cold night air hit her, but the tremor was more than just a reaction to temperature. The only way to keep her head was to stop letting him creep into her thoughts like this. She shut her eyes briefly as she closed the cab door and concentrated on her immediate needs, like the very immediate need to piss. Stepping down onto the asphalt, she wrapped her arms around her shoulders as she crossed to the brightly-lit building.

Where the hell were they, she wondered? It was colder than she'd figured it would be further south, but then maybe going west had kept them on the same latitude. Who cared? She would buy a sweater next store she found, then even if she ended up in Alaska, things could be worse.

Was Alaska far enough from Furnace? Right now, she thought, Jupiter wasn't far enough. Pushing open the swing door, she blinked under the harsh striplights, lighting up the circular display stand for exactly zero customers.

Griffin walked to the door marked with the symbol for women and gave the crude outline, with its A-line skirt and long curled-at-the-tip hair, a contemptuous sniff.

'Hey. That looks exactly like me!'

She banged open the door as though it was personally responsible for centuries of women's oppression, and went to take a leak.

Eddie watched her from the darkness of his cab until she entered the women's washroom, then turned the CB back up.

'. . . so she says, you give me the dog's phone number, buddy, an' you can put it where you goddamn like.'

'Shit, man, that's older than your rig.'

Eddie pressed talk. 'Hey, Jezebel. You out there?'

A pause.

'Who's askin'?'

Eddie rolled his eyes. 'A secret agent for the IRS. Guess I blew ma cover, huh?'

'Weren't that rig they was all talkin' 'bout handled Jezebel?'

'You there or not, Jez? It's Eddie, not the fuckin' bears.'

He waited.

'Hey, me an' my buddy havin' ourselves an argument here. Anybody out there know if it's garlic makes you horny?'

Eddie slapped the wheel in irritation and turned the volume down but not off. He would hear Josh if he called. Meanwhile he would have to keep Loony Tunes in sight. He pushed his hand into the bottom of the nacho bag and scooped up the crumbs.

Griffin sighed with pleasure as a hot stream of urine twisted its way into the bowl. It had been hours since she'd taken a leak, she realized, and hours since she'd eaten. She was hungry, and that monosyllabic son of a bitch at the wheel hadn't even offered her one of his nachos.

Things were not going as Griffin had planned and she shifted on the toilet seat as she tried to clear her head. It didn't work. The strip of runes in Josh's hand came searing back into her head and she bent forward and put her face in her hands. Where was it now? Had it been slipped into something, concealed and passed on? Or had Josh given up? Taken her advice before . . .

She grunted with the effort of trying to lose the image that conjured. This time she managed to push it away, filling her head with the things she would do when she got far enough away. California maybe. Maybe not. Being free was intoxicating and she held to the joy of it to keep the horror of Josh Spiller at bay.

Finishing, she pulled up her panties and jeans, went to the washbasin and rinsed her hands. The mirror above the basin told her she wasn't looking her best. That was bad, but like a lot of things, it was something she could rectify. She splashed her face with cold water, and decided she'd dig in her pack for some witch hazel when she got back to the truck. Feeling refreshed she left the washroom with more spring in her step than when she'd entered, and as she passed by the circular stand, she paused and playfully grabbed at one of the hideous flyers.

'Okay,' she said jauntily, pushing a wet hand through her hair, 'let's see where we are and how we can amuse the nuclear family while we're here.' She read the long piece of shiny paper aloud. 'Want to explore some of the oldest and most mysterious caves in the United States?' She turned the page, smiling as she did so. 'Shit, which state hasn't got caves?'

Her smile died on her lips as she read the second page.

A small map showed the location of ten famous caves, all dotted cheerfully in red along the ridge of the Appalachians. Dropping the flyer on the floor, Griffin tore out another one.

A picture of a happily screaming toddler sliding down a plastic chute begged her to visit the Shenandoah Water Park, open from Memorial Day through Thanksgiving.

She grabbed a handful and scanned them feverishly, panting like a frightened animal.

'Come on a guided nature trail in the beautiful George Washington National Forest . . .'

'Pet live farm animals in our authentic working Dutch farm . . .'

Griffin let the rest of them flutter to the floor, and turned her head to the truck with its engine running on the other side of the glass.

She pressed her hand to her chest as though it would stop her heart racing, and spoke out loud again, this time through gritted teeth.

'You son of a fucking bitch.'

Nelly kept her eyes on Josh as she held the booklet by a corner of its cover page and shook it. Nothing fluttered from its pages. She smiled at him with raised eyebrows, almost in admiration.

'Just testing?'

Josh stared at her. When he replied in a dry cracked voice, he felt like a child.

'What did I do wrong?'

Nelly McFarlane sighed and walked to the sideboard where she'd originally fetched the booklet, and carefully replaced it in its drawer.

'You did nothing wrong, Mr Spiller. In fact you did everything rather well. It's what you were going to do that couldn't be allowed.'

He watched her cautiously, trying to remind himself that the damage was already done, that he had nothing else to fear. His pulse failed to get the message and it thumped like a piston in his ear. Nelly gently closed the drawer and turned to him.

Looking at this woman in her suburban silk nightwear, her hair scooped back and face without make-up, Josh wanted to laugh at himself, to mock the terror lying like heavy syrup in the pit of his stomach. What could be frightening about someone who looked like they were wandering around the ground floor of Southfork Ranch with a cocktail in their hand, waiting for J.R. to come home? He looked deep into her green eyes and decided there was plenty to be afraid of.

'You really should have read it. It's never too late to embrace the Lord.'

Josh felt a stirring of anger and spat his words at her. 'Were you embracing the Lord when you killed that baby?'

Her face softened, like a lunatic being humoured. 'Yes, Mr Spiller. I surely was.'

Turning his face from her, he blew his ire through pursed lips.

She laughed, a small merry sound that was hideously inappropriate to the situation. 'You see, because you don't know the Lord, you understand so little.'

He looked back at her, his anger manifest in his eyes. 'I guess we might just be talkin' about two different Lords here.'

She raised a finger to her lips as though she were hushing a baby . . .

'No, no no. My saviour is your saviour. The risen Christ. The son of God who died in agony, to show us that life is not merely the finite, random thing you and I might mistake it for. I can understand your desire to believe that my Lord might be, shall we say, on the other team, but you would be very wrong.'

'Then I guess I read a different bible.'

For the first time she looked at him with contempt. 'I guess that you don't read it at all.'

He returned the contempt in her stare. 'So the bible says it's okay to murder kids and mess with the devil.'

There was no question in his voice, just the sarcasm of teacher to wayward pupil. It was the only tool he had left to mask his fear.

She laughed, not unpleasantly, which made it deeply unpleasant. 'You think it's the devil on your tail, Mr Spiller? Good gracious no. Let me assure you, it's a very minor demon indeed.'

Josh ground his back teeth together, trying to keep a grip on reality and his rising rage.

She lifted a finger again, reversing the pupil-teacher relationship.

'And in answer to your question, it was Jesus Christ Himself who "messed with the devil" on many occasions.' She turned back towards the room. 'Just think . . .' she said, crossing to a large arm-chair and sitting down as though about to relax for the evening, 'how fearful that dark legion of unseen creatures must have been, when the Son of God made it so very public that they were there to be commanded by those who possessed the knowledge.'

She gazed at him with a burning righteous intensity.

'And, of course, the purity to use that knowledge.'

She leaned back into her chair with a satisfied smile. 'There's nothing wrong with using them as you will, difficult and troublesome as that might be sometimes. Christ showed us that. Although I have to say, even if they make rather unwilling servants they're no worse than the kind of surly help modern America offers. Have you noticed a decline in the attitude of the service industry? I reckon people have lost pride in serving others.'

'You're fuckin' crazy.'

She weighed him up, seemingly oblivious to his insult.

'Did something at the end of the street cause you bother, Mr Spiller? Make you think you'd gone a little crazy?'

His bitter silence made her laugh again. 'Another even more minor entity. Call it our neighbourhood watch. I won't embarrass you and ask what you saw. Its methods are always effective, but a private matter between itself and the unwelcome visitor.'

Josh felt sick. 'Where does Pace live?'

'Do you plan to give him something? A book perhaps? An envelope? After all the sheriff did his best to persuade you that you were mistaken in what you saw? Dear me. That's very ungrateful.'

Josh clenched his fists impotently, then exhaled and bowed his head to his chest as the hopelessness of it all overwhelmed him.

When Nelly spoke again, it was with surprising softness in her voice. 'Why don't you come back and sit down?'

She extended an arm towards the sofa he'd vacated, and since there seemed little else to do that made sense, he walked to it and sat down heavily. He leaned forward and rested his forehead in his palms.

She brought her feet together daintily, like a debutante at a supper party. Josh stared miserably at her slippers. They were of a silk matching her dressing-gown: her voice, however, had no silk in it whatsoever.

'Who told you?'

Even in his own numbing terror, Josh thought of Griffin's safety. 'I worked it out for myself.'

Nelly McFarlane burst out laughing, a chilling, acid sound that made Josh look up with alarm.

'That, Mr Spiller, would be like a racoon working out time travel.'

'Go fuck yourself.'

This time, she seemed a little more riled by his curse. 'I believe, and God forgive my mouth, that it's you who's fucked. In about six hours from now, to be precise.'

He looked across at her, hatred in his eyes. 'And what if I used those six hours usefully, huh? To drive to the city and tell the cops what really happened to that baby? Who's fucked then?'

She shook her head in mock sadness. 'Now that's exactly what I mean. It was that silly thought that got you into this in the first place.'

Josh barked out a laugh. 'So that's the whole story? I die because I wouldn't sign a fuckin' statement sayin' it was accidental?'

'No. You'll die because you didn't believe it was accidental. You see how important faith can be?'

'Then I guess I'll use my time to go and try to convince someone else.'

She smiled a reptilian smile. 'Be my guest. Do you think I want to be around you come sunrise? I only wish I could be there to hear you tell your tale to some case-hardened city policeman.'

She lowered her jaw to her chest in imitation of Josh, and what she did next chilled his blood against his bones. The imitation he'd anticipated, a woman lowering her voice to affect a man's tone, never happened. Instead, she opened her mouth, and from her lips came Josh's voice. Not an imitation, but the real thing. Its depth and timbre coming from the face of Nelly McFarlane was horrible to hear.

'Eh, officer? You see there's this demon following me and this woman in Furnace, yeah that's Furnace, Virginia, you see, like, she actually killed this baby I ran over . . .'

He slid back into the sofa, his mouth agape at the horror of her conjuring trick. She smiled, as though she had been applauded.

'You see? I doubt if that would be a very good use of your last six hours on earth. What do you think?'

Josh licked his dry lips, pressing further into the back of the sofa as though he might escape through it.

'Do you know what would be?'

Josh shook his head so subtly it was barely a motion at all. But Nelly McFarlane smiled with approval at his attention.

'Understanding the Lord a little better.' Josh swallowed and his fingers slowly curled, making two fistfuls of cushion, while he watched the face of his insane hostess whose unsettling trick suggested she had others.

'Will you at least let me try, Mr Spiller?'

He looked at her and said nothing.

She stood up and extended a hand towards another door in the large room, the one her husband had left through. 'There are so many ways to serve Christ. And serving Him truly can bring great rewards. I just want to sleep easy knowing I've explained our way.'

Josh felt his saliva turn acid again with dread, but as he looked at her a warning in her green eyes told him he was being ordered, not invited. Maybe it was mounting hysteria, maybe just the lunacy of the whole damned thing. But Josh began to laugh. He closed his eyes and put his hands on his big knees and let the laughter gurgle in the back of his throat. Nelly McFarlane watched him silently.

'Shit, man,' said Josh, wiping at an eye when he'd done. 'This is too much. I guess you're goin' to do the Bond movie thing now. Am I right? You know. Like, you say . . . "ah, Mr Bond. Since you're going to die why don't I show you what my plans for world domination really are." Fuckin' far out.'

McFarlane looked at her feet, but it was not to conceal an emotion. It was as though she were growing tired of the conversation. Her voice was weary, but to Josh's ears it still held an immense threat, and unless he was mistaken there was an undercurrent of anger. For some reason, that heartened him.

'I am a philosopher. You don't even know what that means, do you? If I dedicated the rest of my entire life to you, Mr Spiller, painstakingly trying to explain even the first rudiments of the Secret Doctrine, you would know as much as lichen knows on its rock. I have no intention of explaining anything to you, any more than I would read poetry to a brick. I was simply going to extend you the courtesy of knowing a little more about my family, and hope that in understanding why they came here, how much they loved Christ, yet were rejected by people who called themselves Christians, you too might think about why you've let Jesus slip from your life.'

'He never returned my calls.'

She looked at him coldly. 'Before it's too late.'

Josh closed his eyes and put a hand to his mouth. It was already too late. She wasn't the one. She hadn't passed him the runes. So why was he here when there were still at least six precious hours left to breathe? Because only she could tell him where Pace was, that was why.

When he breathed in hard to stem his panic and opened his eyes again, she was standing by the door, still extending that elegant hand like a polite hostess at a dinner party.

What the fuck. He was as crazy as she was. But he was curious. He stood up and walked towards the door.

John Pace turned the lock in his study door, although he knew for sure the other three occupants of the house were deeply asleep. Perhaps it wasn't their intrusion he feared. He walked to the wall and stood in front of the framed woodcut Nelly had given him and Ruth for their wedding anniversary three years ago. He knew it was worth more than his house, but it didn't make it any more pleasant. King Solomon sat on a tall carved throne, his arm outstretched in anger, and in agony on the marble floor before him, smoke billowing from its repulsive hide, writhed a creature that Pace knew well. The woodcut was dated 1632, but the clarity of its detail and the crispness of its line made it look as if it had been executed yesterday. So good, thought Pace with a bitter internal smile, it was almost as though the artist had been drawing from life.

The sheriff took a breath and put his fingers to the edge of the frame. He pulled and it swung out from the wall on its hinges, revealing the wall-safe behind. With trembling fingers he punched in the combination to the tiny, blinking digital keyboard, and waited for the heavy door to click open.

He'd wondered if after six months it would still be potent, and in his darker moments wondered if it would even be there at all. But both anxieties were put to rest when the thin and ancient strip of dried skin twitched as though startled by the light. Pace put his hand out hesitantly and grasped the parchment between thumb and forefinger. It fluttered at his touch and made his throat thick with fear.

Did she know he still had it? That thought was almost more nauseating than the power invested in this vile rectangle. But if Nelly had her suspicions, then she hadn't voiced them. At least not out loud.

He hadn't been able to do it. Not again. Not after what he'd seen in the woods. He clenched his teeth and gripped the runes more tightly. She'd only been an archaeology student from Scotland, for Christ's sake, had gotten some research grant from Glasgow University on a paper she was doing called 'The truth about alchemy'. He remembered her face, sweet and plain, but full of youthful enthusiasm as she sat in his office with a styrofoam cup in her hand, telling him about the project in that cute accent that left him lost after every third word.

Did he know, she'd asked between slurps, that their twin town of Furnace on Loch Fyne in the west of Scotland had been associated with a group of radical and powerful alchemists in the eighteenth and nineteenth centuries? No? Well they had really interesting parish records there that named a few of them, in very vague terms of course.

The villagers then had been frightened of them for some reason, too frightened to name them all, and she didn't know why yet. Maybe just superstition. Maybe just because they were different. In fact, she'd said with great solemnity, that was what was going to make her dissertation so modern, so relevant, the way it would examine not only the truth and nonsense of alchemy, but the continuing persecution of those with other world views. She'd shifted in her seat and said she'd been beside herself with excitement to discover that it looked as if maybe some of the people who left Furnace in Scotland settled here in the Appalachians. It had cost her a lot to get here, nearly the whole grant, but did he know you could get direct flights from Glasgow all the way to Boston now? It was great. And she'd sat beside a really interesting man over on the plane who followed icebergs around the world for some oil company. Although she wasn't sure she believed him. Why would he travel steerage? She'd laughed. Could he believe that?

Was his family originally Scottish? It was? Well there you are, then. Maybe he was related to the alchemists. She'd laughed a lovely throaty laugh again. She'd let him see her dissertation when she finished. Maybe he could end up being able to turn mercury and lead to gold. You could give up your day job, she'd said and laughed some more.

Anyway, she went on. The really, really exciting thing was finding a tiny settlement up here of the same name, oh, she begged his pardon, not that it was that tiny or anything, obviously it was a very lovely place to live, and discovering that some of the names in the phone book here were the same as in the parish records. That was brilliant. She was going to get a first-class degree for this, she could just feel it. There was nothing written about this anywhere. Absolutely nothing. Wasn't it exciting that she'd uncovered the connection? If she got a first, then, she said, she might get a job in a big museum in London. There was this boy you see . . .

He'd driven her out, as requested, to the foundations of the first building erected in Furnace, and shot her through the back of the head. Her face had exploded onto the drystone wall that remained from the old byre, and he'd watched as her legs slowly buckled and her body crumpled like an exhausted deer.

But it had been a kindness. His tourist shopping guide to the Shenandoah valley had remained in his pocket, and between its pages had remained the strip of infant skin. He couldn't have let that young student die the way those men died. She had been dead the moment she'd arrived in Furnace. All he'd done was to make it quick.

But now those runes remained. Pace was out of his depth. When she'd prepared them, did Nelly know the name of the victim? Were they specially conjured to summon that black and terrible death to a named one and no one else? He bit his lip. No. That couldn't be so. Nelly had no idea who the student was. It was he, God forgive him, who'd brought the news to her about the girl. She'd let him deal with the whole thing as though it were a minor inconvenience.

He closed his eyes and thought again of his sons. Gently, he clicked the safe door closed, swung the grim print back into place and walked across the room to his desk.

The ghost of Noah's kiss that had been planted on his father's cheek only hours before, for no reason at all, was so real it was almost moist again. With one hand Pace reached up and touched the spot, and with the other he slid the strip of dried flesh into the front pocket of his trousers.

32

'And so you just decided to do a full one-hundred-and-eighty back-track? All the way back from Kentucky.'

'Hey, lady. It's my fuckin' truck. You don't like it you can walk.'

Griffin didn't like it one bit. But her pulse was racing with a mixture of fear and rage as she sat beside this moron, and she was struggling for control. What to do? The parking lot was empty and she couldn't run onto the interstate and hitch unless she wanted to get killed. How far were they from Furnace? She thought hard about the very few times she'd been driven on the interstate, thought about stopping for a leak before her journey, just after they'd joined the highway. Yes, she could just about picture where this might be. Jesus Christ. That meant they were probably only about two miles from the exit to Furnace and Carris Arm.

She felt light-headed with panic, but she dug her nails deep into her palms and fought for calm. She glanced at the dash. The clock said it was twelve-twenty a.m. She breathed normally and let her heart settle. There were nearly five whole hours left. If this jerk got going like he said he would they could still be half way across the next state by then. She tried to keep her voice steady.

'So when exactly can we move?'

Eddie chewed at his moustache. 'Like I say. When I hear on the CB that the truck's comin'.'

She drove her nails deeper into her skin. 'What the hell does another truck need you to drive along behind it for?'

'It's called an escorted load, lady. I don't know why. I didn't make up the truckin' by-laws of the fuckin' US of A. All I know is, I get the call from my company, I jump to it like a hard-on into a female mud-wrestle.'

She tutted and looked away.

'Hell, now come on there, Elizabeth.'

She looked back at him, eyes full of suspicion.

'Well that's your name, ain't it?' He indicated the brooch.

'Yeah. What's it to you?'

Eddie smiled. 'Just makin' conversation. Eddie's mine, by the ways.'

Griffin glanced contemptuously and with great deliberation towards the dash, suffocated as it was with stickers bought, she imagined, at a variety of truck stops around the country. There was one in the style of the Peterbilt logo, except that the elegant silver type in the oval said 'Eddie'. Another, topped with the brand name of a trailer company, proclaimed on two lines, the top being shakier where the purchaser's name was obviously inserted, 'Eddie Shanklin pulls it in public.' There were at least ten others of a similar nature. Griffin looked back at him with heavily-lidded eyes and sighed.

'No shit?'

He ignored her sarcasm. 'Boyfriend give you the pin?'

She looked down at it, and cleared her throat. 'No. It was a twenty-first birthday present.'

Eddie nodded again, then looked across at the brooch. 'Pretty. Gold ain't it?'

'Yeah.'

She looked at him more suspiciously, not liking this new tone. 'It's the only decent thing I've got on me if you're thinking of turning mugger.'

Eddie sniggered under his mask of hair. He pulled up his jacket sleeve and showed her the two fat identity chains around his equally fat wrist. 'See this, sweetheart? This lets me carry around seven and a half thousand dollars right here on my arm. Twenty-two carats that say I busted my ass up and down these highways haulin' shit an' sugar. Reckon I want to punch out a girl for a thousand-dollar pin with someone else's name on it?'

He looked straight at her, and she wrongly interpreted the stern nature of that gaze as retribution for her mistrust.

She looked away. 'I was kidding.'

In his spot mirror, Eddie saw a car pulling into the lot. He'd spent countless nights in this place alone and never seen a vehicle. It was bad luck. He thought fast. 'Say, if you're gettin' antsy, there's a car comin' in. I could check 'em out an' see if they can take you on.'

She sat up. 'Yeah? Hey don't bother. I can ask them.'

Eddie put a hand out. 'Uh uh. This is a mean highway. I ain't lettin' you drive off till I know it's cool.'

Griffin smiled at him. 'Okay. Thanks.'

Eddie started to climb out. 'You'll tell them I'm headed west. Yeah?'

'Sure.'

Eddie shut the door and walked across to the car, now pulled up alongside the glass section of the building, well aware that Griffin's eyes were fixed on him.

It was a small Datsun, and inside a nervous-looking woman sat waiting while her male companion fumbled in his jacket for something. Eddie bent down and rapped on the window. The woman looked nervously to the man who rebuked her and motioned for her to wind down the window.

'Hey, you help me out here?'

The man looked across at Eddie, crouching as he did so, so he could get a view across the woman's lap. She pinned herself back into the seat as though at the mercy of a leper who might touch her.

'Sure. What's the problem?'

Eddie gave an exaggerated sniff and wiped his nose with his sleeve. 'Well my girlfriend there, she's gone plum loco. Says she needs to get some shit, an' get it fast, get my drift? Or she's gonna blow someone away. Now I don't need that to be me. Know what I mean, fella? So if either of you two good folks got anything worth puttin' in her veins or up her nose I'd be grateful to the tune of a couple of hundred.'

The woman started shifting about, pressing harder into the back of her seat.

The man spoke again, but with a new tone of warning. 'We don't do stuff like that, mister.'

'Aw come on, folks. I wouldn't ask, but it's just she packs heat an' I don't want her flippin' out on me, in the truck half way across the fast lane. Know what I mean? Sure you ain't even got a Tylenol?'

The man said a quiet 'sorry' and wound up the woman's electric window from a button on his side.

Eddie gave them a cheerful wave through the glass and walked slowly back to the truck. Griffin was already fussing with her pack.

'Am I on?'

Eddie whistled through his teeth. 'Can't say. They sure ain't dangerous, but I reckon they're weirder than a seven-dollar bill.'

She looked across at the innocent little car, the woman closing the door as she scuttled into the building to the rest-rooms.

'Why? What's up with them?'

'I don't know. They don't seem to approve of hitchers none. Tried everythin'. Even pretended you was with some Christian fellowship or somethin'. Didn't seem to swallow it.'

Griffin rolled her eyes. 'Yeah. Thanks for nothing. Let me try.'

Eddie smiled as he watched her walk across the lot, trying her best to look small and humble. He watched as the man refused to roll up the window. Watched as she knocked on the glass, shouting through it to him politely and gesticulating to the highway. Watched as the woman returned from the rest-room and walked the long way round the car to avoid her. And then watched with huge relief as the car revved up and pulled away.

Griffin was shaking her head as she climbed back in.

Eddie looked across at her. 'You think they were weird?'

Griffin watched the car pull back onto the interstate and shook her head again for effect. 'Off the fuckin' scale.'

Eddie reached behind the seat and rustled in a sports bag.

'Here. You want a nacho?'

These were the private quarters and they were very different from the cosy affluence of the front of the house. In fact, they were breathtaking. The modest door opened onto a huge circular hall at least forty feet in diameter, its floor a gleaming rink of polished hardwood.

In its centre an ancient rug, also circular, displaying intricate animal patterns woven in muted colours, sat directly beneath an enormous gilded chandelier. Josh stared up in awe at the light. It had seven arms arching from a central ball, each arm taking the shape of a unique writhing dragon, from whose mouth hung an elegant lampshade.

A wide hardwood staircase swept in spiral splendour around one portion of the hall, culminating in two upright balustrades supporting gilded metal orbs representing the sun and the moon.

But the hall was not the lair of a witch. Rather it had the feel of the foyer of some huge and expensive corporate office building. He had underestimated the wealth of these houses. This was not middle-class comfort. This was the realm of the seriously rich. Nelly moved in front of him, turned and held a finger to her lips again.

'We must be quiet. Grandchildren. They sleep so lightly.'

Josh looked at her face filled with affection and with no difficulty conjured up the face that had been standing behind the stroller on the morning of the first of May. And having given mental consent to the memory of that image it was impossible to block the tiny, crushed body blackened with sticky blood in its towelling suit.

Josh closed his eyes for a second and held the bridge of his nose. If there were indeed any children in the house, he wondered not that they slept lightly, but that they could ever sleep at all. His presence here had taken on a dream-like quality, and as he opened his eyes again the brevity of his time, the urgency of his mission, however doomed, nearly took his breath away.

Nelly seemed oblivious to his faltering and walked across the hall as elegantly as her backless slippers would allow to stand in front of double doors of oak, each one beautifully concaved to allow for the curve of the wall. She looked across at him without sympathy, and indicated the doors.

'It's not a dungeon, Mr Spiller. It's merely a tribute to my family. I thought it might help you understand.'

He hated her at that moment, more than he had hated anyone in his life.

Had it not been for the events of the last few days, things he had seen with his own eyes, experiences he could not tidy away as anything but the horrible truth, then he would happily have labelled this woman mad.

But if she was mad, then he was also.

He drew himself up and crossed the floor, his Caterpillar boots making the polished wood squeak in protest as though the floor had never before encountered anything so vulgar in contact with its surface.

The room he entered was small and without windows, but lined to picture-rail height in tongue-and-groove wood panelling. Running down its centre was a long and rugged table, crudely formed as if from some poor farmhouse kitchen. It had a variety of objects placed on it in a regimented fashion, each one facing out to the edge of the table, inviting inspection. The walls of the room were tightly packed with photographs and etchings, pieces of cloth and old candle holders, but there was nothing remotely sinister about the room. It was simply a museum, and as dull as any modern, parochial, child-friendly museum, where the exhibits are of no greater value than their part in social history. Josh almost expected to see a cheesey sign imploring visitors to touch.

Instead, Nelly McFarlane did.

'Please. Look around. Feel free to touch anything.'

Josh didn't want to look round. He wanted to run from here, try to find John Pace. But this woman terrified him almost as much as the thing that followed him here.

He cast her a glance and then awkwardly began a circuit of the room. She stood by the door watching like a curator. 'They came here from Scotland in the eighteen seventies. Not persecuted in the way perhaps that the Jews were, but feared and despised. And why? Because of faith.'

Josh looked at the etchings of glum, craggy faces, a few small oil paintings of cottages by a long grey lake, some obscure old astrological charts. The whole collection looked like some mock-nineteenth-century display in one of those sad yuppie stores in Pittsburgh's Shady Side that Elizabeth sometimes dragged him to screaming, to look at perfumed candles and lace pillowcases. They held absolutely no interest for Josh whatsoever. He turned to the objects on the table: a set of crude metal instruments that looked like a child's geometry set, a wooden mortar and pestle balancing on top of a worn leather book. A small jar filled with some silvery powder sat imperiously beside ordinary kitchen implements. If he had expected something wonderful, something that would have explained the mystery of this hellish quagmire, then his hopes had foundered on this table of junk. Josh breathed hard, trying to fight his panic at wasting time. The emotion overtook him, and he turned to McFarlane, his hands hanging at his sides.

'This is it? The bargain-hour bonanza from a Virginian car boot sale?' His tone was vicious, and whether it was that alone, or the sacrilege of its presence in a shrine to her family, the thunder gathered around Nelly McFarlane. Josh stared at her, and his stomach lurched as he saw her face contort with a mixture of rage and power being held, but only just, under control.

He took a step back from the table, but neither withdrew his comment nor attempted to pacify her. He felt sure, witnessing the strange machinations behind her eyes, that she could strike him down with no more effort than swatting a fly. But he knew too, that she would not. What was more, he hated the bitch so much that to hurt her at all was a triple cherry on the fruit machine.

'Do you have a family, Mr Spiller?'

Her voice was the voice of sinister authority.

He tried and failed to make his sound equally forceful. 'Who doesn't?'

Elizabeth. Oh God. Elizabeth and his child.

'Then you'll know how important they are in your life. Past, present and future.'

I don't have much future left, he thought. Nor much family come to that. What the fuck do I care?

She walked to the other side of the table and stood opposite him. 'You think me a murderer because you saw,' she paused, a coquettish grin being born at the corner of her mouth, 'or thought you saw, me push a child to its death.'

'You are a fuckin' murderer. You want me to make up another name for it?'

'People always make up names for things they don't understand.'

She indicated the pictures on the wall. 'My ancestors had to live with plenty.' She grinned horribly. 'Still, sticks and stones.'

Nelly McFarlane stopped grinning and adopted an insane look of solemnity, like a child asking a parent a favour. 'Are you a believer in a woman's right to choose?'

Josh opened his mouth slightly.

'What?'

'I mean, Mr Spiller, are you in favour of abortion on demand?'

Josh's head spun. What was this? It was as though she were casually starting a bar-room discussion, and one that he'd had often. Yes, of course, he would have said, a bottle of Bud in his fist, the woman should choose. It's her body, her life. Yes. Yes. Yes. You guys are fuckin' Neanderthals if you think different. But now. After everything. Did he still think that? Would his argument still hold water in the motel bar? Did he think he was a bystander, or should he have a say in the fate of the life that he prayed still slept soundly in the safety of Elizabeth's womb? He bowed his head, and let his hands rest on the table taking his weight.

'I guess.'

McFarlane nodded. 'Then what if I told you that the child you saw was not a wanted child? That what you saw was nothing more than a rather late abortion?'

Josh saw the face of Amy Nevin's mother, that ugly shape she made with her mouth. The horror and terror on her face as the wheels crushed the life out of that tiny shell of flesh, and he knew McFarlane was lying. But as quickly, he saw Alice Nevin, slumped at the side of the road mouthing 'I'm sorry' to the man who had brought about this catastrophe. He raised his head, his eyes moist.

'What do you mean?'

Nelly looked deep into his welling eyes, then averted her gaze and walked a little further around the table. 'No. Let me ask you what you mean if you use the word "sacrifice".'

He stared back numbly.

She answered for him. 'I'll guess you would mean the giving up of something precious. Something so unbelievably dear to your heart that it would be inconceivable to part with it, were it not for the love of the something greater to which you offered this prize. Am I right?'

He stared back, still stunned into silence by his own torment.

'Abraham knew that. You remember? God asked him to sacrifice his son. The son he loved more than anything in the world?'

Josh continued to say nothing. There was a dread in his heart that was deeper than the dread of his own death, which he had been facing now in some certainty for nearly a day. He could not contain it or comprehend it, but it overwhelmed him.

'And what did Abraham do?' she continued. She smiled as though she were picking out drapes in a store, continuing in a sunny voice, 'The only thing he could do, Mr Spiller. Obey the will of God.'

He looked up at her from his broken face and his voice was weak and pathetic. 'God stopped him before he killed his son.'

She laughed. 'Yes. Yes, he did. So you have read your bible. I apologize.'

Her laughter stopped and she leaned across the jumble of artifacts towards him. 'But if God hadn't. What then? Would Abraham have been wrong in carrying out that deed? God, after all, created Abraham's son. Did He not have the right to call back that ephemeral gift?'

Josh bowed his head again. Unable rather than unwilling to answer. There was silence for a few moments and then she said carefully, 'Look at this.'

He looked up. She held a wooden stick in the air, shaped at the top in the crude representation of a thistle, and was looking at it as if seeing it for the first time.

'A spurtle. They stirred porridge with it.'

She shot a mad smile across at Josh, and if any part of him had secretly hoped that returning to Furnace would restore him to the land of the sane, would reassure him that the threat of his imminent death was mere fancy, it ended there and then like a child's sand-castle being washed over by the tide.

It took him about two or three minutes to get himself out of bed, get to the door and open it. Elizabeth, dressed in a long T-shirt with a sweater pulled over it, looked frantic when he pushed the door open two inches.

'Sim? Are you okay? I've been knocking forever.'

He nodded once.

'What's wrong?'

'Are you sure you're okay?'

He opened the door properly, aware he'd been keeping her out. 'What's the time?'

Elizabeth looked at her feet. 'Half after midnight.' She looked back up at him. 'I'm really sorry I woke you.'

'I not sleeping. You okay?'

'Can I come in?'

He stood aside.

Sim looked awful, but Elizabeth felt worse. Both because of the dream she'd just had, and from the guilt of disturbing this poor sick man. But she needed company. She was scared.

Sim shuffled back into the house, and Elizabeth was at least relieved to see he was dressed. His crumpled clothes suggested he'd been lying down, but she believed him when he said he hadn't been asleep. They went into the kitchen, which like the rest of the house already had its lights on, and sat at the table. Elizabeth wondered if Sim was scared too. It wasn't like him to waste electricity.

'Sim?'

He blinked at her.

'I had a dream, the craziest, sickest dream I ever had. And I know I sound like a ten-year-old. But I'm scared.'

He looked down at the table. 'I scared too.'

She lowered her voice conspiratorially. 'The phone?'

He nodded.

She nodded too. 'That's what I dreamed about.' She swallowed, looking very serious. 'Sim. I thought you'd gone a little nuts back there. Now you're going to think I've gone too. But I have to ask you something.'

'Sure.'

He sounded so weary, Elizabeth felt embarrassed to be there. She picked at her fingernail.

'This dream. I guess I was just thinking about you, and Josh and everything, you know?'

He stared at her, unmoving.

'In my dream it rang, and I answered, and there was all that noise again. So I did what you said, remember? Spoke with my thoughts?'

She closed her eyes and curled her fingers.

'Oh, Sim. This thing. This unbelievable, disgusting ... thing, started to come out of the phone, and it was laughing at me. Saying terrible things.'

'What you going to ask, Elizabeth?'

It sounded to her like he didn't want this. Wanted her to stop talking about the whole thing and go. It was so unlike the man who would normally, any time of the day or night, do anything to delay Josh or Elizabeth just to chew the fat. She opened her eyes and swallowed across at him. 'The thing ... you saw. What was it like?'

He bent his head forward almost as if he'd fallen asleep. But with his chin on his chest he spoke quietly. 'You know what it like, Elizabeth. It like a nightmare man inside an animal, it got mean red eyes that blink sideways, and claws and teeth that stink like it been inside a carcass already, and its skin that don't look like skin, smoking like it been on fire.'

Her hands had gone over her mouth, and her eyes were as wide as they would be without falling from her face. Elizabeth shook her head, willing it not to be so. Her voice was pleading and tiny.

'You can't know that. You can't know my dream.'

Sim let his head come back up and he looked at her. 'That what stopping Josh calling.'

She took her hands from her mouth, got up slowly and walked back and forward a few paces. 'Jesus Christ. We've gone crazy together, Sim.'

'Maybe.'

'How can I ever answer the phone again?'

''Cos if he call again, he goin' to need you to.'

She looked over at him and joined him at the table again. 'That stuff. About talking to him with my thoughts. What made you say that?'

He shook his head and looked down. How old he looked, she thought.

'Dumb village talk, that's all. Used to be if someone put spell on you, made your cattle dry, made your babies sick, worst thing was you couldn't talk to no one you loved. Everyone run away and leave the person alone. Person go crazy with loneliness and fear. But sometimes, people who loved them could think at them and be heard. So they say.'

'You believe that?'

'I don't believe spells was what caused the misery people sometimes thought it had. They just simple people. Just take against someone and think there was curses where there was only cattle colic or diphtheria. But I don't know nothing that say it can't maybe be true.'

She sat back in her chair. 'I can't believe we're having this conversation.'

Sim looked at her as if this was the first interesting thing she'd said all night. 'Me neither. These modern days. Not jungle. I just a crazy old man who make you dream crazy stuff too. Go back to bed, Elizabeth.'

She looked with pleading eyes, then got up reluctantly, a scared child going back to the dark bedroom. Sim did nothing to stop her. She paused on her way out the door.

'You know what the thing in my dream said, Sim?'
He didn't want to know. His face said so. But she told him anyway.
'It said, he's dead already, bitch.'

33

The bad thoughts had stopped. The thoughts its carrier had entertained about killing it. It writhed again comfortably, stretched, almost able to see its own limbs as they continued to form. Sometimes it was uncomfortable. Like when its carrier was thinking hard about how to expel it, or when someone was trying to hurt its carrier. But then even if it couldn't touch yet, couldn't make its physical presence tangible to all, it could still make its carrier dream. And what dreams they were.

It shared the dreams, the way it shared everything. And while they made the carrier sick with terror, they made it feel whole, contented, feeding on that fear.

It asked itself again, for the thousandth time, had it been born before? Its time was not far. And yes. Yes, it was almost sure it had.

'Can I know two things?'

'That depends if the answer is within your meagre comprehension,' she said, still examining the spurtle as though it were a work of art.

Josh had enjoyed the look of anger of McFarlane's face when he insulted her little display. He was going to die. He could do what he liked, and he wanted to see that flash in her eyes again. He would take his time.

'Why did you use me for, what'd you call it? The "late abortion"? Why not just kill her yourself?'

She tapped the wooden stick thoughtfully on her cheek. 'You won't understand this. But the answer is the child must be given up. That is, to take the life oneself is not enough. God knows, particularly in this part of the mountains, the creatures who inhabit these backwoods cabins are bashing their darling dull-eyed babies against the wall in a drunken stupor on such a regular basis, their power might exceed mine a hundredfold if that were the solution. No. You see, it must be taken away from you. Stolen from you. Ripped from you. Wrenched from you. In the absence of like-minded, reliable colleagues who might perform that task for me, I have been forced to find a different, shall we say more modern, method, of giving up.'

She looked across at him.

'You see? The blank stare of the blue-collar worker. The lichen on its rock.'

The stare was not blank, but she ignored its undertow and turned from him to examine a long painting that looked to Josh like two figures bent over a flame. She tapped it with her spurtle and laughed, her back still to him.

'They were mostly puffers in Scotland, you know. Hopeless amateur chemists who understood nothing and searched for everything. I went there you know, a few years back. To Furnace. I shouldn't have, really. It was heartbreakingly disappointing. Rather a nice oyster restaurant at the head of the loch, I recall. Fine fish, ruined by unforgivably poor service. And then the village itself. Dear me. A few modern little houses with their attendant suburban bushes. No trace of the laboratory the town was named after. But then it was only the McFarlanes who reached the truth of the Philosopher's Stone.'

She paused, her voice becoming thoughtful, as though she'd forgotten Josh's presence. 'Imagine having the Philosopher's Stone in their grasp. And all they could do was to make gold. A bottomless well of servitude, every unwilling recruit from the dark legion at your disposal.'

She turned to him, very much aware of his presence, to emphasize her point like a lecturer.

'Part of the price paid by those unpleasant little creatures, the price for choosing the wrong side, you know, falling from grace with the rebel angel.' She turned back to the painting. 'And all they could do was to make gold.'

Josh wondered at that moment why he shouldn't kill her. She was a slight woman. He could jump the table and be on her in seconds. And if he was to die anyway, why not have the satisfaction of taking the mad bitch with him, ensuring that no more junior Furnace citizens rolled under trucks? Josh looked down at his feet. He was no murderer. The baby's death still stuck to his soul like an acid poultice. But as he looked up at the back of her head, watched the set of her slim shoulders beneath her gown, he had an almost palpable sensation that she wanted him to attack her. His fingers tingled with the sensation of it, and her voice, full of expectation and warning, made them worse.

'And the second thing?'

Josh took a breath and wrestled physical violence from his mind, although the urge to hurt her was almost stronger than his urge to breathe.

'When you killed Alice Nevin's baby. Why'd you dress up like an old whore at a pimp's funeral?'

Nelly McFarlane stayed facing the wall for a second then without warning spun round and brought the spurtle down so hard against the edge of the table that Josh jumped. Whatever game of civilized torment she had been playing, she had abandoned it. Josh took a step back from the creature crouching slightly over the table, now pointing the ludicrous wooden stick at him as though it were a wand. Her teeth were bared and her eyes had turned a deeper shade of green, glittering like mica in a boulder. The voice that came from her curled lips was not one he would ever care to hear again.

'You have no idea who you're talking to, do you, you little cunt lick?'

Josh drew enough breath to force a phoney laugh. 'Cunt lick? That's Deuteronomy. Right? Chapter three, verse four?'

Her hand on the table was like a claw, and she continued to look at him along the shaft of her wooden stick, her chest rising and falling as she fought to control herself. It took her a moment, but she succeeded. Before his eyes, the feral predator who crouched ready to strike, slowly changed back to smug suburban housewife. But it did so with a struggle. She straightened up and took a breath through flared nostrils.

'At this time in May, the sun rises here at five-fourteen precisely. The next few hours are not going to be pleasant for you.'

Josh felt his heart reach for his throat. Nelly put down the ridiculous porridge-stirrer and slid her hand into the pocket of her gown.

She pulled out a small plastic container and threw it across the table at him. It rattled as he intercepted it and he looked down at the catch. A bottle of painkillers.

'If I were you I'd take at least eighty and pray they work before the first rays hit you.'

'Where's Pace?'

She ignored him, walked to the door and opened it. 'It's nearly come through, now. I can feel it on you. Try and find some human company for the last dark hours ahead.'

Josh wiped his mouth and walked towards the open door. As he passed by an etching McFarlane held out a finger. 'There, Mr Spiller. You asked why I . . . dressed for the occasion of sacrifice?'

Josh turned to what she indicated. A tiny etching he hadn't noticed before. It showed a man and a woman in what looked like heavy mayoral robes, both standing by the long dark lake, the man holding an orb in his hands, the woman holding a struggling naked infant upside down by one ankle.

'You see, ceremony is everything. They dressed as they felt most powerful in their mortal roles. It enhances the potency of the Great Work.'

He looked away and continued towards the door. As he passed without glancing her way and re-entered the hall, she spoke again.

'I, of course, do the same. Which, to answer your insolent question, is why I dressed as I do when I instruct our financial people. I'm sorry if it's not to the liking of a truck driver. It's Versace. Perhaps it goes down rather better in the boardrooms of Europe than in the diners of Pittsburgh. Not much polyester content.'

He looked back at her once with disgust, then, as a child began to cry from somewhere far distant in the house, he started to cross the hall.

'She told you about the runes, didn't she?'

Josh froze in his tracks.

'Griffin.'

There was a smile in her voice, as she enjoyed saying the word, enjoyed seeing the effect it had on Josh's retreating shoulderblades.

He turned, and his face contorted with hatred. He lifted a finger and pointed at her.

'She's long gone, you sick bitch.'

Nelly McFarlane smiled.

'For her sake, I hope you're right. I really do.'

She closed the door and climbed the stairs towards the cries of the child.

He knew Archie Cameron was watching him, but John Pace didn't hurry, walking slowly around Jezebel's cab, checking it out like a kid at a truck show. He slid Josh's log book into his pocket, zipped up the front of his jacket and took his time crossing the street and entering the office.

Deputy Cameron was sitting at his desk, but Pace knew he'd only just left the window.

'Took your time, sheriff.'

Pace opened the door in the glass partition and walked in.

'Take as long as I damned well please.'

Cameron absorbed the irritation of his senior without comment, then sat back in his chair and clasped his hands in front of him.

'He went to the councillor's house.'

Pace sat down on Lena's empty desk. His deputy was looking smug, as though passing this information had somehow raised his status.

'So?'

Archie sat back up, irritated. 'So he was askin' where you lived.'

Pace looked away, as if bored. He picked up a few scribbled messages from Lena's desk and flicked through them. Archie Cameron pulled at his collar.

'She wants you to drive over there.'

'I gather.'

'You want me to come too?'

Pace shook his head casually, still looking at the bits of paper in his hand as though they were important. If he wanted to take his deputy to boiling point, he was doing all the right things. His tone changed from snippy informer to spiteful child. 'Can't help wonderin' why she needs to see you this time of the mornin', sheriff? Maybe she didn't expect that dumb trucker to come strollin' back in here like he did. Maybe she thought she did her bit, and keepin' him away was yours. Huh?'

'Archie?'

His deputy's face was twisted with scorn. 'Yeah?'

'You figure you'll be sheriff one day, don't you?'

The man held Pace's stare unflinching.

'You got sons. Everyone knows what that means.'

'But if they didn't want the job. If something happened to me? A new family was needed to take over, you'd like it if it was you?'

'Guess it'd be okay.'

Pace got up off his desk and walked to Archie's. He stood in front of the man and leaned forward, his straight arms taking his upper body weight.

'Are you never afraid, Archie?'

The younger man grinned moronically. 'I believe in the Lord.'

'And the things that do Nelly McFarlane's bidding? Do you believe in them?'

'I heard talk.'

The man's grin had faded.

'Listen to me, Archie. You get nothin' for nothin'. You understand?'

Cameron looked back earnestly at his chief. 'I know that. We all know what the councillor gives.'

Pace stood upright. 'Do we? And what about us? What do we give for the few scraps she throws us? Huh?'

Cameron shrugged. 'We just believe.'

Pace bowed his head to his chest, dismissed the reply with a shake. 'No. We live in fear. That's what we pay.'

The deputy stared back at him for a moment, before gesticulating a dismissal into the air. 'Yeah? And who don't live in fear? Huh? Think they'll lose their jobs. Think their kids'll take drugs. Think the gang at the end of the street'll break in and kill 'em. Bein' scared's part of life.'

Pace nodded, then looked up and replied gently, almost sadly. 'Then I guess you will make a good Furnace sheriff, Deputy Cameron. 'Cos when the somethin' we can't even think about comes creepin' up on you in the night, knowin' your thoughts, feelin' your breath, an' waitin' until it can rip at you and turn you inside out; the somethin' that's worse than any nightmare you ever had or any bogeyman a child with a fever hollered at in the dark; then I guess you goin' to shrug and treat it like a big electric bill came through the mail.'

He held the man's gaze a few more moments then turned and walked towards the door. Cameron called after him.

'You just talkin' like this 'cos it's you who's afraid.'

Pace hesitated, looking at the door . . .

'Yeah. I am.'

He left quietly. Archie Cameron watched him go, cleared his throat, shuffled some paper then glanced towards the empty office adjoining his, a doorway of dark and stillness. He ran a finger around his collar, got up and put the striplights on.

34

Nineteen minutes past two. He looked at his watch and he knew that at that precise moment, he had decided to die. It had taken him twenty minutes to walk back the long way round to the truck from McFarlane's house, avoiding the corner though he knew in his heart there would be no ice cream sign there now, and it had been twenty of the darkest minutes in his life.

He could feel the beast constantly, keeping pace with him, moving without sound but never hurrying. Sometimes he caught a maddening glimpse of something running low over a porch, or disappearing with spidery agility into a crawl-space, and his stomach walls touched.

The worst had been only yards from Jezebel. He had tried so hard not to run, and then the sound came again. The unearthly rasping attempt at his name, followed this time by something that approximated a thin laugh.

His body had acted for him, bolting forward towards the distant and false security of Jezebel, but leaving him short of breath, having to stagger against a tree, back up against the trunk to gulp in air. His hands had gripped the rough wood behind his hips and moved against it as he stared back up the street towards the source of the sound. That was when his fingers had touched something rougher than bark. It took only seconds, but the information he processed through the tips of his fingers seemed to take an age to reach his brain. In that time, his skin registered a substance that felt like wet leather pitted with thick, coarse hairs, hot and stinging to the touch and leaving a residue like mild acid on Josh's fingers. He pulled his hand away with a shout only to look down and see two long fingers of a clawed hand slide from view around the wide bole of the tree.

He launched away as though expelled by electricity and ran at the truck, gulping back the vomit that nestled at the base of his throat. It was only on reaching the door and falling gratefully against it that he remembered the movements in the sleeper, that writhing beneath his comforter.

Nineteen minutes past two in the morning, and the stark realization that sobered his fright rather than fuelled it, was that if Jezebel wasn't safe, then nowhere was. The tape in the machine labelled 'Josh Spiller' had come to the end and there was no automatic rewind. The only choice left now, was how he was to die.

Josh stood up and fought to catch a breath.

'Promise me,' Griffin had said, *'you'll think about the first option.'*

What had been unthinkable for thirty-two years now seemed not only plausible, but desirable. Josh didn't want to die, but unlike the demented cowardice that suicide had always suggested to him, to cheat the creeping darkness at his heels by taking his own life suddenly seemed almost honourable.

He'd only ever known one person in his life who'd committed suicide. Tan Levinson had been a company driver who sometimes drove the same route as he and Eddie, and ended up swallowing midnight breakfasts in the same stops or unloading aluminium in the same docks. He'd been a quiet man, had a wife and one son in Detroit, but nothing had ever made either of them think he was ready to pull the rip cord.

Eddie used to call him Springsteen, on account of Levinson always leaving one unused work-glove hanging from the back pocket of his jeans, but any jokes at his expense were waved away amicably with a limp hand as he smiled from behind a veil of cigarette smoke.

And then one January, he'd pulled into the TA at Tuscaloosa, parked between a tanker and a Schneider doubler, taken a hand-gun from his overnight bag and spread his brains over the padded walls of his sleeper. No one knew if there was a reason. Everyone said there had been none. But Josh remembered once, late at night in a stop in South Carolina, that Levinson had stared out the window into the blackness and said something to Josh, apropos of nothing, that had stuck with him:

'If you don't outrun it, it runs over you.'

Josh had cast Eddie a glance, hoping for a laugh, but he'd grunted and carried on reading a truck-trading free-sheet.

'Yeah, Tan. What's that?'

'Life, you dumb fuck. What you think?'

Josh had played with his coffee cup, slightly embarrassed without the jocular support of his partner. 'Uh-huh? So how you outrun it then?'

Levinson had turned and looked at him with tired eyes. 'Get to the finish line first.'

Josh put his head against Jezebel's door, his own name flourished above his bowed skull like graffiti, and wept.

'I thought it best if this weren't found in the truck.'

Nelly took the log book from Pace's hand and raised an eyebrow at it. She looked back up at him and smiled, then cradled it in her lap like an opera programme. 'You have a policeman's attention to detail.'

He looked at her impassively. 'How long's he got?'

She crossed her legs under a black wool dress and tipped her head to one side. 'Now, come on, John. How many times have you helped summon this particular servant?'

'The same one,' he said in a whisper, ignoring the question.

She rubbed a finger and thumb together absently. 'As far as your understanding stretches, yes. The simplest way I can paint it is it's the same species. But that's not quite right either. Lord, I'm not in the mood any more tonight for instructing the ignorant.'

Pace swallowed, and she waited a moment before smiling cruelly. 'You saw it, didn't you?'

He said nothing and she continued as though she hadn't expected a reply. 'And that's good. Because to know is always better than not to know.' Her voice hardened. 'I want you to come into the laboratory.'

Pace shook his head. 'It wasn't a request, sheriff.'

She stood up and led the way out the room. He knew the route well enough and after looking at his feet, alone in her study for a few moments, his legs found the strength to follow.

He walked slowly across the polished hall floor, through the Scottish Room to the far wall, where the concealed door stood a few inches ajar.

John Pace pushed the door open and paused. He had been here only once, ten years ago, and although the sacrifice had been nearly consumed by then, even the cloudy memory of its remains nauseated him. It would be worse now. A fresh sacrifice. A fresh horror.

But soon it would be over, and he dug deep to summon the strength to face his destiny. His jaw moved as his back teeth clenched involuntarily, and Pace walked forward, descending the narrow wooden steps with difficulty, burdened by his thick frame. There were fourteen steps without the benefit of a handrail, ending in a small square landing and door lit by a single naked bulb. He went down holding on to the brick-lined wall for support, and wiped a film of sweat from his upper lip. The whispering had been audible from the top of the stairs, surrounding him and growing in strength as he descended. But now, standing before the half-open door it was almost loud enough to make out isolated words. Pace clenched his teeth harder and knew that would be fruitless. He had nearly bolted last time, afraid for his life. Afraid that whatever belonged to the ugly rasping little voices, lisping those whispers, would appear to fulfil the plans they were hatching.

The words they were speaking were in a language he didn't care to comprehend, and his fists opened and closed against the horror of syllables that he knew no human mouth could form. He lifted his head higher, put a hand out and pushed the door open.

The whispering stopped abruptly as though a tape had been cut, and while he still had the courage he stepped through the doorway and into Nelly McFarlane's lab.

He was right. It was much worse. The last time, he remembered, his entrance had been like breaking a spider's web. Not in the literal sense.

There had been nothing to feel. It was a subtle internal sensation alerting unused senses to an unidentifiable threat. This time as he crossed her diabolical threshold the invisible threat was not subtle. It wrapped him like chainmail. Pace drew in a faltering lungful of air, and across the small room Nelly McFarlane watched him without expression.

'Close the door.'

He fought for breath. The smell in the room was complex and heady, so thick with elements other than oxygen that it made him wonder if it was breathable. He closed his eyes briefly, and as his hand pushed the door shut behind him he concentrated on calming his panic and breathing normally.

She held up Josh Spiller's log book, then threw it down contemptuously in front of a buzzing, illuminated computer screen.

'He wasn't supposed to come back here.'

Nelly McFarlane's voice was light, but Pace could read it better. He looked up and kept his eyes firmly on hers.

This was not a space he cared to look around. It had the feel of a boiler room, indeed the louvred slit of a window that ran along the base of the yard wall above them betrayed to the rare inquisitor who might ponder on it from outside, only that it contained part of a heating system.

Two generations of McFarlane children had kicked a ball against that grate in the stone wall, believing that the thin pipe expelling steam from the centre of the metal slats was nothing more than plumbing.

Or perhaps they believed nothing of the sort. Maybe they could hear sounds coming from that pipe as they bent down to retrieve a ball, or chalk a scored point on the stone. Sounds like malicious whispering voices. Maybe smells that weren't the smells of radiator steam. Was it really better to know, than not to know? John Pace didn't think so.

Even with his eyes firmly on her face and not what lay between them, his skin was crawling and he pressed back against the door, with what he imagined was a subtle movement. She looked at him with contempt.

'I'm finding the mortal fear of the unknown increasingly unattractive, John.'

Pace curled his fingers into the wood of the door and tried to make his reply sound normal. 'Ain't that what we trade on?'

'We?' She smiled. 'I appreciate your solidarity.'

'Nothin's changed I know of.'

She scrutinized his face for a second, an enigmatic expression behind her eyes. But when she spoke it was with the familiarity of a boss to an employee. 'You let him come back here. You make sure you clean up.'

Emboldened by the commonplace nature of her scolding, Pace let his eyes leave McFarlane's face, and, studiously avoiding the horror in the centre of the floor, took in the room's details.

The light source was an incongruous fluorescent tube hanging on two chains from the low, open-beamed ceiling, but despite the broad reach of its harsh illumination, the room was alive with shadows.

A stainless steel counter, like the kitchens of a large hotel, ran the full length of the opposite wall. In its centre was a sink and surgical taps, a tray with implements lying at its side. The computer screen that buzzed and clicked as its display changed, sat at the end of the counter, a thick stalk of cables snaking from its back into a hole in the rough-hewn brick wall. Apart from the stark modernity of that area, the room was a repugnant temple to McFarlane's madness.

Her athanor, the bullet-shaped alchemic furnace that had travelled the Atlantic with her ancestors, was mounted on a block of granite, and he could see a blue flame flickering in its heart as it stood unassumingly in the corner. Both the stone and the wall above the neat metal capsule were furred with a soot-like substance, in which scrawled marks, bizarre childlike writing, had been made with something sharp. Pace swallowed his fear as his instinct told him that Nelly herself had not been responsible for those wild symbols, and he looked away.

On the stone floor in front of the athanor, a pentangle marked out in dark brown smears was littered inside with droplets of mercury as though a vessel containing the quicksilver had been dropped and smashed. Against the wall four of the familiar metal packing-crates were stacked neatly, the ones that would take the plane ride away from here, like they always had, when the dull lead inside had been transmuted into something more useful.

As he looked he was sure he saw a furtive movement in the shadow behind the pile, the portion of a spidery limb being pulled back into the darkness. He looked away again quickly, desperate to focus on something that filled him with neither revulsion or fear. But looking away brought his gaze back to the centre of the room. John Pace expelled air through his teeth with an inaudible hiss.

Nelly McFarlane snapped at him. 'Don't be a child.'

He licked dry lips and surprised himself by finding he still had a voice and a fool's courage. 'You mean me, or her?'

He had no need to indicate what he referred to. McFarlane looked at him with a curious expression which made Pace squirm as he interpreted it as a look of anthropological interest.

Between them was a large flat stone, a soft sandstone lozenge carved around the edge with crude runic symbols. God forgive him, but he had personally arranged for its safe passage from the New York docks after its purchase in Scotland, and now it lay on its back in this room instead of in the field on the edge of Loch Fyne where it had stood for over three thousand years. But if it needed compensation for that blasphemous wrenching from its site and interruption in purpose, it had it in the form of the carefully dissected remains of Amy Nevin, which were stretched out on it like those of a laboratory rat.

The corpse was naked, and most, but not all of the skin, had been flayed and hung in tidy strips on a grid of steel sail-wires that suspended the massive stone from a crossed beam in the ceiling. Remaining patches of milk-white skin adhered only to those parts of the baby that had been most badly crushed, and an incision from breastbone to genitals had been clamped wide open. There was a strange beauty about the red gash of that empty cavity, the way it echoed an exotic orchid, the tiny white ribs like stamens from a bloom. And although the organs that had been laid within the smaller pentangles around the stone were not in themselves shocking, being livid with the bloom of the healthy child they had come from, the tidy, methodical way in which they had been sorted for different use made Pace nauseous again.

'It's rather late to give her advice, John.'

She was still examining him, eager to see what he would do next, to see if his challenging words would expand to a physical threat. Her expression, a slightly open mouth and lowered brow, suggested that she might relish that. What he did made her eyes glaze over with disappointment.

John Pace backed against the door and slid down it to a crouch. Something wet scuttled deeper under the stone's shadow as his view altered to take in more of the floor, and he closed his eyes against the slight trail it had left. He heard her sigh.

'I want him gone before it's time. You've nearly three hours to persuade him.'

He wiped his mouth with an arm and blinked up at her. 'And Griffin?'

'I would hazard a guess and say she's a lot further than three hours away. What do you think?'

Her voice was so hard, the barked, weary instructions of emperor to slave, that the tenderness in his caught her off-guard.

'Councillor? How much more killin'?'

Nelly McFarlane looked over the hanging stone at the rugged man crouched like a frightened child against her door and let her hands fall to her sides. She walked slowly around the fearsome obstacle and knelt in front of him, putting slim hands on knees that stretched his policeman's slacks to the limit in this unpolicemanly position.

'John. Amy was mine to give. You know that. That's why we have power again. Look.' She indicated the room he knew was far from empty.

'Can't you feel it?' She laughed like a young girl. 'They're no more willing, and no less eager to deceive and disobey, but, oh sheriff, I'm so much stronger.'

He looked at her hands on his knees, willing them to stop touching him.

'And the trucker?'

'Would you mourn him if he was a name in a newspaper paragraph detailing the fatalities in a ten-vehicle pile-up?'

She didn't wait for an answer, but shook her head for him.

'No. Because that's the random daily nature of life and death. Just as this is. Just as he might have made the wrong decision on the highway and ended up mince, he just drove into the wrong town. Lord knows you gave him enough chances, but the stupid man simply made the wrong decision over his statement.

'His death at least will be more interesting than a mundane head injury finishing him off in some county ambulance with poor suspension. At least in the last few days, and certainly in the last few minutes of his ordinary little life, he will glimpse that part of the secret and incredible world hidden from the majority of men, that you are privileged to witness, and I am privileged to control.'

Her face was mad with an inner ecstasy that Pace had never seen in her mother. But, as Pace had reasoned so recently that it still seemed like a blasphemy to think it, like most of Nelly McFarlane's relatives who had possessed the power of the philosopher, Morven McFarlane hadn't survived long enough to curb that insanity.

He nodded, eyes down, as though he understood, but she could tell he was lying. Nelly McFarlane could tell a whole lot of things. Especially until the remains of that tiny body were all used up.

'Do you think we do harm, John?'

There was no use in pretending. 'We kill. We keep on killin'.'

She shook her head. Not unkindly. 'We kill rarely. In comparison to some inner-city juvenile gang, or a despotic government, we're angels of mercy.'

'But councillor, Jesus said . . .'

She cocked her head, waiting, and he knew it was useless. The hands he so badly wanted off his legs, tightened their grip on the flesh around his knees.

'The Antichrist will come, John. I've told you this. Often. Make no mistake. And only we will have the financial resources to combat him. And why? Because through the love of Christ we have the Philosopher's Stone, the means to conjure and control not only the tawdry metal that the world holds so dear, but the very dark forces themselves that would side with the Antichrist. Now, you think our Lord would disapprove of the loss of a few unimportant lives when it's part of how we're preparing to defend His return?'

He spoke in a tiny voice, that was almost comic coming from such a large man. 'Not one sparrow falls.'

Mercifully, she removed her hands. Her face was still soft, but her voice had an edge returning to it. 'Then Christ'll know when our trucking sparrow falls at sunrise, and will presumably mourn him.' She stood, smoothing her dress. 'Stand up.'

With the effort of the portly, he obeyed, following her with his eyes as she crossed the room to the aluminium workbench and picked up a small glass bottle next to the sink. She held it cheek high.

'I have the usual assistance if you require it.'

Pace swallowed. 'I don't reckon he's got a gun.'

'In his heart he believes you passed him the runes, John. When he can't give them back, who knows what he might do?'

He could tell there was suspicion growing in her face that he wouldn't accept the tiny bottle of grey liquid, but his hand trembled at his side at the very thought of the revolting concoction that it contained.

'I'll be okay.'

She looked hard at him.

'Interesting. You don't want to take it, John. Yet you know its power. That nothing can harm you for seven hours.'

He stared back at her, silent.

'Nothing human,' she added with malice.

He ground his back teeth again and held out a shaking hand. Nelly McFarlane crossed the room to him, looked down at his wide palm and held the bottle between her thumb and forefinger. 'Make him go to the woods. It's tidier.'

Like a bully stealing a child's playground candy, she closed her fingers around the bottle with a flourish, turned her back, walked to the bench and started to wash her hands under the surgical taps. John Pace looked down at his empty hand, slowly closed his own fingers and turned to go. As he faced the plain door his thoughts became words.

'You ever afraid, councillor?'

When he realized he'd spoken, he turned back into the room. She still had her back to him at the sink, but there was something changing about the atmosphere in the room. Either the light was dimming or his eyes were failing, but the shadows were starting to have their own life, and Nelly McFarlane seemed to be absorbing the dark areas of the room. She turned to him slowly and he pressed back up against the door again as her face was revealed.

Her green eyes were glittering black pricks of hatred sunk in two deep, round craters. Her mouth was grotesquely wide at the corners, curling up in a clownish leer, and beneath her slightly parted lips, Pace feared he could see considerably more teeth than she could have called her own only minutes ago. When the deep, rasping voice came from that mouth, John Pace was already fumbling behind him for the door-handle, his mouth agape in terror. 'Why should I be afraid?'

He grunted in his passion to escape, but even as he found the handle, slammed it down and stumbled through the doorway, part of his rational mind was thinking about that hideous inhuman face, and the very faint something he had so briefly glimpsed behind its eyes.

He had nearly puked his guts in his effort to reach the top step, by the time he decided something. It surprised him, horrified and comforted him in equal measures, but he would swear he was right.

Sometimes, somewhere deep inside her armour, Nelly McFarlane was very afraid indeed.

*　　*　　*

'It's three o'clock.'

'Yeah?'

Griffin rubbed at her forehead. 'Look. Can't you just get on that radio thing and ask if someone else can pick me up from here?'

Eddie looked across at her from behind a magazine he'd selected purposely from the ancient pile behind his seat to offend her, titled *Asian Babes*. 'Hell I'm sorry. Didn't 'preciate you was a payin' passenger. I kinda thought you was hitchin'. You know? Travellin' for free? Takin' other people's gas and drivin' time so you can see the country without playin' jack-shit?'

Griffin folded her arms like a Vaudeville wife and looked out her window at the empty parking lot.

Eddie got back to the centrefold of Sinijta, originally from a village called Kharahyira, who had big naked tits and the bottom half of a sari tied round ample child-bearing hips, but wanted to convince the reader she was interested in in-line skating. He sniffed back some snot in the back of his throat and addressed the magazine rather than his reluctant passenger. 'Anyhows. Can't call out until they calls me. Need to keep on this channel.'

Griffin looked at him with disgust, then looked back out the window. The long dark band that marked the ridge of the mountains was already visible, by virtue of the lightening sky behind it.

Her heart tripped over itself in her chest as she imagined that hot, celestial orb hurtling over the Atlantic towards them, and how its arrival, so eagerly anticipated by every kind of man through centuries, was dreaded by one today, not more than fifteen miles from here.

'I need a leak again.'

Without looking up, Eddie lifted a hand indicating the door, as though she would have trouble finding it.

'Don't go without me.'

He made a small head movement that could have meant anything, and she climbed out in a sulk. As she crossed the cold lot towards the building, Griffin shivered, squinting hatred at the magnolia sky like a vampire.

35

He almost laughed at the things he was thinking. Would she manage to send in all the bills to the dispatcher and get the money due him? Would she knew how to fix the cold faucet in the bathroom when it did the weird hissing thing? Would Dean come to his funeral, and if he did, would he wear that Blues Brothers suit of his and embarrass the shit out of Elizabeth?

Josh sat upright behind Jezebel's wheel, the bottle of painkillers McFarlane had tossed him lying on the road beneath the truck where he'd ejected it with contempt out the window. He was almost delirious with the decision he'd made, but he had to think straight now. Just because he'd decided he was to die his own way didn't mean it couldn't be done properly. An obvious suicide would mean no insurance money, and that was unacceptable. She didn't know it, but when Josh was on the road Elizabeth was not only on his mind, she was on his life policy. Sure, he hadn't made the commitment of marriage, but he'd made plenty of financial commitments, his own particular way of binding them. Commitments that felt more solid to him than a white dress, some finger-food and a bad band for a hundred guests in a overpriced hotel. But they'd never discussed it.

Too late. All too late.

At least if he did it the right way, just drove the truck off the road, it would look like an accident. Then the horrible thought occurred. What if he didn't die? Plenty of guys had survived blistering accidents. Accidents that saw their rigs tumble down canyons and let them walk away with no more than a cut chin and bruised wallet. He closed his eyes against the thought of lying injured, waiting for that nightmare thing to come and do its worst while he lay helpless. With a grimace, he opened his eyes, looking out the window and fiddling with his earring as if he were thinking about nothing more than buying new mud-flaps. And suddenly, with a force that took his breath away, the reality, the awfulness, the sheer gravity and finality of his situation hit him in a wave of grief.

He was no suicide case. He had no idea what went through the heads of those sad individuals who pulled their own plugs, but he was damned sure it wasn't the kind of lucid sorting and planning he had been indulging in grotesquely for the last few moments.

He didn't want to die. But he was going to. One way or another. And he would never see Elizabeth, his love, his friend, his reason for everything, again. Josh Spiller felt then as though he had died already. His heart shrivelled, and the panic that constricted his chest and throat made him want to rip at his own flesh to relieve it. He let go a whining sound through his teeth and his fists opened and closed impotently. Jezebel's door fell open against his weight, as he pressed down on the handle with a desperate arm, and he tumbled out the truck and into the night. He wanted to run, as if running could do him some good, but instead he stood on the asphalt panting, in a semi-crouch.

'Elizabeth!'

His wail echoed in the empty street and the dimly-lit window in the sheriff's office stared back like an eye with a cataract. Josh gasped at the volume of his voice in the still of the night, then he turned from the truck and ran down the street towards the corner where a lone phone booth stood sentinel outside a shuttered store. Josh fumbled in his pockets for money, for anything that might connect him across the states to his love. They were empty.

A newspaper vending machine sat at the doorway of the store and with a bouncing run to gain momentum, he went at it and kicked the metal money box open. The noise was tremendous, but if anyone objected, they did so privately. He remained alone to scoop up the dimes, clawing at them like a Calcutta beggar gathering alms.

Feeding a random number of stolen coins into the slot Josh stabbed out their number. As the machine processed his instruction, he sucked in a breath and held it, staring ahead, absolutely still. There was a sudden heat growing on the skin on the back of his neck, and the perspex backing to the phone booth ticked as it bulged slightly outwards, becoming subtly more concave in the increasing temperature. The curving reflections of the streetlights on its surface shifted with the change of shape and Josh watched as those lights were obscured by something dark. Something moving with nervy, fluid movements behind him in the street and, by its growing size in the tell-tale perspex, coming closer. And then the telephone clicked through its last chirruping computations, and he heard the familiar sound of his own telephone ringing in the sweet haven that was Pittsburgh.

With that connection, a stillness came over the hot air wafting at Josh's face, a halting of movement that echoed his own alert and immobile stance, almost as though whatever had been moving towards him was waiting with him.

The long tone sounded four times, and in each silent interlude, Josh's hand tightened on the handset, pumping the ungiving plastic like a Nautilus device.

It was answered. He let his breath go. The line exploded into static. He screwed his eyes shut and made a fist at the back of his hot neck with his free hand.

'Baby! It's me! For God's sake don't hang up!'

He was yelling against the storm of white noise, an impotent rage temporarily usurping his fear. But it was a brief respite. He opened his eyes to the knowledge that the dark shape behind him was on the move again.

Its reflected form was unfolding from a crouch in the wavy plane of the perspex booth, and although his survival instinct was to turn and face whatever was approaching, with its attendant sounds of claws scraping on asphalt and its sickening wet hiss like a low fire, his failing nerve would not allow him to do so. Maybe it had read his suicidal thoughts. Maybe it didn't like being cheated out of a bargain. Maybe it would show its hand before he could use his own to end the waiting. Whatever the thing's intention, he had to hear her one more time. Had to tell her that she was the only precious remarkable thing in his, until now, unremarkable life.

'Elizabeth! Can you hear me?'

His voice was nearly a sob. But the mockery of the voice that tried to rasp his name behind him was nearly a retch.

'Chooaash!'

The disgusting phlegm-filled word was accompanied by a sound that can only have been a thin laugh. Josh's shoulders hunched in horror and he closed his eyes again, a little boy in bed who thinks that his eyelids will protect him from the dangers of the darkened nursery.

And then suddenly there was another voice. A voice in his ear, coming from the chaos that filled the phone. It was faint and tiny, but he heard it nevertheless. It was calling his name, and it cut through the savage crackling mess by virtue of its sweetness.

'. . . love you. Josh . . . hear me? I love you.'

'Elizabeth?'

He hesitated in his elation, since he knew that although he heard it, there had been no voice in reality.

The sizzling of the line was no less crazed, in fact if anything it had increased its pitch. But the voice that he knew was hers had reached into his head. It came again, and he cocked his head like a bird.

It was broken, fragmented, but he filled the gaps with his own desperation to believe what he heard.

'I don't know . . . you . . . hear me, Josh. But you . . . to know something. Please listen . . . love you. I love you . . . I'm . . . have our baby.'

Josh Spiller started to cry, unable to speak, fit only to listen and pray this was no trick of his crazed brain. Elizabeth's tiny, distant, tinkling voice spoke again.

'. . . you can hear me . . . anything's possible. You understand? Anything . . . fact . . . going to concentrate . . . and . . . might hear someone else . . . crazy . . . listen.'

He kept crying and cocked his head some more as though the angle would somehow assist the message that was being generated in that space in the skull where only personal stereos can reach. There was nothing for a moment. Only the roaring of the phone line's tempest.

Then, a note rather than a voice. But an undulating note like sweet birdsong. In its rising and falling, even though it was as faint as porch chimes from a mile, Josh could feel, rather than merely hear, emotions. They overwhelmed him with their intensity and he gasped. He could hear, feel, a kind of unformed love, a simple longing to be, that he somehow knew in a deep velvety part of him, would turn into a longing to be with him. And there was a clean, deep curiosity in the love he divined in that singing note, a desire for everything there was. For every smell, taste, sight, touch that could be experienced on earth. A desire untainted by knowledge, but a desire that was stronger than any he had ever felt himself or witnessed in any other being.

Josh knew then, without understanding why or how, that he was being spoken to by his unborn child.

His knees gave way beneath him and he slumped down in the booth, the phone falling from his hand and swinging from its cable. He rested his hot head against the metal leg of the booth and found no relief from its equally hot surface. Josh turned his head slowly and looked over his shoulder.

The sidewalk was still smoking from the presence of the nightmare, but the air was cooling around him. It had gone.

Josh Spiller wiped a hand over his face and slowly straightened himself to stand. He stood still for an age, knowing that he was decided. Firm in his resolve.

There was to be no suicide. If he was going to die he would die fighting. Fighting in a rage because, even if it was only in his sick and battered mind, he now believed he had something to fight for. A woman and child.

He looked at the smouldering asphalt with an expression that had been absent from his face, not just for these last days of hell, but for years.

It was the challenge of an aggressive male, and his voice in the still night air had a quiet menace that reinforced the stare.

'Know what, you fuckin' chargrill? The hunted just turned hunter.'

He had two hours. Leaving the phone hanging from its cable, he went to find Pace.

God, she felt dumb. But she was crying all the same. Elizabeth leaned forward, catching the phone with an elbow, and let it fall from the bedside table as she cradled her belly and wept. How could he possibly hear her when she hadn't even spoken? And had it been him at all? It was just a call in the middle of the night that could have been a wrong number from a mobile going through a no-service area.

But she knew different in her heart. She knew it was Josh. She was sure because she so badly wanted to believe it was him. What she couldn't believe was that she had followed Sim's loony advice, and thought her conversation at the phone as she held it, even tried, for Christ's sake, to get her foetus to talk to him. She had gone as crazy as her old Korean neighbour.

'Josh,' she croaked in a tiny voice, and the early swelling of pregnancy allowed her head to fall forward onto her knees.

Yes. So good. So good and delicious. To have made contact with its carrier. To have spoken. To have known that the carrier knew. It writhed again and stretched its growing limbs in the thick syrupy darkness.

Not long. Not long at all. It slept and dreamed of things to come and the end to this darkness. An escape into the light that would be red with blood.

36

Someone was in the truck. In the driver's seat. Josh saw a slight movement in the long rectangle of mirror buttressed from the door like a banner, and he stopped immediately and crouched low. Taking the considerable weight of his body on his thighs, he crept slowly along the side of the cab, doubled up as though winded. As he drew level with the back of the sleeper, Josh huddled lower and hung on to the aluminium running board below the door.

With his new-found purpose, he seemed to have developed the keener senses of the hunter, and the cool air around his face told him that his dawn executioner was not the current and uninvited occupant of his cab. He suspected it was human.

Slowly he lifted his right hand to the long bar at the back of the door, and when he had a sure grip, pulled himself up, caught his fingers under the door-handle, and wrenched it open in one fluid movement.

Sheriff John Pace didn't flinch. Nor, as Josh filled the door-frame threateningly, did he turn his gaze from the dash in front of him, which he studied like a prospective buyer. He inclined his head to the instrument panel.

'How much gas this thing swallow?'

Josh stood, feet apart for balance on the running board, weighing up the threat. This was the man he had, only moments ago, decided to devote the last few precious hours of his life to tracking down and tricking into replacing Josh's death with his own. No need. He had come willingly, and Josh needed quickly to fathom why.

'Depends.'

'Yeah? On what?'

'The load.'

Pace nodded politely at the wheel as though that was more than sufficient answer to a dumb question at three in the morning.

'Need your chair back?'

'What you doin' here?'

Pace turned to look at him for the first time. Even in the weak parallelograms of streetlight that provided the only illumination in the cab, Josh could see that the man's face was haggard, crumpled.

'Like to talk to you.'

Josh's mind raced. The runes were still safely tucked in his inside breast pocket, folded neatly and surreptitiously before he had visited McFarlane, between the paper of a spearmint gum strip. He nodded, and as Pace made a clumsy movement to get up and move to the passenger seat, Josh raised his chin.

'It's okay.'

He stepped down and closed the door, realizing that his breathing was growing faster. Was this to be his only chance? He walked slowly around Jezebel's shiny nose, using the time to think. It wasn't enough. He reached the passenger door long before he reached any decision. But he opened it up anyway and climbed in.

Pace looked across. 'Guess you don't sit there too often, huh?'

Josh returned the thickset man's gaze in silence. His confusion was total. The life-affirming plan to find Pace and return the deadly paper to him had crumbled. Why would he be here if his proximity put him in such peril?

John Pace watched with practised impassivity as Josh's confusion travelled across his honest face and he came straight to the point. 'You got around two hours left, Josh. I reckon you know that already.'

Josh looked out front, saying nothing. Pace studied the side of Josh's face for a moment, then followed his gaze to the empty street in front of the truck.

'Yeah. I guess you do.'

Josh spoke to the windshield, the pair of them sitting like sulky lovers rowing in a parked car. 'I asked before. What you want?'

The sheriff ran a hand over his forehead, back across the top of his head, and laughed. The jolliness of the guffaw made Josh stare at him.

'What do I want?' repeated Pace.

He laughed again, this time with an edge of hysteria, then stopped.

'Salvation.'

There was so little drama in his intonation, only a chilling weariness, that Josh knew instantly this was no trick, knew that Pace was sincere. It could mean only one thing.

But if so, the only explanation Josh could summon from the mire was that Pace wanted an end to his own life. That he wanted Josh to give him back the bomb he'd planted and let it blow him away with the sun. Why else? What would make a murderer draw back the knife at the last instant and offer it to his victim? But if that was the truth, then the question still remained. Why? He decided there was no time to ask it.

Slowly Josh reached into his breast pocket and took out the pack of gum. He stared down at it for a moment, then extended the strip from the packet, betrayed by the way it was fattened by the strip of runes, and held out his hand to the man behind his steering wheel.

'Want one?'

Pace looked down at the gum and then back up at Josh's stern face, something approaching disappointment showing in his tired eyes.

'Like I said. You got two hours. Best keep that real safe.'

Josh lowered the gum, then slid it back into his pocket. 'How'd you do it? In the statement copy? The ticket? Huh?'

Pace sighed and looked away. 'You need to do some listenin'. I'm gonna tell you this stuff not for you or anyone else.' He looked round at Josh again, and fire was replacing defeat in Pace's eyes. 'I'm tellin' it for me. You understand? I ain't no saint. I don't know you, mister. I got nothin' against you, but this thing I'm doin' here? It ain't for you.'

'Like I fuckin' care what you think.'

Pace nodded sagely. 'Yeah. No reason you should hear me out. I done wrong but only on account of thinkin' I was doin' right by those I love.'

The truck bounced as though boarded, but only very lightly. It was enough to make Josh hold up a hand to silence the bleating of his companion. Both men sat in silence, waiting. Nothing moved. False alarm. Josh lowered his hand and looked with hatred at Pace.

'No heat. No smell. It ain't our pal Joey.'

'You seen it?'

Josh's answer was silent, a look that would have withered a lesser man. Pace held the stare and broke it, making Josh look away.

'Just gimme your crap, man. I got two hours to make you take this strip of shit back.'

The two men sat quietly for an age. So much so that Josh started to believe that John Pace had changed his mind.

He was about to break the awkward silence when Pace held his hand over his face as though his body was trying to stop the words, and spoke from behind the fleshy mute of his palm.

'Got kids, Josh?'

Josh's heart leapt. He replied in a smaller voice than he would have liked.

'Nearly.'

Pace kept his hand at his face, fat fingers toying with a wide nose. 'You change when they're born. The door you came through, the one you been gazin' at over your shoulder your whole damned life, you know? Like you say, "when I was a kid I done this", or "when I was a teenager I shouldn't have done that"? Well that door closes on all your memories. They seem irrelevant, dumb even. The only thing worth rememberin' is stuff that hasn't happened yet. You look forward to rememberin' the kids on a beach vacation before you've gone on the damn thing. Know what I mean? You can see the photos in the album before you took them. You imagine how they goin' to remember you. And then before you know it, you hear the creak of a new door, the one you're goin' out of. It creaks real loud as it starts to swing open.'

'Christ,' hissed Josh.

Pace laughed. Hollowly this time, and let his hand fall from his face. 'I'm just tellin' it how it is.'

'Yeah, like I'm beggin' to hear it.'

Josh's sarcasm got through the reverie Pace seemed to have descended into. His tone sharpened and he met Josh's eye.

'I didn't have no kids when I took over my Daddy's job.'

'So you turned murdering scum 'cos you had mouths to feed? Fair excuse.'

Pace lowered his voice and became business-like.

'I never could figure why she needed a sheriff in her pocket. My

Daddy reckoned we was essential. Kept the faith secret. Kept the town respectable. Made the deaths seem plausible. I knew different. She could've done all that just by thinkin' it.'

'McFarlane?'

Pace ignored him, taking the question as rhetorical. 'The real reason she needed us included in her life was simpler. Know what? She was lonely. Lonely, and sometimes scared.'

Josh forgot the sarcastic mask that hid the frantic plans he was hatching. He began to be interested.

'What is she?'

'A woman. A philosopher.'

Josh blinked and Pace came to his rescue, saving him asking the same question again.

'An alchemist. You know what that is?'

'Sure. Guys in tights who tried to make gold.'

'She can make gold. She got the Philosopher's Stone. She can make gold make itself, again and again and again.'

'Then I guess she watches the Shopping Channel.'

Pace ignored him again. 'Nelly McFarlane may be the single richest person on earth.'

'Why only maybe?'

'Could be others. I don't know. When we left Scotland we wasn't the only ones in Europe who had the Stone.'

'We?'

'My family were there in Furnace, Loch Fyne, with hers.'

It was Josh's turn to laugh, and he surprised himself at how the sarcasm and disdain bleeding into his every word from the back of his throat had been replaced with merriment. He was almost amused by this ridiculous scene.

'So she's a rich chemist. This ain't makin' my flesh creep. They been able to make man-made gold for decades. Read *Newsweek* more often. You might find you have to kill less people.'

Pace's tone had a warning in it. 'Like I say. I'm tellin' this for me. You don't want to listen then fuck you.'

'There's that Christian talk again.'

'I am a Christian.'

'Yeah? Me, I'm a Kentucky Fried Family Bucket.'

'As good as, in less than two hours, Josh.'

Josh looked out front again, away from Pace's eyes. As he did so he slid his hand into the pocket with the gum pack, ready for the moment when Pace looked away.

'Go on.'

'Makin' gold ain't the big part. They been doin' it since man first discovered metal. The Egyptians even. I reckon she could teach you or me or just about anyone how to do it in a half an hour. Shit, it's almost harder gettin' the stuff outta the country into them European banks of hers than it is for her to make it. It's the stuff that comes with that knowledge she been messin' with I can't take no more.'

Josh ignored that for the moment. He wanted to distract Pace.

'What's she doin' way up here if she could buy the White House for weekends?'

'She's got places all over the world. I don't rightly know, but I reckon it's something about where she first discovered the philosophic truth that ties her to makin' the stuff there. I know they had to start again when they came from Scotland to here. Had to make a new furnace. Everythin'.'

'Don't you hate when that happens?'

Josh felt the corner of the strip of parchment with his forefinger, and started to tease it from the gum wrapper.

Pace sighed deeply and rubbed his eyes. 'The thing. The demon called to you. It's got itself a name.'

Josh swallowed, staring ahead but listening.

'Asmodeanus.'

'How'd you know? You see a name sewed into its jockey shorts?'

'It's been called before.'

The sadness in Pace's voice made Josh mildly ashamed of his forced flippancy. He adjusted his tone. 'By you?'

'I can't call them. Only she can do that. Only she can write the runes and make the incantations. I just deliver the mail.'

'So she can't get it back.'

Pace looked momentarily and incongruously delighted at Josh's understanding. 'Right.'

'Who'd you deliver to before?'

Pace looked at his feet. 'Two Government guys. Don't rightly know if they were just IRS or somethin' bigger. But she must've done. Somethin' that attracted attention. Came sniffin' round lookin' for God knows what. She didn't say why they had to disappear. Just when.'

'How'd they die?'

Pace looked back up at Josh, and there was thunder in his face. 'Like there's no God.'

Josh's jaw twitched, and he shifted in his chair. 'Why you puttin' yourself at risk here? Why aren't you as far away from me as you can get?'

'I ain't finished talkin'.'

'Then get on with it. There's a meter runnin'.'

'For us both, Josh.'

Josh looked at him questioningly, expecting an expansion of that remark. But none came.

Pace ignored him and cleared his throat. The lecturer preparing.

'There's a part of alchemy that was good. Godly even. True philos-ophers ain't a spit away from priests.' Pace shook his head at that for a reason unclear to Josh. 'You know a pile of modern knowledge came from alchemic mistakes? Yeah? Puffers, they used to call them, on account of them always blowing bellows into their useless fur-naces. Greedy amateurs who didn't know nothin'. Their mistakes discovered all kind of stuff. But just like them puffers maybe found useful chemical reactions without meanin' to, the true alchemists discovered stuff without meanin' to neither. Dark stuff. Powers that were behind what they did but not really part of it.'

'Like Mr Hot Ass?'

'Asmodeanus ain't nothin' but a foot soldier. Comes when he's called. Goes when he's done. I reckon she got a whole army that stick about long as they please, and some of them are generals.'

'Then why aren't we lookin' at Nelly McFarlane, Master of the World?'

Pace exhaled, whether out of exasperation with his ignorant audi-ence, or merely with a release of tension, it was unclear. 'Maybe we will. But there's a price. It's high. And when she stops bein' able to pay it, I guess even she don't know what'll happen.'

'What price?'

Josh waited to hear the answer. His mouth was dry and his temples throbbed. He didn't want to hear it, but his heart knew he'd been part of it, and he had to know. John Pace spoke the word softly.

'Sacrifice.'

Blackened blood. A tiny foot. A sticky towelling suit. He closed his eyes against the memory. Pace continued.

'Every seven years . . .' he paused, took a breath. '. . . you got to sacrifice your own child.'

Josh opened his eyes and looked round quickly. 'But that baby . . . it was Alice Nevin's.'

Pace shook his head. 'She grew it. Sure. But it was the councillor's egg. Got too old to have 'em natural.'

'How?' croaked Josh, though he knew.

'IVF. All she needed was sperm and a womb. She got one from that big dull jerk, Jim, and Alice Nevin provided the other.'

Josh spoke through his teeth. 'And then I killed it.'

Pace shook his head. 'She did. Believe it.'

Josh remembered Alice Nevin's house. The big expensive house with a fancy car in the drive and catalogue toys on the lawn. And then he remembered what he thought had been the baby's father, the babbling nonsense he had shouted after Josh on the day of the baby's death.

'Alice Nevin said "sorry" to me after the death. Why'd she do that, Pace?'

The sheriff mashed his chin and nodded. 'Yeah. I saw her. I reckon she was apologizin' to the whole world for stoppin' her man Bobby Hendry doin' the only thing he could have done to save that baby girl.'

Josh was looking at him, trying to race ahead, to figure a way through this nightmare maze. Pace got there first.

'Has to be done just right, you see. Got to be the seventh child. Baby got to be seven days old on the first of May. Got to be a girl.'

A pause again while he fixed Josh with that weary stare. 'An' it got to be a virgin.'

Josh turned his head away. 'For fuck's sake.'

'Now you listen real good to this. She was on to Hendry. Knew he might try and save the kid by doin' what no decent man would even want to have a bad dream about. But he knew about McFarlane's first husband. How he'd done the same just to let his baby girl live. Knew the rules. Hendry was a dumb son of a bitch, but he had balls. Didn't blow his brains out till the thing got so close he smelled the sulphur on its breath. Found the runes in his paperback novel and even tried to pass 'em back to her. I know 'cos he told me.' He swallowed. 'Wish to God he hadn't. She knows he did.'

Josh ignored his lament. 'Jim McFarlane's her second husband?'

Pace nodded once. 'Samuel was her first. Fathered seven of her kids. Saved the seventh and had his throat cut open in return. That was when she discovered that Hell don't seem to mind the modern miracle of surrogacy. Her power was down to near zero for a year while she got some poor hick kid to grow her a new one.'

Pace looked dreamy again.

'That would've been the time to take her out. God forgive me I did nothin'.'

Josh felt a slight rocking movement from Jezebel again. Tiny this time, but enough to make him cock his head and raise a finger.

'You feel that?'

Pace looked dolefully back. 'What?'

Josh's nerves were in tatters. He pushed aside the gut feeling to fetch his tyre-billy from behind the seat and go check the trailer. He wanted to hear more.

'Never mind.'

He sat and looked ahead, absorbing the information as best he could. Pace waited, almost as though he were expecting something from him.

'What happened to the girl he saved?'

Pace nodded, like he'd been asked how his mother was. 'Griffin McFarlane's just fine.'

If he hadn't been sitting down Josh would have fallen. He felt as though fluid were draining from his spine, his legs heavier than flesh should ever be. From a mouth in which the saliva had turned to acid, he whispered to John Pace: 'Griffin is Nelly McFarlane's daughter?'

'That much's for sure.'

Josh shook his head and leaned forward, elbows on the passenger dash, hands linking at the back of his neck. 'Jesus. Jesus.'

Pace sat quietly, waiting for his companion to compose himself. When Josh spoke, it was almost to himself, his racing mind trying to sort and file the mess of information he'd just been given. He spoke quickly and quietly, directing his words at a windshield that reflected his dark silhouette.

'I know her. You know? Picked her up outside town. Jesus. No fuckin' wonder she wanted outta here. How'd she bear it so long? She must hate that old sow like she was the devil.'

Josh sat up suddenly. Pace was still watching him.

'Shit. You have to keep her away.'

He leaned towards Pace, a desperate plea in his eyes.

'McFarlane knows she told me about the runes. Listen, man, she's dead for sure if she comes back here.'

'Josh.'

'No, listen. You have to . . .'

'Josh.'

Josh stopped speaking and waited.

Pace let him settle, then spoke with the first edge of malice he'd used since they'd started to speak . . . 'That little bitch you care so much about is only in danger if you get to her before dawn.'

Josh stared. 'What you sayin?'

'Think I'd be sittin' here if I'd passed them runes?'

Josh swallowed, processing the implications, and when he spoke it was in a barely audible whisper.

'Griffin?'

'She ain't no Daddy's girl. This is one who wants to be just like Mama.'

'No. Not true. Can't be true.'

Josh was shaking his head. Pace was nodding his.

'I guess the councillor stopped trustin' me after . . . well let's say I reckon I've been fallin' from grace a little. And Griffin was real keen to cast her first runes. She already got the minor powers of the philosopher, and her bein' the seventh child she told me she reckons she's goin' to be even more powerful than Mom. She can make gold like we make toast. Bores her, far as I can tell. More interested in the visitors from the dark places in McFarlane's lab, but she just ain't quite so in control yet of those . . . things. But it'll come. This is the beginning.'

Josh's mouth was open. He stared for a minute, then let out a barking laugh. 'I fucked her, Pace.'

Pace looked back emotionless. 'No. She fucked you.'

Josh clenched his fists. He thought of that betrayal of Elizabeth, and the memory of her voice on the phone came back like a waft of sweet air in a foetid tunnel. 'I'll find her.'

Pace nodded, then licked dry lips before speaking. 'Saw a note on the desk to my deputy from some highway patrollers. Deputy must've been gettin' worried. See, he dropped her off at that restaurant you was in. Reckon since the dumb asswipe carried out that chore he thinks the whole thing's his responsibility, like he's scared of what the councillor might do if her little girl don't get back safe. Anyway, the guys he's been sneakily askin' to look out for her said she been hitchin' back here pretty close by. Reckon she's still on the interstate.'

'Change seats.'

Josh got up to move back into the driver's chair. Pace put out a hand and held his arm.

'I ain't goin' with you.'

It was the voice of self-sacrificing bravado. It made Josh sick. He looked into Pace's old and worn face and wondered if the man genuinely expected him to have admiration or sympathy for a murderer. The decent part of Josh Spiller tried. It failed.

'I don't want you with me. I want you to get the fuck out of my truck.'

Pace let go his arm and his face crumpled. He nodded once, then put a hand on the handle. 'You find her, she got to take them back willingly and unknowingly. You know that?'

'I'll find her. I don't give a shit if she got as far as Florida, I'll find her. And when I do, and she don't take them, then I'm gonna hang on round her bitchin' neck until the dawn comes and we can watch it rise together. I go, she's comin' with me.'

'Yeah.' There was no attempt in Pace's voice at humouring the impossible hope. He opened the door and moved his big body to leave.

'Pace?'

The sheriff looked back.

'What are the runes written on?'

The man lowered his brow and his eyes glinted with something Josh couldn't read.

'Amy Nevin's skin.'

He stepped down and closed the door quietly behind him.

She looked at her watch. One and three quarter hours to go. There was a decision to be made. Was it safer to stay put, knowing that even though he was close, he might as well be a million miles away if he didn't know she was here? After all, he would be dealt with in town. That was a certainty. Or should she try and get on the move again? Griffin thought for a second, frowning at her reflection in the washroom mirror.

Instinct told her she should move, the same instinct that was telling her the truck driver was not being truthful. What was confusing her was what exactly he wanted from her.

If he'd wanted to jump her, he could have done so a hundred times before now. Of course he would have gotten the elegant blade of the stiletto she had concealed up the sleeve of her long-sleeved T-shirt, somewhere in his thick neck for the privilege. But at least that would have explained his behaviour. What bothered her was that he was no slow-witted dork, and despite his act with the porn mag, no lecherous pervert either. She'd watched his eyes beneath his filthy and ludicrous cap, and they were not the eyes of a fool. He was up to something, and Griffin wanted to know what.

She smoothed down the sides of her baggy sweatshirt, before catching herself in the mirror. She smiled. A habit picked up from Mom.

Mom. She smiled a little wider. If this came off well, Nelly was going to be proud. Although there had been something other than parental pride in her mother's eyes when Griffin first transmuted mercury, that had stayed with her; but she shrugged the memory away. One day, and Nelly knew it, Griffin would be the more powerful. The shadows would come to her call and the black sea that was Nelly's to command would come under her younger and more vigorous sceptre. Not for her to wait seven years, worn by childbirth, tied to some ridiculous man just for the raw material for her work. No. She had taken an easier, a more modern route. That made her smile turn coquettish, and she lifted her chin and absently admired her bone structure.

The revving of a diesel engine from outside broke into her thoughts. She knew he wasn't going anywhere. The guy kept turning the engine on to keep his batteries charged, he said. Time to go and check him out. She would walk the long way round his hideous truck and give it the once over. Maybe there'd be something. Maybe not. It was something to do while she waited to make her next move. And looking at her watch again, Griffin McFarlane decided she'd make that move pretty soon.

*   *   *

Pace watched with a doom-laden heart as the truck roared away. Then his heavy heart quickened its beat as he saw the impossibly sprightly figure that had been clinging to the back of the tractor unit, jump numbly down from the moving rig into the darkened street.

Nelly McFarlane smoothed the grey coveralls that Pace had often seen her wear in the garden, thinking even then that they lent her the unpleasant air of an abattoir worker. Now, as she walked slowly towards him in the street, the effect was increased significantly. Jezebel thundered to the corner, turned and disappeared from view, her rumble still audible, its driver unaware of the passenger he'd just shed.

McFarlane waited until she stood directly before Pace before speaking. 'You're not running, John.'

Pace stayed silent.

'You should.'

'Do any good?'

She laughed. Merrily and youthfully. 'No good whatsoever. But I like it.'

'Then I'm glad I ain't runnin'.'

Her smile metamorphosed into a leer, laden with malice and a naked desire for violence that was almost sexual. 'What interests me, John, is why you thought you could oppose me and have any hope of living.'

John Pace shifted his gaze from her malevolent face for a moment, flicking his eyes to the sheriff's office only yards away. The blinds were still. Either Archie Cameron wasn't interested in his chief's death, or more likely, he wasn't there.

Nelly followed his gaze. 'Out on business, John. Along with the rest of your deputies. There's a truck to dissuade from reaching the interstate. Remember?'

Pace's heart sunk further, but he smiled, noticing that his widening grin diminished hers in an exact inverse proportion.

'You gonna die someday, Nelly. Just like me, just like the rest of us. And what then? Huh? Think you'll sleep sweet? Or will them filthy things you got lickin' at your old ass come callin' for some back payment?'

Something flashed in her right hand as she twitched in response. A scalpel. Pace almost laughed with relief. She was going to do it herself. Conventionally. He thanked God that it would be cold steel. Nothing worse. Nothing slower.

McFarlane growled. 'Death is only the booby prize for lowly, crawling, pant-shitting nobodies like you, John. The philosophers cheat it as easily as you scratch your shrivelled balls.'

Pace shifted his weight on legs that had turned to liquid with his concealed fear.

'Yeah? So where are they now then? Huh? Your great philosopher ancestors? Your Mama called lately? Your Grandpappy come home for Thanksgiving? They lie to you, Nelly. Them things that tell you what you want to hear. You gonna die and it gonna be a lot worse for you than me.'

McFarlane took a step towards him brandishing the scalpel in front of her face. 'You idiotic little shit. You think life has only one form?'

Pace kept his phoney smile and promoted it to a small empty laugh. 'They tell you otherwise? Them whisperin' things? Ho. Good one. Real good.'

She lowered her head, a big cat sizing up its prey. Pace lost the smile, fixed her narrowed eyes with his own and spoke quietly, from the heart. 'You gonna burn, Nelly.'

If there was a pause it wasn't one he would recall with the last few sentient moments of his life. Before he could even raise his hands against it, the blade entered his throat deeply just above his Adam's apple and sliced through his vocal cords, turning the scream he would have summoned into a wet gurgle. She pulled it free and let him slump to his knees. With her left hand she grasped his thin hair, pulled his head back and grunted as she made a series of sweeping horizontal incisions that all but severed his head. Her fury was such that she kept slicing until the thick white of his spinal column resisted the scalpel, the blood pushed by Pace's still-beating heart pumping over her hand and arm in hot waves.

Nelly McFarlane stood erect and admired her work. She felt the prickle of tiny invisible claws on her left shoulder and smiled at the obscene excited whispering in her ear. In the periphery of her vision, at an upper window in the large house to her right, a drape twitched.

She spun towards it and stared, her scalpel held out, away from the side of her body, in the manner of a knife-fighter.

The light came on and a figure pulled back the drape, stood where it could be seen and raised an arm limply in greeting.

They knew better in Furnace. Better to declare your presence than to be caught snooping. McFarlane did not acknowledge the wave, but watched unmoving until the figure retreated and switched the light off.

She turned back slowly to the clumsily-folded body of John Pace at her feet, regarding his blood-saturated jacket as she moved its slick material with her foot.

'Don't worry, John. It'll clean up real nice for Ethan.'

37

He knew it was useless trying the CB until he got out from these cursed hills. So Josh Spiller just drove. He drove like a stoned stuntman at a truck show. Jezebel's tyres screamed as she was forced round bends at speeds that required more rubber than she had to give. The trailer pitched and swayed, always nearly on the edge of losing its relationship with the tractor, but then Josh would ease off just enough to let the tortured block of metal hang on in there.

Five fucking dollars.

He clenched his back teeth, remembering the play-acted integrity with which she'd insisted he take it. The thought of her sleeping with him, touching him, caressing him, knowing that she'd condemned him to death . . .

'I'm comin', you bitch. You hear? I'm comin'.'

She had been going north. He'd get on the interstate in about fifteen minutes and then sit on that radio until someone, anyone, could remember where she'd been seen last. His lights swung crazily on the road ahead speeding beneath the windshield, but over the tops of the shrubby oaks, though his mind was trying its best to ignore it, there was an unmistakable luminosity to the sky. The sun was coming.

At the side of the road, the fall-out of Jezebel's headlights made the shadows dance behind the tree trunks, flickering like a penny peep-show. And amongst those moving black lines was a more regular shadow.

Blacker and more substantial than the thin vertical stripes made by the trees, Josh glimpsed its rapid sprinting shape running behind the line of trunks. It was keeping pace effortlessly with the speeding truck with a fluidity that was horrific in its strength rather than graceful.

'Jesus Christ,' he hissed, and stepped on the gas, though there was little more Jezebel could give.

On account of the increased speed, when he rounded the corner and saw the police car parked sideways across the narrow road, the three hundred yards' braking distance was cutting it fine.

Josh straightened his right leg and slammed on the brakes. He felt the trailer slew, aching to jack-knife, and gripped the wheel, adjusting it in turn by enormous and tiny increments, using all his years of feel to halt its lurching impending disaster. Jezebel screeched and bucked and came to a halt. The trailer joined the tractor unit in its bouncing stop, coming to rest at an ugly angle, thwarted, but not entirely dissuaded from its rebellious path.

The police car was still, lights flashing silently, lighting the tunnel of trees with colour like an office Christmas party disco behind blinds. Josh ran his tongue across dry lips. He would have been a fool to have expected a clear exit from Furnace, but this seemed too easy. No bear with a full complement of grey matter would try to stop an eighteen-wheeler with a saloon car. If they were relying on his conscience, the fear he might kill the occupants by ramming it, then they'd chosen the wrong guy, the wrong day, the wrong situation.

He waited, and still nothing happened. In those pregnant seconds, he scanned the area ahead, a curious calm keeping his eyes narrow and his pulse steady. There was only one vehicle, sure, but beyond it the road curved sharply again, and between the trees, caught by the flashing lights, Josh thought he could glimpse the reflective glint of more metal.

He pondered that for a moment, then turned his attention back to the silent car in his way. It was their move, but in case they needed a reminder he was here he revved hard, a deep, growling boom that made him proud to be sitting in Jezebel's guts.

The lights on the car cut, confirming that it was occupied. Without its gaudy, blinking show, the vehicle looked as insubstantial as a child's cut-out, made two-dimensional by the harsh glare of the truck's lights. But with the police car's flashers and headlamps out, Josh could just make out a silhouetted, moving figure inside. There was a beat, a fraction of a pause, and then an echoing voice wavered above the engine noise.

'Just shut it down, Spiller.'

The loudhailer was crackly and comical. Josh exercised a crooked smile at the earnest delivery of the announcement, then revved again in defiant response. The police car door opened on its far side and before Josh could identify the driver Jezebel's windshield exploded into a thousand tiny, glittering squares. The bullet thudded into the headrest of his seat and Josh cried out, hands instinctively shielding his face against the shrapnel of glass.

Through the football-sized hole in front of him, he saw the dark figure connected to his car by the loudhailer cable press the mouth-piece against his lips again.

'I said do it, you dumb shit.'

Josh slid down low in the seat, panting. His pulse was no longer still, but his resolve remained steady. He would ram the fucker. Two more shots pounded into the cab in quick succession, one bursting almost directly through its predecessor's hole in the back of his chair, the other going wide and smashing the cool-box at the side of the sleeper in a brittle and complex explosion.

Josh punched the cushion of the passenger seat with a bellow of rage, slammed his feet down to the pedals and grabbed the gear shift.

'Baby-killing fucks.'

It was as though Jezebel had been waiting to be released: she roared and lurched forward. With so little distance to gain momentum, Josh stamped on the gas and crashed through as many gears as the yards allowed, and as he braved sliding his head level with the hole in the windshield, he saw that it was enough. The figure with the gun bounded away, caught in the headlights like game, and Josh quickly sat upright again to grip the wheel, as Jezebel bore down on the car, hungry for the collision.

He had hoped the car would be bulldozed sideways, had imagined it spinning conveniently into the trees and out of his path. But as the windshield filled with the dark undercarriage of the car as it flipped over on impact, and the cab rose steeply to mount the vehicle it was crushing, Josh accepted it was going to be a whole lot messier.

The tractor unit bucked crazily as its speed carried it up and over the diminishing pile of police-liveried metal. Josh's lips drew back from his teeth in a silent cry at a carnage he had prayed daily throughout his working life he would never encounter, but had now instigated, and he held the wheel tightly, riding the nightmare. The noise was a combination of screaming metal, an engine howling as the wheels it commanded lost contact with the ground, and, threading through the cacophony like punctuation, three more gunshots.

But Josh was holding it together. It was happening fast and his speed and power were in his favour.

The crushed car had turned turtle and a third of it was still caught beneath the truck. Although Jezebel's trailer and tractor were in equal distress riding over the top of it, making a shape like the two sides of a pitched roof, it was the car that was giving in. It shuddered and bounced, then scraped out from under the ten wheels of the tractor, letting the cab slam back down to the road. The back end of the swaying trailer nudged what was left of the wreck as it passed, and with an aching right foot Josh begged Jezebel to give him what she had left.

There was still plenty. She roared away from the tangle of metal and Josh obliged by finding the gears to help her. By the time the truck had started to round the bend, it was too late for caution.

Josh was right on two counts. Firstly, that no fool would put their money on a saloon car stopping an eighteen-wheeler, and secondly, the sight of metal glinting through the trees had been no illusion.

'Jesus.'

It was all he had time to say before Jezebel's nose smashed into the barrier of felled oaks blocking the road. At the edge of the great construction the manned logging JCB that had pushed the trees down twitched its hanging arm slightly in response, as though smugly delighted by the result. The front of the truck nosed chaotically through the horizontal wooden puzzle, Josh holding his arm across his face as the tumbling tree trunks pounded the rig. Even as he let go the wheel to protect his face Josh could feel the trailer going.

The choreography of large vehicles crashing is nearly always balletic, a macabre elegance created by the anarchy of unchecked momentum. But there was an ugliness in the way Jezebel's trailer started to part from the rig. The angle of their separation was like a healthy person's cruel imitation of a spastic. It jack-knifed at speed, swinging around the rig like a compass arm until smashing with unexpected fury against the JCB. In the cab of the great yellow logger, a figure at the levers made a star shape with its arms and legs before being crushed into the sandwich of twisted metal, and Josh's cab lifted as the wheels on the righthand side left the ground. As it rose, its inevitable aim to turn over and put an end to Josh's hopes, Jezebel screamed and tore in half.

The trailer was gone, still moving, finishing its task of crushing the beast that had laid the wooden trap, but severed untidily from its own brains in the form of the tractor unit. Freedom from the broken trailer was the cab's salvation; aborting its toppling course to disaster it crashed back down, ploughing crazily into the logs.

Grunting, Josh grabbed the wheel again in an automatic gesture of survival, and powered down on the throttle. He could feel from the listing rig that he'd lost tyres, but until he found out how many he kept the revs up, gasping as the tractor lurched and smashed at the trees.

It was over in seconds. The dam of logs, strong when united, were diminished when divided, and with one final growl the tractor unit scrambled over the cobbling of the last three rolling trunks to freedom.

Cold air howled through the broken windshield and the sound of gunshots echoed behind him as Josh floored it along the road, calculating by feel as best he could just how many tyres had given up the fight. He figured two, and since he was still driving, it couldn't be the two fronts. Luck. The first in days. If he still had the main wheels at his command, then he reckoned he might make it with eight. His mind was on fire, hot with a mixture of adrenalin, and for the first time, hope. An area under the truck, directly beneath the passenger seat, was thudding and banging in an alarming fashion, so that Jezebel lurched and steered like a supermarket cart, but he kept his foot down, mindful only of the distance he had to put between himself and the mess on the mountain road behind him. Josh fingered the radio and although he was still in that curiously dead area for the CB, it crackled obligingly to confirm it had survived.

One headlamp was miraculously still operational, albeit without cover of glass, and in the dim and faltering beam he stormed along the winding road towards his impossible task. There had been no time to assess further the futility of that task, the ridiculous notion that he could still find the needle in the haystack. It was enough just to drive. To get away from Furnace. That was enough.

The luminous veil thickening above the trees confirmed the sun's growing proximity, and before him Josh could almost see the road without the aid of his wounded headlamp. And as if to remind him of the nature of his flight, a hundred yards ahead a shape too big to be a man, too low and humanoid to be a deer, loped across the gloom of the darkened road. The adrenalin was still lava in Josh's veins, and with a scream of rage he stepped on the gas and aimed for where it had crossed, not caring about the pointlessness of trying to run down something that wasn't there. Yet.

The crippled shambles that was Jezebel boomed towards the interstate, while the darkness watched from the cover of oaks with something more than eyes.

The ice-box lit her face as she opened the door. The choice was not impressive; an obscure can of soda Josh must have brought in from the truck, a nearly empty carton of orange juice, the remains thick as syrup, or a small bottle of still water. Elizabeth pulled out the water, shut the door, and crouched with her back against the fridge.

How could she sleep? She felt elated and terrified at the same time. Even if she'd been talking, correction, thinking, into the ether, the actual act of admitting she was keeping her baby had ignited her.

But it was more than that. Elizabeth genuinely believed that the words she'd spun from her heart had somehow found Josh's ears, and now she was writhing internally, trying to work out exactly what was making her entertain such a bizarre theory. Her madness in that respect was almost more alarming than her physical predicament.

She lifted the bottle of water to her face, rolling its cold condensation-bloomed plastic over her cheek. There was terror in her breast for Josh, and it was all the more acute for its nameless and irrational nature. The rectangle of kitchen window was lighter than the room, a half-hearted Pittsburgh sunrise on its way, only just starting to bleed through the polluted sky, and she regarded it with melancholy.

Elizabeth lowered the bottle, glancing at the label as she broke the sealed cap with a twist. Highland Spring. Five hundred millilitres of ordinary water that had made it all the way across the Atlantic from Scotland. Briefly, she studied the tiny painting of a Scottish landscape below the water's grand title, a delicate rendition of snowy mountains fronted by pines and wild flowers, then closed her eyes as she lifted the bottle to her lips.

Modern life was weirder than anything Sim could come up with. Two cupfuls of water from another continent soothed her dry throat, while the sweet, clean water from her own faucet lay in the pipes undrunk. Weird, as Nesta often said, was all a matter of degree. She stood up and moved to the window. She had decided that going to bed was futile: she wanted to watch the sun come up. In fact with the same atavistic, unidentifiable instinct that told her Josh was in trouble, that Josh had been the caller, that Josh had heard her crazy thoughts, she knew she had to watch the sun come up. She put down the water and leaned against the sink, still and calm, watching.

Nine feet below, another figure stood in an identical position, staring from his identical window, and trembled like the leaves of a delicate herb.

She hated him. He was dead, yet his words were having an effect. For that alone, if she could have killed John Pace many times over she would gladly have done so. But he was beyond her fury now.

'You gonna burn, Nelly.'

McFarlane made fists and held them rigidly by her sides as she walked. The branches of the shrubby trees clawed at her as she bullied a path through their bulk. But she was impervious to them. She began to berate the dead sheriff as she walked, and such was her distraction that she was oblivious to the fact that she was speaking out loud.

'Think I'll burn, John? Huh? Think I don't know the rules of the game? That I deny my own fear?'

She laughed, shaking her head, one hand uncurling from its fist to stab the air in front of her at her imaginary listener. 'Fear, you fucking coward, is the currency of this world and theirs. You hear me?'

Her voice was nearly a shout, and its volume reeled her back in from the rant. She stopped momentarily, wiped her face with the palm of a hand, then walked a few more steps to a group of rocks standing proud of the tangled undergrowth. This was the right place. Here, she could compose herself as she prepared, and look down into the valley, the sun rising directly behind her.

It was cold. Doubly so for her, since apart from a leather belt around her hips, hung with seven small items, Nelly McFarlane was naked. Today, it was necessary. Just as the Jews strapped their prayers to the skin of their heads to make the sense of their God's word more potent, so she needed to have the first rays of sun touch her body without the barrier of material.

Because it was a Calling Day, a day when the hot elemental she had conjured and held would come through to the light. Oh but they were sly, these low creatures. They had to be watched, to be monitored, and her readiness against insurrection was a habit she had never broken on a Calling Day. The runes bound them to her will only for the time allowed and then, with the dawn, were released. Maybe one day Asmodeanus, or one of his thousand evil brothers, would foil the return to darkness that followed that release. But for that they needed knowledge, and more. They needed human restraint.

For it was the kill they made that broke their hold on the light and sent them screaming back to the pit. Not because they had been judged. Nothing so moral. Simply that they had touched their carrier, broken the otherworldly laws of physics that repelled the solid from the illusion, and denied them the right to exist in anything other than unclean spirit. One day, perhaps, an elemental would uncover that knowledge, would come through and spare its carrier. Nelly would be ready. She would have to be. That would be the day it would come for her.

Pace's blood still stained her right arm almost all the way to the elbow, and she looked at it now as she stepped up onto the cold, flat stone. She caressed the blackened patches gently and spoke again, looking into the distance and nodding at her imaginary listener, this time in a crazy whisper, a sentence that merged almost into one continuous sound.

'Yes, yes, yes, I can be afraid, John. You see me now? Yes I am, yes I am. I see the bestial abyss of demons' faces, hear the hunger in their whispers. How they exist to destroy.'

She lifted her head and looked down into the valley, where the lights of vehicles moved slowly along the interstate. But John Pace was not listening. John Pace was dead, and for some ineffable reason, that fact was making Nelly McFarlane uneasy. She was irritated with him, even in death. Irritated that he'd forced her hand, that he'd made it necessary to kill him. Maybe, she thought, if he'd been a woman he would have understood. But men were weak. When would they accept their sex can never make a lasting pact with the dark world? But still they try, despite the fact that there were never any powerful male philosophers. All charlatans, cheats and frauds. Puffers and ineffectual warlocks, but never philosophers. And why? She put her finger to her lips as if hushing a child and spoke aloud from behind it, telling a secret.

'Know why? Men are destroyers, John. Your similarity cancels the bond with demons. You're given life by woman, but you can't create life. Don't you see? You have nothing to bargain with. Nothing.'

She smiled and blinked benignly, then dropped her hand to the leather belt and found a thin strip of dried skin, curled and hideous, hanging from an ornate gold hook. McFarlane lifted it to her face and kissed it. She held it there, pressed against her cold cheek, then looked down the darkened valley again. It grew lighter as she watched.

'Griffin?'

She called out loudly, almost angrily, into the dewy air as though her daughter were genuinely there, then after a pause, a silence in which no one replied, she lowered her voice to a conspiratorial whisper.

'You're nearer than you should be. He's on his way, Griffin. Racing towards you with the delusion of saving himself.'

She smiled to herself. The Keystone Kops hadn't managed to stop him. Griffin knew, as she did, that Nelly could stop the trucker right now if she chose. But she chose not to. Her daughter would finally grow up today with the man's blood, and Nelly hoped Griffin would make herself watch it happen.

It was a privilege she wouldn't have enjoyed if she'd handled the calling better, but she was young. She'd made a mistake. Griffin would learn from the horror of what she would see coming with the sun.

Nelly's face hardened and she dropped her voice to a rasping, barely audible whisper, her hand closing on the strip of skin. 'But remember this, Griffin. You live because I let you, your power grows only as long as I let it, and like the child you are, you think I don't see into your heart.' She laughed softly. 'But I do.'

She lifted her arms in front of her, clasped her extended hands together and cocked a wagging forefinger towards the valley.

'Just don't ever fuck with Mama, sweetheart.'

38

He pulled his hat lower over his eyes and sighed.

'So the store manager says to the first interviewee, ifin you found a ten-dollar bill on the floor would you give it back or keep it, an' the girl says, well guess I'd hand it back. Well the next girl up says, I reckon it might not necessarily be the store's anyhow, might just be some rich Jock dropped it or somethin' an' I guess it'd do more good in my pocket than his. So the question is this. Which girl got the job?'

Eddie snorted under his moustache. Dawn CB. The pits.

'Come on, man. Finish the fuckin' gag.'

'Girl with the biggest tits. That's who.'

Eddie smiled in spite of himself.

'Anybody know if the chicken-house northbound is open?'

'Closed, buddy. Ride your overweight with pride.'

'Hey, driver. That store-girl joke stank bad as my ass.'

'Anyone . . . Listen . . . There was a hitcher. Northbound 'bout ten hours ago. No . . . Wait . . . Maybe six.'

Eddie's eyes opened.

Laughter at the urgency of the driver's tone fought for space on the bored channel.

'Would that be maybe five?'

'Got an emergency hard-on there, driver?'

The first voice came back on, agitated, almost manic.

'Listen, would you? Listen. About five-eight, short brown hair. Big pack. Just tell me if you fuckin' saw her, okay?'

Eddie sat up and snatched the handset. 'Spiller? It's Eddie. Go to our channel, man.'

'Hey. Is this a fuckin' play on the radio or is anybody doin' their job out there?'

'Eddie?'

Josh's crackly, indistinct voice sounded incredulous, but if channel 19 noted the panic of his broadcast, it didn't much care.

'Well listen up, drivers. Faggots' hour started early.'

Eddie retuned quickly and waited, his heart beating fast. He held his breath for what seemed an age and then Josh's weak signal crackled in.

'Eddie? You really there?'

Eddie pulled his beard with some delight and sat back in the comfort of his air-sprung chair.

'Unless I'm someplace else. Listen, 'fore you move another mile, this is real important. Where you at?'

''Bout a mile from 23 northbound. But Eddie, I ain't got much of a truck left.'

'What the fuck happened, man?'

'Not important. She's still movin'. You near?'

'Five minutes north. In that fuckin' tourist pull-in we used to hate, you know? Never has any shit-paper in the john?'

'Then lend me Kong, Eddie. I got to find that hitcher.'

Eddie was taken aback by Josh's easy acceptance of his location, disappointed his proximity hadn't been met by a whoop of delighted disbelief. But then Josh wasn't sounding much like Josh any more. And something big must have gone down to make him so casual about busting up Jez. He bit back his feelings.

'Yeah, like in your dreams maybe I let you behind this wheel. But hey, Spiller? Want to hear somethin' that'll crack a smile across that ugly puss-cake of yours?'

'I don't have any fuckin' time left for this, man.'

Josh was practically crying. Even though the signal was poor, Eddie felt a knot tie in his stomach at the unfamiliar distress in his friend's voice. What was going on?

'She's here, Spiller. Muffin' or whatever the fuck she's called. I got her with me, along with that gold pin she stole.'

There was a long silence. Long enough to make Eddie think he'd lost Josh's signal. Then Josh's voice, low and distant.

'In the cab? Now?'

'Naw. In the john. Probably wipin' her ass with a handbill on white water raftin' like everybody else.'

'Eddie?'

Josh sounded almost calm. Eddie relaxed a little.

'Yeah.'

'Ever kissed a guy?'

'Not even ma Daddy.'

'Get ready for a first, man. You might just have saved my life.'

'Fuck off and drive, Spiller. Two miles from the exit ramp.'

Eddie replaced the handset with a satisfied smile, unconsciously fingering his bottom lip as though Josh's kiss had already been planted.

He was still smiling pleasantly when his door opened, but the lips drew back and remoulded his half-visible mouth into a snarl as the knife slid between his ribs.

Griffin used both hands to push the blade home, and she was glad. It took more strength than she imagined to penetrate clothing and flesh, but her double-hander provided sufficient force.

She watched Eddie's face contort as he turned to her, his hands grabbing at air in front of him, then pulled the blade free with a grunt and sank it deeply into the base of his neck. He made a futile move to rise, to grab hold of her, and she withdrew the knife, quickly stepping back down from the running board.

Eddie Shanklin followed her involuntarily, his big body toppling sideways from the considerable height of his cab, landing painfully in an untidy heap on the asphalt. His face was pressed to the ground, his knees folded beneath him, pushing his back into an ugly arch. Griffin bent low, out of curiosity, to hear the gurgling sound that was bubbling from his lips. Blood frothed in his beard and she pushed at his bulk tentatively with her foot to get a better view. It rocked him over and the man slumped onto his side, the thick red blood from his chest wound welling out beneath a trapped arm, the mess from his neck blackening his jacket.

She bent lower, level with his face. 'Aw, now don't be mad with me, Eddie. Treat it as a kind of greetings telegram from all those women out there I know you drivers respect so much.' She wiped the blade of her knife on his trouser leg and stood up. 'Thanks for the ride.'

She stepped over him, pulled herself into the cab and closed the door.

The keys were in the ignition and Griffin smiled. Sure, her plans had gone a little pear-shaped, but there was no denying this was exciting. She was going to get out of here before Josh arrived, and she was going to do it in his dumb accomplice's truck. She'd watched him drive, and although it was a manual shift with about a million mystery gears between top and low, she reckoned there wasn't that much to it. Her slim hand touched the plastic gorilla hanging from the key ring, then gripped the plastic key-fob and turned it.

The starter motor wheezed into life, churning obediently under the hood but failing to start the engine. Griffin cursed and tried again. The same. She was starting to sweat now, half from a growing panic, half from a core of embarrassment at the feebleness of her attempts to get the truck moving.

She tried once more and then noticed the immobilizer – a small panel with seven numbers mounted inexpertly beneath the steering column.

'Shit. Shit. Shit.'

She banged the wheel with a fist, then pushed open the door and jumped down. Eddie was twitching and gurgling, his arms trying to cross his body for instinctive comfort, and failing. Griffin bent to his face again and pulled it round roughly by the blood-soaked beard.

'Tell me the immobilizer number, you bastard.'

Eddie opened an eye and blinked at her through blood and agony.

She let go his beard and pulled out her knife. 'Tell me, or I'll cut your tiny dick off and feed you it.'

Eddie swallowed with difficulty, the blood burbling in his throat. The noise he used every last ounce of his energy to form from that frothy mess sounded incomprehensibly like 'khuck yaw'.

Griffin got the message. She paused a moment, contemplating how best to hurt him, to make his last moments of life unendurable, when the roar of a wounded engine made her freeze. She looked up, startled but not surprised, and watched ferally from the pre-dawn gloom of her crouch as Josh's wrecked truck entered the parking lot.

Griffin McFarlane moved fast, keeping low and sprinting for the only cover, the wooden washrooms, like she'd trained for it. Slamming open the doors, she disappeared inside as Josh halted the mess of Jezebel alongside the mess of his friend. Jez's engine cut for the last time and he climbed cautiously from his cab, assessing what he was seeing in the half light, a light that was increasing with alarming acceleration.

Josh stood for a moment, weighing up the silence, puzzling over the open door of the cab. Then realizing what the dark shape on the ground was, he whined at the back of his throat like a wounded dog, stumbling in his haste to get to Eddie, and coming to rest on his knees in the gore of the fallen man's blood. Josh's whine became a wail. He stretched his hands out impotently as though to heal with them.

'Eddie. Talk to me. Eddie. Jesus.'

Eddie twitched in response, his mouth making shapes soundlessly. Panting in panic and fury, Josh put a hand behind his friend's head and gently pushed back the soaking jacket. The wound on his neck was bleeding profusely, but not pumping. Josh mentally ticked it off. It wasn't an artery.

'S'okay, man. S'okay. You're goin' to be fine. S'okay.'

Eddie moved again, gurgling this time.

'Shhh. Shhh. Keep it together, man. Come on.'

Josh moved the jacket further, searching for the source of the main injury and found it in Eddie's side. Worse. Much worse.

Could be a punctured lung, could be anything. Up until minutes before, Josh regarded the universe as a place where only he needed immediate help, but until the sun came up, which was going to happen in a matter of minutes, Eddie needed help more. He ripped off his jacket and folded it under Eddie's head, then pulled off his sweatshirt and laid it carefully over his friend's trembling body.

'Stay still, man. I ain't goin' anywhere. You hear? I'm right by you.'

He stood up, climbed quickly into the cab and grabbed the CB, trying to stay calm but aware he was screaming into it like a fighter pilot.

'All drivers. I got a man dying of stab wounds in the parking pull-in two miles north of exit 23, highway 81. You got that? Two miles north. Like I need an ambulance right now or I'm gonna fuckin' lose him. You hearin' me out there? This ain't a stunt an'

I got no time here to reply. For fuck's sake somebody help me.'

He dropped the handset, oblivious to the cacophony of response, and jumped down to Eddie's side.

'Eddie. They're gonna come, man. I know they're gonna come.'

Eddie moved his mouth, straining to speak, and Josh shook his head.

'Don't. Stay still. I know, man. I know she's here and I'm goin' to deal with her, okay?'

Eddie tried a nod, then moved his eyes towards the open cab above him and successfully formed a word.

'Gun.'

Josh's pulse, already racing, quickened further. Eddie had been stabbed, not shot. What was he trying to say? He looked up at the rig and understood. Eddie was agitated, anxious that his instruction had registered. Josh touched his face gently and calmed him. 'Save it, Eddie. I got you, man. I remember where it is. Okay?'

Eddie closed his eyes and made a thick sound in his throat.

Josh looked at him tenderly for a second then climbed back into the cab, his eyes adjusting to the changing light, constantly searching the empty parking lot and wooden building for any sign of his enemy. He had to be careful. If she could take out a guy like Eddie then she was a formidable opponent.

Josh paused. The ludicrous nature of what he was doing struck him hard. He was about to find Eddie's gun, and go hunting a twenty-one-year-old murdering psycho. But a psycho to whom he needed to pass back a strip of dried skin, and have her take it willingly and unknowingly, or he was about to become more shredded than his oldest friend.

And the craziest part of all? It had to happen now. Right now, in the next few minutes, before the ridge of mountains he could see to his right, already illuminated from behind, exploded with the first light of the new day.

If it hadn't been for Eddie lying in his blood at the door of the cab, Josh would probably have held his head and laughed. But there was no mirth to be had in this madness. Josh knew now it was impossible to save himself. But if it was the last thing he did, he would take Griffin McFarlane with him into oblivion.

He sat in Eddie's chair, took a deep breath, then with his right hand felt behind the seat. Josh closed his eyes, and exhaled as his fingers closed around cloth wrapped around something hard and heavy. He pulled it out, unwrapped it and held the gun in his hand, feeling its deadly weight and cold metal against his palm, and with a hand that was surprisingly steady, he clicked open the bullet chamber.

Josh stared at the round ends of Eddie's shiny bullets, snug in their cylindrical homes, then looked towards the dark wooden building at the end of the parking lot. In the gloom of the cab something shifted behind Josh Spiller's eyes, a flitting ghost of movement that was echoed around the corners of his mouth. It was a twitch of muscle that was beyond a smile, beyond madness or revenge, nothing more than the muscular response of a predator to an electrical message from its brain.

There was a slit in the wooden walls of the men's washrooms, invisible from within when the darkness of the parking lot competed with the strip-lit interior. But Griffin had punched out the lights, her fist wrapped in her sweatshirt, and since the dawn was winning over the dark, she had found it easily. By crouching on top of a toilet cistern, she could survey nearly the whole parking lot through it.

She cursed through clenched teeth. He had been in the cab a minute ago, his shape easily recognizable as it moved slightly behind the wheel. But she had become uncomfortable in her bizarre position, had taken a second to adjust herself, and when she looked again Josh had gone. Griffin ran a hand over her face and stepped quietly down from her undignified pedestal. There was no need to panic. What could he do? He could force-feed her the runes and it would make no difference to the outcome if she hadn't received them correctly.

Willingly and unknowingly. Yeah, sure. She smiled at how the dumb piece of beefcake would try. In a few minutes he was history and part of her bristled with the excitement of what that would mean. She was going to see what few mortals had seen. Asmodeanus in the flesh. But better than that. She would see him at work.

There was only one area of risk. The bearded trucker had been easy. He hadn't known she was listening at his door. Hadn't expected her to be there, to have a knife, to have murder as her chore. Without that advantage she wondered how she would have fared, and now the upper hand of surprise was gone, Josh Spiller had height, weight, muscle and the blind rage of revenge on his side. She fingered the long point of the knife and wondered if making a break for the far distant trees across the fields wouldn't have been a better decision. But no.

The possibility of missing the physical manifestation of her first hot elemental was too much of an incentive to stay near.

All Griffin McFarlane had to do now was to stay alive longer than the man she'd condemned to hell. She slid the knife carefully up her sleeve and started to study her surroundings more closely.

In other circumstances, Josh would have acknowledged that the light was sublime. Painters, photographers and film-makers had rightly named this moment in the day 'magic hour', celebrating the limbo between light and dark, the miracle of a sky mixed with turquoise and cream and pink, when the air itself seemed charged with illumination of its own. In such a light, the humble and crudely-designed wooden building was lent a magnificence it didn't deserve. Against this backdrop, the striplights that remained on the central glass area endowed the whole structure with a beautiful melancholy, a contrast of blackness and highlights that resembled the surreal dusk restaurants from Edward Hopper paintings.

Beyond the building lay the still, dark, naked fields that stretched to the edge of the hills, their dew-soaked grass making ready to catch the first rays of light. But as Josh stood openly before it, unafraid of being detected, his gun-hand by his side, the idyll was further undermined by the stench that had started to fill the air.

There was no room in its foulness for the bright, sharp smells of morning. There was only decay and disease and throat-catching tendrils of burning flesh. It was as bad as it had ever been, but it felt keener, closer. It felt more real. Josh steeled himself for a glimpse of its hideous form, waited for a moment, then quickly cancelled the physical reactions his automatic response to fear had kick-started.

Its failure to appear was a viscous tease in itself, but there was little time to contemplate the demon's last taunting. It was time to find Griffin.

The central section was an open stage, brightly lit, with nowhere to hide. She was in one of the washrooms. That was it. One or the other. And whichever it was, he would tear it apart until he found her. He walked calmly to the glass doors and entered. The ladies' room was to his left, the men's to his right. Josh didn't even hesitate as he chose the men's. Griffin, he suspected, would have done the same.

He pushed the wooden door open slowly, unsurprised to find the room in darkness. The door was on a spring and it nudged back against his shoulder in its effort to close again. Josh lifted a leg and kicked it, a rage behind the force that not only severed the flimsy spring from its fixings, but bent the hinge on the door, leaving it leaning from its frame at an angle. There was a mirror nailed to the end wall opposite the door above two sinks, and he saw himself silhouetted in the door-frame. That was good. If he'd made a mistake and chosen the wrong washroom, he'd see her in the mirror as she dived from the door behind him.

'Can you smell its breath, Griffin?' He didn't shout, but his voice was loud and startling in the silence of the room.

'Huh? You feel it comin'?'

He took a step into the room, his boot crunching on the broken glass of the smashed overhead light.

'I can feel it real close. But then I guess now you know what it's like to feel your executioner so close you feel him breathe. 'Cos I'm right here, Griffin. Can you taste my breath?'

He took another step. His eyes adjusted to the darkness, taking in the two urinals on the wall to his left, and the more important fact that the three toilet stalls on his right were closed. Slowly he crouched down and, through the gap beneath the stalls, scanned the floor. There were no feet. He straightened up, senses on hyper-alert.

'Maybe you still remember what it tastes like.'

Josh kicked the first stall with the same fury he'd unleashed on the door. It banged open and smashed against the wall, before slamming back again and coming to rest half open. The stall was empty.

'Sweet, wasn't it?'

He stepped in front of the second stall with another crunch of glass, glancing once at the mirror for movement outside, the gun held level with his chest.

'Never thought when we fucked that we were goin' to kill each other. Crazy, huh? Ain't exactly what I call safe sex.'

He hesitated, leaving a beat between his words and his next action.

Josh took two quick steps forward and smashed his foot into the second stall door. It banged twice in protest and revealed its emptiness. His eyes flicked to the last stall, and as he looked, the door swung slowly inwards by an inch or two.

Turning slowly and crouching low, he inched back towards the swinging door, both hands gripping the gun.

It was the right hand, the one cradling the trigger, that took the knife as he pushed forward into the stall. Griffin brought the blade down with a scream, impaling the steel in the soft skin and muscle between Josh's thumb and forefinger. The gun fell from his hand and he cried out, as Griffin let go the hooded sweatshirt hanging on the door's hook that she'd clung to, legs tucked up in a crouch, since he entered. Josh's eyes were closed with the pain, but he grunted and squirmed against her as he felt her slip past him, bending to retrieve it.

And then Griffin was outside the stall and he felt the barrel of the gun sticking in his ribs.

'Come out of there, you shit-faced loser.'

She was panting so hard, her words were spoken on both the incoming and outgoing breath.

Josh stared at her, unblinking now in the half light as he held his wounded hand against his chest, the knife still up to its hilt in muscle. She stepped back, the gun raised towards his chest, and gestured with her head, giving herself time to regain her composure.

Josh stepped out, allowing her enough space to move behind him and press the gun to the small of his back.

'Pull the knife out and drop it on the floor.'

'Fuck off.'

'Do it.'

Josh glared at her, and paused, concentrating on getting his breathing steady again. His head was pounding, the searing pain from his hand making him nauseous. Without taking his eyes from hers, he tentatively touched the handle of the knife with his left hand. Even the tiny movement was agonizing. Josh gritted his teeth, then quickly pulled on it. The cry that left his lips, despite being muffled by the acoustics of a small room, was a bellow, and the knife clattered to the floor. He gasped with pain as he heard Griffin bend quickly behind him and pick it up.

She gave a small ugly laugh. 'Think that was sore. Just wait, Josh.'

The laugh again.

'Now move.'

The gun poked at him and he looked at her with an expression that made her break the rod of their locked gaze. She flicked her eyes to his forehead and motioned again with a shake of the head. With as much dignity as he could muster, he walked out of the washroom into the light.

Josh's voice was croaky. 'Why you think I'll do what you say just 'cos you got the gun? Maybe I want to get shot.'

She opened up the distance between them now they were in a bigger space and gestured towards the swing door.

'Yeah? Maybe you do. But I figure you're still hoping for the cavalry to come. You want to see me die, don't you? And pulling a dumb move'll only make me shoot you. I reckon part of you thinks all this is make-believe. That demons don't exist and maybe you're going to live. It's the human spirit, Josh. Hope. I'm counting on it to increase the pleasure of seeing you die.'

He walked to the door and pushed it open with his hip, then hesitated and looked back. 'Why outside?'

She smiled like a reptile and pointed a thumb backwards to the line of hills behind her through the other wall of glass. The sun's rays, if not the orb itself, were now clearly visible.

'It's going to get a little crowded in here in a minute.'

They walked around the building and ended up in a patchy area of grass behind it, invisible to the parking lot, nothing now but the dewy fields between them and the hills. Griffin stood back from him, pointed the gun squarely at his chest, her head cocked to one side in amusement.

'Well? Got something for me?'

Josh glared at her, nursing his hand.

'No? No book to give me? No map or box of matches? Not even a packet of candy?' She laughed at his silence. 'Aw come on now, Josh. While the sun is still on the other side of that hill, you still got the chance to pass me that little piece of skin I'm sure you've got hidden somewhere very special indeed.'

The ugly sarcasm in her young voice made Josh almost as nauseous as the pain from his hand.

'Why'd you do this, Griffin?'

The smile left her. 'I do what I please.'

'Murder pleases you?'

'Power pleases me.'

Josh snorted a laugh. 'You're nothin' but a dumb little kid with a gun. You got as much power as my farts.'

Griffin straightened up from her coquettish stance and thunder rolled behind her eyes. 'You know nothing, do you?'

Josh made a mock-thinking expression. 'Eh, let's see now. Your Daddy screwed your baby ass, your Mama killed your Daddy, your Mama's gone as crazy as a shark in a toilet, an' you reckon you goin' to run the world or somethin'. In other words you're one sad fuck-up. How'd I do?'

Griffin's mouth contorted into a slit of hate and as she put two hands to the gun she looked for a moment as though she would shoot him. Then something broke in her face and she softened again.

'Good, Josh. Real funny. But I got a little secret for you. Want to hear it?'

'Sure.'

'He's coming now. You're right to say you can feel his breath. And you know how we can command dumb brutes as ancient and evil as Asmodeanus?'

'You cut up your babies.'

Josh had made himself sound bored. The ire in Griffin's eyes told him his tone had worked, but as he watched she replaced the petulant anger with a more adult mask of authority. It made her attractive again, that juxtaposition of effortless beauty and the earnestness of a young girl trying to be taken seriously.

Taking a step back, she let her weight rest on one leg, her hips pushed provocatively out at an angle, and the girl he'd picked up and laid was almost visible again. Almost but not quite.

'Know what? It's crazy, but I never really got out of Furnace much. It was hard. You know? We didn't mix much. But I used to watch the trucks go by on the interstate. Used to climb up onto the ridge and see them move along in line. You do that, you guys, don't you? You stick together.'

Josh said nothing. His hand was swelling into a puffy mess.

'I guess that's 'cos you're all just kids, huh? You feel big up there, high in your seat, looking down on the rest of the world like you were real men.'

She laughed and shook her head.

Josh spoke quietly. 'What you did to Eddie. You're goin' to die for that if nothin' else.'

Griffin regarded him for a moment, then did a mock shiver. 'Help. Save me.'

Josh looked down, anywhere to get away from that face contorted with delight in its own primitive sarcasm. Griffin was silent for a moment, then spoke in a different voice. A softer voice, but more genuinely menacing for it.

'Who told you I passed the runes? Who sent you after me?'

Josh replied to his feet like he didn't care. 'Pace.'

She smiled. 'Then I guess he's already dead.'

Josh looked up and winced internally. He reckoned she was right. 'So tell me your secret.'

Griffin continued to smile, pleased to have his attention back, and sighed theatrically. 'It's tricky, you know. The seventh baby's the powerful one, the one that counts. My mother got round that, after . . . after she lost me as sacrifice.' She hesitated, looked at he ground, then looked back up with renewed vigour. 'She's not well, my mother. If she was just a housewife, you know, a regular aproned Mom? I guess she'd be hiding the Valium in the linen cupboard. But as it is she just keeps making gold. Crates and crates of fucking useless, unspendable, dangerous gold. If she keeps on she's going to get us caught.' Griffin looked distant and angry for a moment, then returned to her theme. 'But that's nothing to do with us. Is it, Josh?'

She grinned and adjusted her grip on the gun.

'You've seen plenty country hicks. Have babies like they jar pickles. Dumber than dirt and eager to please when they know the company my mother keeps. You see, my second eldest brother died when he was twelve. Since I survived that makes every baby she has, and kills, the seventh child. She simply surrogates. Neat, huh? But you see, Josh, I can't wait around to have six ugly, squalling brats before I get the one I need. You, of all people, given your current situation with, what's her name, Elizabeth? You understand that.'

'You're so fuckin' sick.'

She ignored the genuine hatred in his voice. 'So I've been sharing eggs around. Without Mom knowing, of course. Donated six healthy eggs over the last two years, and what do you know? Six healthy babies are growing and shitting for their proud parents somewhere in this fine state.'

Josh remained silent. It seemed to disappoint her.

'The seventh, Josh. Don't you want to know where it's coming from?'

His eyes flicked to the mountains behind her. The rim was beginning to shimmer.

'Your ass?'

Griffin did an astonishing thing for a woman holding a gun to a six-foot man. She walked across to Josh and slapped him hard across the face. She moved back quickly as his bloody hand came up, but it merely went to his cheek where the blow had fallen.

She watched him for a moment, unsettled by her careless display of temper, and composed herself before she spoke again. When she did, it was in a patient teacherly manner, studied and calm. 'There's good news, Josh. You see you'll live on. At least for seven short days. I slept with you because everything was just right. My cycle, my temperature, everything. Unless you shoot blanks, which as we both know is not the case, then your baby is going to make me considerably more powerful than my dear mother.'

She patted her belly in a mockery of proud motherhood. Josh stared at her, struggling to contain his horror. The saliva was drying in his mouth, but he kept his voice as calm as hers, although his heart was bursting in his chest.

'Big deal. It won't be seven days old on the first of May.'

Griffin looked delighted. 'No. You're right. It won't. What a scholar you are for a dumb fuck of a trucker. But that's the gift my mother unwittingly gave me. You see I'm the seventh child. I was seven days old on the first of May. Read any shabby tome on the lowly art of witchcraft and you'll see that my power allows me, unlike my very ordinary mother, to sacrifice any time I want.'

She grinned like a mad woman and Josh tried to sound like he cared little about this new and nauseating nightmare.

'A witch, huh? Neat.'

She ignored his irony. 'Witch? There are no witches, Josh. None with any power. Oh, the log book and the phone? Like I said, that's standard witchcraft that comes with the spell. Kids' stuff. But I'm no witch. I'm a philosopher. The highest form of alchemist. And now I get the driver's seat.'

Josh looked hard at Griffin for a moment, letting his eyes take
in the elegant curves of her cheek, the sheen of her hair lit gently
from behind by the brightening sky, then leaned back against the
wall and slumped down the rough wood pulling his T-shirt up to
his armpits. He lowered his head and spoke wearily into his bent
knees.

'You don't get jack-shit, Griffin.'

He held his head with his uninjured hand, and continued in a voice
that was close to tears, talking as if to himself. 'Sweet Jesus, there's
been so much killin' already. Can't make myself proud of this.'

She stared at the top of his head, then spoke with a nervous
laugh. 'What the fuck are you talking about?'

He looked up at her and blinked. 'Willingly but unknowingly.'

The rim of the mountains started to glow with a piercing line of
orange. Griffin glanced behind her and then back at him. 'You're
a dead man. You're not scaring me.'

Josh slumped even lower, his body a weight he felt he could no
longer support. He gestured lazily with his good hand, but it was
weary rather than casual. 'Look in the gun, Griffin. In the bullet
chamber.'

In the near distance a wail of sirens oscillated in the morning
air, and Griffin, her mouth open and panting, looked left and right
quickly as though they were already upon her. Josh prayed silently
that Eddie had stayed with the game.

'You're lying.'

Her voice was two octaves higher than normal. Josh looked back
at her with agonized eyes and shook his head with the minimum
of movement. Griffin's hand began to tremble uncontrollably and
she steadied it with the other as she started to walk backwards,
putting a new distance between them. Her foot caught a stone and
she fell back, dropping to one knee. A panicked glance at Josh, still
sitting motionless, his back to the wall, confirmed that he had no
intention of using the moment, and the implication of that made
her start to whimper.

'No.'

It was a tiny word, spoken in a small voice.

She glanced down at the weapon in her trembling hand, and
with her gaze dividing itself between it, Josh and the burning rim
of light behind her, she broke the gun open.

The chamber was empty. Empty that is, of bullets. But in one of the six dark cylindrical chambers there was something else.

Rolled tightly, as tightly as a thin cigarette, was Josh's returned gift. Seven inches of dried human skin, marked in blood with symbols of power that were older than man.

With her mouth open, a small circle of terror, Griffin's eyes were darting back and forth from the gun's chamber to Josh's face. One trembling hand extended slowly towards Josh and a thick noise escaped from the back of her throat as she struggled to speak.

'Take it back.'

Josh bent his head and shook it slowly above his knees, not so much as a denial to the order they both knew had been spoken pointlessly, but in black despair for them both.

There was a high-pitched whining, and as Josh looked up, Griffin's mouth, the source of the one-note noise, became a down-turned grimace from which unchecked spittle dribbled to her chin. The gun fell from her hand, and like a broken watch-spring the sickly roll unravelled from the bullet chamber, fluttered once, then blew along the ground out towards the darkened fields on a wind Josh could not feel. They both watched it go, still, like listening animals, the string of spit hanging from Griffin's contorted mouth glistening in the growing light like a dewy web. Her whine became a bestial pant, then she tottered for a moment, turned, and ran floundering after the tumbling strip.

As he watched her stagger away, arms flapping as though broken, for one breathless moment Josh believed the whole thing was a lie. A great, big, messy, inexplicable lie, a tangle of madness with nothing to ground it except the belief of those like himself, falling into the trap with their faith in the implied unseen. There was no demon coming, no alchemists misled to do business with uncontrollable forces. There was only the mess of death. Real death, at the hands of real human beings, and his own insanity.

And then Josh felt his blood freeze.

He pulled himself to his feet slowly, and peered at Griffin. She had stopped suddenly more than a hundred feet from him, halted violently in her tracks as though she'd struck a wall.

Josh blinked, his breath held in check as the stalled silhouette of Griffin McFarlane was temporarily granted a sainthood, haloed and back-lit by the first sliver of a spectacular sunrise. Josh had no idea what to anticipate, but the visual confusion that reigned in the next few moments would have been beyond his guesswork.

At first it seemed as though she was increasing in size, that the dark outline of her slight body was being inflated like a balloon. Then, widening with horror, Josh's eyes differentiated between the indistinct silhouette of Griffin and the dark figure that was growing directly between her and the hills, expanding from nowhere like bacteria growing beneath a microscope, stealing the light from her outline as it drew its own.

Its shape was humanoid, but only just. Massive limbs hung nearly to the ground; a small, horned and misshapen head was held low, so low it was almost below the two massive shoulders that supported it.

And undulating around those shoulders was the unspeakable suggestion of withered, flightless wings. It crouched, yet it towered at least three feet above its prey.

On the tendrils of morning air, that shift of moisture-filled gas too weak to be called breeze, yet too restless to be called still, came the stirring of an odour. He knew it, knew how it would increase and sicken him even as its first nauseating particles brushed the sensors of his nostrils. Josh slapped a hand to his face, covering his nose and mouth, and, turning from the unholy sight in the field, leaned heavily against the rough wood of the building.

The touch of something real, the coarse texture of the hardwood slats against his shoulder, the stabbing of pain from the wounded hand that he hugged to his breast; these sensations sobered him. He screwed his eyes shut, willing himself to wake from the nightmare, but already the stench had circumvented the crude protection of his hand and filled his nose and mouth. Josh struggled for breath, his mind bubbling with the broth of unholy images that accompanied the smell. And then came the first scream.

He should have buried his head in his hands, should have tried the best he could to blank out the overture of fear and suffering that was to have been his.

But Josh made a mistake. He looked back into the field.

Asmodeanus worked silently, but his victim was less restrained. Griffin's screaming had become deep and guttural, an expulsion of air which contained no pleading, no hope that its sound would bring aid. Instead, it was hollow and forlorn, the sound of an animal crazed by agony. Josh felt his gorge rise, and the panic in his throat that her wailing ignited threatened to make him run to her. He willed himself to remain static, an audience of one with a ring-side seat.

Smokeless flames were engulfing the complex shape made by the two figures. Pale, almost invisible licks of sickly brightness shimmered around their two bodies like a mirage, and Josh squinted against the confusion of light and dark until with narrowed eyes and almost against his will he gradually made sense of the image.

The movements made by the huge black shape were almost sexual. It held Griffin's writhing body around her arching back with one massive arm, as the other tore at her torso with the ease of a farmer plucking feathers.

Her skin was blistering and blackening, boiling up into globes of heat-stretched membrane before bursting like dark fruit, as the limb of the demon that tore at her grew thick with the harvest it found amongst her flesh. Strings of gristle and intestine dangled from its thrashing claws as it rooted around its plaything.

The arm that supported Griffin was now busying itself at her back, ripping great trenches from shoulder to hip, while the flesh it touched ignited and smouldered like melting plastic. She could scream no more. Whether the light of sentience had gone from her forever, or the mechanism for sound had merely been cut, Josh didn't know. But his relief in its passing caused him little shame.

Although noises remained on the stillness of the morning air, the popping of bursting skin, the slick lapping of evisceration, it was rendered bearable by the absence of Griffin's agonized response. Josh swallowed back his bile, unable to stop looking, unable to run.

And then it dropped her. The hollowed sack that was Griffin's body crumpled to the ground and the monster paused for a moment, considering it.

Gradually, the glass wall to Josh's right lit with blue and red as an unseen assortment of emergency vehicles that had announced their coming only moments ago, arrived in the parking lot. But despite the carnival of colour that danced on the earth beside him Josh could not take his eyes from the form that defied the laws of physics, reason and faith.

If it was aware of the arrival of more humans, then it gave no indication.

It crouched forward, a hunched gargoyle, with knees bent to its ears, and started to tear at the smoking remains with its jaws. But even as Griffin's body rose and fell with the choreography of its ripping, there was a change in the substance of the beast.

It was no less real, its form casting a shadow before the orange rays of the risen sun. But there now seemed to be purposeful form in the thin flames that licked at it. It appeared that it was being consumed by its own fire, the edges of its misshapen body blurring like darkened, opaque glass. The ground around it was becoming indistinct also, becoming part of the beast and its prey, and yet more fluid and giving than dawn-hardened earth should be.

It was departing. Being called back. Josh wanted to shout in triumph, to scream childish obscenities as it started to writhe in its own death throes. But before he could even form the words or make a fist, the head that was bloodied with sizzling human flesh turned slowly towards him and straightened on its impossibly thick neck.

Two slits of red hate focused on Josh. The pupils were in glittering contrast to the dull black flesh, and the mind that reasoned behind them was naked through their ruby light. It narrowed those eyes and opened its mouth in a wide, lascivious leer, and as Josh's heart made a decision whether to continue to beat again or not, one long, flesh-clogged claw came level with Asmodeanus's eyes, and pointed at him.

Josh slumped to the ground, pulled both his arms across his head and screamed from the back of his throat. The wail pierced the still morning air with a volume that was rendered unearthly.

In the parking lot, the cop who heard Josh's cry drew his gun, motioned to his partner and backed slowly around the edge of the building. Their caution departed at the sight of the man slumped on the ground, to be replaced with a violence of action that literally took from him what little breath Josh had left. Two pairs of hands hauled him to his feet, pushed his face and hands against the rough wall, while two voices barked instructions, shouting like sailors over a storm.

'Keep your fuckin' hands up. Do it!'

'You stay like that, mister. Hear me? You stay right where you are, nice and still. We ain't goin' any fuckin' place but here. I said, you hearin' me?'

Blood from his hand trickled down the uneven surface of the wooden slats, and Josh's face, pressed to the wall, was squeezed into a ludicrous shape, a silent comic-book approximation of a man shouting.

His eyes moved from the grey texture of the wood to the vast reflective plane of the glass wall next to him where shapes in the distance moved against the reflected circle of sun. And as he watched without wanting to, in truth aching to look away, the silhouetted shape diminished, began to recede, struggling as it did so, into the dark ground – the unimaginable violence, the ancient and inescapable horror, rendered nothing more than a mound of writhing matter, masked from casual eyes by the brilliance of the risen sun.

'Help her,' he whispered weakly into the wood, and his words were lost in a muffled croak.

One of the men behind his head was already barking into a radio, the other pulling roughly at Josh's arm to handcuff him.

'Okay now,' he said as he pulled down Josh's wounded hand and realized that no cuff would encircle such an obscenely swollen wrist.

Hands frisked Josh's body, and the man muttered 'clean' to his partner.

Josh smiled at that. Clean. He would never be clean. He had saved himself. But the dark filth that had ripped and torn and seared and devoured, had touched him and left its mark. The policeman stepped back.

'There ain't no place to run. You just come round real easy and you gonna keep breathin'. You make a move an' you leave here in plastic. Got me?'

Josh nodded, lowering his arms slowly and turning to face the men. He kept his eyes on the ground. He had no wish to look back out towards the sun, towards what he knew would now be an empty field with nothing to find. Instead he waited to be led away, the dirt beneath his feet the only thing he dared to see.

'Move it slow now, mister. Real slow. It's over.'

'It's over,' repeated the companion.

No, thought Josh. Not over. But then he could forgive them for thinking it.

They, after all, never knew her mother.

*   *   *

The light. The light had come and it was the light of birth. Asmo-deanus had writhed in the dark pit of his gestation, alarmed but not bereft, that his carrier had changed. There was still the birth to come. That was safe. That had not been cancelled. And as he grew and became as solid as the flesh he would consume, he raged at the growing knowledge that this birth would once again mean his death. A return to the dark place where the silence was an eternal scream and the heat and the pain had no texture.

And he used that hate as he was born, wallowing in its power to grow and tear and burn and drink in the pain of this filth that was a human, that species of dung that dared to have flesh and life of its own and call him from the dark to do its bidding.

So he came into the light, and he ripped, and he shredded, and he burned, and he screamed a silent scream of even greater agony than his prey, as the human's pathetic and cowardly death pulled him back towards the pit.

There was no hate greater at that moment than its own hate, and he took it with him, howling back into the dark place he was bound to forever, believing with the low intellect he possessed that someday he would find a way to make his release into the light permanent.

Eddie had gone by the time they bundled Josh into the police car. The kinder of the two cops said he might make it if they got him to Harrisonburg, said Josh had better pray he made it and could talk, if Josh's mumbled story about a third assailant was true, and Josh had nodded, closing his eyes in a silent movement of thanks. Thanks both for the answer from a policeman who was softening to his prisoner's obvious lack of violence, and for the fact that Eddie was still alive. Now, gliding out from the crowded parking lot, he held his roughly-bandaged hand to his heart and gazed out the window at the forested ridge of the Appalachians, radiating the sunlight erratically from its long and textured back.

How long before she came after him? A month? A year? A lifetime?

Josh Spiller took a breath through his nostrils and made a pact. There was life at home. New life that needed love and needed him. He had been given this life back and he wasn't going to live it in fear. The sunlight filtered through the wire squares of the grille separating him from the two policemen, and Josh blinked through it, remembering. Last time he'd been in a police car he'd ridden up front. Riding shotgun with Sheriff John Pace instead of huddled in the back like a criminal. It seemed a lifetime ago. It *was* a lifetime ago.

He closed his eyes again and the face of John Pace drew itself on the pinkness of his inner lids. It was laughing, distant and hazy, but unmistakably laughing. The effect the unremarkable vision had on him was suddenly and inexplicably comforting. This unheralded emotion washed over him like a cold wave, so external to his line of thought that it gave Josh a start. He flicked his eyes open, startled, but curiously toughened in his resolve. Josh looked at the necks of the two men up front, then turned to stare out the dirt-crusted window towards the mountains, taking a lungful of air in through his nostrils.

'Won't work, Nelly,' he whispered to the black hills. 'I feel safe.'

And even if it was merely the act of believing it as he said it, and nothing more, somehow it became true in his heart.

There had been several stages to her fury, but the calm at the end was what surprised her. The first stage, when she knew for certain, had been a confusion of mad rage and disbelief. Then a sickening relief had crept in, a warped comfort in the knowledge that she was safe from her daughter's rapidly growing power.

What followed as a direct response was the most sickening of all. Grief. A sadness so powerful had gripped her that it had made her lament for a hidden core of sorrows that had been entombed for half her life. Nelly McFarlane had wept and screamed and torn at her breast, crying for her children, her womanhood, the bonds that she had ripped at to feed her fire. But it was an emotion that was too expensive, and she blotted it quickly, regaining her composure to concentrate on its replacement. The delicious heat of revenge.

It was the searing ire of that revenge that had made her stalk the room blindly, searching her mind for the thread of a plan to weave into a noose for the trucker. Then her eye had fallen on the man's log book, the souvenir brought to her by Pace, sitting in silent triumph beside her computer.

McFarlane had trembled for a moment, then picked up the pad of cheap paper and thrown it violently across the room.

It slapped into the wall and fluttered down to the floor, its torn and tattered pages like the wings of a careless bird smashed against a window.

And then Nelly felt time stop.

The whispering ceased in the lab. There was an abrupt end to the scuffling and shifting of the invisible entities that found solace in proximity with the machinations of her dark craft.

McFarlane licked her lips and looked at the seven-inch strip on the floor. The one that had fluttered from the pages of Josh Spiller's violated log book. She stayed still for a very long time, then walked slowly across the room and bent to retrieve it.

Griffin's death had proved her eyes were capable of tears, and they came again, but she was smiling through them, not weeping. It was so perfect that she might have embraced him if her arms could defy the grave, but it was doubtful John Pace would have returned the gesture. He was safe in his oblivion, safe and certain that the runes spelling Nelly McFarlane's ugly death could never be passed back.

Never.

Because she was the one who had taken a scalpel to her only hope.

'Well, well, sheriff,' she whispered. 'Very good. Very good indeed.'

She straightened up and smiled.

Councillor McFarlane held the runes in her hands like a losing lottery ticket, then let them drop gently to the floor, her fingers open, palms turned down. Her posture was straight and proud as she walked to the drawer beneath the computer, opened the box inside, took out its contents and stood for a moment. As she handled the gun, she was almost tempted by habit to make an adjustment to what she saw flickering on the screen. Then Nelly McFarlane laughed in a short staccato burst, and gently switched it off.

She cast one brief glance at her baby's remains glistening on the table, then raised the gun to her mouth.

'Will I burn, John?'

She arched an eyebrow in contempt, then closed her eyes.

No one in Furnace heard the muffled shot and even if they had, they would have thought little of it. All over town, people carried on with their breakfasts and their plans for the day, little knowing that, for the moment at least, Furnace was on its own.